# The Murder Queens

Michael Gallon

Lock Down Publications and Ca$h
Presents
# The Murder Queens
A Novel by *Michael Gallon*

The Murder Queens

**Lock Down Publications**
**Po Box 944**
**Stockbridge, Ga 30281**

**Visit our website @**
www.lockdownpublications.com

Copyright 2022 by Michael Gallon
The Murder Queens

**Lock Down Publications**
**Like our page on Facebook: Lock Down Publications @**
**www.facebook.com/lockdownpublications.ldp**
Book interior design by: **Shawn Walker**
Edited by: **Sandy Barret-Sims**

Michael Gallon

## Stay Connected with Us!

Text **LOCKDOWN** to 22828 to stay up-to-date with new releases, sneak peaks, contests and more...
Thank you.

# Submission Guideline.

Submit the first three chapters of your completed manuscript to ldpsubmissions@gmail.com, subject line: Your book's title. The manuscript must be in a .doc file and sent as an attachment. Document should be in Times New Roman, double spaced and in size 12 font. Also, provide your synopsis and full contact information. If sending multiple submissions, they must each be in a separate email.

Have a story but no way to send it electronically? You can still submit to LDP/Ca$h Presents. Send in the first three chapters, written or typed, of your completed manuscript to:

**LDP: Submissions Dept**
**Po Box 944**
**Stockbridge, Ga 30281**

*DO NOT send original manuscript. Must be a duplicate.*

Provide your synopsis and a cover letter containing your full contact information.

Thanks for considering LDP and Ca$h Presents.

Michael Gallon

# INTRODUCTION

## MURDER QUEENS
## THE FLORIDA HOT GIRLS

The story you're about to read is based on actual events that took place between 1998 through 2013. The Rise and Fall of the Florida Hot Girls is not only the true-life story of what they went through during their fifteen-year career, but it also reveals what their owner and manager went through. His demise, along with their fall from grace, is chronicled from the first book to the last.

Their phenomenal story is told by none other than the man who started one of the most talked-about dance groups ever, Michael Valentino, the founder of the Florida Hot Girls.

The Florida Hot Girls were a select group of beautiful women who danced their way into the hearts of many. Not only did they turn heads, but they also broke necks with their sheer beauty, style, and grace.

The story chronicles the lives of the characters as they traveled from state to state and club to club. Not to mention, the wild bachelor parties that took place all over Florida and throughout surrounding states.

This is the true story of The Rise and Fall of the Florida Hot Girls—the actual, true-life story of what them Alphabet Boys *didn't* want you to know.

Michael Gallon

# PROLOGUE

We had just pulled up to the guard gate when I rolled my window down to put my security code in. I noticed there wasn't a guard at the gate.

"That's strange, Redd," I said.

"What's that, bae?" She turned away from what she was looking at through her passenger window.

"There's always a guard at the gate but I don't see one tonight."

"Oh yeah, you're right, she said, after she noticed the gate had been left unsecured.

I pulled into my driveway and pushed the button on the garage door opener before proceeding to drive inside the garage.

Within minutes, the ladies and I were inside the house. We put our bags down and proceeded to settle in.

Out of nowhere, I got hit across the side of my face. I fell to the ground, holding my jaw in sheer pain. Sexy Redd had gone through the den area and somehow managed to get upstairs without being noticed.

"Get down and stay down!" the heavy-voiced man said as he stood up over me with a chrome plated .380 pointed at my dome. "You bitches put your hands behind your fuckin' back and don't fuckin' move! Tie their asses up," he yelled to one of his henchmen."

I rolled over to four masked gunmen standing inside my house. I looked over and realized Mignon, Strawberry, Nicole, Entyce, and Jasmine had all been tied up.

Still somewhat dazed, I thought to myself, *where in the hell is Sexy Redd?*

The leader of the masked group sat me up in one of the dining room chairs. "Okay, Mike, this can be over in a few minutes, or we can take all fuckin' night kicking your ass and fuckin' these pretty ass bitches since you don't never let nobody fuck 'em. Your black ass know what time it is, nigga, so let's not waste each other's time or get nobody killed over a few measly dollars."

"Hey, man, hold up," one of the henchmen yelled to the leader of the group. "It's supposed to be six bitches in here with this fuck ass nigga. Where that bitch they call Sexy Redd?"

The first guy turned around to poor Strawberry and asked her, "Where is Sexy Redd, bitch?"

"I don't know who you're talking about," she said with her head looking downward. *WHAP!* He slapped poor Strawberry so fuckin' hard across her red face, she fell to the floor. Blood squirted from the right side of her lip and face, as tears of anger filled her eyes.

"C'mon, man, you didn't have to slap the shit out of her like that!" I yelled.

"Shut the fuck up, nigga! I'ma slap yo' punk ass just like that, if that bitch of yours don't show the fuck up in five fuckin' minutes," he barked in my face.

"Man, she ain't here! You don't see her, do you?" I snapped.

*SWAT!* The next thing I know, the big, black ass muthafucker slapped me across my face with his pistol and my jaw began to swell instantaneously.

"Man, listen, if it's the money you want, man, y'all can have it!" I said. "Just untie me and I'll get you the money," I told him, trying to bargain with him. He instructed a slim nigga to go upstairs to check for any other females who might've been in the house.

Doing as he'd been told, the slim guy quickly ran up the stairs, carrying a rusty, old ass gun that looked like his grandfather might've given it to him. Once he was up there, I could hear his footsteps as he walked from room to room, looking for anyone else who might've been hiding inside the house.

"Now, Mike, back to you, pimp," the lead man said, "we understand there's a safe in here somewhere." He paused and looked around as if it would magically fall out of the air. "We want everything in it, plus all the cash these pretty ass hoes made over the weekend. I heard they made quite a bit," he said, "somewhere in the neighborhood of three-thousand dollars apiece, right?"

As I listened to him talk facts, my mind raced. *Damn, this nigga even know how much money everybody made over the weekend. One of my girls must have set us up.*

By now, the ladies were crying their eyes out—everyone except Jasmine.

"Hey, we don't wanna die over no fuckin' money. Y'all niggas can have this shit," Nicole said angrily. Her face was wet with tears and her pretty face was smeared with snot and makeup.

"Mike, please do something," Strawberry said. The blood from her lip oozed down her chin, and the mascara she'd been wearing made her look like she had racoon eyes. Her lip grew bigger by the minute, and she reminded me of Eddie Murphy in the movie "The Nutty Professor".

"Y'all bitches stop crying and shut the fuck up," the gunman said. He looked from one girl to another, which caused his eyes to move around rapidly. "Y'all don't be acting like this when y'all be taking our fuckin' money in the strip club and shit," he said. He pointed his gun at Strawberry's head. One of the guys sounded so fucking familiar, and he was the same one who looked at the girls and unzipped his pants.

"Man, let me put this dick in one of these bitch's mouth, since Mike don't let these hoes do no fuckin' after the club." He laughed. "Let me see how this bitch with the fat, red ass can suck on this big ass dick," he said, as he stepped closer to Nicole. "Open your fuckin' mouth, trick!"

"Muthafucker, I'll take a bullet to the head before I suck your little ass, dick-in-the-booty-having-nigga, bitch," Nicole said with anger in her voice. She coughed up some yellowish-colored phlegm and spat at his black ass.

"Hold on, nigga, we came here to get this bread, not fuck these hoes," the leader of the group said to his partner. His partner still had his limp manhood out. He tried to get it up so he could make Nicole take him up on his offer.

"Man, after we get this money, I'ma fuck that little red, loud mouth bitch in her fat lil' ass!" the familiar voice said, as he zipped up his Wrangler jeans. He wiped the phlegm off that had landed right on top of his shoe.

Realizing how long the slim dude was taking upstairs, the leader of the group yelled out to him. "Yo', nigga, you found anything yet?"

"No, not yet!" Just as the words had left his mouth, a loud, thunderous *thud* sounded from upstairs. The floor above shook, and a picture fell from the wall. The skinny nigga came tumbling down the stairs hollering in agonizing pain as he hit the bottom of the stairwell.

"What the fuck!" the leader of the group shouted. His eyes bulged from his head, as he gazed at his partner lying on the floor. When he bent down to assist his homie, Sexy Redd came running down the stairs, taking them three at a time, with a chrome .380 automatic aimed and loaded. She came down so fast, it was as if she'd had wings.

"Drop your muthafuckin' guns or I'ma split your Goddamn heads in two like a fuckin' watermelon," she shouted, as she simultaneously jumped over the guy.

Perplexed, they dropped their weapons.

The guy on the floor yelled out to his homies. "Man, this pretty ass bitch broke my fuckin' jaw and pushed me down the fuckin' stairs. I think my fuckin' leg is broken too," he said, as his leg lay twisted up by his head. "The rest of my body is facing another fuckin' direction," he said in disbelief, and began to cry.

"All you broke ass niggas move your black asses over there out of the muthafuckin' way," Sexy Redd yelled out to them. "Baby, are you alright?" she asked. She handed me the chrome .380 automatic and I pointed it at the nigga who had hit me in my fuckin' head.

# CHAPTER ONE

*"Everything that looks good isn't always good"*
*April 1999 Orlando, Florida*

"Good morning, babe, how'd you sleep last night?" I asked my wife, Camisha. She had walked right by me as if I wasn't even there. Yet again, I had found myself sleeping on the couch all alone while she'd slept cuddled up on the other couch with her son, Tazz—short for Tasmanian Devil, for which he was. Since we'd been married, it seemed as though I had grown accustomed to the routine of our sleeping pattern.

I had met Camisha about a year prior at one of my favorite nightspots in Orlando—Club Amvet's, a nice twenty-one and older club. I still remember the first night I met the most beautiful woman in the world, at least that's what I thought at that moment...

It was Saturday night, ladies' night. All the fine ladies of Orlando had come out to get their grown and sexy, on and popping. It was a warm summer night, and of course, I was dressed to impress. My body was draped in a black-and-white-pinstriped two-piece suit, and my feet rocked a pair of black-and-white Stacey Adams that shined so bright you could see your reflection in them.

I was standing by the bar with my homie Aaron, scoping out the females I would take home that night. That was the beauty about Club Amvet's—most of the women had jobs and about ninety percent of them had their own place. So, we didn't have to worry about any gold-digging women being in the club that night.

Aaron was so amped up; he couldn't sit still. He couldn't keep his hands to himself, and he just had to touch every female who walked past him. He'd either tap them on the shoulder or touch them on the ass and shit.

"Calm down, homie," I yelled to him over the loud music. "You gonna scare all the pretty ones off acting like that."

Now, on the other hand, I always played it cool. I had been to that particular club many times and I was a pro at getting the ladies.

The club was packed wall to wall with women and I might as well have been the only man in the club 'cause I didn't see any other brother in there as fly as me.

My boy Aaron stood beside me looking just like Phillip Michael Thomas, the nigga from Miami Vice, even though most people always said he looked like Al B. Sure. He was dressed in a nice pair of black slacks, a white shirt, a white jacket, and no tie. His shirt was opened at the neck to show off the small gold chain he had on. The penny loafers he'd worn made him look like he'd just stepped out of a Michael Jackson video. He was a cool, laid-back brother with light skin, green eyes, and curly jet-black hair. Now don't get me wrong, his looks were on point, but he was slacking in his dress game. And I gotta admit, when he wasn't all hyped up the women would stop and chitchat with him. He had his own business, his own crib, and he seemed to be on the right path in his life. But as soon as he got that juice in his red ass, lights out. Being his own boss, he did things the way he wanted to.

Now, me, I'm brown-skinned, with brown eyes, and low wavy hair. The waves in my hair were so deep, women said they got seasick from just looking at them. Standing five feet ten inches tall, I weighed one hundred eighty-five pounds with a nice, chiseled body, and not one inch of fat anywhere. And don't get me wrong; I had my own place and money too; except I punched a time clock every day and worked a nine to five.

I was still sipping on my first drink when, suddenly, Ms. Camisha J. walked in. She looked to be about five feet eight, one hundred thirty-five pounds. Her skin tone was a high yellow. The sight of her nice round ass caused my mouth to fall open, and as I stared her down, all the cool in me went straight out the door.

For half an hour, all I could do was watch her as she walked through the club, chitchat with her girls, or just stood on the wall and watched everyone else; however, the third time she walked by, I made it my business to stop her and introduce myself.

"Excuse me, Ms. I'm sorry, but are you married or seeing anyone?"

"And why are you asking." She replied with sass in her tone.

"I didn't wanna be rude and impose on anyone else's wife or girlfriend."

"Since you put it like that, *no*, I'm not married, and *no*, I'm not seeing anyone at the moment, sir."

"Well, let me introduce myself. My name is Michael. Michael Valentino."

"And my name is Camisha," she replied, "nice to meet you, Michael."

"Now that we've introduced ourselves, may I have this dance?" I asked and smiled.

"Of course, Michael, especially since you were so polite."

We walked to the dance floor, and I couldn't help but notice how nicely shaped her body was. I turned and looked back at my boy Aaron, who was still standing by the bar looking all crazy and shit, probably wondering how I had pulled the baddest female in the club. Hell, as far as I was concerned, she was the baddest female in Orlando.

Unlike Aaron, I was always trying to find Miss. Right to make her Mrs. Michael Valentino. But she had to be the perfect female to make me complete. I thought I had found that in Camisha. After meeting her that night, we became inseparable and began seeing one another exclusively. Fast forward, after a year of dating, we decided to get married. It was the worst mistake I could've ever made, the beginning of the end.

Once I married Camisha, she showed me a different side of her that I just couldn't deal with. She was always in a bad mood, and always complaining about our money situation. Simply put, she was never happy. Because of her, I eventually ended up leaving a lucrative job, working for the State of Florida, to become my own boss. She changed the course of my life.

One Saturday afternoon she wanted to go to the county fair. I tried to tell her I'd paid all the bills and there wasn't any money left over to go to the fair. As usual, she wasn't trying to hear that.

*"Well, I know where we can get some extra money from, Michael."*

*Here we go,* I thought.

*"Just take my wedding ring to the pawnshop and you can go back and get it on your payday,"* she'd said, as if she'd just thought of a brilliant idea.

To keep from hearing her mouth any further, I pawned the ring. Of course, I never got it back, and from there, things just kept getting worse.

Nevertheless, we did end up going to the fair that day, but I didn't enjoy one minute of it. I should've known earlier on that she wasn't Mrs. Right when my mother wouldn't even agree to meet her. *Mike, when it comes to you and your sister's relationships, keep me out of it. I didn't put you in them, and I sure as hell can't get you out of them*, I recall her saying.

My mother was a smart lady, and, oh, how I wish I had listened to her when it came to her opinion of Camisha.

There's also another time during our short-lived marriage that comes to mind. The two of us had been cooped up in the house on a Saturday afternoon and she approached me with an invite.

"Michael, would you like to go to the club as a couple tonight? I've been at the hair salon all day and I'm dying to show off my new hairdo."

"Sure," I replied. "It's been a while, so I'd love to accompany my wife to the club."

I wanted our night out to be as pleasant as possible, so I decided to go the extra mile to score some points. Right away, I rushed outside to wash my car. Afterward, I got myself cleaned up and proceeded to pick out the right suit to wear. Most importantly, I had to make sure I had enough money in my pockets to keep Camisha happy. Mainly, because she spent it faster than I could make it. If I had known how reckless she would be with the money I would have stayed single. I would give her my check every payday as if she was the bank. I swear, I can't ever remember a time throughout our entire marriage when I was able to keep my own money in my own pocket.

Anyway, while I was in the bedroom looking through my suit collection, I overheard one of Camisha's lonely ass girlfriends knocking on the door before she was let inside. The slight smile I had on my face immediately turned into a frown. *Maybe they'll just talk for a few minutes before Camisha sends her tired ass home.* Imagine how mad I was when she still hadn't left after being there for four hours. "Damn, this bitch ain't gone yet?" I mumbled to myself as I glanced at the watch on my wrist.

"Hey, baby, it's eight o'clock," I said, making my way into the room they were in. "You know it takes you at least three hours to get dressed."

"Michael, it's cool," she replied. "Since you can see that I have company, you go ahead and to the club without me."

"But I thought we were going together?"

"Yeah, but my girl is here so I think I'm just gonna just chill with her."

To say I was angry would've been the understatement of the year. Camisha knew I didn't like to go to the club by myself, and it had been her idea. If I knew she was gonna back out at the last minute, I would've called my boy Aaron, or Ed, another clown ass nigga I'd hang out with from time to time.

After we debated for an hour, I was like fuck it, I'm riding solo. I must admit being loyal to her wasn't an easy job and it took everything I had in me to do so, especially since she wasn't making love to me anymore. Even despite her holding back on sex, I had remained dedicated since day one. Never cheated or even looked at another woman. Now, here she was throwing me out the door to head to the club all by myself, knowing temptation was a muthafucker.

On the way to the club, I thought back to the time one of my clients came into my office with a proposition I couldn't resist. I had cut her food stamps off because she wasn't in compliance with the rules of receiving assistance from the State...

*"Excuse me, Mr. Valentino,"* she blurted out, as she walked in complaining and fussing.

*I found it a bit odd when she took it upon herself to close the office door behind her. I was busy at my desk with my head down.*

*My eyebrows lowered and the corners of my mouth tightened*

slightly. *"Yes, may I help you?"* I asked, without taking my eyes off the task at hand.

*"My name is Ms. Sharon Connolly. My food stamps have been placed on hold because I didn't bring in the worksheet for the job search."*

I inhaled, and slowly exhaled, before looking up in her direction. She had made herself comfortable by sitting down in the chair on the other side of my desk. Her legs were crossed, and I couldn't stop my eyes from taking in their thickness. She was as beautiful as could be—caramel complexion, hazel-brown eyes, and shoulder-length hair. My mouth fell open as if I was looking at the face of Janet Jackson or Halle Berry. I was both stunned and speechless.

She brushed an index finger across her bottom lip and bit down on it as she looked at me. Next, she licked her lips, allowing her tongue to dance across them. Her hand moved slowly down the length of her legs.

*"If I open this,"* she said, pointing at the flower between her legs, *"will you turn my cash assistance and food stamps back on?"*

Before I could find my voice, she spread them open widely. To my surprise, she wasn't wearing any panties. Now, here she was sitting right in front of me with her legs wide open, displaying the nicest pussy I had ever seen.

*Damn, do I eat it, kiss her, or just start fuckin' her right here in my office?* All kinds of thoughts raced through my mind.

Then, a voice rang out over the intercom. *"Mr. Valentino, call on line two."*

*"Hello, this is Mr. Valentino,"* I answered, as I tried to sound as normal as possible.

*"Hi, honey, are you busy?"* It was Camisha, and I was as nervous as hell.

*What in the hell does she want? She never calls me at work,* I thought, but dared not say it aloud. Instead, I answered, *"No, not really,"* I lied. *"Just looking over a client's case so I can turn her cash assistance back on. Why, what's up?"*

*"Well, I'm on my break and I just wanted to make sure you were*

*at the office before I came over to take you out to lunch."*

*"Oh, okay. How far away are you?"*

*"I'm in the building as we speak."*

*Damn, I guess I won't be cheating today, I thought. I looked over at Camisha and covered the mouthpiece of the phone with my hand. "Yo', close your legs," I whispered. "My wife is about to come to my office."*

*"What was that, baby?" Camisha asked.*

*"Nothing, honey. I was just talking to a client who was just about to leave."*

*"Oh, okay. So which office door do I come to?" she asked. "Oh, never mind," she said before I could reply. "Here it is, I found it." She walked in just as Ms. Connolly was getting herself together.*

*"Hello, I'm Mrs. Valentino, nice to meet you," she said, introducing herself to my client.*

*"Hello. It's nice to meet you too," Ms. Connolly replied.*

*"Am I interrupting?" my wife asked.*

*"No, not at all," I quickly replied. "Don't be silly, Camisha."*

*She quickly gave us both a nice smile but her expression seem to say 'yeah right, you were about to hit that lil' cute thing'.*

*Hell, I should've hit it since you ain't giving me none, I thought.*

*"Mr. Valentino, do you think you'll be able to turn my assistance and food stamps back on?" my client looked at me and asked.*

*"Why of course, Ms. Connolly. Since you showed me your job sheet, I should have them both back on in no time." I smiled.*

*"Thank you. And I must say, you have such a beautiful wife, Mr. Valentino."*

*"Oh, why thank you." I turned my focus on Camisha and added, "She can be beautiful some of the times and ugly at others."*

*"Enjoy your lunch, Mr. Valentino. And thank you once again for helping me with my case."*

*"You're quite welcome, Ms. Connolly. And you have a nice day as well."*

*Camisha smirked as she looked from me to my client. "It was nice meeting you and thank you for the compliment," she quickly chimed in.*

*Ms. Connolly walked out the door and my hard-on left right along with her.*

Damn, she was fine. I can't even lie, I thought about shawty the rest of that day. I wish like hell I could've entered that pretty little hole of hers. Driving to the club, thinking back on that day, had my emotions on overdrive. How in the hell had I let that pretty lil' thing get away from me?

Now, I'm about to be at the club by myself, mad as hell Camisha even let me out solo just so she could stay in with her girlfriend.

On top of that, I was already mad about the plans she and her girlfriends had to go out later in the week to gawk at male strippers.

When I pulled up at the club it was already packed, as usual. While looking for the perfect parking spot, I gazed at all the beautiful females on deck. *Shit, they out here tonight.* I mean, the line was backed up with beautiful ladies waiting to get inside so they could get their groove on.

As I walked by all the clubgoers, I heard a few women talking to each other.

"Girl, ain't that Mr. Valentino from the Wages Program?" one girl asked the other.

"Damn sho' is, girl. That's him with his fine ass," her friend replied.

"I thought he was married," the first girl inquired.

"Girl, he is married, but I don't see no wife with his ass tonight." Both girls giggled.

Since I was trying to get inside the club before it got too packed, I breezed right on by them like I hadn't heard them talking about me.

When I entered the club the D.J. had the place turned up already. Feeling like all eyes were on me, I walked straight to the bar. As I headed to the bar I smiled at all the ladies I made eye contact with. Rubbing my two fingers across my lips coolly, I felt like Morris Day and shit.

"Yes, yes, the club looks kind of right tonight," I said to myself, as I leaned on the bar and ordered my drink.

"Hello, beautiful, can I get a Sex On the Beach, please?"

"Yes, sir, coming right up! Will there be anything else I can get you tonight?"

"Well, since you asked," I replied and added, "is there any chance you would write your phone number down for me so we can meet up for dinner and drinks?" She smiled at me and stepped away to make my drink.

"That'll be five dollars, sir."

I pulled out a twenty-dollar bill and placed it in her hand. "Keep the change." I winked and grabbed my drink.

"Excuse me!" she called out, as I began to walk away. "You forgot something." I turned around. "I thought you wanted my phone number?"

"You know I do, so, where is it?" I asked with a devilish grin on my face.

She slid a piece of paper over to me. "You better call me. And make sure you don't lose it."

I eased the paper in my pocket, smiled again, and made my way to a corner of the club. I sipped on my drink as I eyed the women in the building. Standing a few inches away, the same two women I'd passed in line were pointing in my direction, talking to one another about me and the outfit I had on.

"Girl, he be dressed like that at work too," the one pointing at me said.

"Nah, for real?" the other replied.

"Yes, child! He be doing the little Wages Seminar, explaining the Wages Program. And girl, we can't hear nothing he be saying. We be all in his mouth checking his smooth ass out and shit. Girl, they say he be acting all shy and shit like he tryna be loyal to his wife."

"Well, if that's the case, why he all up in here tonight by himself?" the second girl asked curiously.

"I have no idea, but if I get a few more drinks in me he might be getting up in this lonely female tonight," the girl doing the most gossiping said.

However, listening to the two females talking had my curiosity aroused, but my attention was suddenly focused elsewhere.

"Girl, you so crazy"—the two women high-five each other and laughed out loud—"how you know that man would wanna be with you anyway?"

"Shit, he don't have to want me to want this pussy," the first girl said, "and it can be *all* his if he wanna get up in it. He just don't know it yet."

While I was standing there listening to the two chicken heads talk about me, Miss Pretty-Ass Sharon, the client who had been in my office the other day, walked in looking like a million bucks. *Damn, could I be so lucky as to see her again? And in the club at that? Maybe coming to the club alone wasn't such a bad idea after all.* My thoughts raced around my head a mile a minute.

I quickly finished my drink and headed straight for Ms. Connolly. "Excuse me, Ms. Are you here alone?"

She turned to look at me and her smile melted me instantly. "Well look who's in here tonight. Mr. Valentino with his shy ass."

"Nah, let me explain why I reacted the way I did the other day. My wife be tripping," I told her. "And if she would have caught us in any kind of compromising situation neither of us would be here right now."

"I understand, Michael. I'm just teasing you," she said. She giggled. "For real though, if you were my husband, I wouldn't even let you work up there 'round all them single thirsty ass bitches."

"Should I take that as a compliment or are you teasing me again?" I smiled coyly, faking the shy guy I'd been deemed.

"I'm dead ass serious, Michael. You should hear how some of the women be talking about how nice and shit you be looking."

"Hell, as a matter of fact, I heard some of that talk tonight," I said, "by the two over there in the comer." I pointed at the two chicken heads.

"See what I mean, and not to mention how sweet they say you are to them when it comes to helping them with their case."

"Well, I do try to help the ladies out as best as I can. Everyone needs to eat." Changing the subject I said, "So, can I get you a drink?"

"I really don't drink that much, but I guess one little drink won't hurt me."

"Fine. One drink coming right up." I ordered her an Amaretto Sour, a smooth little drink I fell in love with over in Germany during my Military days. "Here you go, beautiful."

"Thank you. And where is your wife tonight?" she asked with raised eyebrows. "And don't tell me she let you come out all by yourself?"

"Well, she was supposed to come with me, but one of her girlfriends came over. So, she decided to stay in with her and do the girl thing," I said, getting upset all over again.

"Sorry to hear that, Michael. I hope she knows what she's doing. A nice-looking man like you, all alone in here with all these women . . . umph, she's better than me."

"Since you put it like that, where's *your* man? I could say the same thing about your man and your lil' cute ass." I flirted. "Why would any man leave you all by yourself up in here? Hell, it's a lot of thirsty ass niggas up in here looking for Ms. Right."

"Yep. You are absolutely right. I just can't find the right guy. So, I decided to come in here and get my grown and sexy on. My homegirl was supposed to meet me but I don't think she got here yet."

"Okay, I see. But since she isn't here yet do you mind if I tag along as your bodyguard?"

"That's fine with me, Michael, but I'm not fighting no women in here over you," she said and laughed.

"Same thing here, Sharon. I don't want no guys trying to fight me over you either."

We laughed and joked around while kicking back in the club. While I kept her company, I had to admit I was having a nice time drinking, chilling, and laughing at different people in the club. I hadn't even thought about my wife standing me up for her lonely girlfriend. Sharon was keeping me company and keeping my mind off my troubles at home.

"Michael, if you're so lonely at home, why don't you just leave your wife?" Sharon asked. Her curious expression caused me to ponder her question before answering.

"Yeah, I've thought about it, but, honestly, a part of me really loves her."

"You know . . . that's the first time I've heard a married guy openly admit he loved his wife."

"So why aren't you married, Sharon?"

"I'm just waiting on Mr. Right, Michael. Maybe you can hook me up with one of your friends."

I'm thinking to myself . . . *yeah right, the only friend I have is my boy Aaron, and he's head over heels in love with his girl Tasha.* Then there's my homeboy, Ed, who's so stuck on his self, he only dates women he thinks he looks better than.

"I don't hang with anyone, Sharon. But when I do run across a nice brother who I feel will treat you right, I'll do my best to hook y'all up."

"Now may I have this dance, please?"

"I thought you'd never ask, Mr. cool."

As we walked to the dance floor, I couldn't help but notice how fine she was. She was, what we call down in Florida, "phat da def", a slang phrase used for a woman with a banging body.

After dancing with her for a few songs I needed some fresh air. We walked off the dance floor together and she must've read my mind because she suggested exactly what I was thinking.

As we walked outside of the club, to my surprise, Mrs. Camisha and her lonely ass girlfriend just happened to be riding past the club.

"What's wrong, Michael? You look like you saw a ghost or something," Sharon said, noticing the look on my face.

"Nah, I just saw my damn wife and her lonely ass girlfriend

drive by. I'm sorry to dip on you like this, but I gotta follow her and see where they going," I said and began walking away in rapid steps. It was nice seeing you again, Sharon," I called out over my shoulder, "hopefully, I'll see you again soon!"

I ran off so fast I didn't hear the response. If I had to guess, I'd say she told me to call her when I got the chance. Whatever she said, I didn't care at the time. I was too busy trying to get to Camisha.

I sprinted to my car full speed while wearing a pair of expensive ass Stacey Adams, in a nice ass suit, trying to catch up to my wife before she got away.

I got inside my car and started it up before barely closing the car door. *Where could she be going and why did she wait three hours before leaving the house?*

She made a left turn onto John Young Parkway. Then I knew exactly where she was going. Straight to her mom's house to drop off her two kids before heading out to the club. "Oh no, not tonight, young lady," I mumbled out loud. And by the time she got to her mother's house, I was pulling up in the driveway.

Her girl was in the car listening to the radio so she didn't see me walk from behind the car and head to the front porch. Camisha had gone to the back of the house to take her kids inside, so I waited out front so I could surprise her when she ran back out.

I heard her yell to her mom that she'd be back the following morning to pick her kids back up. As she made her way back to her car in a hurry to get to the club, I bolted off the front porch like a flash of lightning.

"And where the hell you think you going, Miss Lady?" She was completely caught off guard, so she tried to turn the tables.

"Oh, no, homebody! I just saw you outside the club with that same little hussy who was in your office the other day, playa," she said all loud and shit. I saw y'all walking outside the club together, so what? Were y'all two about to go get a hotel, or was you gonna fuck that food stamp-receiving bitch outside in your car?"

"Neither one, Camisha," I answered, clearly caught up. "I was about to come home to be with you."

"Yeah right! Well too bad, 'cause I'm going to the club so I can help people with their food stamps too."

"Oh, now you got jokes, Camisha? You might as well cancel your club plans 'cause you going back home with me, Miss Lady!"

She quickly threw her hands up. "And who gonna stop me from going to the club, Michael?"

"Damn, Camisha! We 'bout to throw hands 'cause I said you not going to the club?"

"Yes," she replied sternly.

*Damn, this girl about to fight me over going to the club.* "Well let's get it on," I egged her on. Now, why did I say that? I must've forgotten how nice she was with her hands, and she was most definitely nice. After all the ass whoopings she took from her first baby daddy, she mastered the skills of championship boxing.

I was about to get a first-class ticket to one of the nicest ass whoopings I'd ever received. I quickly pulled down her halter top. I thought revealing her breasts would stop her from wanting to fight me.

Wrong! Those pretty ass titties of hers fell out and she went into fight mode and started swinging on me.

"Hold on, Camisha!" I yelled out. "Cover them thangs up."

She wasn't having it and she kept right on swinging. Me, on the other hand, was bobbing and weaving like Ali.

"Man, forget this shit, Camisha! I'm leaving you and them badass kids of yours. I'm going to the house right now to get my clothes and then I'm out!"

I jumped in my car doing about one hundred miles per hour, trying to get home before she did. When I got there, Camisha was right behind me.

"Oh, so you call yourself leaving? Okay, get the hell out and don't come back," she yelled.

And before I could move to the left to counter her punch— *WHAP!*—she got me smack dab in my right eye. The blow caused a loud ringing in my ear. Then she broke my pinky finger, before stabbing me in the back with a knife.

She threw all my clothes out the door, along with my big screen TV, and all I could do was stand there bleeding from my back, wondering what I would do.

First, I picked up my clothes, then I placed my broken big-screen TV in my car, and headed to the hospital to get fixed up.

Pulling out of the driveway, I realized I couldn't see out of my right eye due to it being closed from the right hook she'd landed to my face. I knew I needed to get it seen so I took my chances and drove there anyway.

On the way there, all I could do was think about that cute ass of Sharon's, wishing I would've stayed at the dub with her instead of being in a fight with Camisha, a.k.a. Mike Tyson.

By the time, I reached the hospital, my eye had swollen up so bad, the doctor wanted to call the police. He said I looked like I'd been jumped by at least four guys at one time.

Once I told him it was my wife, Camisha, he couldn't believe it.

"You mean to tell me that pretty young lady who came in here the other day for a spider bite did this to you?"

"Yep, that's Camisha," I replied, looking all sad and shit.

"Damn, that girl has some skills," he said, as he started to work on me.

I was in bad shape—a swollen eye, broken pinky finger, and a stab wound in the back—all from a woman I considered the baddest female in Orlando.

*Yeah right, the baddest thing about Camisha was how nice she was with them muthafuckin' hands.*

Michael Gallon

## CHAPTER TWO
### THE BUSINESS

After the doctor patched me up at the hospital, I needed to find a spot to lay my head down for a few days. There was only one person that came to mind at that time. My dear cousin, Edward Valentino, also lived in Orlando.

I knew he would let me stay with him for at least a few days until I healed up. He lived in a nice, gated community off International Drive, which was about thirty minutes from the hospital.

When I finally got there, it was somewhere around four thirty in the morning. I had been knocking for about three minutes when he finally came to the door. Edward stood a massive six feet five and weighed two hundred fifty pounds. He had curly black hair and hazel-brown eyes. He was raised as a mamma's boy, so he made sure he kept his lavish three-bedroom apartment spotless—a habit he not only got from his beautiful mother, but from his three older sisters, Cyntrena, Yolonda, and yours truly, Felicia, as well.

"Who is it?" he yelled from the other side. "Knocking on my damn door at four thirty in the morning," he snapped. I could hear his footsteps stomping toward the door.

"Ed, it's me, Mike," I yelled back. I was excited and nervous because I didn't exactly know how bad I looked at the time.

"Who?" he asked as if he didn't recognize my voice.

"Mike, your cousin from Lakeland!" He opened the door still half asleep and shit.

"Man, who in the fuck did you get in a fight with?" he asked, as he finally focused on the hideous look of my swollen face. He looked me up and down from head to toe. I held my head down because I still couldn't see out of my right eye.

"Man, what's up?" I reached my hand out and dapped him up.

"What's up, hell! I need to be asking your beat-up-ass that question, don't you think."

"C'mon, Ed, man . . . Is it that bad?"

"Hold on, cuz . . . do I need to go get my pistol so we can go get them fools who jumped your ass?"

"Funny, Ed. Man didn't nobody jump me. My damn wife Camisha did this to me," I replied in a flat, soft tone. I was sad, and I was hurt.

"Damn, you didn't press charges on her ass? 'Cause, it looks like she beat the brakes off of your ass," he said, as he ushered me inside his lavish three-bedroom apartment.

"Nah, man, I love her too much to be pressing any charges on her. And besides, she's my wife. So why would I wanna put them nosy ass police officers in my fuckin' business?"

"Man, forget that. The way she got you lookin', it's clear she don't give a damn about yo' black ass," he said. He walked to his kitchen to get something to drink.

"You might be right, Ed, but she's still my wife. Hey, pour me some of whatever you about to drink 'cause I can use it right now."

"Damn, you just got beat up, and now you thirsty too?" Ed laughed.

"Whatever, Ed. So you got jokes, right?" I chuckled, as he poured me some orange juice. I drank it even though I was hoping for something stronger.

"Man, you can't even go out nowhere lookin' like that. Have you seen yourself in the mirror yet?" He shook his head from side to side. "And what's that shit on your damn pinky finger?"

I looked down at my hand. "Oh, she broke my pinky finger right before she stabbed me in the back."

"Damn, c'mon, cuz. You let her do all that to you and you didn't even attempt to call the police?"

"Nope, I just picked up the clothes she threw all over the front lawn, put them inside my car and drove off to the nearest hospital with my eye swollen shut."

"Man, you crazy as hell. I'ma call your sister, Cynthia. I know damn well she'll drive over here from Lakeland and put them paws on your so-called wife." Ed pulled out his cell phone.

"Nah, Ed. Man, that's the last person I want to know about this, man. You know how crazy Cynthia can be."

Which was so true. The last time my sister put her hands on another female she almost chopped the poor woman's arm slam the fuck off. And the crazy thing was, she was the one in the wrong for fuckin' that female's man. Nope, Cynthia Valentino was not the one to fuck with, especially when it came to family. And she would go ham if she saw me looking like I had just stepped out of a horror movie.

"Well, man, I'ma go back to bed and get some sleep."

"No problem, cuz, and thanks for letting me stay here for a few days. I appreciate it."

"No problem. What was I supposed to do? Let you go back for a rematch with Iron Mike Tyson?" He laughed at his joke.

"Funny, cuz, I see you love telling jokes early in the morning."

"Shit, you can see that but you couldn't see that right jab coming could you?"

"C'mon, man, I know it looks bad but I'll be okay in a few days."

"I guess so, cuz. I'm just joking with you, Mike. Shit, you the real comedian in the family. I'm surprised you ain't cracked a few jokes about it yourself."

"Yeah, whatever, Ed. I'll see you after we get some sleep."

"Sounds good, cuz. I wanna let you in on a little business venture I been thinking about us doing together anyway. If shit work out both of us can be making some real money 'round here."

"Since we already up, tell me about it now. You know I'm always game to try something new," I said, eager to know what he was talking about.

"Nope, you gonna have to wait 'til later. Believe me when I tell you, you gonna love it. It's something right up your alley," he said, as he stood up and walked towards his bedroom.

"Yo', Ed, you know I'm still at the Wages Program, so, whatever it is, I'ma have to fit it around my busy schedule," I said behind him.

He turned around just as he opened his bedroom door and asked, "How much is that job paying you, Mike?"

"Right now, I'm at fifteen dollars an hour with a few perks here and there," I answered proudly.

"Okay, hold that thought, and when the sun comes up, we'll talk about gettin' to some real money. It'll be our own money we'll be making, you gonna have fun doing it, *and* you'll thank me in the long run." With that, he went into his bedroom and closed the door behind him.

A couple of hours later, I woke up eager to hear what my cousin had to tell me about the new business venture, but, to my surprise, he had already left for church. He hadn't even woken me up before he left. I wouldn't have gone anyway, not looking the way I did, so I took my happy black ass back to sleep.

The right side of my face was swollen so badly, I had to sleep on the left side. As I lay tossing and turning in Ed's guest bedroom, all I could think of was Camisha, and I hoped she was thinking of me too. As I lay there with thoughts of her on my mind, I dozed off praying that when I woke up, my face would be gone down, but to no avail.

When I woke up a few hours later, it seemed as if my face had gotten bigger. I thought about calling Sharon, or even the female bartender who had served me my drink that night, especially since she'd told me to call her. But every time I started to call one of them, I would glance at my swollen face in the mirror and quickly throw my phone down in disgust.

*Who am I fooling?* I kept thinking to myself. *I can't see nobody looking like this.* And I meant that literally. And I damn sure didn't want them to see me. Camisha had done a job on me. It was as if she knew by marking my face up she wouldn't have to worry about me trying to get next to any other female. At least, no time soon.

During the time I spent at Ed's he never did sit down and explain the business venture he had for us. He just kept putting me off, telling me that in time he would explain it to me. So, with nothing else to do, I just healed up and decided to go find my wife since I was still madly in love with her. Even though she had put her hands on me, she still meant the world to me.

The first place I went to look was her job. As I walked into the Super Walmart where she worked, I spotted her at her usual cash register. I walked up behind her just as one of the customers in her line alerted her that I was approaching.

"Hi, Michael," she said when she turned around and saw me.

"Hi, Camisha," I replied, trying to hold back tears of excitement. Seeing her again for the first time in days made me emotional. I have to admit though, every time I saw Camisha my heart melted. You know how you get that funny feeling like you're about to lose your breath? Yeah, well that's the feeling I'm talkin' 'bout and that's exactly what I felt every time that I saw that beautiful woman.

"Michael, I'm so sorry about the other night and I just can't live without you in my life," she said. She had forgotten about the customers in line because as she focused on me she appeared to have put them on pause as if they weren't there.

"I can't take not having you in mine either, Camisha. I missed you so much these last few days," I admitted. Total strangers were listening in as we confessed our love to one another.

"So why don't you just come back home, Michael? I miss you and so do the kids."

"Say no more, boo. I'm on the way there right now," I said without a second thought. "What time do you get off?"

"I'll be home at five this evening."

"Okay, I'll be there waiting on you," I replied. I left the store and headed for the house we lived in.

Driving home "As Soon as I Get Home" a song by Baby Face, played through my car's stereo system. I couldn't help but wonder if she was going to change or if our relationship would remain the same.

I was so tired of the same old routine night after night and day after day. We would argue and then she would sleep on the couch wrapped up with her son, Tazz, while I was on the other couch wrapped up all by myself. The whole house would be silent except for the sound of the television watching the three of us sleep. As if that wasn't enough, she would still wake up the next morning in a fucked-up mood and wouldn't even say good morning to me. Each time it happened, it would leave me in such a foul mood I would get to work and take it out on my helpless clients.

Camisha arrived home just like she'd said, at five o'clock on the dot, but, as usual, she had an excuse for the not wanting to stay home. This time she'd told we needed to go to her mother's house for something. The truth was our air conditioner was broken and she didn't want to stay at the house because it was so damn hot in there. So, we left.

When we arrived at her mother's house, her mother started adding her two cents before I could even get in the door good.

"Mike, if you don't take those shades off inside the house," she said. "There is no need for you to be acting all cool inside of my house, young man." Without saying anything to Camisha I just walked away to the kitchen, trying to play things off. Of course, her mother was right on my heels. So, I went ahead and pulled my shades off.

"Good Lord, who hit you in your eye, Michael?"

"My mamma put them paws on him the other night, Grandma! You shoulda seen it," Shayla, Camisha's lil' badass daughter said, all out loud and shit before I could reply. "Mamma was tearing him up," she said as if her lil' black ass was happy her mom had beat the hell out of me that night.

Her hands rested on her hips and her eyebrows scrunched downward as she looked toward Camisha. "Paws? What in the hell are *paws*, Camisha?"

"We just had a little misunderstanding, but we Gucci now, Momma," Camisha answered short and quick.

"Not with the poor man's eye looking like he just lost a heavyweight fight with Iron Mike Tyson."

*Damn*, I thought, *why is it that everybody keeps comparing my eye to somebody who got hit by Mike Tyson*? Did it look that damn bad? I was lost in my thoughts while Camisha's mother got on her about putting her hands on me like that.

After a few hours had gone by, we returned home to a hot ass house.

Five minutes after we got home, my phone started to ring. I took a quick peek to see who was calling and to my surprise, it was my cousin, Ed. I pressed the answer key.

"Cuz, you busy?" he asked as soon as the lines connected.

"Nah, just getting in, why what's up?"

"You ready for me to talk with you about the business we 'bout to get off the ground?"

"Okay, I'm all ears, go ahead."

He started talking about Strippers and began telling me how much money we could make by taking them to the different strip clubs throughout Florida.

He touched on how we could take them to bachelor parties and make even more money from charging men who requested their services. I listened attentively.

"Check this out, Mike," he continued, as he broke the numbers of the profit line down, "if we charge each girl thirty-five percent of what she makes each night, that should be roughly a thousand dollars a night," he concluded. His tone dripped enthusiasm and his energy level was on a hundred.

"Damn, Ed, they make that much each night they go dance?" I asked as visions of Franklins danced around in my head. See, I had never, ever, ever been to a strip club, so I was like a newborn baby to the game when he brought the idea to me. But my math was on point

"Yep. Give or take, it's not always that much, but it's always good money," Ed insisted.

That was a damn lie but I wouldn't find that out until later on down the road—the hard way. I would later come to learn that most nights some of the women dancing for us wouldn't make nearly that amount of money; in fact, it was closer to a loss than a win.

"So, Ed, what would we call the women who gonna dance for us at these clubs and parties you talkin' about?"

"Shit, man, I don't know. You can't think of a nice name that would entice people to wanna see what they about?" He asked as if to say 'I came up with the idea, didn't I.'

"Hold on, give me a minute or two to think of something that will catch the attention of the whole world," I answered and began contemplating.

"Ed, I got it!" I said louder than intended.

"What, cuz? Remember, it has to be the perfect name that will just melt in a nigga's mouth," Ed replied.

"We'll call them the Florida Hot Girls," I proclaimed.

"Oh shit, sounds good to me. Ain't there a song called "Looking for a Hot Girl" by Cash Money out right now?"

"Yep, it sure is, man. It'll go perfectly with what we 'bout to do. That can be the theme music for the dancers," I said getting more excited by the minute. "When do we start?"

"As soon as we get some ladies together," he answered.

"Do you have any right now who would make the team?" I inquired.

"Not right now, but I do have a few in mind, Mike. I'll call you back tomorrow and let you know what I come up with, cuz."

"Aight, holla at me first thing tomorrow," I said, as I hurried off the phone before Camisha could come in the room and assume I was on the phone with a female.

So that was the night I came up with a name that not only caught the attention of many men and women but also got the attention of them damn Alphabet Boys who eventually kicked in my goddamn front door. Not only did it melt in a nigga's mouth, but it stayed burned in their minds to this very day.

Needless to say, I never got that call from my cousin, Ed and he never assisted me in any kind of way when it came to the Florida Hot Girls. Anyway, just keep reading and you'll see exactly what I mean.

The minute I hung up the phone with my cousin, my mind went to work on the type of females I would recruit. My marriage was on the rocks, and even though Camisha claimed things would change, I knew better.

# The Murder Queens

I couldn't believe that after one month of being married to her, it was about to come to an abrupt halt just like that. We had gotten married in January and would be divorced by February of the same damn year.

*** 

AFTER A FEW WEEKS OF THE SAME old bullshit at home and the constant flow of women on my case log, my life changed forever.

One Monday morning, I walked into my office and my supervisor was standing at the front desk as though she was waiting on me. Boy, was I right.

"Excuse me, Mr. Valentino, I need to speak with you before you start your day," she said, just as I walked by the desk.

I thought to myself... *What in the hell have I done now? Shit, it's always something getting me caught up.*

She cleared her voice and crossed her arms over her chest like a mother about to scold her child. "Mr. Valentino, it has been brought to my attention that you did something very disrespectful to one of your coworkers the other day," she said sternly.

I displayed a concerned look on my bewildered face. "I don't recall anything out of the ordinary, Mrs. Smith. What was it they say I did that made them feel uncomfortable?" I asked.

"Well, Mrs. Hansberry said you walked into her office the other day and threw two extra-large Magnum condoms on her desk and then walked away smiling." She cleared her throat again.

"I was just teasing her when that happened. I was telling her about my days as a male stripper and those were the type of condoms I had to wear over my manhood while performing."

"Well, Mr. Valentino, I don't know anything about that, but we don't allow our staff members to come in the workplace and indulge in anything that displays a sexual nature," she said with a grim look on her big ass face.

"I'm very sorry, Mrs. Smith. It won't happen again."

"I know it won't happen here again, Mr. Valentino, because you've left me with no other choice but to transfer you to the downtown office—effective immediately," she said in inevitability.

"Let that be a lesson to you, Mr. Valentino, and please don't let your private life affect your future here with this company. When we hired you to do the Wages Seminars and assist the special needs women with job placement, we thought we had hired the right man for the job. Don't let me down. You came highly recommended from the Goodwill Wages Program out of Hillsborough County."

As I walked out of her office feeling humiliated, I knew exactly what she was trying to say. It appeared that whenever she felt like it, Ms. Camisha had been coming to my office, quite frequently, showing her ass and shit.

"Excuse me, Mr. Valentino, what was your stage name?" she asked, just as I started to close her office door.

*I know damn well she ain't just ask me what I think she did.* I thought. "Excuse me, ma'am?" I asked in the same stern tone she'd used with me just moments prior.

"You heard me, Mr. Valentino. What was your stage name?" she repeated. A smile wrapped around her large face.

"My stage name?" I was confused and wondered if Mrs. Smith was an undercover freak.

"Yes, your stage name . . . when you were dancing."

I started blushing and gave her one of my sexiest smiles. "Oh, they used to call me Sexual Chocolate." I continued to smile.

"Now why did they call you that, Michael?"

"If I tell you that, you might get offended."

"No, please tell me. I'm curious to know why they called you that."

"Well, Mrs. Smith, ain't that why I got transferred in the first place?"

"Okay, Mr. Valentino. I understand if you don't want to tell me why they called you that."

I closed the door so I could go to my office and retrieve my things. Before I walked away, I peeked my head back in the door and said, "Excuse me, Mrs. Smith . . . it was because chocolate melts in your mouth, not your hands."

"Get out of here, Mr. Valentino, you're so crazy." She smiled at me as though she wanted me to get up on her desk and give her a little private show right there in her office.

I could still hear her laughing as I said my goodbyes to my co-workers. Well, the ones who weren't offended about me having shown the Magnum condoms.

Truth be told, Mrs. Hansberry wanted to see how that condom looked on my manhood while it was enlarged and up in her stomach, and so did Mrs. Smith. I thought about it as I walked to my car. I sat there for a minute or two and laughed like Denzel Washington in the movie, "Mo Better Blues," before driving away.

Michael Gallon

## CHAPTER THREE
### STEAK, LOBSTER, AND SHRIMP

By now I had moved out of Camisha's house and purchased an apartment, not too far away from her home. She had put her hands on me once again, and I wasn't having it anymore.

My new place was okay since it had the basic things I needed to get me by and all the things a single man like myself needed. The important thing was that it was mine and I could come and go as I wanted to. All I had to do now was break it in with a pretty ass female. The first one that came to mind was Ms. Sharon's fine, cute, sexy ass.

I had her number stored in my phone as "Phat Da Def," but I hadn't spoken to her since the night Camisha put her hands on me. Nevertheless, I dialed her number. I was nervous just thinking about speaking to her.

"Hello?" She answered her phone on the very first ring.

"Hello? Is this Pha— I mean, excuse me, is Sharon home?"

"This is Sharon. What did you say before you said my name?"

"I was thinking about something else," I said, "I'm so sorry." I could hear her laughing under her breath.

"Okay, so who is this?"

"It's me, Sharon. Michael from the Wages office."

"Oh. Well, hello, Mr. Track star. I was wondering when you were going to call me."

"Let me explain that night to you really quick. I was trying to catch up to my wife before she got ghost in the streets. When I finally caught up with her at her mother's house we got in a big ass fight. I eventually ended up in the hospital from the beating she put on me that night."

"I'm sorry to hear that, Michael. Are you okay now?"

"Yeah, I'm doing alright. I've since moved on to better things. I'm sorry it took me so long to call you. I've just been so busy moving into my new apartment and all."

"Oh, so you've moved out of the home you shared with your wife?"

"Yeah, I just couldn't take it there any longer. So, I did the next best thing and left her and them badass kids of hers."

"So, you called me when you got yourself settled in at your new place?"

"Yep, and you're the first female I've called since moving here. Matter of fact, you're the *only* woman I've even talked to, period."

"So, what's on your mind, Mr. Michael."

"I was wondering if you'd like to come over and have dinner with me?"

"I would love to, sir. What's on the menu?"

"I was thinking about cooking up some steak and lobster along with some shrimp."

"Michael, you know you don't know how to cook all of that."

"Ms. Sharon, you would be surprised at all the things I know how to cook."

"Okay, that sounds good. What time do I need to be there for dinner?"

"I'd say 'round 'bout eight o'clock."

"Sounds good, Michael. Let me call my babysitter. Send me your address and I'll be there at eight o'clock. Is there a special way you'd like me to dress?"

*Yeah, come like you did that day in my office, with no panties on*, I wanted to say. Instead, I kept it cool and said, "No, not really, just bring that pretty face of yours and dress as casual as you'd like. I'll see you soon, Sharon. Peace.

When we hung up, I jumped up and down like the Dallas Cowboys had just won the Super Bowl. It was already half-past six so I had still needed to get to the Winn Dixie Supermarket to pick up the steaks, fresh lobster, and, of course, the shrimp.

Since I lived over in the Pine Hills area, I never knew who I might run into while out and about. There was always a chance of meeting some fine-ass females while out shopping, so I threw on something casual to head over to the grocery store.

As I pulled into the parking lot, I couldn't help but notice all the fly ladies out shopping for groceries.

"This is just the type of place for a nigga to get his mack on," I said to myself while looking for a place to park.

Within a few minutes of entering the store, I was on this cute, lil' Spanish chick who just couldn't stop smiling at me. I always used my last name when it came to mackin' the ladies since they seemed to think it was so cool and all. So, I walked over to her, spit a few words at her, and just like that, she was on my line.

"I'll be calling you real soon," I said after spittin' my game to her.

Walking away, she looked back at me and said, "You better call me too 'cause I'ma be waiting on that phone call, Valentino."

I made my way through a few of the store aisles and picked up the foods I needed. After paying for it in the checkout line, I headed for the door. Making my exit, I accidentally bumped into the last person I expected to see. Yep, you guessed it—Camisha and her badass little son, his grown ass self.

"Well, hello, Mr. Michael. You must be enjoying yourself since you got your own spot now?" she said in a sarcastic tone.

"Hello, to you, too, Camisha." I tried to remain cool, calm, and collected.

Before she could say anything else, her badass son, Tazz, had already started kicking me in my leg and shit. Just as I reached out to grab his little mannish ass, she blurted out, "You better not touch him, Michael!"

"Damn, you just gonna let his badass kick me all in my shin and shit, and I don't get to say nothing to him?"

"Michael, you know he's just a baby."

"Camisha, that little nigga is five fuckin' years old. He ain't no fuckin' baby!" I limped to my car and shit, and looking back at her, yelled, "That's exactly why we didn't make it! 'Cause you keep treating your son, who looks like a grown-ass fuckin' man, like a damn baby!" I quickly got inside my car and pulled off before they decided to jump me right there in the parking lot.

When I arrived back home, I was still looking behind me to make sure they hadn't followed me back to my crib. Hell, I wasn't taking any chances. Tazz was so short he could've played the stunt double on the movie *Lil Man*. He looked exactly like Marlon Wayans with a big ass head on a little ass body. He was so short, she could've put his lil' ass right through the windows, and he would've gone right in and unlocked my fuckin' doors like he lived there and shit. So, of course, I didn't feel safe until I locked the door and the damn window.

When the time the fear in me had calmed down, I got busy in the kitchen and got dinner ready for Ms. Sharon. I had the steaks marinating so they'd be ready to put on once she arrived, and then I steamed up some rice and mixed vegetables. To get the mood right, I let the soothing sounds of Keith Sweat play through the surround sound.

It was already eight-fifteen, so Sharon would be pulling up in the next few minutes. She'd texted me thirty minutes earlier to let me know she'd dropped her daughter off at the babysitters and was on the way.

I was as nervous as a muthafucker waiting on her to arrive. I double-checked my bedroom so everything would be on point when I got her in there. Next, I checked my condom box—extra-large Magnums, perfect. Ms. Sharon didn't realize that with the steak, lobster, and shrimp, she would be getting ten inches placed inside of her muthafuckin' stomach for dessert.

While I was in the mirror making sure my look was good, my doorbell rang. *Showtime!* I must admit, it had been a long time coming, especially since I hadn't been with anyone other than Camisha.

I opened the door and was pleasantly pleased. She was dressed in a pair of tight-ass jeans and a nice see-through shirt, and the cutest smile was etched across her face. Her hair hung down the spine of her back and she looked like she'd just stepped out of *Jet Magazine*.

"Hello, Michael, or should I call you Valentino?" she said by way of greeting.

"As pretty as you are, you can call me anything right now and I wouldn't even be mad at 'cha," I quickly replied.

Sharon was a beautiful female. Nice and slim, she looked as if she weighed about one hundred thirty pounds and stood five-feet six and a half inches and had a nice light-skinned complexion. The size of her breasts looked to be a 34B, nothing smaller or larger than that. And to go along with all that, she had a nice, beautiful pair of light hazel-brown eyes that shined ever so brightly when the light shined off of them.

She came in and had a seat in my living room while I prepared our dinner. I turned the volume down on Keith Sweat and turned on the TV for her.

"I must admit, Michael, you got it smelling good in here. I found your apartment by following the scent of the food," she said while looking around trying to adjust to the niceness of the surroundings.

"Well, I do aim to please, Sharon."

"If it tastes as good as it smells you've got me hook, line, and sinker," she said. She smiled at me from the sofa.

I returned the smiled, you know, the one like Prince had in the movie *Purple Rain*, when he and Apollonia were at the lake and she jumped in naked—my favorite movie by the way.

"Michael, you're a mess," she looked at me and said.

"Yep, that's usually what they all say after they eat this steak and lobster, and a little shrimp."

"Now, what's that supposed to mean, Mr. Michael?"

"Aw nothing, I'm just joking around," I said.

She made her way into the kitchen and watched me cook. Right on time, Jaheim and Keisha Cole came through the CD player, and their duet titled *I've Changed* blared through. She started singing and dancing like she was in the club and shit, moving them hips from side to side. The next thing I know, she started grinding up on John Boy, that's the name I had given my manhood. Within seconds, he started to wake up and stood at attention like the soldier he was.

"Alright now," I said, "if you wake up 'ole John Boy, you gonna have to deal with him."

"Who is John Boy?" she turned around and asked unknowingly. "Is he here with us?"

I pointed down at the bulge in my pants and her eyes grew as big as pancakes.

"Damn, Michael. I hope you got a big leash for John Boy 'cause he seems to be pretty big," she replied.

I picked her up and took her straight to my bedroom. She had a smile on her face as I placed her down on my bed. I turned my back to change the song to "Tonight" by Ready for The World, to get the mood right. I watched in delight as she proceeded to pull her thongs off, and it was a sight to see. She then unhooked her bra, and her breasts stuck out from her chest. They were perfectly round and looked so beautiful and firm. Her body was picture-perfect, as she stood before me butt-ass naked.

"Thank you," I couldn't help but say.

I reached for the Magnum condoms and she looked at me with her pretty little hazel-brown eyes and said so softly, "Michael, be gentle."

"Gentle is my middle name, just don't break my heart," I replied.

Before I could put the condom on, she took my manhood and placed it between her soft wet lips, and started to give my manhood some mouth-to-mouth resuscitation.

It was so good she had me climbing the walls, and my little black ass was talking in German from the way she was working me and shit.

"Sh-sh-shit, d-d-damnit, aww shit, hold up." I tried to push her head back. "Let me do you," I said all excited and shit.

"Michael . . . Michael, no. Not yet, wait a minute, please."

I flipped her lil' red ass over on her back and went for broke. I was eating her pretty lil' pussy like that nigga that be on them porn flicks—you know, the nigga they call Pretty Ricky. He made it big in the porn business doing a few underground porn flicks directed by this dude named Clyde Johnson.

Now, back to Sharon. First, I sucked her little clit until it was swollen. Then, I started blowing in her sweet ass until she couldn't take it. After that, I went back to slurping on her pussy until she pushed my head out of the way and screamed, "Michael, I'm 'bout to skeet all over your bed."

I jumped up to move out of the way, and before I knew it, she was gushing everywhere. *Damn, she skeetin' all over my brand new satin sheets*, I thought to myself.

As soon as she finished, I pushed all 10 inches of rock-hard dick up in her and watched as her mouth fell open.

"Oh, my God," she whispered in my ear, "it feels like you're in my stomach."

"Well, if I'm not there by now, I will be in a few more minutes," I replied.

For the next hour or so, we had hot passionate sex.

"Michael, I can't take no more," she panted, "it feels like you're knocking the bottom out of me."

"Hold on, baby. Give me like five more minutes. I wanna hit that sweet thang from the back."

Without rejection, she rolled over and got in position. Allowing the weight of her body to rest on her knees, she tooted her ass up high in the air, and gave me direct entry inside her slippery tunnel. She had another orgasm before I could get off my first one.

"Michael, please baby, let's take a break for a minute."

"Babygirl, I'm about to explode right fuckin' now." I screamed so fuckin' loud I think I must've scared her 'cause she jumped clear across the bed.

"Michael, are you okay?"

"I am now, Sharon. You the best," I told her.

"When was the last time you had some, Mr. Michael because you were up in me like you were trying to beat my guts up."

"Sharon, like I told you at the club, my wife never wanted to make love. She always had some type of excuse."

"Wow, she doesn't know what she was missing. I've never had a man make love to me like that."

"Why thank you, Ms. Sharon."

After she cleaned us both up, we went into the kitchen and enjoyed our steak, lobster, and shrimp dinner. We fell asleep about an hour later watching one of them Pretty Ricky porn flicks.

# Michael Gallon

## CHAPTER FOUR
### THE SETUP

I woke up the next morning yearning for more lovemaking with Ms. Sharon. The touch of my hands on her luscious soft hips caused an arch to form in her back—a clear indication that let me know she welcomed the thought.

After a few minutes long stroking her from the back, she turned around, looked at me, and said, "Michael, please take some of it out, you're gonna have me sore all day." I knew she was being truthful since I had put in some serious muthafuckin' work.

"Okay, let's get in the shower and maybe it won't hurt as much," I said, not wanting to lose the moment.

Taking her by the hand, I led her to the shower so we could continue to quench our thirst for one another's affection. I wanted to take advantage of every minute I had with her since I had to go to work later that day.

After about forty minutes of acting like two dogs in heat, we finally took some time to take showers.

Once done in the bathroom, we headed back to my bedroom to dress. I picked up the pants I'd worn the night before and reached in the pocket to retrieve some money. All I had was a pocketful of fifties, so I casually pulled out two crispy fifty-dollar bills and handed them to her.

A sour look spread on her face and her smile turned upside down. Her head tilted to the side as her hand rose and landed on her hip. "Michael, what is this for? Are you trying to pay me for sex," she asked.

I laughed before I answered her. "Sharon, that's for your babysitter. She watched your daughter all night, remember?

"Michael, my babysitter is my mother, silly."

"Oh, my bad. I didn't mean to offend you in any kind of way."

"No problem, keep your money, Michael. I just hope this wasn't a one-night stand," she said, as she pulled her panties up on her nice, red, round ass.

"Not at all, precious. I would love to see you again. Hell, I was hoping to see you again tonight if that's all right with you?" I asked, sitting on the edge of my bed, gazing at her sheer beauty.

"I'll see, Michael. Call me before you get off. I've got a few interviews today, so I don't know what time I'll be finished with everything I've got to do."

The two of us finished getting dressed and I walked her out and to her car. After saying our goodbyes, she leaned in and gave me a sweet kiss on my lips. I hugged her once more and headed back upstairs to my apartment.

I couldn't believe how nice and fine she was, and to think, she was about to be all mine. Not to mention how nice her sex game was. It had been a long time since I'd a woman who knew how to move her body along with mine, so being with her would be an exciting challenge.

The only problem I had was would she be cool with me being the manager of a group of butt-naked females. It was a secret I would have to keep from her because I sure as hell didn't want to lose her fine ass.

***

THAT MORNING, I ARRIVED AT MY new downtown office right at nine o'clock. I walked into the building and the front desk clerk looked as if she should've been working for a store inside of the mall.

She had beauty and stature and stood around five-eight and weighed around one hundred forty-two pounds. Even though she was a white female, she still caught my eye. From the first time I ever acknowledged the opposite sex, I always thought being with a white girl would lead to serious trouble. Not only from people of my race but from the opposite race as well. I had always dreaded the harsh reality of a sister ever having to find out that as a black man I had crossed over to the opposite race. I would never be able to live that sort of stigma down.

So, in other words, the beautiful white female who smiled at me from across her desk made me realize that being with her was off-limits.

"Good morning, sir. How may I help you?" she asked.

"Yes, I'm Michael Valentino, the new case manager from across town."

"Yes, sir, we've been expecting you," she stated politely. "Follow me to your desk please," she said. She smiled as though she knew I was undressing her with my eyes.

Now, in the new downtown location, I wouldn't have my own office like I'd had at the locations before this one. So, I would have to get used to having a desk that was surrounded by other co-workers.

I made myself comfortable and got right to work, working on the cases that had been left unattended for at least two months or so. My caseload was a whole lot bigger there, due to it being our downtown office which meant more clients.

My new supervisor at the downtown office was a little, short, fat, white lady who stood around five-foot-two and a hefty one hundred sixty pounds. Her cold deep-blue eyes seemed to constantly look at me as though I had shit or something on my face. She had given me the impression that she didn't like my kind of people *if* you get my drift.

As the day went on I felt as though something was wrong, like everyone in the office was watching me, waiting for me to fuck up so they could fire me. And as it turned out, that's exactly what they were planning to do. After my black ass got transferred I became a marked man within the company.

Little did I know, they had already set up a plan to get rid of me and it was about to be put in motion. That's when *she* walked in. *She,* meaning the cute black female they'd sent there to put their plan into effect.

She stood around five feet six and had a petite weight that looked to be around one hundred thirty-five pounds with a 34B breast size.

"Excuse me, sir. Are you my case manager?" the young dark-skinned woman asked, as she sat down at my desk. With my fingers entwined as though I was the shit and knew my shit didn't stink, I smiled at her kindly. I looked her over as though she was a hundred-dollar steak dinner at some fancy restaurant.

"I don't know. Let me check my computer. What's your name, please?"

"Seneavu Miller," she said smiling and showing all her teeth like she had won some coupons for free chicken at Popeye's. As she sat there, I couldn't help but ask myself would she fit in as a Florida Hot Girl?

"Yes, Ms. Miller. I'm your case manager," after a few minutes later of browsing through my caseload. "How can I assist you today?" I asked.

"Well, I went to purchase some groceries earlier today and they told me my food stamps had been terminated." She looked confused as explained what happened.

"Let me check your case and see what's going on with your food assistance." I looked through my computer so I could determine what the issue was with her food stamps.

"Ms. Miller, it looks as though your last case manager put a sanction on your case because you didn't comply with the Wages Program."

"Excuse me, sir," she replied, with the same confused look. "What do you mean? Could you please explain what that means?"

"Yes, I'll be more than happy to explain what happened. It appears you haven't been looking for any jobs nor have you been to any of the job seminar classes.

"Well, sir, I've been looking for a job, but no one seems to be hiring at the moment." She shifted her weight from one foot to the other.

It seemed to be the right moment to pop the question on her black ass. And I knew from looking at her she was a perfect candidate to become a Florida Hot Girl.

"Excuse me. Let me ask you something off the record." I sat back in my chair and crossed my legs.

"And what would that be, sir?" she said, while pulling her chair closer to my desk so she could hear what I had to say.

"Well, since you can't seem to find a job, have you ever thought about being a dancer?"

Her eyes lit up like a Christmas tree. "Yes, I have. Do you know someone I could talk to about that?"

"It just so happens, I'm about to start a dance group called the Florida Hot Girls. For starters, the girls will travel from club to club, and they'll also be booked for bachelor parties and other types of private parties. Does that sound like something that might interest you?"

"Hell yeah," she answered loudly. Some of the workers look in our direction. "Sorry," she said quietly. "I'm interested. How do I get in?"

"Okay, listen. Leave me your phone number and I'll give you a call tomorrow so we can meet up. I'll come by and give you a little interview. You know like . . . check out your body and shit. And then we can go from there."

"Don't you have to work tomorrow around this time?" she asked, trying to appear as though she cared about me and my job.

"Yeah, but I'm gonna call in tomorrow to clear up my schedule so we can get together."

"Okay, my number is 3052449024," she said rattling off the numbers as if it were a race.

"Hold on sweetheart." She had spit out the numbers so fast, I had to ask her to pause. "I didn't get 'em all. "

"I'm sorry." She smiled coyly. "I get like that when I'm excited."

If only I had known then what was ahead for me. If I had, I would've never taken that damn number that day.

As she walked away, I couldn't help but notice how fine she was but, at that time in my life, I wasn't in to dark-skin women. So, I brushed off the thought of fuckin' her the next day.

She had a nice ass and a bangin' body but she was black as hell. I knew if she got hired her stage name would be Midnight or Dark Chocolate.

*  *  *

It was finally five o'clock and time for me to clock out and head home. I couldn't wait to get out of that damn office and start recruiting more females for the group. I gotta admit, it felt good driving to my own apartment and not having to worry about Camisha or her badass kids. I didn't have to deal with her nasty ass attitude, and the only person I had to worry about was myself.

On the way home, my phone started to ring. I quickly looked at the caller ID and noticed it was none other than Ms. fine ass Sharon, so I answered it on the second ring.

"Hello."

"Hey, you. How was your day?" The pleasant voice on the other end was music to my ears.

"It was okay. The downtown office just stayed so busy with clients coming in with the same old problems. How was your day, beautiful?"

"It was all right until I had to come home and soak in the bathtub, due to the way you beat my little cootie cat to death last night and this morning," she said. As I drove, I tried not to laugh.

"Babygirl, I'm so sorry. It's just that it had been a long time since I'd had some real good sex."

"Whatever, Michael. Don't tell me something just to make me feel good. And anyway, why did you transfer to the downtown office?"

"You really don't want to know that right now," I told her. "But I'll tell you later on down the road. But seriously, boo, you are the bomb, from the way you kiss to the way you move your body in sync with mine. And especially the way you put John Boy in your mouth and worked him."

"I hope John Boy hasn't been in any other females lately," she spat. "Shit, I don't wanna be catching nothing up in my mouth, Michael."

"Sharon, believe me when I tell you I haven't been with anybody except my soon-to-be ex-wife."

"All right, Michael, I'm just gonna have to trust you. What are you doing tonight?" she asked.

"Right now, I don't have any concrete plans. I do have to make a few calls to some people about a new business I'm trying to start. Other than that, I'm free. Why, what's up with you tonight?"

# The Murder Queens

"I was trying to see you again if that's cool with you, Michael?"

"Okay, Sharon. Let me get home and make a few calls, and afterward, we can go from there. Is that cool with you, Boo?"

"Yes, Michael, that works for me. I'm on my way to the daycare to pick up my daughter now. I'll be waiting on you to call me, playa."

"Now there you go, why I gotta be a playa?" My Denzel Washington, slash Malcom X, smile spread over my face as I continued driving down Colonial.

"Because since you about to be a single man you probably 'bout to be off the chain."

"Sharon, listen. . . . I really enjoyed myself with you last night and I'm looking forward to spending more quality time with you, and your daughter, in the immediate future. So, please don't feel that way."

"All right, Michael. I'll be home waiting on you so don't make me wait too long." With that said, we said our goodbyes and ended the call.

I could tell her heart had been broken from a previous relationship. At that moment, I promised myself I would not be the next guy to break it.

As I turned the key in my door, I couldn't help but think, *home sweet home.* Once inside, I placed my briefcase down on the coffee table and went straight to my bedroom. I turned on my CD player and put in a slow-mix CD *Back in My Arms* by the group Silk. Allowing the music to relax me, I headed to the shower to wash off the remnants of the day. As the water cascaded over my body, I thought about the previous night I'd had with Sharon and how she'd put her love down on me.

Listening to the song as it blasted through my apartment, the mere thought of her turned me on. *Damn, she ain't even here and she got my manhood growing. Shit, this girl already got me pussy-whipped.* I laughed out loud and fought the urge to stroke myself, knowing I needed to save that load for Sharon.

The last person to do that was my ex, Camisha, and one other chick name Nene who I was fucked up about when I was in the Army, stationed at Fort Riley Kansas.

I was surprised Sharon hadn't asked me about the business I was talking about. But as long as she didn't ask, I didn't have to tell her. Hell, if she had already developed feelings for me, there was no way I could tell her about a business based on butt-naked females being around me.

After I showered, I grabbed a bite of the leftovers from the food we'd eaten the previous night. Next, I got on the phone and began placing calls to the females who fit the mold of becoming a Florida Hot Girl.

The first female I called was a cute little redbone named Renee. Renee stood about five-six and weighed around one hundred thirty-five pounds with a beautiful face and sweet personality. I just knew she would be a perfect fit for the group.

She lived over by the fairgrounds in a rundown beat-up apartment and I don't know why anyone would want to stay there. I guess that's why she was in the Wages Program in the first place since she was living in such a horrible place.

And, to top it off, she stayed with someone, so I figured she had it rough and really needed to make some money. After speaking with her, she told me to pick her up around seven thirty that evening.

When I pulled up to the parking lot it gave me chills. The people at the complex stared at me and tried to see who I was there to see. The local drug dealers turned their heads to hide their faces, thinking I was a probation officer or the cops.

As soon as I knocked on the door of her apartment, someone yelled for me to come inside. I looked both ways to make sure my environment was good, then proceeded to go inside.

Upon entering I got a good look at who it was that had yelled for me to come in. It was her roommate and she was huge. She looked like she was about two hundred or so pounds, standing a mere five-feet-four. She was getting her hair done by a fine ass female named J.K.

"Have a seat, sir," her roommate said.

"Hello. How are you fine ladies doing this evening?" I asked.

"We're fine, sir. You must be the guy who's gonna be taking Renee to the local strip clubs to make some money, huh?"

"Yes, ma'am, that's me." Before I could even get comfortable, J.K. started grilling me as to how my business worked. Her first question was straight from the hip.

"So, Mr. Michael, you're taking a bunch of females to different strip clubs to shake their asses for a few dollars?"

"Damn, Ms. Lady, why do you have to say it like that? I'm the guy who's gonna be taking them to make some serious cash," I replied to her.

"I wish I would be in a damn club taking off my clothes for a few dollars and shit."

"Yeah, I must admit, J.K., it's not a job every female can do. But for the women who *can* do it, there's a lot of cash for out there to be made."

Minutes later, Renee waltzed out of her room looking like a damn baby doll. *Damn, she's gorgeous*, I thought.

"Hey, Mike," she said, showing the pretty white teeth in her mouth.

"Hey, Renee. I didn't know you were that damn good looking. Hell, you gonna be making all the damn money."

She smiled as she walked over to me. "Sorry to keep you waiting. I hope you're not mad at me," she said. She placed her arms around me and gave me a nice hug. I could smell the Chanel perfume she'd adorned her body with after she'd gotten out of the shower. I couldn't wait to get her back to my crib.

"Why of course not. As fine as you are, I would've waited for you all night," I said. I imagined how nice it would be to have her in my bed. It was a thought I seemed to have whenever it came to meeting the females who came through the group.

\*\*\*

WE WERE ON THE WAY TO MY CRIB, and I couldn't wait to see how fine the pretty little thing would be with her clothes off. During the drive home, I put in Prince's *Sign of The Times* CD and put it on "Adore", one of my favorite songs by him.

She started to sing along with the song as I drove. I looked over at her and gave her a shy smile.

"Do you know how to sing, Michael?"

"Well, since you asked, a lot of people say I sound just like Prince when I'm singing one of his songs."

"Well, let me hear how you sound so I can be the judge of that."

I started singing and, soon enough, she was staring at me as though Prince was actually riding in the car with us.

"Damn, Michael, you do sound like him," she said surprisingly. "You sound good as hell! Hearing you hit them high notes got me wet down there already," she said.

I made a right turn off Silver Star Road into my driveway.

"So, you live out here in these apartments?" she asked.

"Yeah, I just moved here a few days ago," I told her.

"I heard they're some expensive ass apartments. They look nice on the outside. I can't wait to see what yours looks like inside."

She was right. They did look nice on the outside and I was feeling the same way about her. She looked nice on the outside, but how did she look without them clothes on? She was about to get out when I ran around to her door.

"Hold on, young lady. Let me get that for you."

She smiled at me. "You are such a gentleman, Michael. I knew it was something about you I liked."

As I opened her door, she opened her legs and I caught a glimpse of her cute, shaved vagina since she didn't seem to be wearing any panties.

She saw me looking. "I'm so sorry, Mike. You were not supposed to see that, not right now anyway."

"I didn't see anything. What are you talking about?"

"Whatever, Michael. I saw how big your eyes got when you saw my you-know-what."

"Renee, I promise you, I didn't see your cute little shaved vagina."

"Well, how do you know she's shaved?"

"Girl, you know I saw all of that pretty little vagina of yours, *and* that wet spot you were talking about." We smiled at each other as we made our way up the stairs to my apartment.

Moments later, we were inside of the love palace, a.k.a. my apartment.

She was shocked to see how I had it decorated. The living room was laced with nice rugs I'd purchased from an African art store off Colonial. It had also been furnished with some nice furniture from Badcock home Furniture & more.

I had a black leather sectional that surrounded a nice big screen television, and a glass table with a black panther mantle underneath it. On the walls were pictures of nice artwork I'd picked up from the Wicker Hut.

"Michael, this is nice. Who helped you do all the decorating? It looks like a female lives here with you."

"Believe it or not, Renee, I did all this by myself. Wait till you see my brass waterbed."

The dining room table was set up with plates and silverware a wine glass sat on the side of each, similar to the setting you'd see at a fancy restaurant.

A nice flower arrangement sat right in the middle of the table, surrounded by candles. The whole ensemble gave the distinct impression of a nice candlelit dinner.

"Michael, I'm impressed. You have such a nice apartment and it smells so good in here. You go, boy," she said. She was clearly surprised that a single man could have such a tastefully-decorated pad without the help of a female.

From one corner of the room to another, she looked around in awe of my crib. I just stood aside and allowed her to take in the surroundings.

Next, she walked down the hallway. "Oh, my God! You do have a brass waterbed!" She yelled out like a child in a candy store. "And it even has mirrors in the top of it, so you can see yourself fuckin' in bed."

"No, Renee. The mirrors are there so when I'm making love to that special lady, she can look up and *watch* me make love to her."

"Michael, you're a mess. I've never seen a waterbed like that.

Can I sit on it?" she asked in a giddy, childlike tone

"Hell, you can do more than just sit on it. Why don't you just take off those clothes and let me check out your body, so I can see just how fine you really are."

As soon as she started taking off her clothes, I immediately saw the problem she'd have being a stripper. Her stomach was laced with stretch marks that looked like balled up homework paper from school. Her breasts hung low on her chest as if someone had spread them on with a spatula.

I was shocked. How could she be so damn pretty and not have a pretty body? Damn. Then she looked at me and asked me the million-dollar question.

"So, Michael, do you think I'll make some money?"

I couldn't let her know the truth. And the truth was her body was jacked the fuck up, but it would have to do. She was my one and only dancer at the time. So, I lied to her.

"Yes, Renee, you're fine. You should make some money, but I don't know how much money you'll make."

She continued to stand in front of me as naked as could be, so I told her to go ahead and get dressed. Instead of doing what I'd asked, she quickly climbed her butt-naked ass onto my bed.

"Nah, Mr., why don't you take off your clothes and join me in this nice big ass bed of yours," she said.

Damn, if she only knew how her body had turned me off. I tried to make up an excuse but she wasn't having that.

"Are you sure this is what you want to do, Renee?" I asked. I tried to keep a straight face.

"Michael, it's what I've been wanting to do since the first time I met you at your office. Now stop bullshitting and bring that dick over here," she demanded.

Minutes later, I was in bed with her. I tried to knock her back out. The deeper I went inside of her, the more she chewed on my ear.

"Renee, not so hard, baby. You're gonna chew my fuckin' ear off," I screamed. I was actually trying to punish her for making me fuck her.

"I'm sorry, Michael, but it feels like you're touching the bottom of my stomach." She couldn't help but look at herself while I was fuckin' her. "Oh, my goodness, look at my face," she said, when she caught a glimpse of her reflection in the mirrors above the waterbed.

"Oh shit, I'm about to cum, Michael!"

"Go ahead, baby, and do you," I told her as I kept pumping in and out like a jackhammer.

"Michael, Michael, hold up please," she begged, "you're to-to de-deep inside of m-me," she panted. "Damn, I'm cummin' all over your big ass fuckin' dick inside of my stomach."

When I turned her over and started hitting her from the back, I watched myself in action in the mirrors. *Damn, I'm really punishing her little cute ass*, I thought to myself.

Finally, reaching the point of ecstasy, I pulled out of her thirty minutes later just as my phone started to ring. I looked over to see who was calling me and saw Sharon's name of the screen.

"Excuse me one minute, I really have to take this call."

"No problem, Michael. I need to calm down for a few minutes anyway," she said. With a big smile on her face, she watched me walked out of the bedroom door.

"Hello." I answered once I was sure Sharon wouldn't hear Renee.

"Hey you. What's up? Did you forget about me tonight?"

"No, Sharon, I had to meet with a few people regarding the new business venture I'm trying to get off the ground."

"Oh, okay. By the way, I never asked you about that. What type of business is it anyway?" she asked as I sat butt-naked thinking about fuckin' Ms. Bad Body.

"Oh, it's the type of business that will require me to do some traveling and stuff."

"Well, what kind of business is that, Michael?" she probed.

"I'll explain it to you one day when we both have some free time."

"Michael, are we still getting together tonight? It's already nine forty-five and I still got my daughter with me."

Just as I was about to answer her question, in walked Renee with my silk sheets wrapped around her naked ass body.

She bent over and whispered in my ear. "Can I have some more of big daddy, please?"

"Shhh," I whispered quickly. "I'm still on the phone. Give me a quick minute and I'll be right back in there with you," I said.

She put her head down and walked back to the room like a little puppy who had just gotten in trouble.

"Yes, Sharon, let me wrap up this meeting and I'll call you back and let you know what time to come over."

"Okay, Michael, and tell John Boy I said hello."

"I'll tell him, and we're both sorry to hear about your kitty kat being swollen up."

When Sharon and I ended our call, I went back to my bedroom to give Renee some more of what she was looking for. She called him *Big Daddy*, but the rest of the world knew him by John Boy. . .
.

## CHAPTER FIVE
**RENEE**

Not long after my call with Sharon, I was back in my bedroom taking poor little Renee through it. Hell, she was getting what she had asked for, more hot, passionate sex. We finished up around ten thirty that evening, and by the time on my watch, it was getting late.

I knew Sharon was probably getting impatient since I hadn't called her back yet. And looking at the way Renee had made herself so comfortable in my bed, it looked as though she was trying to spend the night.

"Excuse me, Boo. We need to be getting ready so I can take you home," I said politely.

"I was hoping I could spend the night with you, Michael," she said, looking like that sad puppy again. I already knew she was going to try that.

"I would love for you to stay over, but I gotta get up early in the morning for work."

"Okay, Michael, I see. So now that you done fucking the shit out of me, you ready to kick me out and shit." She rolled her eyes as she jumped up and snatched her clothes from the floor.

"Renee, that's not what it is," I said. "Seriously, I have to be up very early since I work downtown now." The way I saw it, I was telling the truth.

"Oh, that's right. You did say you had moved to the downtown office. I'm sorry, let me hurry up and get dressed," she said. She arched her back and bent over far enough to give me a birds-eye view of that fat ass pussy from the back.

"I promise, as soon as I get off tomorrow, I'll be sure to call you so we can go shopping for your outfit," I said. I rubbed my dick at the thought of hitting that ass again before taking her home.

"What outfit, Michael? What are you talking about?" "Your outfit for this Friday night when I take you to the club to dance, silly."

"Oh, so you buy the outfits for the other dancers too?"

"No, I'm only buying your clothes 'cause you're gonna to be my lil' boo thang." She smiled at me while putting her bra on those flat ass titties of hers.

"Now isn't that sweet, Michael. You can be a sweetheart, can't you?" she replied.

Shit, I was trying to hurry her ass up out of my apartment before Sharon got there. When she finally got all her clothes on, we were out the door headed back to her humble abode.

I could understand why she didn't want to go back home where she lived. Those apartments were hideous. As bad as they looked, I wouldn't want my dog staying out there.

After I dropped her off, I rushed back home to wait on Sharon to arrive.

She had told me, since I waited so late to call her back, she would be bringing her daughter too. Fortunately, that wasn't going to be a problem since we couldn't fuck that night anyway, due to her pussy still being swollen up from the night before.

Once she arrived, we put her daughter to sleep and then watched some television.

"I really love falling asleep in your arms, Michael," she said, looking into my eyes right before she fell asleep.

"I really love having you in my arms too, Sharon," I replied.

She kissed me good night, curled up in my arms, and closed her eyes. We fell asleep in each other's arms the way couples in love do.

The next morning, while her and her daughter were still asleep, I was in my living room calling my job to let them know I wouldn't be in.

"Good morning, Wages Program, how can I direct your call?" the receptionist greeted.

"Yes, this is Mr. Valentino, Case Manager for the Westside region." "Yes sir, good morning. How can I help you?"

"Could you please let Mrs. Stephens know I won't be in today. Seems as though I've caught a cold."

"I'll let her know, Mr. Valentino. I hope you feel better soon, and have a nice day," the young receptionist said before hanging up.

I jumped back in the bed with Sharon and her daughter, anticipating seeing Seneavu later that day. I lay there smiling from ear to ear thinking about how fine Seneavu was, and how she would look in my bed in the doggie style position. I dozed off dreaming about fuckin' her.

I awoke to the smell of bacon and eggs cooking in my kitchen. At first, I thought I was dreaming until the aroma hit my nose again. I turned to my side looking for Sharon and realized she wasn't there, and neither was her daughter.

I jumped out of bed and went to the kitchen. I found her standing over the stove stirring up a pot of grits while her little princess sat in the living room watching cartoons.

"Hey, what's this?" I asked, watching her cook.

She turned to me and smiled oh-so-cute.

"What does it look like, Mr.? I'm cooking breakfast for my man and my daughter."

"Damn, it looks good too. I can't wait to get me a plate of them eggs, bacon, and grits."

"Whatever, Michael. Sit down and let me fix you a plate. I wanted to feed you before you go to work."

"What about cutie over there? Isn't she eating?"

"She already had something to eat. I'm gonna get you straight before I have to leave and drop her off at daycare."

"Thank you, boo. It looks good. I can't wait to taste it. I must admit, it's nice to have someone to cook for me since Camisha never really cooked for me or her badass kids."

"Well, since I'm in your life now, Michael, you will never have to worry about having someone to cook for you."

She gave me one of those wet kisses before she left the kitchen to dress and leave. It was still fairly early, around eight forty-five in the morning, and I had my day all planned out. Once Sharon was gone, I had plans to call the chocolate female from the day before and put in more work while digging off inside of her stomach.

About twenty minutes later, I was walking Sharon and her daughter to her car. As she placed her daughter into her car seat, she turned to me and said, "Michael, I really enjoyed myself last night even though you called me all late and stuff. Will I see you later tonight?"

"Once again, I'm so sorry about that. I promise I'll make it up to you."

"Whatever, Michael. I'm gonna hold you to that. Oh, and by the way, I stole one of your Pretty Ricky fuck flicks. Now I know where you learned how to eat pussy so damn good. You be watching that nigga, don't you?"

"Damn, so you stole one of my tapes. And hell no, I didn't learn how to eat pussy from watching that nigga. My skills are way better than his. Hell, he be eating all in a bitch ass and shit, that nigga be doing the most when it comes to eating a female's pussy."

"You right, he is a lil' bit too freaky for me too, Michael. I just think the way he be fuckin' them hoes is sexy as a muthafucker."

"Whatever, Sharon."

She smiled as she got into her car and rolled down her window. "I know one thing. You better not be fuckin' or eating on no other female other than me. Now give me a kiss so I can go."

I leaned my head inside of her car and kissed her in front of her daughter.

"Ewww, Mommy, you kissed that man!"

"That man is Mr. Michael. Do you like him?" she asked her little girl.

"I'm gonna tell my daddy you kissed Mr. Michael on his lips."

"Whatever." Sharon laughed.

"Have a nice day, Bae. I'll talk with you later," I told her.

As soon as she turned out of my parking lot, I ran back upstairs to my apartment so I could call Ms. Seneavu Miller. Like I said, I had my day all planned as to how I was going to get her back to my apartment so I could check out that fine ass body of hers.

I dialed her number and waited for the phone to ring, but as soon as it rang, I was sent to voicemail. I tried again, hoping she would answer but it went straight back to voicemail a second time.

*Damn, she knew I would be calling her today around this time, so why isn't she answering the damn phone?* I sat there for another minute or so wondering why she hadn't picked up.

Since she wasn't answering her phone, I decided to use the day for more recruiting. Little did I know what would be waiting for me the next day at work. If I had known, I wouldn't have ever taken her phone number.

***

IT WAS WEDNESDAY MORNING, the first day of the rest of my life, meaning, I would never get that day back again, good or bad.

I put on one the brand-new suits I had purchased the previous weekend. Dark blue, white shirt and a light-blue tie and, of course, my signature Stacey Adams.

As I walked to my small ass cubicle that morning all eyes were on me, including my short ass supervisor's.

I sat down at my desk, turned on my computer, and put my password in. As I sat there waiting for it to come on, I got a nagging feeling that something was off.

*Something is wrong. Why isn't my computer coming on?*

"Hey, Paul. Is there something wrong with the computers today?" I asked a co-worker.

"Nah, Mike, my computer seems to be working just fine," he said, as he sipped on his third cup of hot Java, which he drank every morning faithfully. That was probably why his teeth had a very dull yellowish stain on them.

He smiled at me with those front teeth of his just staring at me. At one point, I had actually thought those yellow stained teeth had a mind of their own given the way they stood out in his mouth.

Anyway, out of nowhere, I heard my supervisor's voice. "Mr. Valentino, can I have a word with you please?"

"Yes, ma'am," I said. I stood up from the cubicle I called a desk. As I walked into her office, everyone seemed to be looking at me as though I was about to be shot in the head.

"Have a seat please, sir," she said politely.

"Thank you, ma'am."

"Mr. Valentino. Yesterday there was a young lady who came to see you about her food assistance, correct?"

"Yes ma'am," I answered, "a Ms. Miller, I believe."

"Yes, it was Ms. Miller. While she sat at your desk discussing her case, you mentioned something to her about becoming a stripper, correct?"

*Damn, that bitch ratted me out, fuckin' black ass bitch,* I thought to myself. I kept a straight face and answered truthfully. "Yes ma'am, I did mention it to her since she claimed that she couldn't find a job."

"Well, before she left, you acquired her phone number, an act that goes against the policy of the Wages Program. I hope you understand when I say 'this is not a place where you obtain one's phone number for social or recreational pleasures."

"Yes ma'am, you're correct."

"Then, on yesterday, Mr. Valentino, you called in and said you wouldn't be at work due to being under the weather. Furthermore, you've attempted to call her several times."

*Damn, how did she know that? Did her and that bitch live together or something?*

"Yes, ma'am, I did," I said solemnly. What more could I say? I was stuck. I couldn't say a damn thing. I was cold busted.

She cleared her throat and inched closer to her desk, allowing her elbows to rest atop. "Mr. Valentino," she said, looking me directly in the eyes, "you leave me and the Wages Program no other choice but to terminate your employment here with the company. Please obtain your personal belongings and leave the building immediately. We'll mail your last check to you."

The conversation left me broken down and I felt rejected.

"Yes ma'am, thank you," was all I could muster up. I kindly backed my chair away from the frog faced lady's desk, went to the fuckin' cubicle to retrieve my things, and hauled ass out of there so fuckin' quick, it looked like I had just robbed a bank. I tried to get as far away as possible.

And just like that, I got fired. What was I going to do now? My only fuckin' backup plan was the idea of getting a group of females together and calling them the Florida Hot Girls. *Damn, I got to make this shit work for me now.*

The first person I called was my fuckin' Cousin Edward Lee since he had been the one who had told me about the so-called business venture to begin with. He was convinced we'd make a lot of fuckin' money. So, now I needed to touch base with him to find out if he had any females lined up to start taking to the club.

"Hello?" He answered his phone on the first ring.

"Ed, it's Mike. What's up?"

"Nothing, cuz, just sitting around chilling."

"Hey, man, I just got fired, so I gotta make this thing with the girls work." I let out a frustrated breath.

"Sorry to hear that, cuz. That's fucked up, man," he replied.

"How many girls do you have ready?" I asked again.

"Man, I don't have no girls lined up right now," he said. It almost sounded like he was laughing under his breath.

"What?" I said in raised tone.

"Yeah, cuz, I ain't even been out tryna recruit no females." His tone was too nonchalant for my taste.

"Damn, man, you were the one who said this would be a sure way to make some serious cash," I said in an irritated tone.

"Yeah, but I didn't think you would go and get fired from your job." He chuckled as if shit was funny.

"Yeah, me either. Hahaha," I said with a little sarcasm in my voice. "No problem, Ed. Let me get off this phone so I can go find some females so I won't end up back at your house sleeping on your couch."

"All right, cuz, good luck. Call me back after you find a few girls," he said. I could just picture his sweet ass smiling on the other line. "If I come up with some, I'll call you immediately," he said. For the record, even to this very day, Ed has never called me regarding one damn female (Thanks, Cuz).

Now, I was desperate for some females and had no job. And if I didn't come up with something soon, I wouldn't have a place to stay either.

I was all alone, just me, and this one redbone female name

Renee—the one with the stretch marks on her stomach that look like balled up homework paper from school.

That night, after talking to Ed, I made a few phone calls. I went over a few things I had lined up, and I checked in with Renee to make sure she was still good for Friday night.

She sounded so excited when I told her she would be the first female I'd be taking to the club to dance. Shit, if truth be told, she was the only female I had lined up yet.

After talking with her for about an hour, it was on to a few other females I'd met. Once I ran the business down to them, they, too, wanted to give it a try. I told them I would call them when I was ready to check out their bodies.

Next, I needed to call my lil' Boo thang, Sharon. She answered on the very first ring and blurted, "I was wondering when you were going to call me."

"Hey, I'm sorry, but I've had a very long day and I was trying to get to you before it got too late in the evening," I told her honestly.

"I understand, boo, it's okay. Is there anything me and this tight pussy of mine can help get off your troubled mind?"

"Now see, there you go. You told me she was still swollen up and couldn't have any visitors."

"Michael, for you, I'll make an exception because I know you'll be gentle with her tonight," she said in a lust-filled tone of voice.

"Okay, Ms. Mind reader, what time will you be over?"

"I'm on the way. Give me like forty minutes."

"Okay, Sharon. Did you eat yet?" I asked.

"Yes, I did, and I made you a plate. So I can bring it when I come, if you like, Michael."

"That'll be fine. Thank you, Boo. I'll see you soon."

"Okay, Mike, I'm 'bout to leave right now."

"I'll see you in a few," I said before hanging up.

She arrived forty minutes later. Just like she'd said, she brought me a plate of smothered pork chops, rice and gravy, some good ass collard greens, and some cornbread. I must admit, not only was she fine as hell, but she could also cook her ass off, straight wifey material.

Once again, we fell asleep after having some good passionate sex. And Wow! It was some of the best sex this side of Medulla, Florida. I mean it was just that good. It was the kind of sex that made a nigga wanna slap his momma and ask, 'why you ain't tell me about females like Sharon'.

***

IT WAS FINALLY FRIDAY NIGHT and it was showtime for Ms. Renee. I arrived at her place around eight o'clock. I was decked out in my fresh ass pimp suit, with the penguin coattail going down my back.

Renee stepped out in a nice little black miniskirt. Her skin glowing, and her long, jet-black hair flowed down her back. She looked picture perfect, just right for them white boys at the strip club I was taking her to on Dale Mabry in Tampa.

Just as long as she didn't have to get naked she would be fine, my plan was to take her to the club, drop her off, and then head to Club Kathleen in Lakeland, so I could recruit some more females for the group.

When we got to the club, there was already a nice bit of cars in the parking lot, so I knew the club had to be packed. I turned to her while she was still seated over on the passenger's side. Noticing the nervous look on her face, I took her hand and gave her a little pep talk.

"Okay, baby, listen . . . all you have to do is go to the manager and let him know you're interested in dancing."

"But I'm scared," she whined, "I've never done anything like this before," she said. Her voice cracked and she moved around in the seat displaying her nervousness.

"Renee, listen, boo, you're beautiful and you're gonna be just fine. There is no way the manager won't let you dance in the club. So, stop looking like that and go in there and make that bread. I'll be right here until you get hired, okay?" I gave her hand a gentle squeeze to reassure her and kissed her for good luck. When she opened the car door to get out, I wished her the best before she walked her lil' slim, petite, red ass inside the club.

Thirty minutes later she ran back to the car and hopped back in. "Michael, they hired me on the spot! The manager said I have the perfect look for what they're looking for," she said, all excited and shit.

"Okay, Renee. See, I told you there was nothing to worry about."

"I know, baby," she said showing all thirty-two of her pearly whites, "I was just so nervous. He didn't ask to see my body or anything! He said my face was my ticket to being a superstar."

*Damn, he said all of that to her*? I thought. *Hell, maybe he sees more than I see, or maybe he just likes balled up homework paper.* Hell, all I cared about was getting Renee's foot in the door so I could bring more of the girls to the club.

"Okay, Michael, I know that you have to get to the club so that you can recruit more females, so give me a kiss and I'll see you later," she said, as I started the car so I could leave.

She was already out the door when she turned around and yelled, "Oh, by the way, Michael, you better not be at the club flirting with no girls unless they joining the team!"

Damn, I knew she thought we were in a relationship, but that's exactly what I *didn't* want her to think.

On the way to Club Kathleen, all I could think about was how much money Renee would be making that night. Having her bringing in so much money, I would be set. "Shit, I'm good. Who needs cuz? I'll just do everything by myself," I said to myself, as I merged onto I-4 headed to Lakeland.

Forty-five minutes later, I pulled into the parking lot of Club Kathleen. I was feeling myself as I had my number one dancer at the Strip Club, and I was about to recruit some more females so they could join her. *I got the perfect job and I'm just getting started!* I thought to myself.

Upon walking into the club, I saw the usual people inside. I hadn't been there since moving to Orlando, so I knew I would, somewhat, be a new face to some of the new females on deck. As I stood over by the bar area surveying the club, I couldn't help but notice my baby girl's mother standing across from me staring me down.

She looked at me as though she expected me to walk over to her and start up a conversation. Me, being the cool, calm, collective brother I was, stood my ground and pretended not to see her lil' short, cute, black ass.

But how could I not see her ass standing there wearing a nice, tight-fitting ass pair of jeans. The jeans hugged her round ass and caused it to stick out. To complete the outfit, she'd worn a nice Baby Phat shirt and Prada shoes.

In other words, she looked as good as she had the first day I'd met her on my way to work. It had been five years since the day I met her at a local gas station in Mulberry Florida. She was on her way to Badcock while I was on my way to the Department of Transportation, where I worked as a Finance clerk for the 8th District of Florida.

Amelia stood a mere four-foot-seven and weighed around one hundred fifteen pounds, with a bra size of 32B. Her skin complexion was a dark pecan-tan. She had a nice soft ass that felt tender to the touch, and the longer I stood there talking to her, the mere thought of making love to her again started dancing in my head. Standing there looking at how nice she looked in the skin-tight jeans, I thought about the times we would get together and do the damn thang.

We had hooked up a couple of times and during the process, I fathered a beautiful baby girl named Aerial.

Aerial was a beautiful child, and I enjoyed every minute I had her around me. However, Amelia knew whenever Aerial was around me, other females would pamper her. And one thing she did not want, was for Aerial to consider another woman as her stepmother.

As we tried to ignore one another, neither wanting to be the first to approach the other, she finally walked over to me and said, "Well, hello, Mr. Michael.

"Hey, Amelia, I said dryly. I turned my head away from her,

trying to look at all the beautiful women in the club.

"Oh, am I stopping you from getting your mack on, Mr. Playboy?"

"No, Amelia, what's on your mind?"

"You know what's on my mind. I haven't received my child support check and you haven't been by to see your daughter," she said. She rolled her eyes and rolled her neck from side to side.

"Well, it might be a while before you see a check since I just lost my job."

She folded her arms across her chest and looked at me as if she wanted to slap the shit out of me for losing such a good job. "Damn, Mike, every time you get a good job you always seem to fuck it up," she snapped.

"Sorry, Amelia. I'll try and do better next time since you're standing here talking to me like I'm your child!"

"That's not it, Michael. It's the fact that your daughter needs money for school and other things."

"Damn, does she go to a private school or something?" I asked as I stared down at her short ass.

"No, she doesn't. But you know as well as I do, I want her to have the finer things in life."

"And so do I Amelia!"

"I can't tell," she said loudly. "You should be breaking your neck trying to come and see her."

She was right about that.

"Well stop taking your ass to every club that's open and stay home with her so you can save some money," I said.

"Whatever, Michael! Just pay your damn child support. Either way, me and your daughter will be just fine, with or without your black ass!"

"Okay, you're right." I finally caved in after thirty minutes of going back and forth.

I dug in my pocket and pulled out three crisp hundred dollar bills and handed them to her. She snatched them out of my hand so quick, for a minute, I thought she had robbed me.

"Okay, that's what I'm talking about. Now when can I expect

more?" she asked. Her eyes grew the size of pancakes as she stared at the fresh hundred dollar bills in her small ass hand.

"Damn, Amelia, I just gave you three hundred dollars. The sad thing is, poor lil' Aerial probably won't see any of that money!"

"Whatever, Mike. I'm taking my baby school shopping in the morning when I wake up," she said.

"How is she doing anyway?" I asked just as she turned to walk away.

"She's doing fine. Why don't you come by and see her after the club?" In judging the way she responded, I knew exactly what that meant.

"Yeah. I'll see how the night pans out and go from there."

"Whatever, Mike. I'll leave the key under the mat for you," she said, as she looked down at John Boy.

"Fine, if I don't make it, just tell her I said hello and I'll be by to see her soon.

As she walked away, I couldn't help but notice the lil' shorty standing over by the DJ booth, looking lonely.

Seconds later, I was in her ear telling her how nice she looked. She looked into my eyes and looked me up and down. "Shit, you don't look so bad yourself with that fly ass suit on."

"Well thank you, ma'am. I always try to dress to impress. May I have the pleasure of knowing your name?"

She looked at me and gave me a cute lil' grin. "Valentino, stop playing! You know who I am. *Damn, this chick knows me and I don't remember her at all.*

"Oh, so that's how you do it, huh?" I replied.

"Excuse me, Boo, what do you mean? What? Do we know each other from somewhere?" I asked looking all stupid in the face.

She stepped back and placed her hands on her hips. "Valentino, my name is Carmen, remember? I'm from Plant City! Damn, you just fucked me like three months ago!"

I stood there for a minute or two.

"Oh shit, Carmen! Girl, you look so different now. What in the hell did you do? Pick up some weight or something?"

"Yes, I have since the last time you saw me. It wasn't like you cared anyway. Especially after the way you left me in the hotel that night after you fucked me."

"Carmen, it wasn't even like that. See, something came up when I went to get you something to eat. My phone started ringing, and when I answered it, it was my baby girl, Aerial. She was calling to ask me to pick her up from her best friend's house. She was supposed to spend the night with her, but when she got there she wanted to go back home."

"Whatever, Michael. All I know is you left me there, and I never heard from you again after that night."

"Just let me make that night back up to you. Here's a hundred dollars." I held the bill out to her. Put it in your pocket and I'll give you more once you come work for me."

"Work for you how?" she asked.

Realizing I had piqued her curiosity, I explained my group to her.

"Hell yeah, I've always wanted to be a fuckin' stripper. When can I start?"

After giving her a few more details, she gave me her digits and I walked away to move on to the next female.

She yelled out as I was walking away, "Hey, Mike! When can I see John Boy again?"

"Hell, if I have enough time tonight, you might see his big headed ass tonight." I smiled and walked away in pursuit of the next recruit.

"Walking throughout the club, all I could do was think about Renee and wonder how much money she'd made. When my phone started vibrating in my pocket, I took it out to see who it was, and to my surprise, it was my lil' boo thang, Renee.

"Yes, she must be calling to let me know how much money she made so far," I said to myself.

"Hello, what's up?" I greeted her.

"Michael where are you at?" She sounded real scared and shit.

"I'm at the club, Boo. What's wrong?"

"Come get me, I can't do this. I'm walking around the club and these people act like they don't even see my red ass!"

Taken aback, my mouth dropped. "What? Ain't no money in there or what?" I asked, trying not to sound angry at her.

"That's not it, baby, it's me. I don't wanna do this. I'll just find me a regular nine to five." Her voice trembled, and I could tell she was on the verge of tears.

"Okay, Renee, just calm down. I'm on the way," I said.

I didn't even bother to try and convince her to stay and let things play out. Unfortunately, Ed hadn't told me all the ins and outs of business. He'd basically assured me that all we had to do was take females to the club and they would make the money.

It was the third mistake I'd made when it came to the business. *Of course*, I thought. *I gotta take females who want that type of life, not the ones who don't care if they make money or not.*

When I picked her up I could see the hurt and pain in her eyes. I didn't want to stress her out any more than she already was, so quietly, I just let her sit as I drove back to Orlando. Halfway home she attempted to explain what had happened.

"Michael, I—

"Don't worry about it. We'll figures something else out later," I said.

She placed her head in my lap. When she tugged at the zipper of my pants, I knew she wanted to put John Boy in her mouth.

"Not right now, Renee," I said, as I quickly pushed her head away. I was too pissed off. I'm not in the mood," I told her as kindly as I could.

She sucked her teeth and replied, "You're mad at me, aren't you?"

I couldn't tell her the truth, so once again I lied to her. "Nah, not at all, Boo. It's just that I'm driving, and I don't wanna cause an accident on account of you giving me some good ass neck."

"Well, can I go back home with you so .e can figure out our game plan for tomorrow and have some breakfast?"

"Nah, Renee. I'm beat right now. I'll just call you tomorrow and talk with you then."

Forty-five minutes later, I was dropping her off at those raggedy ass apartments.

"Okay, baby. Call me first thing in the morning and make sure to drive home safe," she said, as she opened the car door to get out.

I gave her a quick smile and drove off. Now, all I needed to do was find a female who actually wanted to be a true Florida Hot Girl…

## CHAPTER SIX
### MISS KITTY

Now, I can't remember where and how I met Ms. Kitty, but where ever it was, I was glad as hell I'd met her. She had been born to be a dancer, and that's exactly what she was—a dancer and a very good street hustler. At five-three, she couldn't have been any more than one hundred thirty-five pounds. Her breasts fit her petite frame perfectly; I'd say a firm 34C. I mean, she had some nice, soft, big ass titties and a nice round, fat soft Jell-O-like ass.

I approached her and gave her the spill about the group and how I wanted the females in the group to be.

"Yep, sounds like what I wanna do. Just tell me what I need to do to get in the group, Mr. Valentino?" she asked me looking oh so damn fine. I quickly replied to her.

"All I have to do is get you back to my apartment, check your body out, and we'll go from there," I explained.

She quickly replied, "Let's ride, my nigga," And that was all I needed to hear.

Minutes later, we pulled up at the love palace a.k.a. my apartment, ready to partake in some sexual positions I'd rather not speak on. In other words, I was about to put in that muthafuckin' work.

Just as we were getting out of the car, she took it upon herself to tell me she didn't have anywhere to stay at the moment. Her revelation was music to my ears.

"Well, you know I live alone, Ms. Kitty, and if everything goes well, we might be able to work something out."

"So, you don't have a girlfriend or wife, Michael?"

"Nah, Ms. Kitty. It's just me and ole John Boy."

"What? You have a roommate named John Boy?" She waited for an answer.

"Nah, it's just an old saying I use from time to time. She smiled at me as we walked up the stairs to my apartment.

Once we were inside, I gave her a quick tour of my place. Afterwards, I could tell she liked what she'd seen by the way she'd marveled at everything. Before I could explain more about the group, she was already butt ass naked.

With nothing on except her birthday suit, I couldn't help but stare at her nice ass breasts. It was as if they were calling out my name saying, *Michael, Michael, come get some of this sweet baby milk in your mouth...*

"Excuse me, what did you just say?" I asked, still gazing at her breasts.

"Mike, I didn't say anything," she answered and looked at me as if I was crazy. "What's wrong with you? Are you hearing things?"

"Hell yeah, I thought I heard you say something about some baby milk."

She burst out into laughter. "Boy, you tripping. I didn't say nothing about no damn baby milk. I was asking you if you wanted to taste this pretty little pussy of mine?"

"Yesum, I be much obliged if I's could eat sum of dat dere pie, ma'am," I answered, as if I was her slave or something.

She lay back on my bed like she was about to make a movie or something. She spread her legs as far as they could go and showed her shaved vagina up close and personal.

I licked my lips and then put my head so far up her vagina, you would've thought I was an unborn baby being pushed out of her womb. She squirmed from side to side, up and down, and all kinds of ways trying to keep me from hitting her G-spot, you know the point of erotic pleasure.

After I got her to that point, I raised my head up and started kissing on those soft ass lips of hers. I sucked her bottom lip as though it was a piece of hickory smoked bacon. She looked me straight in my eyes as I went back down on her. I could tell she had never experienced anything like that before.

She didn't know if she wanted to cum or kiss me. She grabbed the back of my head and pressed it up against her clitoris. As she released her first orgasm, I held it inside my mouth and leaned up to kiss her. I let the taste of her juices roll off my tongue and into her mouth so she could enjoy the taste as well as I did.

The more I kissed on her, the longer my penis started to get. Before she knew it, I had entered deep inside her again. The Beautiful Ones (by Prince) played in the background. She grabbed my ass cheeks and tried to push me further inside of her.

"I wanna feel you all up inside my stomach, Michael," she said, as she looked me in the eyes.

"I want the same thing, beautiful," I whispered. I dug deeper and deeper until I knew I had hit the bottom. She flinched and squirmed trying to keep me from hitting that spot once again.

As I pounded her, I sucked on her breasts at the same time. Having one orgasm after another, she begged me to give her a few minutes to calm down. I obliged momentarily, but within minutes, we started up again. I kept right on banging her soft tender ass. Then I started going in circular motions as I dug off in her as if I was starring in my own motion picture.

She matched my rhythm as if she wanted to out-fuck me. Back and forth, side to side, and then back in circles, I could tell I was turning her on.

She opened her eyes and saw her reflection in the mirrors up above her head. "Damn, I never knew I looked like that having an orgasm."

I know, freaks you out. huh," I replied.

"Michae,. what are you doing to me? I've never—

"I know, shhh … be quiet and watch this." I pulled her legs up and placed them on my shoulders and pushed deeper.

"Michael, I think you're in the bottom of my stomach. I'm about to cum again," she screamed out.

"I was like, go ahead, we'll cum together."

"Oh, my fuckin' God," she cried out lustfully.

"Shhh, I know … just lay there for a minute and catch your breath, Ms. Kitty."

"I've never had five orgasms while having sex," she said, as she tried to catch her breath.

"I know!" I laughed. "You had all the fun, young lady. While you were having five, I only had one!"

"You mean to tell me that you only got one nut off, Michael?"

"Yep, it's cool though. I'll get the other one when we go for round two."

"Damn, so you think you just gonna fuck the shit out of me and then drop me back off?"

"Nah, shorty, I just wanna make sure you never wanna leave me and John Boy."

"And who in the hell is John Boy? You keep talking about him." I pointed to my penis lying on my leg and smiled.

Still somewhat hard, I picked my penis up and said, "Ms. Kitty, meet John Boy."

She looked at me, kissed John Boy on the head, and said, "Nice to meet you, Mr. John Boy."

I looked back at her and replied, "He said it's nice to meet you too."

Afterwards, we got in the shower, washed each other off, and put our clothes back on.

"Since you've fucked all my insides out, can you at least feed a sister, Michael?"

"Sure, would you like for me to cook you something eat, or would you prefer to go out to dinner?"

"Can we go out for something to eat, please?" she asked. So, we left my place and headed out to my favorite Caribbean Restaurant.

Ms. Kitty ordered the jerk chicken dinner while I had to have my favorite—oxtails, rice and peas, cabbage, and cornbread. We must've sat there and ate for at least two hours, laughing and getting to know one another.

Around nine thirty that evening, we were back at my place. I took her straight back into my bedroom and picked up where we'd left off. Moments later, I was hitting Ms. Kitty from the back.

"Michael, could you get back on top of me please? "'Cause it feels like you're hitting my rib cage," she moaned out.

"Sure, baby, anything to please you." I got back on top and went to work. I gazed at her as I filled her up with all ten and a half inches of dick. I couldn't help but notice how she looked at me in the mirrors as I was putting it down.

Hell, I could see why she wanted me back on top. She wanted to see herself in the mirror. Ms. Kitty was a freak and didn't know it but I did. I also knew she was about to become a muthafuckin' Florida Hot Girl. John Boy had just initiated her entrance into the group.

I thought to myself. *Good boy, John Boy, good boy!*

Michael Gallon

## CHAPTER SEVEN
### THE RECRUITS

The next morning, Ms. Kitty woke up to some scrambled eggs, bacon, and sausage, some fuckin' off-the-chain hash browns, a side of hot buttered toast, and some freshly squeezed orange juice.

She turned over in bed when the aroma of the food hit her cute little button nose.

"You cooked me breakfast, Michael? Where's your plate?" she asked. She yawned and her breath smelled like the night before.

"Well, I would eat something, but I ate too much last night. I gotta watch my weight, you know?" I laughed and rubbed my stomach. "I can't get too big 'cause the females won't wanna work for no fat ass nigga!" We laughed.

"Oh, so you gonna get *me* all fat and you gonna stay in shape for the females?" She giggled and took a bite of the toast.

"No, silly. You're just fine, believe me," I said, "I'll let you know if you get too big and out of shape."

"Michael, let me ask you something?" She paused and chewed up the bacon in her mouth.

"Go ahead, lil cutie."

"Are you a pimp or something like a pimp? 'Cause I don't wanna be pimped by nobody. Shit, if I wanted to sale my pussy for money, I could do that by my damn self," she said with a tone of certainty.

"Kitty, I'm not a pimp. And that's what I *don't* want people thinking. I'm just simply taking you girls to the club to dance."

I explained to her once again that all the money her and the other females made would be theirs. I let her know that all I would require was a small tip out fee from each of them.

"For example, Kitty, if you made five hundred dollars, how much of that do you think you'd have to pay me?" I quizzed.

"I don't know, Michael. I'm gonna say somewhere around two hundred dollars?"

"Wow, that sounds like a nice number, but wrong. Out of the five hundred, all I would want is sixty dollars."

"That's it? Sixty dollars?" At my answer, her eyes widened, and she laid her fork down.

"Yep, babygirl. Sixty dollars is all I would require from a five-hundred-dollar dance night."

"Shit, that's what them other females gonna be making. I'm definitely making more than that, partner. Shoot, I'm ready to start right now." Feeling more at ease, she wanted to know how many girls I had on the team and when the first show would be.

"Hold on, lil' mama," I said, so she wouldn't get ahead of herself, "first, we need to recruit some more females for the group."

"I don't have anything to wear, Michael." Quickly, her excitement had turned to disappointment. The corners of her mouth drooped on her pretty lil' face, and the glow that had just been in her eyes faded. That is until I pulled out a brand-new outfit for her to change into. "How did you know my size, Michael?"

"Let's just say I took a wild guess. Go try it on and see if it fits. Then we can go to the Magic Mall and buy you a few more new outfits and do some recruiting at the same time."

She ran off to the bathroom to try on her new outfit. It had actually been meant for Renee, but since she'd gone to The Chili and bombed out, I figured Kitty could put it to good use. Hell, she'd earned it since I had literally fucked her brains out.

When she came out of the bathroom with the outfit on, I knew without a doubt, it was the perfect fit. She waltzed around the room like a brand-new person. Her confidence seemed on a higher level, and she couldn't wait to get to the Magic Mall to get more clothes. Afterwards, she'd be ready to let the world know she was the manager of the Florida Hot Girls.

\*\*\*

IT WAS A GOOD DAY TO BE AT The Magic Mall Plaza, and it was already crowded. There were wall-to-wall females throughout. Some were there shopping, and some were just browsing. Not to mention, those who were only there to be noticed because they had nothing else to do.

"So, Kitty, do you see any females in here worth talking to

about being in the group?" I asked.

"Yeah, I see a few who could definitely make the team. I'm just not sure what to say."

"That's not a problem, baby girl. Just point them out and I'll take it from there.

"There's one right over there." She pointed toward a lil' cutie over by the shoe department.

"You talking about over there right by them Prada shoes?" I zoomed in on shorty as if I had X-ray vision.

"Yeah, the lil' red chick right over there," she answered..

"Okay, I see her. Yeah, she does look kind of cute, doesn't she?" I checked her out from a distance. "Okay, here goes nothing." I walked up behind in mack daddy mode. "Excuse me."

"Who me?" the cute red female said.

"Yes, ma'am. *You*," I said. I flashed her my best smile. "How you doing today?"

"I'm fine. What about yourself?" She looked from me to Kitty.

"Fine, and thanks for asking."

"You're welcome," she replied. She turned away from me and bent over to look at a pair of shoes. Noticing her pussy print through her outfit caused my manhood to rise.

"Could I talk with you for a few minutes about a job?" I asked.

"Sure. What type of job is it?" she asked. Her expression displayed her surprise at my question.

"Have you ever thought about being a dancer?"

"What? A stripper?"

"Yes."

"Yes, I have. Why? You hiring dancers for a club or something?" She sounded too excited about the prospect of becoming an Exotic Dancer.

"Nah, but I got something better than that. My name is Michael," I said, "and this is Ms. Kitty." Kitty smiled and gave her a girly wave.

"Hi, my name is Nicole. Nice to meet you both."

"Our sentiments exactly," I said. Kitty looked at me clearly lost by my vocabulary.

I proceeded to explain the business and she was in hook, line, and sinker.

"So how do I get in?" she asked while smiling at the both of us.

"All I have to do is check out your body and then we can go from there."

"Well, I gotta be honest," she said, " I've never danced naked in front of a lot of people before."

"Girl, you'll be fine. I've never danced naked in front of anyone but my boyfriend, so you'll be all right," Kitty reassured her.

The three of us walked out of the Mall and headed to my car.

I pulled out onto Colonial, headed back to my apartment in Pine Hills. Nicole and Kitty conversed casually. Of course, I couldn't keep my eyes off of her because she was so fine. I couldn't help but stare at her from my rearview mirror. She was a beautiful, young-looking lady who I couldn't wait to get back to the crib so I could see her naked.

She stood around five-foot-four and weighed around one hundred twenty-eight pounds. She had a fat ass and wore a size 36B bra. Her skin was smooth, and her complexion was a light-reddish color that made her look more inviting. She was a perfect specimen for the next Florida Hot Girl.

When we pulled up in the parking lot of the apartment complex, the usual dope boys were out hanging around the apartment when one of them yelled out to me.

"Yo', Mike, what's up playa?"

"Hey, what's up playboy?" I hollered back.

"Nah, you the playa. Who you got with you?" he asked. He passed the blunt he was smoking to one of the other dope boys.

"Yeah, man, they some of the females I'ma have dancing in the group I was telling you about a few weeks ago.

"Damn, cuz, they all gonna be looking like them two? If so, they gonna make a lot of fuckin' money," he said, eyeing Kitty and Nicole up and down. "Cause them two hoes right there fine as hell," he added.

It must have lit a fire under Kitty's ass when he called them hoes because she went off on his ass.

"Hey, homie, listen up real quick. We not no fuckin' hoes and we damn sure ain't no fuckin' bitches. So don't put that in your mouth," she scolded him. "And remember that when I'm dancing in front of yo' ass and taking all yo' fuckin' money, dope boy." She rolled her eyes and strutted away like the badass she was.

His boys laughed at his ass as the girls and I went inside my apartment. "Man, I'm gonna fuck the hell out of her lil' fine ass; just watch what I tell you," I heard the guy Kitty was clowning on say to his homies.

Once inside the apartment Kitty and Nicole went straight to my bedroom. I went to the kitchen and got myself something to drink.

"Baby, you might wanna come in here and see just how fine Nicole really is," Kitty yelled out from the bedroom.

"Okay, I'll be in there in a few minutes," I called back, "and I'll be the judge of that," I yelled from the kitchen.

I finished off my drink and made my way to the bedroom.

Nicole had undressed and she stood in the center of the room butt-ass naked.

"Well I'll be John Brown," I said, taking in her voluptuous body. "Nicole, how in the hell did all that body get into that outfit you had on?"

"Believe me, Michael, it wasn't easy," she said. She turned around and gave me a better view of how nice her ass looked. "So, do y'all think I can make some money?" she asked.

"Yes, and a lot of it!" I said loud enough to show my enthusiasm. However, it was hard to control my manhood and prevent him from changing into the Incredible Hulk inside my pants.

Before I could say another word, her and Ms. Kitty were kissing each other like they had already met. That's when it dawned on me that Kitty was bisexual, and that's exactly what I needed on the team—a bisexual female who could pull in the females and get them hooked on her ass so they wouldn't want to leave—another mistake I made.

Little did I know, Nicole would not only be a Florida Hot Girl, but she would also become the most vital asset to the team. Because as time went on, and more females decided they wanted to be a part of the team, it became difficult to fire them. Specifically, because she was bisexual and in love with Ms. Kitty and didn't want to leave the group. I just didn't know it that beautiful Saturday afternoon when I hired her.

Before I knew it, Nicole and I were both on the bed eating on Kitty like she was a slice of birthday cake and it was our birthdays. Nicole had one of Kitty's soft titties in her mouth, and I had her pussy in mine. We were eating on Kitty as if we were two zombies.

We recruited eight girls after that afternoon—just enough to fit inside the car and finally showcase The Florida Hot Girls. The next thing I had to do was find a spot to take all the beautiful women so they could dance and make some money.

Someone had given me the number to a club in Tampa called Apollo South. I called the club and asked how I could get the girls in to dance. The manager informed me of the days they could dance, and after a brief conversation, it was set. The Florida Hot Girls would make their first club appearance at Apollo South.

Kitty and I went straight to work after that day. Nicole along with a few of the other females I recruited, decided to move in with us, a decision that worked out perfectly. Now, all I had to do was set up a practice show so the girls would be ready for Apollo South.

Having the girls living with me, I began to put Sharon off more and more. She continued to call and wanted to know when she would be able to come back over; however, I could never give her a straight answer. I couldn't let her know about Kitty and I couldn't let Kitty know about her. I had to keep all confrontation at bay as much as possible to ensure I didn't draw unwanted attention. I didn't want what I had going on in my neighborhood to get back to the wrong people.

Now that we had our first club lined up, it was time for us to get our grind on. I called all the females and informed them of the schedule. In the meantime, I was eager to do our first show. I figured the best place to do one would be my apartment.

# The Murder Queens

Since I already had a big screen TV, the music, and of course the females, all I needed to do was have an event and make it happen. Because there was already a pay-per-view boxing match airing on TV the upcoming Friday and Saturday night, I decided to do a show at my spot. I let the ladies know they would be dancing, and I also got the girls to sell tickets for five dollars at The Magic Mall for the Saturday night TV event. The guys who showed up without a ticket would have to pay ten dollars at the door. Now, the beauty of it all was that, if the guys who bought tickets didn't show up, all that money would be free profit.

The females would make their money from dancing, and they would also receive a small percentage from the tickets they sold. So, everything was perfectly set—another mistake I was about to make as the manager. Rule number one: Never shit where you lay your head.

\*\*\*

WITH EVERYTHING LINED UP, I waited for Saturday morning like a child waited for Christmas morning. I always loved Saturdays since it was basically the start of the weekend. To top it off, all the beautiful females would be hanging out throughout the town. I was always out looking for the next dancer for the group, so being at the Mall that Saturday wouldn't be any different.

The females were busy selling tickets, promoting the fight, and letting the guys know they'd be stripping during the fight. While they were busy handling that, Ms. Renee continued to ask me about her position in the group.

"Okay, listen, Renee. . . . I told you when we first met there would be more females besides you on the team," I explained. I was somewhat aggravated by her constant nagging.

"I know that Mike, but who is this Kitty bitch? She's already acting like she's in charge of all the females in the group"—she gazed over at Kitty with hatred in her eyes—"I thought I was the head bitch in charge?"

*'How in the hell you tryna be in charge when your scary ass couldn't finish out a whole fuckin' night when you went to the club,'*

I wanted to ask, but kept my thoughts to myself. Instead, I lied to her once again.

"Yeah, you will be baby. It's just that Kitty has more experience than you and she gets along well with the other females."

"Or is it just that she likes to suck pussy and have hers sucked by the other bitches, Michael?" she said with anger in her voice. She got so loud, other people inside the Mall were staring, clearly eavesdropping on our conversation.

"Damn, Renee, who told you that? Hell nah, that's not it," I said.

"Bullshit, Michael! I can't fuckin' tell since her and that Nicole bitch already asked me three times if they could eat my pussy and suck out of my ass, damnit!"

"Damn, they really turned up if they wanna suck out your ass!" I couldn't help but laugh at their freakiness.

"Shut up, Mike. That shit ain't fuckin' funny so stop fuckin' laughing!" Renee was thirty-eight hot by now.

"I'm not laughing, it's just strange that they would want to suck out the ass of a total stranger, Renee," I replied in between laughter.

"I know right. I mean, you really know how to pick them. Instead of the Florida Hot Girls, we should be called the Florida Hot Freaks!"

The two of us walked along the aisles. Renee was giving me an ear full, and I just couldn't stop laughing.

"C'mon, Renee, cut it out. Just chill, man, damn," I told her, still laughing. I stumbled over some chairs that had been left in the aisle.

"Don't think I don't see how she looks at you either, Michael!"

"Renee, it's not that serious."

"Okay, well since it's not *that* serious, why did she tell Carmen you made love to her the first night you met her?"

"Damn, she spreading rumors like that?" I pretended not to know what she was talking about.

"Yes, and she told the rest of the females that you and her are together and not to even think about you sleeping with any of them."

"Renee, listen, boo. Seriously, our first show is tonight, so let's make this money first and then we'll go from there. So promise me you won't show your cute red ass and start any trouble."

"I can't promise you that, Michael. Since the first moment I saw you at your office, I knew I wanted to be by your side. I thought by dancing, I would be with you day and night. I can see that probably won't be happening because of this Kitty bitch since you let her take my place," she said with tears in her eyes.

When I saw the tears run down her face, I realized how serious she was about me. She had acquired feelings so fast, I hadn't noticed until it was practically too late. And Renee wouldn't be the only heart I broke when it came to being the manager of the Florida Hot Girls.

As time went on and the group became more established, there would be several females I'd go on to dose my heart to. I just wish I had known how bad it would feel when the tables turned and my heart was broken by one of the girls, known as the Florida Hot Girls.

# Michael Gallon

## CHAPTER EIGHT
### INTRODUCING THE FLORIDA HOT GIRLS

I gave Renee two hundred dollars and told her to buy her something nice for the two upcoming shows. I needed to get away from her so I could find out how the girls were coming along with their ticket sales.

When I finally found Kitty, she gracefully handed me the money from her ticket sales.

"Wow, you sold that many tickets?" I asked.

"Yes, baby! And a lot of the guys said they would just pay at the door."

"Perfect, well I guess we're all set then."

"Yeah, and by the way, Michael, we recruited some more females for the group."

"Outstanding, babygirl, you're just an all-around badass female, aren't you?" I smiled. I was proud of what she'd done.

"You know I gotta make sure things are all in place if I wanna be the manager of the Florida Hot Girls," Kitty said, as her and the other females walked beside me.

When I had finally counted all the money the girls had made from selling the tickets, I expected a nice turnout for the first show.

Now some fifteen years later, I look back on that first day and think to myself, if only me and the girls had known our world, as we knew it then, would be turned upside down.

I was still lame to the game, so I didn't know what to put together for the event. Hell, I thought having the females there was all I needed.

We had been back at the apartment for a few hours or so and it was going on eight o'clock. The girls were getting dressed for the night's show. I was busy making sure there was enough seating. There would also be condiments for the guests to enjoy while being entertained by the ladies.

"Baby, did you get enough one dollar bills so you can make

change for the guys tonight?"

"Oh, snap ones," she repeated. "Don't they bring their own ones?"

"Yeah, the ones who are gonna be tipping, not me," I answered. However, that was another mistake I would never make again. In the future, I would always have ones available when throwing a party where females would be taking their clothes off.

Ten minutes later, my doorbell rang. I answered it and it was some guys looking for the party.

"What's up fellas?"

"This where the party at, right?" the guy standing in the front asked. His smile revealed a set of greenish, stained-gold teeth.

"Yes, it is, do you guys have tickets?" I asked.

"Nah, how much are they?"

"Ten dollars per person, my man."

"Okay, it's five of us," he said.

"That'll be fifty dollars, my man."

"We were told there was gonna be some butt-naked females up in here tonight," one of the guys said from behind his friend.

"Yep, that's what's up. You fellas need any change?"

"Nah, Pimp, what time does the show start?" another guy asked. His breath smelled like hot cow shit.

In about ten minutes," I informed him. "Shit mouth," I said under my breath.

"Hey, what you say, lil homie?" he asked. He must've heard me.

"Nothing, my dude. I said somebody must've stepped in some dog shit 'cause I thought I smelled something foul up in my spot."

"Oh, 'cause I thought you said my breath smelled like straight cow shit," he said, as he went to sit his stank-breath ass down.

"Come on now, homie. Why would I say that about you? I don't even know you like that to be playing with you," I lied.

"That's what's up. But yo', check it, if you got some females up in here, bring 'em out, man 'cause we got the paper on deck," the guy who seemed to be the leader said.

"Hold on, young man, I gotta wait for a few more guys to show

96

up before I bring out all them beautiful young ladies," I said, with a lil sarcasm in my voice.

"I understand lil' homie, my bad."

Just as the loud mouth guy finished talking, Kitty yelled out from my bedroom. "Hey Mike, we almost finished in here! How much longer before you start the show?"

"I'm waiting for a few more guys to show up then it's on and poppin'!"

"Okay, baby! I was just wondering, 'cause the girls saying they ready to shake their asses for some cash! One of 'em said she wanna do something strange for a lil' change."

Damn, I wanna see what that's all about," the shitty mouth dude said, as he leaned over in his homie's ear.

The lyrics of Cash Money blasted in the background and "Looking for A Hot Girl" blared through the speakers.

The doorbell rang again. I opened the door and there was twenty more guys trying to get into my apartment.

*Damn, do these niggas really wanna see some butt naked girls, or they really wanna see the fight on pay per view?* I wondered but knew it was latter.

I don't know who was more excited, me or the females I had dancing for me that particular night. I called my supposed-to-be business partner, Edward Lee Valentino, but as usual, he couldn't make it to the show. By now, it was clear Ed had just been blowing smoke up my ass when he'd told me about the business, which we were supposed to be doing *together*. Hell, I didn't need his sweet-smelling ass anyway.

I went in the back to my bedroom after hanging up the phone with him. I took one last look at the females in the room, all dressed to impress.

"Let's make this muthafuckin' money," I said. After a brief meeting with them, I went back to the living room to get things started.

"Listen up, fellas," I shouted over the music. "May I have your undivided attention please. You all could've been anywhere else in the world tonight, but y'all decided to be here with me and the

Florida Hot Girls! So, please, show your love for Ms. Kitty, Nicole, Lil' Red, Ms. Tight Pussy Felicia, Sexy Redd, Charlie B, Carmen, and of course, Tiny! The Muthafuckin' Florida Hot Girls!" I shouted louder.

Man, when those girls came out of the room, they looked serious as hell. Their facial expressions said it was all about the Benjamins, but their bodies said *come get it*. They didn't waste time dancing on this guy and that guy. They moved as if they were dancers at the strip club already in their prime. Money flew everywhere and the girls spread their ass cheeks and pussy lips from one side of the room to the next. Guys were making it rain. Hell, some of them made it storm from the way they threw money in the air. I was busy making sure the girls picked up the money just as fast as it hit the floor.

When Juvenile's "Back That Ass Up" played in the background, the feelings and emotions that ran through me at that very moment was the best high I could ever phantom. I had some of the baddest females in Orlando dancing for me. They were making mad cash and I was having the best time of my life.

The females screamed, "Mike, my bag is too full to hold any more money!"

"That's fine, Sexy Redd, let me change you out!" Before I realized it, I had just about changed all the girls' bags.

The guys yelled for more ones as the girls yelled for me to change the song.

Then Mr. Shitty mouth yelled out, "Man, you might as well turn the fight off. Sheeiit, all these badass females up in here, we don't wanna see no fight. We wanna see these badass females get butt ass naked!"

Mr. Shitty mouth was absolutely right, no one was even watching the fight. They were all too busy watching all that pussy all over the floor. And me, well . . . you know what I was watching . . . all that damn money being thrown all over the place..

"Yo', G-Money," one of the guys yelled out to his homie, "man, these two females over here doing girl on girl!"

Even before I got over to where the two females were, I already knew it had to be Kitty and Nicole. I pulled one of the guys back to see who it was, and I was shocked to see that it was Kitty and Lil' Red. Kitty's head was so deep in between poor Lil' Red's legs, all I could do was stand there and collect all the money the guys were throwing at them.

The guys made it rain from toe to toe. And it was at that very moment I realized what my cousin meant about the amount of money that could be made each night.

Then, Kitty and Renee went over to the corner to do their thing. The whole crowd along with the other females were all getting turned on. Before I knew it, the girls were doing each other in every corner of the apartment.

The party was going good until someone shouted, "Hey where the VIP rooms?"

Then the guy Kitty had cursed out a few days ago, chimed in and yelled ou, "Hell yeah, 'cause I'm about to take this party to the next level! Shit, these bitches up in here eatin' up all the pussy. Shit, I wanna eat some pussy too and fuck some pussy after I eat all up in a bitch's ass and shit!

Sexy Redd was standing beside me when the guy shouted out his request. "Now that's a foul mouth ass nigga right there," she said, "talkin' 'bout eatin' a bitch ass and shit! No telling where his nasty ass mouth fuckin' been!"

"Hold up, fellas, we ain't got no VIP rooms located inside the apartment. I thought I explained that to you guys already," I said, just as the music stopped in the middle of one of the songs.

"Hold on, my brother . . . you mean to tell me you ain't got no VIP rooms in here at all? What if we wanna take it to the next level?" one of the guys asked. The others just sat there waiting for an answer.

"Fellas, fellas, hear me out real quick. I'm not a pimp, and these girls are not here to perform any sexual activities. I'm not trying to catch any pimp charges for prostitution or anything of that nature. I explained that earlier, so if anyone is upset, I'll be more than happy to refund your money."

"Hey, Mike, man, fuck what that nigga talkin' about. Please

turn the music back on so these females can come back out here and get this money. Hell, I'm having a good time just like this. If that nigga wanna trick with some hoes, tell his crackhead ass to go down to Orange Blossom Trail and trick with them dirty ass hoes," another guy hollered out.

"Okay ladies back to work, show time," I said to the girls, after the brief intermission.

Boy was I glad that was over. Hell, If I needed security, I would've been shit-out-of-luck. Especially since I had fired my security guard earlier that night. The fool had ate one of the girls out in the bathroom and broke my damn toilet tissue dispenser.

*It was around nine-fifteen and I was making sure everything was all right with the females. All of sudden, I heard a loud Bamm! coming from the bathroom.*

*"What in the fuck was that? I said, as I went to investigate the loud thunderous noise that came from my bathroom.*

*To my surprise, when I opened the door, Tiny was sitting on the toilet seat with her legs wide the fuck open. My damn security guard, Bernard "Fats" Walker had his head so far up inside her vagina, it looked like she was giving birth to his big black ass.*

*"Man, what the fuck are you doing to her lil' short ass?" I asked, with a surprised look over my face.*

*"Man, I just had to taste her, dawg," he said, "then one thing led to another, and before I knew it, she had her legs wrapped around my head, man. I was eating her out like I was at Golden Corral or something," he explained, as he wiped her juices from his mouth.*

*"Man, get your dumb ass up!" I shouted angrily. "Look how you done fuckin' broke my damn toilet tissue dispenser!" He looked around and saw the damn thing laying on the floor.*

*"Oh, that's what the noise was," he said dumbfounded. "Hell, I was holding on to it while I was sucking out of her ass," he said. He picked it up and tried to fix it.*

*"Hey, man, it's broken, I tell you what," I told him, "just go ahead and finish what you were doing and then you and her can kick rocks before we get the show started."*

*"C'mon, Mike, man, what? You firing both of us?" he asked. Breathing hard in my damn face, he stood there looking stupid and his mouth smelled like ass.*

*"Yep, you should have known better! And Tiny knows goddamn well I said 'no sexual activities with nobody. I don't care if you are the damn security guard, there is not supposed to be anything sexual between y'all, at all!"*

*"What about you, Mike?" Tiny asked. She slid her thong back up over her fat ass pussy. It had been staring at me and I stood there with my mouth wide open and my dick rock-hard.*

*"What are you talking about, Tiny?" I asked with my head coked to one side. I continued to look at how nice her vagina looked in the red thong.*

*"If I was fuckin' your black ass you wouldn't fire me!" Damn, she was fuckin' right. How could I fire her when I was just as guilty as she was. I had been fuckin' some of the girls in the group before I ever hired them."*

*"Okay, Tiny. Fix yourself up and get ready to make some money," I said. "You're not fired, but Fats you gotta go, so bye!" He turned and looked at me with those big ass eyes of his.*

*"Man, that's so fucked up!" He wiped Tiny's juices from his mustache and beard.*

*"Sorry, playa, that's how it has to be."*

*He walked to the door and turned around. "Can I at least stay here for the show?" he asked.*

*"Yeah, it's ten dollars," I said. He paid the ten dollars so fuckin' fast, I thought he was one of the guys who was paying at the door. Then he flopped his big-headed ass down in one of the seats.*

*"Hell, this is what I wanted to do anyway," he said, "watch all these fine ass bitches you got up in your fuckin' crib, nigga!"*

As the time continued to move on, so did the party. Before I knew it, it was time to shut it down. Some of the females were getting tired while some were still making the money. The guys started dwindling down after they had given all their money away. I was getting tired from counting all the damn ones. So, I decided to shut the show down around three thirty that morning.

As the guys were leaving, one of them yelled out, "Hey Mike, when you having another Florida Hot Girl Party?"

"I really don't know, young man, but it'll be real fuckin' soon. Just remember the name *Florida Hot Girls*!" He left, and I locked the door. I instructed the females to count their money so that I could collect my tip-out fee.

"Oh, Mike, I got your tip-out fee right here," Carmen said. She held up a hand full of ones.

After about ten minutes of collecting the fees, I had a grand total of two thousand dollars and some change. Not so bad for a first show, and there would be many more to come.

As the females got dressed, I had a brief meeting with them and informed them of the upcoming show that was taking place at the Apollo South later that night. They were all happy about the money they'd made.

"Mike, we ready to go right now. You bullshitting," a chick named Do-Dirty said.

"Hell nah, not after all that pussy eating that was going on, I'm ready for some rock-hard dick up in this sweet tight ass pussy," Kitty said. She stood next to me as I finished up the meeting.

"Yeah, Mike, hurry up and take the girls home so you can get back here. Me and Kitty wanna speak to John Boy for a minute or two," Lil' Red said. She stood up and placed her hand on Kitty's soft Jell-O-like ass and ushered her to my bedroom.

As soon as she said it I was out the door in a flash trying to get back there for the threesome. When I finally got back there I ran straight to my bedroom. However, both of them were fast asleep in each other's arm. I stood there and watched them.

"Damn, I guess I'm too late," I said. I hung my head down. Then I heard the cutest lil' voice a man could ever hear coming from my couch.

"Well, Michael, I guess you must have just missed being with the two of them, but you can join me on the couch if you like."

I turned around and a cute Puerto Rican chick invited me to join her on my couch. It cute ass Sexy Redd.

Sexy Redd was the finest girl in my group at the time. She stood around five foot eight and weighed around one hundred forty pounds with a beautiful caramel complexion.

Her breast size was about a 36B, and she had a nice ass like a fuckin' sister. You could say she was a sister since she was mixed with Puerto Rican and black. So, you know she was a badass female I would have on my arm one day.

"What are you still doing here?" I questioned. "I thought you went home?"

"I was about to go home but since we have a show later tonight I might as well just stay here with you all."

"That's fine with me," I replied, as she sat on the couch and counted her money.

"So how much money did you make tonight?" I asked. She looked over at me with a cute smile on her face.

"So far, eight hundred dollars and some change. That's for you and me," she said sweetly.

"No, Sexy Redd. That's all your money, baby. You already paid me."

"You heard me, Michael. It's just a matter of time before you realize I'm the one you need on your arm, playboy. Now get some sleep 'cause we got a busy day ahead of us," she said.

I lay there on my couch and watched her count her money. I thought to myself, *damn she is the baddest female in my group, but what about Kitty and Sharon?*

I must have dozed off thinking about my situation, because when I woke up, it two in the afternoon and my phone was ringing off the hook.

As I reached for my phone, I fell off the couch trying to answer it. "Hello," I said sounding all groggy and shit.

"Good afternoon. Is this Mike?"

"Yes, what time is it?" I asked the voice on the other line.

"It's around two-fifteen in the afternoon," the nice voice on the other line said.

"How can I help you?" I asked the caller.

"Yes, my name is Lil Kitty, and I heard you were looking for females to join your dance group."

"Yes, that's true. And what did you say your name was?"

"My name is Lil Kitty," she said with authority in her voice.

"Okay, Lil Kitty. We already have a Ms. Kitty in the group."

"Okay, so you can't have two Kitty's in your group?" given the way she questioned my authority, she really sounded like a boss and shit.

"Okay, I tell you what, we have a show tonight down in Tampa. I have to take the girls to the Magic Mall to do some shopping. Could you meet me there so I can see how you look? Then we can go from there." I told her.

"Yes, I could meet you there. If I look good enough do you think I could do the show tonight 'cause I really do need to make some money for my son's birthday party."

"That's fine. I'm pretty sure we'll have enough room for you. By the way, how did you get my number?" I asked.

I overheard some females at church talking about how they had hooked up with you. They said they had made a nice bit of money last night. I asked them for your number, and they told me to give you a call."

"Okay, I was just curious as to who gave it to you, that's all," I said. I got up off the couch and went to use the bathroom.

"What time do you think you guys will be at the Mall?" she asked.

"Well, it's two thirty-five right now. I'm about to wake the girls up so they can start getting ready. We should be there around three thirty. I'll be at the watch counter checking out watches while I wait on you."

"Okay, how will I know it's you Mr. Michael?"

"'Cause, I'll be the only guy standing there waiting on you, Lil Kitty."

"Okay, Mr. Smarty pants, if you say so." We hung up.

I looked over at Sexy Redd still asleep on the couch. Her legs were partially open. I could see why they called her Sexy Redd. She was sexy as a muthafucker lying there sleeping. As sexy as she looked, I wanted to unzip my pants and slide my stiff manhood all up inside her. But before I could get closer to her, I heard the voice from hell behind me. "All right, Mr.! I told your black ass I wasn't playing when it came to you and John Boy!" Damn, Ms. Kitty had woken the fuck up. I guess I wouldn't be fuckin' Sexy Redd that day.

Michael Gallon

# CHAPTER NINE
## MY GIRL CHAZZ

Everything was going just fine for a young street hustler like myself. I had just woken up, and I had spoken with another hot female who wanted to join the ever-growing team of beautiful women called the Florida Hot Girls. So, I was about to gain another female but just didn't know it at the time. I found out as the girls and I were busied ourselves and we ran around the house trying to get ready to head to the Mall. My doorbell rang, and at first, I thought it might be one of the guys from the party we'd had the previous night. I looked through the peephole and saw someone totally different.

"Who is it?" I asked.

"It's Ronald and Chazz," the deep-voiced gentlemen said behind the door.

"Who in the hell is Ronald and fuckin' Chazz?" I mumbled to myself. I took another look through the peephole to see if I recognized them. When I confirmed I didn't, I said, "Yes, can I help you?"

"Yes, is Mike here?" one of them asked. "We wanted to speak with him about someone we know possibly dancing in his group."

I opened the door and introduced myself to them.

"This is my daughter, Chazz," the gentleman said. "We live over in Eatonville and we heard about the dance group you have." He was a tall, slender built gentleman. He ushered his daughter into my apartment.

"Yes, I do, sir," I answered proudly. The group is called the Florida Hot Girls." I introduced him to a few of the girls who were still at my apartment.

"Wow, I must admit," he said, looking from one girl to the other, "you've got some beautiful women on your team." He smiled big while rubbing his hands together. "Well, that's exactly why we're here. My daughter, Chazz, would like to join your group." He was direct and to the point.

I looked her all up and down. She was beautiful and slim with a dark caramel complexion. On the taller side, she looked to be about five foot seven. I guessed her to be one hundred thirty pounds. She had nice perky titties and a very soft ass.

"She does have the look and body of a Hot Girl," I said, after I'd looked her over from top to bottom. "Can you dance, Chazz?"

"Yes, Michael," she answered, speaking up for the first time since they'd arrived. "I've been dancing for a few years at different strip clubs. I just wasn't making the type of money I desired," she said, displaying a cute smile.

However, as time went on, I would soon find out exactly why Chazz hadn't been making the type of money she desired. Let's just say she had the same slight problem a lot of people seemed to have when it came to the "sticky-icky-icky", in other words, Chazz was a born-again weed head. She smoked weed every single day as soon as her eyes opened. She had to have something inside her lungs that made her fuckin' head spin.

After giving her an interview, which she shined brightly in, it was decided she would be the next Florida Hot Girl. Hell, to me she *was* the team since she had more experience than anyone else on the team. When it was time for the two to leave, I walked her and her father to their car.

"Oh, by the way, I have a sister name Stephanie. Her and her best friend Peekachu wanna be dancers too," Chazz said. She kindly informed me of a few more females who also wanted to become Florida Hot Girls.

"That's cool," I told her, "just give them my number and tell them to hit me up as soon as possible."

I ran back up the stairs to my apartment so I could finish getting dressed. The team was getting full but I still needed a major spot to take the girls to if I wanted to keep the money rolling in.

***

WE FINALLY MADE IT TO THE MALL around four thirty that Sunday afternoon. Me and the ladies headed in different directions. Of course, I went straight to the watch counter to meet Lil Kitty and, hopefully, other potentials.

I stood and admired the nice timepieces. A Chinese man sat behind the counter eating a large bowl of plain, dry ass noodles.

"Can I show you anything, sir?" he asked.

"Yes, sir. How much is the gold watch with the diamonds inside it?" I pointed to the watch. The diamonds were blinding, and it immediately caught my eye.

"Aww, yes," the man said with a thick accent, "it is a nice piece, sir. One of my most expensive watches," he said, with a half-ass grin on his wide face. He took the watch out and placed it around my wrist. He, too, admired how nice the watch looked against my caramel skin.

"The price tag is two thousand dollars, sir. We do have layaway if you like." I looked at his ass. *My black ass ain't said shit 'bout no fuckin' layaway*, I thought.

Before I could respond, I heard that same cute ass voice I'd heard over the phone earlier, coming from around the corner, over by the shoes.

"Oh, that's nice, Michael. How much did he say it was?" I turned around and it was Sexy Redd as she walked towards me. I stuck my arm out so she could see the watch in the light.

"He said it was two thousand dollars, young lady. Where did you come from?" I asked with a surprised look on my face.

"I was over by the shoes checking out some red bottoms for tonight's show. She continued to admired how nice the watch looked on my wrist.

"We'll take it if you take the price down to around fifteen hundred dollars, sir," Sexy Redd told the Chinese man. He quickly agreed to the price.

"You do take cash, right?" she asked sarcastically.

"Hey, Redd, what you doing? You don't have to get this for me," I said.

"Michael, listen, money means nothing to me when it comes to you. But you need to let your girl Ms. Kitty know when she slips up, I'm gonna be right here to snatch your black ass away from her," she said and winked at me. "And by the way, sir, there's no need to put it in one of those little cheap ass boxes. He'll be wearing that one out the door," she said. She reached in her purse and pulled out a stack of crisp hundred dollar bills as if she had printed them up herself.

After paying the slim Chinese man for the watch, we walked throughout the mall. She told me she was from a small island outside of Puerto Rico. Her father was a bigtime business man and ran a very large company that her and her younger brother would take over one day.

As we walked and talked, I could feel the stares from all the guys we passed by. She drew mad attention everywhere she went.

"So, what if we run into Ms. Kitty?" I asked. "What is she gonna say?" I waited for her response as I tried not to notice how nice her ass looked in the Gucci Jeans she was wearing.

"If she know like I know she better not say a damn thing to me," she said with a lot of attitude, "because she don't want to see these hands of mine. And I don't want to get put out of the group for fuckin' up your lil precious boo thang. No need to worry though, Michael. She's on the other side of the mall at the nail salon. So chill, Mr. Scary Ass," she added. A smile spread across that cute lil face.

In the middle of our conversation, my cell phone rang. I looked at it to see who it was and it was Lil Kitty.

"Oh shit, Sexy Redd! I forgot I was supposed to meet Lil Kitty at the fuckin' watch counter!"

"Hello."

"Mike, I thought you were going to meet me at the watch counter. I'm here but where are you?" she asked.

"Kitty, my bad, I'm right around the comer. I'll be there in like two minutes!" I hung up the phone before she could reply and headed back to the watch counter.

"As I was saying, Michael," Red said and continued to express her feelings towards me. "There's something about you that attracts me to you. I haven't figured it out yet but I will."

"Okay, Ms. Sexy Redd. Thank you for the watch but when do I have to pay you back?" I asked.

"Michael, consider the watch a token of my affection. One day you'll pay me back, plus give me what I want from you." Damn, whatever it was she was hinting at, I wanted to give it to her right there in the mall. Of course, there were entirely too many people around. So, whatever I wanted to give her would have to wait until another time.

As we approached the watch counter, I spotted a cute, spunky female waiting on me. "Excuse me, Mike, right?"

"Yes, and you must be the one and only Lil Kitty?"

"Yes, that would be me," she said, with a smirk over her small but pretty face.

"My, my, my, she's a lil cutie, Michael. No wonder they call her Lil Kitty," Sexy Redd said, as she looked her over.

"Oh, Kitty, I'm sorry. This is Sexy Redd."

"Hello, Lil Kitty, it's nice to meet you," Redd said while extending out her hand.

"Hi, Sexy Redd. It's nice to meet you as well," Lil Kitty replied back. The two shook hands.

As they got acquainted, I stepped back to get a closer look at Lil Kitty's body.

She stood around four foot ten and weighed at least a cool one hundred fifteen pounds. Her chest displayed the cutest little perky titties I had ever seen. She had a nice small booty to go along with her nicely proportioned body. What she lacked in size and weight, she definitely made up with her beauty. She was so small and pretty, she looked a bit like Chilli from the group TLC. Her hair was long and curly and it had a nice shine to it. She was definitely born to be a Florida Hot Girl.

"So, what do y'all think?" she asked. "Can I be down with the team, Mr. Michael?" She placed her hands on her hips and twirled around.

"Oh, so you know you all that and more, huh? Let me confide with my management team. I'm positive they won't have a problem with you joining the team." Just as the words left my mouth, Ms. Kitty and the other girls walked up, and every girl had bags in both arms.

"Hey, baby. This must be the female you were talking to earlier about dancing," Ms. Kitty said with sarcasm in her voice.

"Yes, it is, Ms. Kitty. Lil Kitty, meet the one and only Ms. Kitty. Ms. Kitty, meet Lil Kitty. They looked at one another and smiled as they greeted one another with a hug. Before you knew it, all the females followed suit and introduced themselves to Lil Kitty and she introduced herself to them.

"Doesn't she look like the girl Chilli from the group TLC?" Sexy Redd chimed in.

Nicole was the first to respond. "Yeah, she does look a lil bit like her now that you mention it."

"Well, Michael said he needs to confide with the team before he can let me know if I'll be joining the group," Lil Kitty said.

Ms. Kitty quickly grabbed Lil Kitty by the arm and said, "Girl, don't worry about him. By my standards you are on the team. What size do you wear so we can get you an outfit for tonight's show?"

As all the ladies walked away, all I could do was smile. *The squad is really coming together.* I couldn't wait until later that night so the Florida Hot Girls could take over Tampa. *My girls gonna make a name for themselves in the stripping game,* I thought.

I leaned back on the watch counter, held my head up, and smiled at what I had put together all by myself. It dawned on me that I was about to play a game that played for keeps.

With the new life I was about to start, I had given up so much to obtain so little. All the money, cars, and nice houses, along with the countless beautiful women who would share my bed and my life, hadn't been worth the price I would have to pay in the end.

My new life of wealth, fortune, and fame would cause me to regret ever deciding to become the manager of the world-famous Florida Hot Girls. I just never thought I would have to pay the ultimate price for being surrounded by beautiful women.

"Okay, this will look so cute on you, Lil Kitty. Here you go. Try it on and come back out and let me see how it fits you," Ms. Kitty said. She smiled as she eyed Lil Kitty's ass when she walked away to the nearest dressing room.

"Hey, Ms. Kitty, you think the guys in Tampa will like this?" Nicole asked Ms. Kitty while showing off a nice two-piece outfit she had put on.

It depends, Nicole. Girl, you know damn well your ass is sticking out way too much in that outfit." She laughed and slapped Nicole on her fat red ass.

"I know, girl. . . . but that's the name of the game, baby. You gotta show what you got to get what you want if you want that cash," Nicole told Kitty. She turned around so her ass would be facing the mirrors.

Lil Kitty stepped back out of the dressing room with her outfit on.

"Now that looks cute as hell on you, Lil Kitty," Ms. Kitty said told her. Lil Kitty walked around so she could see her narrow ass in the mirrors outside the dressing room.

"You really think so, Ms. Kitty?"

"Hell, yeah girl. You know that shit looks nice as hell on you," Ms. Kitty replied. The sight of all that ass caused her to lick her lips and smile deviously.

By now the time on my brand new timepiece let me know it was time for us to get back home. We needed time to grab a bite to eat before getting ready. Then the Florida Hot Girls would make their debut at club Apollo in beautiful Tampa, Florida. Sexy Redd gathered up the ladies and I  recruited more females for the group and got phone numbers from guys wanting to see the shows.

When we finally exited the mall I heard someone yell out my name.

"Hey, Mike!" I turned around and saw a big brown skin dude with four of his homies. They were coming straight at me and my girls. *I hope this big ass nigga's girlfriend ain't one of my dancers, and I hope like hell she ain't tell the nigga I fucked her.*

"Yeah, what's up, homeboy?" I questioned him as he approached me. Do I know you?"

"I don't know," he answered, "you ever heard of Disco and the City Boyz?" he asked. The big smile on his face dismissed my negative thoughts. Knowing Disco throughout the years, he would always have a genuine smile whenever he spoke. It was just his character.

"Oh snap, yeah, man," I replied, as if a lightbulb had suddenly gone off over my head. "I hear you all the time on the radio!" I said. "I see your name all over the local flyers promoting clubs and shit."

"Yeah some of my boys told me they were at your party last night and you had some beautiful ass females there. He continued to smile as he talked to me.

"Yeah, you could say that,"

"I was gonna try and make it, but Saturdays are one of my biggest nights," he said.

"Yeah, you really missed a nice show,"

"I heard! Hey, listen, do you have a spot for your girls to dance at on Wednesday nights?"

"Nah, not right now. Why, what's up?" Now, I was curious.

"Because we do Wednesday nights at the Caribbean Beach Night Club. That would be a nice spot for your ladies to dance at and make some serious cash," he said and extended a card to me. "Here's my number. Call me tomorrow, man. I'ma speak with my boss about getting y'all up in there on Wednesdays."

"Sounds like a plan to me," I said without delay. "What time do you want me to call you?" I asked to confirm.

"'Round 'bout two thirty," he said.

"By the way, Mike, you got some nice looking females with you."

"Thanks, man!" I reached my hand out and dapped him up.

"Wait until you see the whole squad," Ms. Kitty said with her usual sassy attitude.

"I can imagine. Where the one they call Sexy Redd?" he asked, rubbing his hands together.

"That's me," Sexy Redd said waving her hand. "Nice to meet you, Disco. "So, what have you heard about me?"

"Nice to meet you, Sexy Redd. I just heard you were a sight to see. And by the looks of it, they didn't lie," Disco chuckled out, "you are a very beautiful female."

"Why thank you, Disco," she said. She smiled at him and stood closer to me as the rest of the females tried to get his attention.

"Mike, I definitely think we should have you and your females at the club."

"I agree with whatever you say, Disco. Make it happen for us, playa." Now I was the one smiling. I was proud of the attention the girls were getting, and it was all due to me.

"So, did you hear anything about any of the other girls," Nicole asked. She stepped around Ms. Kitty so Disco could get a better view of her.

"Yes, I did sexy. You must be the one they call Nicole, huh?" he asked.

"How did you know?" she asked.

"'Cause the boys said Mike had a girl on his team that was short and light skinned with a stupid fat ass. So, that has to be you."

"Yes, that would be me. And as far as this stupid fat ass goes, I'm gonna put it all in your face once you get us in the club," she said, as she bent over and shook her ass in front of him and his boys.

"Aww shit, Mike! Man, let me go before I ask for a private show right here in the damn parking lot." He walked away laughing as he headed toward to his truck.

Driving home that Sunday afternoon, I could hear the Orlando girls telling the other girls there would be a lot of money in the club if they got the chance to dance there. In the meantime, I had Tampa on my mind and couldn't wait to get there. I was ready for the Apollo South to get a good look at the World-Famous Florida Hot Girls.

Michael Gallon

## CHAPTER TEN
### APOLLO SOUTH

The ride down to Tampa was quiet and somewhat laid back. The ladies talked amongst themselves about how much money they were anticipating making that night. Even the new chick we met from Haines City, Florida, the one we called Strawberry.

Strawberry was a different breed of female. First of all, she stood around five foot seven inches tall. Weighing one hundred forty pounds, she had a smooth, dark-yellow complexion. With breasts a 32B in size, a nice firm ass topped off her feminine look.

Her hair was long, jet black, and silky, and it was all hers by the way. She would always frown at the thought of ever putting weave in her hair since hers was so long and pretty. The moment she joined the group, I knew she would be a challenge to work with.

We had met her one day driving through small ass Haines City, Florida. She was living in a rooming house full of men. Walking down the hallway you could smell the scents of every roach infested room in the small wood-framed building she called home.

She had expressed to one of the girls that every day she lived there, she had gone from room to room and pillow to pillow, so she could have somewhere to lay her head. So, you can imagine how fucked up her life was when we came through and rescued her.

The day we met her, we took her back to Orlando with us. She put the past behind her and decided she was never going back to that awful place she called home.

Now she was with us headed to Tampa, talking about how she couldn't wait to get there so that she could start making her some real money. On the way to Tampa, she claimed she was going to shut the club down due to all the money she was going to make. Little did I know, Strawberry, Nicole and a few others, would be more than just Florida Hot Girls, they would become Queens before it was all said and done.

I made a left turn off Hillsborough onto 40th Street. I could see The Chili up ahead in the distance. As we pulled into the parking lot, the club wasn't as crowded as we'd anticipated. I assured the females that it was still early, and not to judge the outcome by the number of cars that were already there.

One by one, the girls started getting their bags out of my car. Then we heard a deep voice come from around my white 1994 Lincoln Continental.

"Excuse me," the six foot four tall security guard said to us. "You ladies must be the Florida Hot Girls," he guessed.

"Yes, we are," Ms. Kitty said, while throwing her bag over her shoulder.

"The manager and the house lady have been waiting on you all to arrive. Let me check your bags in and get you ladies in as soon as possible."

He looked down at me. "You must be Mike, right?"

"Yes, sir," I said, as I looked up at the big ass muthafucker.

"The manager is waiting on you at the bar," he said.

"I'm good. I'll just go in with the group. I don't won't anything to happen to them. You know what I mean? I'm kind of like their security guard too."

"I understand, my brother. You do have quite a few beautiful women with you, so I don't blame you for wanting to keep them safe."

"Follow me," he said, as we walked behind him. Dude was big ass guy and looked like he should've been somewhere playing professional football.

The ladies and I walked in and I could hear the females and guys oohing and ahhing at the number of females I had with me.

"Damn, Rollo, where in the hell did all those pretty ass females come from?" I overheard one of the patrons sitting the bar say to Rollo, the club manager.

"I think those badass ladies are the Florida Hot Girls," Rollo answered.

"The Florida what girls?" the man asked. He sounded confused as to what was going on.

Rollo turned back to face him. "Man, the muthafuckin' Florida Hot Girls," he answered. His annoyance was evident in his tone.

The security guard led me to the bar and introduced me to Rollo. "Hey, Rollo, those are the Florida Hot Girls from Orlando, and this is their manager Mike." He pointed to the girls and then me.

"Hey, Rollo, nice to meet you." He stuck out his hand to greet me.

"Same here," he said back. "When you said you had some females you didn't lie. Boy, you sure do have a nice stable of beautiful women," he said loudly.

"Yes, I must agree with you, Rollo. They are beautiful. Let's just hope they can dance," I said. I held back a half-ass smile because I knew I had some badass females on deck.

As I listened to him explain the house rules, I couldn't help but notice the other women he had dancing for him in the club. Some were cute, but there were a few others who looked like they'd just jumped off a Turnip truck and decided to walk inside the club and make a few dollars. Don't get me wrong; they were nice looking and all, but they just weren't the type you would want to be throwing your hard-earned cash at.

Just as Rollo was about to wrap up his meeting with me, up walked Ms. Kitty with her hands on her hips displaying the signature face she displayed whenever she was upset.

"Mike, we have a problem."

"What's wrong now, Kitty?" I asked.

"These bitches from Tampa are complaining. They said we're in their way, and we're stopping them from making their money."

"Hold on," I said, "is everyone still dressing in?"

"Yes," Kitty answered.

"Okay, just go ahead and continue doing what you were doing and I'll handle the rest."

"By the way, Kitty, this is Rollo, the manager of this nice establishment." I introduced the two.

"Hello, Mr. Rollo. It's nice to meet you. And let me just say thank you for allowing us here inside of your club. We're gonna turn this muthafucker out," she said. She was confident about the entire group.

"So, you and your girls are about to do the damn thing in here tonight, huh?" Rollo asked, as he pulled his cigar out of his mouth.

"Yes, that's if your females allow us to dance and do what we came here to do."

"And what was the problem again?" Rollo asked. His eyes were fixated on her nice thick ass, and the camel toe that protruded through the two-piece outfit she was wearing.

"Your dancers said we're in their way and they can't make any money with us being here," she told him again.

He called out to one of his dancers. "Cymone, tell Moet to come over here for a minute please."

"Kitty you go back in there and tell your girls to finish dressing. Big Rollo is gonna take care of your problems right now," he said.

"Alright, thank you." She walked away, and I could see Rollo's eyes light up as she switched her Jell-O hips from side to side. He looked over at me and shook his head in disbelief at how fine she was.

"As soft as her lips and ass are, I should call her Cotton Candy," I said to Rollo with a smile on my face. Then out of nowhere, the cutest female in the club walked over to where we were.

"Rollo, you sent for me?" The beautiful female's name was Moet.

Moet stood around five foot eight and weighed one hundred forty pounds. Her hips looked like two midgets had been hooked to her back. Her skin color was a pure-red tone, and her breast size had to be at least a 36B. Her hair hung down the right side of her beautiful face as if she was an angel who had fallen from up above.

"Yeah," Rolla said, once she was in front of him. "What's this I hear about you guys giving the new girls problems?"

"Nah, it's not like that, Rollo. All we were saying is the money gonna be short tonight due to the club having an abundance of females," she said and rolled her eyes at me.

"Listen, Moet, the more females we have in here, the more business for everyone associated with the club," he explained.

"Okay, Rollo."

120

"Now go tell the girls from Tampa, if they have a problem with the Florida Hot Girls being here they can go find another club to dance in," he said in a stern tone. Right then and there, I knew Rollo was my type of guy. First, he let me bring my females to his club and dance, and then he wouldn't charge them any bar fee since they had come all the way from Orlando.

Sunday's and Tuesday's were gonna be nice. Now, all I needed to do was lock in the remaining days and we would be set.

After sitting there for about thirty minutes, I looked around the and tried to get a feel for the club. Afterall, it was the first time I'd ever been in a strip club.

As I sat lost in my own space, I heard, Don Juan, the DJ come over the sound system.

"Ladies and gentlemen, boys and girls, please put your hands together and give a warm welcome to the Florida Hot Girls! And I need somebody to bring me a thousand dollars in ones because it's about to be off the chain in this muthafucker tonight!"

Seeing my females come out one by one gave me goose bumps all over. The sheer excitement of witnessing my girls take over the stage and the club gave me a feeling of pride I'd never felt. They were shaking their asses and making their booties clap, and I must admit I felt some type of way as I sat there and watched my girls on stage.

By now the club had a nice crowd and money flowed everywhere. There were females on stage, some danced in front of the stage, and both women and men threw money at my girls. My girls worked the stage like a professional band, and to my surprise, even the other dancers threw money at my girls.

It was just as exciting as it was entertaining. I guess Ms. Kitty was right when she'd told Rollo that her and the crew we're going to turn the club out.

When the girls were finally off stage, every table wanted one of the Florida Hot Girls at their table. I had so many females inside the club that night, it became relevant to me to enlist more people to help me facilitate the everyday operation of what I had put together.

"Mike, this is what I'm talking about! The club is off the chain," Lil Red said, as she counted the ones she had in her purple Crown Royal bag—each girl used one as her money bag.

"Well, Renee, like I told you the first time I took your lil' red ass to that other club, you *can* make money, you just have to put your mind to it," I said, seeing how excited she was about all the money she'd made. At the same time, I imagined how nice it would be to fuck her again.

But the thought was quickly erased from my mind when Ms. Kitty walked up to the bar.

"Thank you for not giving up on me, Mike," Lil Red said as she walked away. Ms. Kitty sat her nosy ass next to me, eyeing me as though I had already fucked poor lil' Renee a.k.a. Lil Red.

"You're welcome, Renee, now go make your money and I'll get with you after the club."

A few minutes later, a slim, drunk looking brother stumbled up to the bar where Kitty and I were seated. He stood around five foot eight and weighed somewhere in the neighborhood of one hundred eighty pounds soaking wet. A Durag underneath a baseball cap covered his bald head. His skin complexion was a light-brownish color maintained from hardly ever being caught in the sun.

"Hey, man, how did you get all them badass females to become dancers?" he asked. His words were slightly slurred.

"It wasn't easy, my man," I answered him. "All I know is I told them about the club and the amount of money they could make."

He stumbled backwards and extended his right hand toward me. "Let me introduce myself," he said. "My name is Smitty. I got an after-hour spot down the road called Lou Doc's."

"Okay, nice to meet you," I said, as I shook his hand, "the name is Michael, and as you can see, I'm the manager of those beautiful women over there who call themselves the Florida Hot Girls.

He looked over to where some of my girls were standing. "I know. They're the ones walking around making all the money, and that's why I walked over here to you. I think I got a sure way me and you can make a lot of money, and have fun doing it," he said.

I leaned over toward Ms. Kitty, who still had her lil' nosy ass sitting by me at the bar. "Excuse me for a quick minute while I talk business with this drunk ass nigga."

"Yeah, Mike, but please make it quick, 'cause I need to speak to you about something before it slips mind."

"Yes, Kitty."

"I'm serious, Mike."

"I heard you, Kitty. Just give me a few minutes. I promise I got you."

Me and Smitty chopped it up for a few minutes. In doing so, it was clear he wanted me to bring my females to his club so the two of us could make some extra cash. He informed me that his club opened after Apollo closed and stayed open until five in the morning.

"I tell you what, let me talk it over with my dancers, and I'll let you know something before we leave tonight," I told him.

"Alright, but I'm telling you, Mike, both of us can make a lot of money— and trust me, it's a nice spot." He sipped on his drink and walked away.

I needed to check on the girls since they were running around the club from table to table making money.

Sexy Redd was in the back and she had three dope boys making it thunderstorm on her fine caramel-complexioned ass. Ms. Kitty was on top of one of the pool tables letting niggas palm her soft Jell-O ass. So, whatever it was she'd wanted to talk about, I was pretty sure she'd forgotten about it by now since she had so much attention on her.

Lil Kitty was by the stage area wrapped up with a lil' ugly ass slim nigga who was borrowing money from his homeboy so he could tip her. Chazz was over in the corner smoking on some bad ass weed with another dude .

Lil Red was off to the right of me and she had her arms wrapped around a ball player who seemed to be mesmerized by her beauty. Nicole was on stage and ten other niggas surrounded the stage as they threw money at her feet.

Strawberry was over in the DJ booth talking with Don Juan,

while the rest of the ladies were doing what they had come to the club to do, make that fuckin' money.

Do-Dirty was over by the entrance of The Chili, sipping and talking with a few shady ass looking niggas who I hadn't paid any attention to.

Before I knew it, it was two thirty in the morning and the club was getting ready to close. I was still collecting the girls' tip out fee.

"Ms. Kitty, have all the girls get dressed and meet me right here at the bar when they're done," I shouted over the loud music.

"Okay, anything else?" she asked.

"Yeah, there's still a few of them who haven't paid their tip out fee yet, so make sure you collect that for me please."

"Okay, I'll be right back," she said, as she turned and walked away. Her hips swayed from side to side.

Twenty minutes later, me and the girls were headed to my stinking Lincoln ready to head back home. I had already told Smitty we'd do his club on Tuesday since it was the next time we'd be in Tampa. The girls rushed to get in the car as the guys from the club surrounded the vehicle trying to get their phone numbers, or convince them to stay in Tampa with them—which by the way, wasn't permitted for any female in the group at that time. There was a rule that said no female was to partake in anything sexual. To establish the rule, before becoming a Florida Hot Girl, I had every girl sign a waiver form specifically stating what they couldn't and could do.

As I backed out onto 40th Street headed towards Hillsborough, I looked back in my rearview mirror to see all the ladies counting their money.

One of them shouted out, "Damn, I made three hundred fifty dollars!"

Another one yelled out, "Hell, I made seven hundred fifty dollars!" All the girls screamed out the amount of money they'd made.

Another shouted, "Shit, I only made fifty fuckin' dollars!"

All of us burst into laughter and I almost wrecked the car.

"Who in the hell only made fifty dollars?" I asked. I tried to gain my composure while some of the ladies continued to laugh.

"I did, Mike," Strawberry said, as she looked around at the other females counting their money.

"Damn, Strawberry! How in the hell you only make fifty dollars?

"I don't know, I was dancing like everyone else," she said. She held her head down in shame.

"Yes, you were dancing, Strawberry, but when we were picking up our money you were too busy flirting with the DJ. And he wasn't tipping, he was too busy sipping on whatever he had in his cup," Nicole said. The other girls listened but continued to count their money.

"Oh snap, that's why I wasn't making no money!"

"Yep, and that's fucked up, Strawberry, 'cause your tip out fee is forty dollars and then you still have to pay for your breakfast," Carmen said.

"Don't worry, Strawberry, I gotcha," Lil Red told her.

"Thank you," Strawberry replied as she turned toward Lil Red.

"No problem. I might not be the manager of the group, but I feel like somebody should be watching out for us to make sure we *do* get up all our money," Lil Red emphasized.

"And you're absolutely right, Lil Red. So, from now on, I'll make sure you guys get your money right. I should've been paying closer attention to you all as you guys were dancing," I admitted.

"That's my fault, Mike. I should have told you earlier that Strawberry really didn't know how to dance," Ms. Kitty replied.

"No problem, Kitty," I said, "that just means that one of you guys will have to teach her how. That way, she can make some serious cash 'cause we definitely can't have her running around not knowing how to dance."

"I just don't understand it though, Mike. When I was in there with Don Juan I made sure I got my money. Honestly, that's where I made most of it in the first place," Lil Kitty said, as she continued to separate the big bills from the small ones.

"Yeah, you probably got some of my money in your little ass hands, Lil Kitty," Strawberry said. She looked over at all the money

Lil Kitty had collected.

"I don't know how in the hell you would think something like that, Strawberry. I made sure he gave me my money before I walked my happy ass out of that booth!"

"You're right, maybe I should have done the same thing, huh?"

"I guess so lil' one!"

"I will next time, and y'all better believe that shit," Strawberry said.

In the meantime, we couldn't wait to get to The Waffle House so we could get something to eat, and minutes later, I was pulling up into the parking lot of the restaurant. It was located in my hometown of Lakeland, Florida.

Everyone was tired and hungry as we headed inside to get breakfast. I was the first one to order. I told the waitress I'd be having the pork chop breakfast. Ms. Kitty ordered grits, eggs, and bacon, and then the rest of the girls placed their orders. I couldn't help but look around at the nice selection of females I'd assembled. *Damn, it would be to nice have a few more ladies on the team,* I thought to myself. I picked up the bottle of hot sauce and sprinkled some on my pork chops and eggs. Then I leaned over to Lil Red and asked, "Are you sure you wanna pay for Strawberry's breakfast?"

"Yes, and why are you asking, Mike?" she countered.

"First, 'cause Ms. Strawberry just ordered almost twenty-five dollars' worth of food, and second, if her apple-headed ass would've been dancing she wouldn't need nobody else to pay for her breakfast."

"And you're probably right, Michael," Lil Red said. "But since it was her first time, I'm pretty sure she'll do better the next time."

"Okay, Lil Red, from this day forward, Lil Ms. Strawberry is your responsibility."

"No problem," Lil Red said nonchalantly, "is there anyone else you want me to watch over, boss?"

"No Ms. Smarty Pants," I said and let out a chuckle. All she could do was smile.

Then she whispered across the table, "Thank you once again for letting me come make this money. I still love you even though you dropped me for Ms. Kitty," she said. She continued to eat her breakfast without knowing she had struck a nerve by expressing her true feelings to me again.

I realized she wasn't so bad after all. My dumb ass just fucked up by letting Ms. Kitty slide in her place. That would be lesson I would repeat time and time again while being the manager of the Florida Hot Girls.

On the way home, the drive was quiet and somewhat calm. All the girls had dozed off to sleep, or at least, so I thought. I happened to glance over at Sexy Redd and she was wide awake.

"So why are you still awake beautiful?" I asked.

"Because somebody needs to stay awake with you to keep you from falling asleep."

"Thank you for your concern towards the group's safety, Redd."

"No problem, baby. And besides, I wanted to keep you company so if you needed someone to talk to I would be here for you."

Redd and I talked all the way back to Orlando, and before I knew it, I was dropping the first female off. I couldn't wait to finally reach home since I needed some rest. I had been on the go for the past few days.

*** 

IT WAS TWO IN THE AFTERNOON when I finally rolled out of my bed and heard the commotion coming from the living room. The girls were up, still counting the money they'd made the previous night.

I went to the kitchen to find me something to drink so I could wet my dry throat. It dawned on me that maybe we should've been concentrating on getting a bigger place since most of the females were staying with me.

"Ladies, excuse me for a quick minute," I said loud enough for everyone to hear me. "Since we're all making enough money, I think it would be a good idea for us to put our money together and invest in a bigger place.".

"Mike, I've got the perfect area in mind," Sexy Redd spoke up. "My father owns a few properties over in the Metro West area. Let me talk to him later today 'cause I'm pretty sure he can make something happen for us!" The other females stared at her like children, taking in her every word. She began to describe how nice the homes in the Metro West area were. I could hear the excitement in the girls' voices as each one began planning how they would decorate their rooms.

On the other hand, I was thinking about my next move for the group. *Yeah, Metro West would be a nice place to stay, but how would we fit in such a nice upscale community*, I thought to myself. I looked at all the females living in my one bedroom apartment, I realized everyone was basically sleeping on top of one another.

As I pondered over our living arrangements, my phone rang. I answered, "Hello."

"Hello, is this Mike?" asked the female voice on the other line.

"Yes, young lady, but who is this?"

"It's J.K., Mike."

"J.K. who?" I replied.

"Mike, stop playing. You know who I am. You met me the other day when you came out here to pick up Renee."

"Oh, the J.K. who said she would never be up in a club shaking her ass for some dollars." I was sure my sarcasm rang through loud and clear..

"Yes, Mike. Well, I changed my mind, and I wanna be a Florida Hot Girl," she confessed, solemnly.

"Damn, how quick the tables turn," I laughed out.

## CHAPTER ELEVEN
### J.K. AND FRIENDS

Still on the phone, I listening to J.K. explain how she needed extra cash to pay off some of her bills. She professed that just doing hair didn't bring in enough to get by. So, she decided dancing for me would be a nice little come up for her.

We must've talked for another thirty minutes or so before she added, "I also have some friends who might wanna dance too."

"Fo'sho J, just make sure they look as good as you do. More than anything, make sure they've all got the bodies to even be called a Florida Hot Girl. I'll talk at'cha later," I said. "By the way, I'ma call Disco as soon as I get off the phone with you to see if we have Wednesday nights at the Caribbean."

"If you can get that spot locked up for Wednesday nights, all of us gonna make a lot of money," she said, "because everybody and their mamas be up in that club on Wednesday nights, Mike."

"All right, J.K. let me get off this phone so I can call Disco to find out if we got the spot or not. Until then, get your crew together so we can make this bread."

"You so crazy, bye, Mike," she laughed and replied. J.K. had a squeaky voice with a laugh that could brighten up any man's day just from hearing it. It would be something I would end up getting used to in the years ahead.

Coincidently, as soon I hung up the phone with her, Disco called me with the good news. As luck would have it, his boss was cool with the girls dancing at his club on Wednesday nights. The event would be called "Disco and the City Boyz featuring the Florida Hot Girls in Disco's Boom-Boom Room".

He explained that I would control the profit off the door and give the club a small percentage for allowing my dancers to perform there. Once I had all the information down, we agreed on the time I would show up with the females and go from there.

After I explained everything to the females, it was on. The come up we so desperately needed had just been established. Now it was all up to us to make things profitable for everyone involved with the

Florida Hot Girls.

As soon as I was done speaking with the few females who lived with me, I went back into my bedroom for some quiet time. As usual, Ms. Kitty entered in with her mouth poked out again.

"Mike, can I speak with you for a few minutes please?"

"Yeah, go ahead, Kitty. What is it now?" I asked. I laid back in my bed with my hands folded behind my head, prepared to listen to her complaints.

"Mike, why is Sexy Redd always here? Doesn't she have her own place to go home to?"

"Hell, Kitty, I don't know. She said she likes being here around you guys."

"Well, I don't like it. I really think she's trying to push me out of the group. She makes me feel really uncomfortable, Mike."

"Kitty, stop it. She really is a good person, and I think we can really go places once everyone starts to see eye to eye."

"What-the-fuck-ever, Michael."

"Kitty."

"Kitty, my ass! A bitch can tell when another bitch is trying to push up against her man."

"Kitty, calm down, boo. It's nothing like that, I promise. Just relax. Things will be okay."

"Okay, Michael, I'm telling you . . . the very next time I feel any kind of way about her ass, I'ma put my foot so deep in her lil' red ass, it's gonna take a fuckin' doctor to pull it out of her pretty ass." Kitty was furious.

"Damn, Kitty. You gonna put it how far up her ass?" I asked. I stood up and laughed as I looked over my balcony.

"It's not funny, Mike. I'm dead ass serious," she said. Her lil' soft ass lips poked from her cute ass mouth.

"Okay, Kitty, I heard you. Man, go back out there with the girls and see if they wanna go shopping." She left the room and left me to my thoughts.

After talking with Kitty, I tried to lay back down across my bed to get some rest. A few seconds later, she was back to let me know her and the girls were gonna head up to the mall to do some shopping. It was fine by me. Having the apartment to myself meant I would finally be able to get some rest and quiet time.

I must have dozed off as soon as they left because I never heard them leave. I had been asleep for a few hours when J.K. called me back to let me know she had spoken with her friends and they were all down to join the group.

She must've been reading my mind because before I could tell her I wanted to see them before we left for Tampa, she started talking again. "Mike were right outside of your apartment. Can we come inside so you can meet the girls?"

"Damn, J.K., I was asleep. How y'all find my apartment anyway?"

"Renee, silly. Damn, Mike, did you forget I was with her the day she came over here so you could check out her body?"

"Oh, yeah. You right, you guys can come on up. You know what number it is, right?"

"Yes, Mike, we're at your door right now. Come open the door."

When they walked in, I observed J.K.'s friends still rubbing the sleepiness in my eyes. They were all attractive as hell, but there was something about the last female who had come through the door. It felt as though we knew each other from somewhere, but, at the moment, I just couldn't figure out where. A strange feeling of déjà vu swept over me as if we had crossed paths in our pasts. But where did I know her from? As J.K. continued to talk, a part of me was listening while the other part was trying to figure out the bizarre puzzle in front of me.

She introduced her friends to me and told them to turn around so I could see how fine they were.

"Hell, you too, J.K. I need to see your fine ass body too, so turn that phat ass around so t I can check it out."

They laughed as they turned around one by one. Now, don't get me wrong, they all had nice bodies, including the friend from Ocala. She was something nice to look at, and that's exactly what I wanted to do.

At about five-seven, her weight of one hundred forty-five

pounds carried over nicely. A 34C sized breasts bulged out perfectly from her chest. Her ass was meticulously proportioned on her backside, and it made you just want to walk up to her and squeeze it. She had everything going for herself including the cute smile that revealed itself on her beautiful face. Even when she laughed out loud, it made you want to laugh right along with her.

She was just your average girl but with qualities that could make a man want to settle down with her cute ass.

"Where is Ms. Kitty and the rest of the girls?" J.K. asked. I had finished looking over the all of the females she'd brought with her.

"They went to the mall to get outfits for tomorrow night's show in Tampa."

"Oh, I know me and my girls going too, right?" J.K. quickly asked.

"Yes, J.K., you and your crew will be going too."

"Mike, you never told me if we'd be dancing at the Caribbean."

"My bad, J.K. Yeah, we'll be dancing there on Wednesdays. So get your game tight 'cause we 'bout to make some serious cash."

"I know that's right, Mike. I told you if you get that club, it'll be on and poppin' fo'sho."

J.K. and her girls looked around my living room, admiring how nice my place was compared to other single bachelor pads they'd been in. But me, I couldn't help but stare at the dark skinned chick who looked so fuckin' familiar to me. And I couldn't help but notice how she kept looking at me from the corner of her eye. Whenever we made eye contact she would put her head down and try to play it off. Could it be she thought she knew me from somewhere too and didn't want me to put two and two together?

*If she was to dance on the team her name would be Midnight or Chocolate since she has such a dark complexion,* I thought.

*Midnight or Chocolate...* That's it! Man, I knew right then and there where I knew her black ass from! She was the black girl who had come to my office right before I got fired and never showed up to meet me.

I quickly walked around my counter, closer to where she was standing.

"Excuse me, can I speak to you for a minute, please?" "Who me?"

"Nah, not *me*," I said in a dull tone, "*You*. Follow me. It'll only take a few minutes," I told her, unwilling to disguise my anger.

We went straight into my bedroom and before I could even ask the first question she began rattling off everything I wanted to know.

"Michael, I know you're probably confused as to why I never met up with you that day when you told me you were going to call me."

"Yes, I was just about to ask you what happened. You know they fired me for getting your phone number, right?"

"I didn't know at the time but they eventually told me what really happened."

"What do you mean what *really* happened?" Now, I was really confused.

"Basically, Michael, they set you up."

"What?" I was totally shocked by what I was hearing. *What would make the Wages Program wanna set me up?* Well, I wouldn't have to wonder long because I was about to find out.

"Yes. They had me act as though I needed help and told me to give you a phone number which wasn't my phone number—it was your supervisor's cell phone number.

They told me to play along with you to see if you were flirting with the clients. So, when you called her number for me the next day, they knew why you hadn't come in to work because you were trying to hook up with me instead," she explained in detail.

"And they used you as the one to set all this up and get my black ass fired?"

"Basically, Mike. I'm sorry. If I had known they were trying to do you like that, I would have never helped them."

I couldn't believe what I was hearing. My job set me up like that just to see if I was flirting with my clients? I was devastated how they could do me like that after all I did for the company. For all my hard work they repaid me by setting me up and firing me.

I wondered how this female could do me like that then expect to work for me after helping some fuckin' crackers fire me over nothing. It was the first time I had actually dealt with someone stabbing me in the back, but still ended up letting them work for me. I must admit the females J.K. brought to the team were suitable for what we were about to start. Nice bodies, perfect attitudes, pretty faces . . . there was only one problem though, space. I definitely had to get a bigger vehicle in order to transport all the females joining the group.

But how sure was I that I could really trust every female on the team? Hell, one of them had already showed me her true colors.

Seneavea walked back into the living room and J.K. knocked on my door.

"Come in."

"Hey, Mike. Seneavea told us what happened. Are you okay?"

"Yes, I'm fine J.K. I just can't believe my old job would do me like that. And what makes it so bad is the fact that they had a sister help them set me up."

"Yep, that's fucked up, Mike. Is it okay for her to still be on the team?"

"Yeah, J.K., it's fine. Hell, it ain't her fault. I should've paid closer attention to what was going on around me. Hell, if I hadn't got fired, we wouldn't be here having this conversation." As soon as I said those words, Ms. Kitty and the rest of the females walked inside the apartment laughing and talking amongst each other.

"Hello, ladies, how's it going?" I greeted them.

"Fine. Judging by all the bags she has on her arms, I can tell who made all the money last night," one of the females with J.K. said, as the ladies put their bags down.

Nah, girl. It was Lil Red and Sexy Redd who made all the money. We just got what was left," Ms. Kitty said to the females sitting in the living room.

"No, I didn't. Sexy Redd's fine ass made like a stack last night," Nicole said. She smiled at the other girls in the house.

"Damn, you made a stack in that little ass club?" Strawberry asked Sexy Redd. Excitement was written over her face.

"Well, to tell you the truth, I made *two* stacks inside that small ass club last night," Sexy Redd bragged and laughed.

"Damn, how did you pull that off?" Nicole asked. The other girls sat back to hear Sexy Redd's answer.

"Well, ladies, it's like this. The bad bitches work the floor while the ones who get laughed at sit over in the comer like a lab rat that no one wants."

"Come to think of it, you were constantly working the floor last night," Nicole said, as she walked to the fridge to get something to drink.

Sexy Redd had just schooled every female inside the apartment. Each looked at the other and realized what she'd said was facts. It was true. All the bad bitches were constantly walking the floor making money. The ugly ones just sat on their asses merely talking about the females who *were* getting money. Knowing Sexy Redd had made that type of money along with making those type of comments, we knew who was the real boss of the group was.

Now the female who pretended to be the boss needed to know who the real boss was. Then maybe she would fall in place and play her position. But instead, she would be pushed out of the group the hard way.

\*\*\*

TUESDAY NIGHT AT APOLLO SOUTH WAS PACKED. The word had gotten around town that there were some new females from Orlando dancing at the club.

When we arrived at the club, the reception was a whole lot different than it had been Sunday night.

The dancers who were already there greeted us with open arms, while the guys in attendance couldn't wait for the girls to get dressed. It was just a whole different persona from the dancers in Tampa. They seemed like they were glad we were there. I was just glad Club Apollo South had realized the Florida Hot Girls were about to take over.

Michael Gallon

## CHAPTER TWELVE
### TIGHT SHIP

Instead of ten girls with me, now I had fifteen. All of them were dressed to impress as they walked inside Apollo South. The guys stopped what they were doing just to see how many I had with me. I must admit I did feel some kind of way as I strolled into the club with all those beautiful women on my arm.

The club had prepared a special dressing room for my ladies. Doing meant there wouldn't be any problems from the local girls when it came to my girls being in the club.

As the girls dressed to take the stage, the local DJ got the crowd hyped.

"Okay, fellas, make sure you got your ones on deck 'cause the girls just walked in! It's the moment we've all been waiting for, and the Florida Hot Girls have arrived!

They will be out momentarily so make sure you have your drinks, your money, and everything else in place before they come out. Let's show these fine ass ladies from Orlando how we do it down here in Tampa!"

While he was hyping up the crowd, I was on top of the girls. "All right, y'all got ten minutes to dress so make sure you guys put lotion on them ashy asses. We sure as hell don't need that up on stage," I said jokingly but meant every word.

"Oh, Mike?"

"Yes, Sexy Redd."

"Can we do things a little different tonight?"

"Do what a little different, Redd?" I asked.

"Instead of all of us on stage at one time, can we somehow break off into pairs?"

"That sounds like a plan," Kitty said.

"And why is that, Lil Kitty?" I asked curiously.

"First of all, some of the girls don't want to be on stage 'cause they don't know how to dance, like Strawberry for example."

"Damn, Lil Kitty, you didn't have to put me out there like that," Strawberry replied with an attitude.

"It ain't like that, Strawberry. I'm just trying to get everybody some money," Lil Kitty replied.

"It's like this. We have fifteen girls with us tonight and there's not enough room on that little ass stage for all of us to get on. So, Mike, you give the DJ a list of all the girls who wanna go up on stage. Then the ones who don't can just work the crowd like Sexy Redd said yesterday," Nicole replied, while pulling her panties off right in front of my naked eyes.

"Sounds like a good idea, Nicole. I'll do just that."

"Sexy Redd, get me a list of the girls who want to go up on stage."

"All right, ladies, y'all got five more minutes to get dressed, so make sure y'all got your money bags. Remember, if any of your bags get too full, come see me at the bar and I'll change your ones in. Are there any more questions?"

"No, Mike, we good," Lil Kitty replied. She wiggled around as she tried to straighten up her thong; for some reason, it would always be crooked in her small ass.

"All right, when I come back in here it's show time," I told them before walking out.

I walked back to the DJ booth to give Don Juan the list of names of the girls going on stage. Guys started asking me all types of questions about the girls.

"Man, how you get all those females to come down here with you to dance?" one guy asked.

"Man, how can we get some of them to leave the club with us?" asked another.

The men asked question after question. But one question I most definitely had the answer for was none of my girls was leaving the club with anyone besides me.

The ladies knew the rules: no giving out phone numbers, no getting phone numbers, no VIP rooms, and no leaving the club with anyone for any reason at all. I was running a very tight ship. Due to not wanting to be called a pimp, I didn't allow the females to participate in any sexual activities. I never wanted to be put in a situation where I would have to explain my business to the police.

Even though I didn't want to be called a pimp, guys still called me that just because I always had a gang of females with me.

One guy summed it up best for me one night after leaving a nightspot called the Sugar Shack, a place I would take the girls to later down the line.

I walked into the Sugar Shack with my girls. "What's up?" a tall, dark skinned brother with long ass dreads asked me out of nowhere.

"Nothing much, player. What's up with you?" I replied with a surprised look on my face.

"My granddaddy always told me to speak to a pimp when I see one. That's why I'm speaking to you, pimp," he said as we walked by.

That name was something I was gonna have to get used to. And that's what those fuckin' agents told me the morning of May 3rd, 2013 . . .

*As the officer who tried to ruff me up was getting his self together, one of the other officers came in.*

*"Are you through roughing up our suspect, Big Mike?"*

*"Funny, Agent Burgess."*

*He was a lot quicker than I thought he was and I had underestimated his size.*

*"Okay, let me handle this my way," Agent Burgess said. The other officers walked his big ass to the ambulance that waited on him outside.*

*Meanwhile, I was sat there with no clue as to how things had gotten to that point. The one thing that kept running through my mind was what did they want with me?" Whatever it was, I was about to find out.*

*"Okay, Mr. Valentino, I'm Agent Burgess and this is Agent Bill Thompson. How are you doing this morning?"*

*"How in the hell do you two dickhead officers think I'm doing? Your SWAT Team blew the doors off my fuckin' condo. Then, you guys send in that big six foot four big ass brother to put in work on my ass. But his ass got a rude awakening when I put these hands on*

*his big fuckin' ass.*

*"Then you two guys decide you want to talk with me?"*

*"Mr. Valentino, we understand you have a lot of questions. So do we. First, let me say 'we're going to forget what you just did to Agent Mike Smith. I want to be the first to apologize for that. I tried to tell him about your military combat skills but he wanted to do things his way which ended up getting him a trip the hospital. Seems as though you may have ruptured an artery in his chest area."*

*"If he would have just kept his hands to himself, his ass wouldn't be going to the hospital with a life-threatening injury," I said*

*"You're probably right, Mr. Valentino, so let's just get on with what we know about you and forget what transpired between you and Agent Smith."*

*"Okay, since you know so much about me, please tell me what I've done to cause you agents to bust into my house like I'm selling major keys of dope up in here."*

*"First of all, we've been monitoring your daily activities for the last year. We have reason to believe that you and a few of your friends are running an illegal prostitution ring." As the one agents was talking, another one came in and said something to his partner about the vehicles I had parked outside of my condo.*

*"Excuse me, Mr. Valentino, is there any reason why your Mercedes Benz out front won't start?"*

*"What in hell does my Benz have to do with this bullshit?" I snapped with anger in my voice.*

*"Oh, I'm sorry, sir. I forgot to mention we have a seizure warrant on both of your vehicles." They looked at me with shitty ass grins on their faces.*

*"What the fuck?" I said loudly.*

*"Yes, we believe both vehicles were used in the transportation of females for your prostitution organization. We'll be more than happy to explain everything to you. So just relax."*

*My head fell down onto my chest as I thought back to that night at Apollo South . . .*

# The Murder Queens

On the way back from the DJ booth, I caught Smitty coming through the door with a nice lil' short hood chick on his arm. He made sure I saw him when he yelled out to me.

"Hey, what's up, Smitty?" I shook his hand.

"I want you to meet one of my strippers."

"Oh, you got dancers now, Smitty?" I asked.

"Yeah, man. I had to start recruiting some for the after-hour spot. You still bringing your girls through tonight, right?" he asked.

"Yeah, I guess so since you said there's gonna be some money there tonight."

"Of course, Mike. I'm about to get Don Juan to make the announcement right now so we can have a nice crowd there. Oh, by the way, like I was saying, this is Tarshay, one of my new dancers."

"Hello, Tarshay. It's nice to meet you," I said with my gaze on her.

"The pleasure is all mine, Mr. Michael," she replied. A shy grin covered her cute little face. I would find out sooner than later that Tarshay was far from shy. She was more so the aggressive type when it came to getting what she wanted.

After speaking with her and Smitty, I knew it would only be a matter of time before she would become a Florida Hot Girl.

While standing there, the DJ came over the loudspeaker and said, "Ladies and gentlemen, boys and girls, give it up two times for Sexy Redd and Ms. Kitty coming to the stage!"

We turned around and watched as Sexy Redd and Ms. Kitty took over the stage. They performed like two professional female strippers from Miami. The way they shook their legs and made their asses move while the rest of their bodies remained in one place was off the chain.

Guys ran up to the stage area and threw mad money at them as they danced to Jay Z and BW1.

Smitty was like, "Damn, Mike. That Sexy Redd is a bad bitch! Where you get her from?"

My mouth hung wide and my eyes stared at Sexy Redd's fine ass. While on the stage, she had the crowd going wild under her magical spell. Moving from side to side, for a minute. I couldn't even see Ms. Kitty's short ass. All I could see was the sheer beauty of Sexy Redd.

"I don't know," I finally answered Smitty, "I just told some people I was looking for dancers and she just showed up out of nowhere."

"Come on, Mike, stop lying. Someone as beautiful as she is gotta be from somewhere."

"Seriously, my brother. I don't remember where I met her. All I know is she just showed up and said she wanted to be a dancer."

"Well, wherever you met her, I wish I had four girls just like her," Smitty said with Tarshay standing right there beside him.

She looked at him like she wanted to say, 'hell, I'm not woman enough for your short, baldheaded ass?'

Anyway, while Sexy Redd and Ms. Kitty were on the stage showing out, the rest of the team was working the crowd. Watching my girls get that bread was like poetry in motion.

They were working the crowd as though they were seasoned veterans at their profession. Hell, even Strawberry was over in a corner with about three dudes. From the looks of it, she was getting all the money t they had between them.

My girl, Chazz, was over by the restroom area dancing on some old ass nigga. She was smoking his blunt and taking his muthafuckin' rent money at the same damn time.

Ms. Tight Coochie was on top of a couple's table showing them why she was called "Ms. Tight Coochie". Her legs were spread wide open as she played with her pussy. I mean, she had the guy *and* his girl wanting to eat her pussy and lick her ass right there in the club. I just stood back chillin' and laughing my ass off. I had a front row seat, and I could see each of my females in action inside the club that night.

Your girl Do-Dirty was over in the back of the club by the jukebox. She was ass naked showing the Tampa niggas why she went by the moniker "Do-Dirty". Shit, the way she had her big, soft juicy ass in their faces, had them nigga's mouthwatering.

From my peripheral, I could see Lil Kitty and Nicole dancing on top of the pool tables in the back of the club. The table had so much money strewn about it, I had to go pick it up before the guys had a chance to pick it back up and throw it again.

Tiny and Carmen were over by the dressing room. From the way they were positioned on top of one of the speakers, I could tell they were pretending some girl-on-girl action.

J.K. and her crew of girls were busy turning in their ones so they could put more money into their money bags.

It was a wild night and it had just started when Don Juan shouted, "Okay, give it up one more time for Sexy Redd and Ms. Kitty."

As the two got their money off the stage, guys beckoned them to their individual tables to dance. Kitty motioned me over to collect her money.

As I was picking up her cash, Smitty approached me and whispered in my ear. "Mike, don't tell me you fuckin' both of them fine ass females."

"Nah, Smitty, I'm just fuckin' one of them for now."

"Well let me have the one you *ain't* fuckin'," he said laughing.

"Nah, Smitty. There's two things you need to know about me, playa. I don't share my candy or my money with nobody. In other words, I'm a selfish ass nigga when it comes to my pussy and my muthafuckin' money."

Don Juan walked back over the speaker system and looked out at the clubgoers. "Coming to the stage next, give it up for Ms. Tight Coochie and Lil Kitty," he said just as they sashayed out.

As they both walked towards the stage one of the broke ass niggas yelled out, "I bet that Coochie won't be tight after I get finished with it!"

Ms. Kitty quickly responded. "Nigga, you ain't got enough money or swag to get up in that tight ass pussy."

While the two of them were going back and forth with one another, I spotted Smitty over at the table where Sexy Redd was dancing. I could tell he was trying to get a peek at her pretty pussy. I walked right up behind him and Sexy Redd noticed me watching her. When she sat her ass up on the table, people started crowding around her to watch her do her thing. She spread her legs so far apart, everyone could clearly see how pretty her pussy print looked.

When this one nigga bent his head over pretending to eat her out right there on the table, suddenly, out of nowhere, Strawberry stepped in with her big ass head.

"The only person eating this pussy tonight is me, so you might as well back the fuck up, lil' homie."

I smiled and walked away. As I did I heard Sexy Redd call out to me. "Michael, take my money bag for me, please!" she shouted over the music, "it has too much money in it." I grabbed her bag and walked away. Strawberry attempted to lick her pussy but she quickly pushed Strawberry's head away.

"There's only one person in this group qualified to eat this pussy and he just walked away with my money bag," she said with sass.

Strawberry pulled her head back in rejection. "My bad lil' mama, I was just trying to hype the crowd up so the guys would throw us some big bills."

"No harm, boo. I'm just fuckin' with you," Sexy Redd said.

"So, can I taste you?" Strawberry asked. She was excited too.

"No, bitch, I'm not gay, and like I told you, there's only one person in this group who'll be eating this pussy."

Now, over in the other corner, Ms. Kitty was finishing up her dance at the table. When she was done, she walked up to me.

"I see how you and your little Puerto Rican bitch always up in each other's face. I'm telling you, Mike, you gonna make me fuck that pretty little bitch up. And I really don't wanna put my hands on somebody else's child."

"Kitty, listen, boo. I'm the manager of the group and when y'all need something, I'm the only one here to handle the problem."

"Well, I hope you're there to handle the problem when I put my hands on your girl." She walked away acting all mad and shit.

I had to try and solve the little problem between them. Sexy Redd wasn't aware of how Kitty felt about her, and Kitty didn't know how Redd felt about her.

Basically, Redd wanted Kitty gone so she could have me to herself. And a part of me wanted Kitty gone too so I could get on with running my group the way I wanted to.

Sitting at my table watching everything in front of me, Smitty stumbled back over to me. "Mike, listen. We can make a whole lot of money together since you got the females and I got the club. It's a sure thing," he assured me.

As I sipped my drink and watched all the pretty females inside the club that night, I wasn't really trying to hear nothing Smitty had to say. I was too focused on the beauties in front of me.

"Yeah, Smitty, I hear you. Just make sure me and my females make some money. I would really hate for us to waste our time in your club if there ain't no money to be made." Before he could respond, Don Juan sounded out over the speakers again.

"Coming to the stage, one of Tampa's finest, by way of Texas, give it up for your girl Mignon!" She would be the next edition to the ever-growing group known as the world-famous Florida Hot Girls.

Michael Gallon

## CHAPTER THIRTEEN
### MIGNON

I placed my drink down on the table and admired pure beauty as she walked out onto the stage. She was gorgeous. With a tall and slender height of five foot eight, one hundred forty pounds filled out each and every curve and gave her a model-like stature. Her hair was long, pretty, and jet-black. Her 36B breasts looked like two perfectly-ripe mounds. She had one of the nicest asses I'd ever seen.

Just as I got comfortable to watch her mesmerize the crowd, Sexy Redd strutted over. "Michael if we could somehow get her on the team we'd be complete. Don't you think?" She smiled.

"I agree with you, Sexy Redd. She's a beautiful young lady, isn't she?" I turned my focus back toward Mignon. My jaw seemed to drop without my control, and John Boy was excited too because he stood at full attention as I watched the stage.

"Excuse me, Smitty"—I tapped him on the arm lightly—"do you know the female on stage dancing?"

"Yeah, that's Mignon. She's been dancing here since she got here from Texas. Everybody in here has been trying to get at her but no one seems to be able to get next to her. I guess the right man or person hasn't pulled up on her yet."

"That's because she hasn't met a man like me yet," I said under my breath while sipping on my drink. As we stood gazing upon her beauty, my mind tried to come up with a plan to get her on the team.

Suddenly, Sexy Redd said, "Let me handle this one for you, babe. You sure you want her on the team?"

I looked over at Redd and gave her a nice sized smile and said, "Go do your thing, ma. Make it happen."

"Anything for you, papi," she replied. She walked away looking so beautiful herself. I watched her and dreamed of the day when I'd push all ten and a half inches of my manhood up in her stomach.

When Redd walked away to put her plan into full effect, Smitty still stood beside me.

"Damn, Mike. How many females you need on your team?"

I couldn't tell if he was impressed or jealous, nor did I care.

Michael Gallon

"Smitty, like my daddy always told me, you can never have enough of two things in life, 'money and beautiful women hanging on your arms'."

"Sounds like your daddy was a smart man, Mike."

Fifteen minutes later Ms. Mignon was at my table telling me how she'd love to travel with the Florida Hot Girls and make mad money while doing it.

"Only one problem, Mike. I would have to stay with you since I don't have my own place," she confessed.

"Nonsense, beautiful. That's not a problem at all. I would love for you to stay with me and the rest of the Florida Hot Girls. I wouldn't have it any other way," I said, while looking at how fuckin' fine she was.

John Boy just wouldn't be still as she smiled at me like I was a hot plate of buttermilk biscuits and syrup. Having sealed the deal, Sexy Redd walked by me, winked her eye, and blew me a kiss. I responded back with a smooth nod of approval.

With all this going on, I hadn't noticed Ms. Kitty heading over to my table with another female from Tampa.

"Excuse me, baby. This is Entyce."

"Excuse me, Mignon. Hello, Entyce. Nice to meet you," I said politely.

Mignon and Entyce hugged each other. Being the business man I was, of course, I stepped back to check out her Entyce's physique. She stood about five foot six, weighed around one hundred twenty-five pounds and carried breasts in the size of 32B. She had a cute shape and a country look about herself. I knew she would be a perfect fit for the group.

After explaining the details of the group to them, Mignon said to Kitty, "Hey, I watched you dance on stage. How do you make all that ass jiggle like that?"

"Aw, girl, that's nothing. Since you're about to become a Florida Hot Girl, I'll teach you all the lil' tricks I know. And then you can teach me the ones you know." Kitty flashed her a sexy smile.

148

Kitty, Mignon, and Entyce walked away laughing amongst each other and talking about how they were going to make all the money. Then Tarshay walked up behind me and whispered in my ear, "I wanna be a Hot Girl, too."

"Don't worry, you'll be one soon, 'cause Smitty doesn't know how to handle your cute lil' sexy ass."

"So you're telling me you can handle all of this, Mike?" She turned around so I could get a good look at how fine she really was. Tarshay was a short hottie from head to toe. She stood around the same height as Lil Kitty. She weighed around one hundred twenty pounds with pretty ass titties and a fat chunky ass I just had to have.

"Yes, I can handle it with no problem," I said.

"Well, if you're so sure about yourself, let's step outside and find out." She had dared me.

"Now, Tarshay, did you just call me out?"

"What? You scared of lil' ole me, Michael?" she asked flirtatiously.

Five minutes later we were outside, parked around the corner inside of the van I had rented. She unzipped my pants while looking deeply into my eyes smiling.

"All right, young lady . . . if you wake him up you're gonna have to deal with him," I told her. I waited for John Boy to turn into the Incredible Hulk.

"And who is *him?*" she asked.

"John Boy." I smiled a crooked smile.

"Who in the hell is John Boy? I thought your name was Michael."

"It is. I'm talking about all that meat you got in your hands."

"Boy, you are so silly," she said. She laughed out loud. The next thing I knew, she had put my manhood deep inside her mouth. Moments later, she had a mouthful. She started working her jaws as though she could handle all of me, but when she felt the full size of my erection swelling inside of her mouth she quickly pulled it out.

"My God, what just happened?" she asked, with eyes as big as pancakes.

"John Boy just changed into the Incredible Hulk, that's what happened. In other words, young lady, you woke him up. I told you."

"I'm sorry, Mike, but I can only fit half of that in my lil' ass mouth."

"No problem, boo. Pull your pants down and I'll just fuck the shit out of you instead."

"Hell, I'm not sure if I want all of that up inside my lil' ass stomach right about now."

"Trust me, I'll be gentle. Just lay there and relax," I said as I helped her take off the tight ass jeans she was wearing. The whole time, she stared at me knowing she'd bitten off more than she could handle.

I gently pushed my manhood up inside of her. She turned her head and let out a small scream. "Oh shit, Michael. Please, owww," she groaned.

After getting all of me inside her, I moved my body 'round and 'round.

"Man, just fuck the shit out of me. Fuck the love making shit, Mike. Fuck this pussy like it's all yours," she said demandingly.

"Say no more. I'm about to knock the bottom out of your lil 'short muthafuckin' ass.

Thirty minutes later, I had her ass trying to tear a hole in the seats of the van.

"Damn, did you cum yet?" She panted.

"Nah, I'll let you know when I get there," I told her.

"Please do, I want you to cum in my mouth. N-n-no ne-need to let a-a g-g-good n-n-nut go-go to w-w-waste," she said. "Ssss, she gasped for air."

Damn, not only did she have good sex, she was also a freak. Could it get any better for me? While I was still beating her from the back, she reached underneath her legs and massaged my nuts. She was oooing and awwing so good, it turned me on and I couldn't hold back any longer.

"Aww shit, I'm about to cum."

"Pull it out and take your condom off. I want that nut inside of my mouth," she said, as she grabbed at my manhood.

As soon as I got the condom off, she greedily placed me inside her mouth so she could taste every drop of my juices. I burst all over her face and in her mouth. "Not my face, silly. I want it in my mouth," she said, as she tried to suck me bone dry.

"Let it go, Michael. I got the rest. "That's what I'm talking about," she said, as she sucked it up.

"Damn, girl, you really 'bout that life ain't you?"

"I'm about whatever it takes to please my man," she replied.

As we fumbled around in the van for our clothes, we could hear Smitty on the outside calling for her.

"Damn, girl, your man out there sounding like he just lost his best friend or something," I told her.

"He'll be all right. Shit, that fool really gonna be sad when I tell him I'ma be working for you instead of him."

I pulled my pants up. "Well, don't tell him tonight, wait a few more days before you break the news to him."

She nodded her head in approval. "Yeah, you right. I wasn't gonna tell him tonight anyway. I was gonna wait 'til sometime next week," she said, as she cleaned herself off.

"Cool, I'ma get out and head back inside the club before my girls start looking for me. I'll get with you later."

"Michael, now that we've got that out the way, my question to you is are you good?"

"Yes, young lady. Anyway, what's that supposed to mean?"

"I'll show you once we start working together." She attempted to get out. However, when she took her first step, her leg gave out. Once she gained her composure, she walked bowlegged back into the Chili as if she'd been riding a horse or something.

"Girl, you are something else, I said. "I'ma see you back inside."

I walked away feeling like I'd just lost ten pounds. One thing was for certain; she really knew how to work that sexy lil body of hers and that nice smooth mouthpiece she had.

Once I was back inside the club, I found Ms. Kitty waiting by the entrance.

"And where have you been, mister? Half of the team has been

looking for you to change out their ones. The other half wanted to let you know they've already made their bar fee."

"Okay, tell them to meet me at the back of the club," I replied. I placed a kiss on her soft ass lips and continued to the back of the club. Before I could make it all the way to the back, Sexy Redd pulled me by the arm and stopped me.

"All right, mister, you were gone entirely too long. Don't let me find out you were outside fuckin'."

"Redd, you know I don't kick my game like that. Chill, lil' mama. The club 'bout to close so go inform the girls to dress so we can get to the next club."

"Okay." She turned to walk away but quickly turned to back to face me. "Oh, and Mike, don't think I don't see what you be doing. Don't slip up and get caught 'cause when you do, you're gonna wish you'd never met me."

While the girls were getting dressed, I kept myself busy talking with Rollo.

As he and I talked, we were interrupted by Entyce.

"Mike do you guys have enough room for me and Mignon?" she asked.

"Yeah, there should be enough room for both of y'all. If not, I'm pretty sure we can figure something out."

Once Entyce and Mignon had officially joined the team, it would only be a matter of time before they, along with Nicole Strawberry, and Sexy Redd, would not only be known as Florida Hot Girls, but they would also be known to the world as "infamous".

"Okay, Mike, everybody is dressed and ready to go," Ms. Kitty said.

"All right, Ms. Kitty. Tell the girls to load their bags inside of the van and make room for Entyce and Mignon."

"So, we still going to Lou Doc's tonight, right?" she questioned, 'cause I got a few guys who wanna spend money on me," she stated knowingly.

"Yes, Ms. Kitty. Once we all in the van we can leave."

"Oh, Mike? I also got a few guys who wanna spend some money on me and my girl, Nicole," Lil' Kitty said loud enough for

Ms. Kitty to hear her.

"Oh, you a baller now, Lil Kitty?" I joked.

"Nah, I just got niggas who wanna spend their hard-earned cash with me and my girl, that's all I'm saying."

Once all the girls had climbed inside the van, we were off to Lou Doc's.

"Damn, Mike," Ms. grown-ass Strawberry shouted out, "somebody's nasty ass left a condom right here in the back seat and I sat right on top of it!"

Ms. Kitty looked at me with fire in her eyes. "Humph," she grunted and rolled her eyes.

"Now I guess we know where Mr. Valentino was when we were looking for his sneaky ass," Ms. Tight Coochie said.

"His nasty ass was out here in the van trickin'."

"Oh shit, all hell is about to break loose," I said. I looked around for someone to help me with what was about to take place.

Michael Gallon

## CHAPTER FOURTEEN
### NOT MY CONDOM

It was early, in the wee hours of the morning. The girls were in the back of the van debating about the used condom Strawberry had accidentally sat on. I had to think of a way to calm them down before Kitty showed her lil' red ass.

"Come on, girls that's not my condom, and I for damn sure wasn't out here fuckin' some trick," I lied. "Y'all know this a fuckin' rental, so maybe somebody else left it in here!"

"Well, why wasn't it in here when we left Orlando, Mike?" Ms. Kitty replied. "With your smart wannabe ass," she added.

"Hell, I don't know. I just know it ain't mine," I answered defensively. I knew damn well it was mine.

"So, what, some random-ass man got in here and fucked somebody, and then just threw his nasty ass Magnum Condom on the seat?" Ms. Kitty probed as if she were a prosecutor in court. The rest of the girls just sat there listening to her go off on me.

"I guess so, Kitty."

"Yeah, right, Mike!" she said. Her eyes were low, and her arms crossed over her chest and it was evident she was fuming. "Let me find out you fuckin' one of these bitches behind my back and it's gonna be me and her!" she said, "then it's gonna be you and me!"

"Well, Kitty, you don't have to worry about me. I'm not fuckin' him," Tiny replied. Within minutes, the rest of the ladies followed suit and removed themselves from the equation.

*I'ma have to fine Strawberry for running her fuckin' mouth,* I thought, as I gazed at my reflection in the rearview mirror.

By the time we got to Lou Doc's it looked like everybody from Apollo South had followed us there.

"Alright, ladies," I said, "I'ma go inside and check things out. Sexy Redd, you come in with me so you can find out where they want y'all to dress at."

Upon walking inside the club, Smitty was already at the door collecting money and directing traffic into the club.

The club was much bigger than Apollo South. Once inside,

there was a nice size dancing area down the stairs. The upstairs was more spacious since it was primary for the girls who wanted to dance on the pole. There were VIP rooms off to the side for those who wanted a more private encounter with a female of their choice.

The feeling I got when I entered different compared to the feeling I'd got at the Apollo. Maybe, it due to the fact that I hadn't seen any security at first. That is, until I saw the big ass nigga named Eru from North Carolina. Eru played with the Bucs and did security on his off time.

"So, Smitty I see you already here making sure things flow well."

"Yep, Mike, I told you the club's gonna make money as long as you bring them badass females of yours up in here." He sounded excited.

"Excuse me, Smitty," Sexy Redd said. She stepped up to him. "Where do we get dressed?"

"Hey, Eru, show Ms. Sexy Redd the dressing room for the females, please."

Eru showed Sexy Redd the dressing room. Smitty and I continued to talk about how much money could be made between the two of us.

Sexy Redd came back just as Smitty and I were doing a walk-through of the club. "Michael, things seem to be in order, so we can change upstairs."

"Okay, babe. Get the rest of the girls and have them dressed in within twenty minutes, please."

"No problem, boo," Sexy Redd said. She headed back outside to get the rest of the girls from the van.

"Yo', Mike, she is beautiful," Smitty said, still smitten by Redd's beauty. "She dating anybody at the moment?"

"You're gonna have to ask her that, Smitty," I told him. "You know she's half Black half Puerto Rican, right?"

"That's why she got that beautiful skin complexion," he said, while grabbing his crotch area.

It was the second time that night that Smitty had asked me about Sexy Redd. Hell, I didn't want him fuckin' one of my girls the way I had just fucked pretty ass lil' Tarshay—especially not Sexy Redd anyway. He could've taken Strawberry and we could've called it even, but he sure as hell wasn't fuckin' my beautiful Sexy Redd.

After all my ladies got inside the club and started dancing, time seemed to fly by. Before I realized it, it was already five in the morning and way past my bedtime. The club was closing down and so was I. Half of the females I had with me had already made enough money. So, when the time came for us to leave, no one complained since they were ready to head home also.

I had to admit it had been a very interesting night. Nevertheless, it would be the first night of the bizarre events that would take place within the lives of the females who called themselves The Florida Hot Girls. And because I was their manager, I would also encounter those events. Things changed that night. I was learning the game, but at the same time, I was becoming a part of the game.

*The future is looking bright for me and the girls,* I thought to myself. I merged onto Interstate 4 and headed back to Orlando early that Wednesday morning. I just didn't realize how much it would change my future. The hold The Florida Hot Girls had on me caused me to lose sight of what could possibly lay ahead for the girls and me.

While driving down Interstate 4 with my attention locked on my destination, a scripture from the Bible crossed my mind: "For what shall it profit a man, if he shall gain the whole world, and lose his own soul" (Mark 8:36).

If only I would have stopped and paid attention to what it actually meant. If I had, maybe there would've been a different ending to my life.

Wednesday morning, not much longer after the sun had risen, I was finally back in Orlando dropping the females off at their different homes. As the radio played, Disco's voice rang through the speakers, and he shouted out the girls who would dancing at the Caribbean Beach Night Club. The girls couldn't believe their names were being called out, one-by-one, over the radio.

"Mike, we need a truck with the Hot Girls' name on the side of it so people will know when we're in their town," Lil Kitty said. She sounded like she couldn't wait so the whole Orlando could see her narrow ass, half naked. She was so hyped, the other girls got hyped too. As I turned onto John Parkway, I had to calm them down.

"Sounds good, Lil Kitty but we don't need that type of attention right now. We need to stay as low key as possible," I explained, "too much attention draws the wrong type of crowd," I said, a lesson I would learn sooner than I wanted to.

"So, I see Disco put us in the mix, huh, Mike?" Nicole asked. She laid her head on my shoulder and smiled.

"Yeah, he did that, didn't he beautiful?"

"Mike you know we gotta go shopping for some new out fits for tonight. There's no way we going up in that club if we ain't got no fly ass gear on," Sexy Redd said. Of course, the rest of the girls agreed.

"Yeah, I know. Y'all figure out what time y'all wanna go to the mall," I told them.

"Sounds like a plan to me," Ms. Kitty said.

We dropped off Chazz in Eatonville and headed to our apartment. Once I made the right turn on to Silver Star, I knew I was home-sweet-home. It had been a long night that lasted into the early morning, and it was past time for me to get some much needed rest.

I fell asleep before my head hit the pillow. It was as if my body shut down from being so exhausted. Since the house was so quiet, I figured the girls who were living with me fell asleep just as fast as I did.

*** 

I FINALLY WOKE UP AROUND ONE THIRTY in the afternoon. I heard noise from the shower running and saw hot steam coming from under the closed door. I rolled over expecting to see Ms. Kitty. Since I didn't feel her soft, luscious body next to me, I figured she had to be the one in the bathroom with the shower on.

I staggered out of the bed and headed for the shower with nothing on except my sport briefs. I hoped to join her short ass in the shower. Just as I reached for the door knob, the faint sounds of moaning and groaning came from my bathroom. *Damn, now I know this lil' bitch ain't in there fuckin' some other dude while I'm right here in the fuckin' house.*

I opened the door and I was greeted with a pleasant surprise. Ms. Kitty and Nicole were butt-naked having their way with one another. Nicole stood vertically as Ms. Kitty crouched underneath her sucking the wet juices out of her pretty shaved vagina.

At first, I stood there in sheer amazement and couldn't believe my eyes. I rubbed them  to make sure I wasn't dreaming. Then I pinched myself to make sure I was fully awake. My manhood began to take notice of what was taking place.

"Come on in, baby. We won't hurt you," Ms. Kitty said.

"Kitty, you know how you feel about me being around the females in the group," I said.

"Boy, I'm cool with it as long as you're doing something with them in front of me. It's when you do it behind my back that I trip about. Now get your silly ass in here with us."

"Yeah, Mike, hurry up and close the door. It's cold," Nicole said. Soap suds flowed down her pretty ass titties. Hell, I didn't know which one was harder, my manhood or her pretty ass titty nipples. Either way, it didn't matter.

Ms. Kitty took my erected manhood and inserted it into her warm mouth. She sucked on it as though it was the last big black dick on earth. While she was sucked my dick, Nicole washed my back. She watch Kitty work on John Boy. She seemed to be enjoying every single minute of the attention Ms. Kitty was giving him and he continued to grow bigger in her small mouth.

"Kitty, you look like you could use some help with all that wood your mouth," Nicole said. Kitty grabbed my manhood by the base and took it out of her warm mouth. The way she held it in her hand made it look like a Louisville Slugger Bat.

"Come on and get you some if you want to. It's enough for the both of us."

Now why in the hell would the two of them do me like that? What had I done to deserve that kind of treatment? Hell, it wasn't my birthday so why was I getting treated like a muthafuckin' king?

I stood with my head back as they took turns on John Boy, enjoying the treatment I was receiving.

"Kitty, just move out of the way, I just have to have that big black, long-hard dick up inside of me," Nicole told Kitty.

"Alright, girl, don't fall in love with my dick. I'm just letting you get a little bit of it right now." Remember who that dick belongs to," Kitty replied. Nicole smiled as she arched her back up against the shower walls and threw her leg up over my thigh. I pushed the tip of my dick up inside her soaking wet, tight-ass pussy.

She grabbed my arms and squeezed the shit out of me. By now, I had both of her legs wrapped around me, and half of my dick was stuck up inside her. With the water from the shower pulsating down my back, I pushed all of my dick up inside of her while holding her up in air.

I pushed up in her. She wrapped her arms around me and laid her head on my shoulder as I commenced to fuckin' the shit out of her. At first, she looked me directly in my eyes as Frenched kissed me as if we were madly in love with one another.

She whispered in my ear. "I been waiting on this moment since the first day I met you in the mall."

"For real."

"Yes, Michael. I can feel you in my stomach and it feels so damn good. Please don't stop," she said, as I continued to go deeper inside of her virgin-tight pussy. Minutes later, she looked me in my eyes once again and said, "Oh shit, I'm about to cum."

"Just hold on and enjoy it, baby. I'm not going to hurt you. I just want you to know how much I really enjoy fuckin' your fine ass."

Little did I know, Nicole was a virgin for real, and it was hard for me to take in the fact that I was her first.

"Michael, take it out and hit me from the back, please," she said, as I pulled out, Her secretion covered my manhood. I placed her down, turned her beautiful red ass around and bent her over the sink. Then I placed my right hand in the small of her back as I arched her over. I inserted the tip of my manhood back inside of her tight vagina.

At first, she let out a light scream as I entered inside of her.

"Shhh, the other girls will hear us," I told her.

"Fuck that, Mike. Shit, the head of your dick is like the size of a fuckin' candy apple. It just hurts when you first go in me," she said, as she turned her head around to see our reflections in the mirror.

She turned back towards me and French kissed me again. I had all my dick up inside her. I must admit, it was some of the best sex I had ever had. I fucked her from the back and deep throated her mouth with my tongue.

As I continued to pound her ass, Ms. Kitty was on her knees behind me massaging my balls. She placed warm, gentle kisses all over my back.

"Baby, fuck the shit out of her," Ms. Kitty said. She grunted as though she had a dick inside her too. "Let's take this shit to the bedroom," she said. She turned the shower off and wiped my back off. I carried Nicole to the bedroom with my dick still enlarged up inside of her tight ass vagina. I lay down on my back and Nicole began to ride my dick. Slowly, she went up and down.

Ms. Kitty came out of the bath room with a dildo strapped on her lil' ass body.

"Damn, Kitty what you about to do with that?" I asked. My eyes grew as big as saucers.

"I'm about to fuck the shit out of her little fat ass. Just keep on going, Nicole. Is it okay if I fuck you in your ass?" Nicole's eyes grew wide when she saw the size of the dildo Ms. Kitty wanted to stick up her tight ass hole.

"I don't know, Kitty . . . I never been fucked in my ass while being fucked in my pussy. Honestly, I was a virgin in both of my holes."

"Girl, I have been wanting to fuck you in the ass since the day we met your cute ass in the Magic Mall," Kitty said. She rubbed some lubricant over the dildo. *Damn, Ms. Kitty a real fuckin' freak,* I thought to myself. As soon as she entered Nicole's fat ass, she wrapped her arms around my neck and placed her head down on my chest.

"Oh shit, Kitty, I can feel you up in me too!"

"I know. It feels good doesn't it?"

"I have never had this done to me before. I can't believe I'm getting fucked in both holes at the same time," she said, as her grip on me grew tighter and tighter.

"Damn, Kitty, let me hit some of that fat ass too," I told her.

Nicole got up and bent her ass over the bed as I inserted my manhood inside of her swollen rectum.

"I hoped you ain't cum yet, Michael, 'cause I want you to fuck me too," Kitty said.

"Nah, I ain't even thought about cummin' yet. And believe me when I tell you, I wanna fuck you too. Don't think Nicole is going to be the only one who gets all this long, big, black, hard-ass dick."

## CHAPTER FIFTEEN
## GOLD TEETH AND DREADS

Moments later, I was pulling my stiff erection out of Nicole and making sure I wiped him clean before I placed him inside Ms. Kitty's wet throbbing vagina.

While I was making love to Ms. Kitty, Nicole limped her sore ass body to the bathroom so she could soak in a hot tub of water. As Ms. Kitty and I continued to fuck another forty minutes, a half-dressed Mignon burst into our bedroom.

"Oh, excuse me," she said. "I should have knocked first. I'm so sorry. I didn't know you guys were busy," she said, as Kitty climbed off a hard John Boy.

Kitty walked towards Mignon who appeared to be shocked. Completely naked, Kitty said, "Girl you good. We were already finished. I'm about to get in the shower. You wanna join Nicole and me?"

Damn, that Kitty was something else. We had just got done fuckin' and she still wanted to take Mignon in the shower while Nicole was still in there soaking.

Kitty took Mignon by her hand and led her to the bathroom. Mignon turned around and looked at me as I lay in my bed. My manhood stared her right in her beautiful eyes. As soon as the bathroom door closed, Kitty and Mignon kissed as if they were two high school girls madly in love.

Poor Nicole just lay in the tub soaking. Nicole was so exhausted after Kitty and I had fucked her, all she could do was gasp for air. However, there was too much steam coming from Kitty and Mignon's passionate moment with one another to get much air.

She thought about the way Kitty and I had made love to her two virgin holes. Once Ms. Kitty finished fuckin' her in the ass, my big, black, hard, long dick was pushed right back in her fat ass.

Now I don't know what went on between the three of them in the bathroom that day, all I knew was I had really enjoyed fuckin' the both of them that afternoon.

That Wednesday was like no other day. The girls were getting publicity from the radio station and just by word of mouth alone. The first sign of their super stardom was when they arrived at the Florida Mall. They arrived at the mall around four thirty that afternoon. As the eight females walked in together, the men and women couldn't help but stare. They carried themselves like they were super models.

Some of the guys already knew them by their stage name. Because of that, it boosted the attention they received that day and their rise to fame was set in motion. The persona that they displayed made them appear as though they had been destined for something big, even before they'd made their debut at the Caribbean Beach Night Club.

Time was moving fast as the girls shopped for something nice to wear for their first night at the club. It was seven thirty-five that evening when they finally returned home with their arms filled with shopping bags.

I greeted Ms. Kitty as soon as she hit the door. "Did you guys get me anything?"

"Yes, we got you something to wear, but we didn't know what color suit you had planned to wear tonight."

"Okay, so what did you get me?" I asked.

"We got you three pair. We hope you like them," she said as she pulled out three pair of muthafuckin' socks.

"Man, y'all got me some socks?" I asked. "I already got a drawer full of them," I said sarcastically.

'Shut up, Mike! It's the thought that counts," Kitty said, "just be thankful that we got you that." She walked to the bedroom to get dressed.

I took the socks and looked at them. "Yeah, y'all right, so thanks for at least thinking about me. Now I have something to tell you guys," I said. "Sexy Redd called me when y'all were out. Her father spoke with the realtor about getting us the house out in Metro West."

"Okay, Mike, so what did she say?" Nicole asked. She leaned against the wall to hold herself up due to the lingering pain caused by Kitty and me earlier that day.

"Ladies, make as much money as you possibly can, 'cause I gotta meet with the realtor tomorrow to give her the deposit to move in."

"Oh, that's what's up, Mike," Strawberry said in an excited tone. "We definitely gonna make enough bread  so we can  move out of this small ass apartment and move into something big." She jumped around like she had won the lottery or something.

"Hey, Mike, how  many bedrooms does the house have?" Mignon chimed in.

"Redd said it has at least eight bedrooms—five upstairs and three downstairs."

After explaining everything to the girls, it was time for them to start getting ready for the club. I went inside my closet to pick out a suit for the show.

Kitty walked in behind me and wrapped her arms around me. "I really enjoyed the way you put it down on me earlier," she said lustfully. "Do you think we can do it again sometime really soon?"

"Damn, you really like getting down like that?" I questioned her.

"I like doing whatever pleases my man, Michael. By the way, how many females do you have dancing tonight?"

"So far, it looks like about twenty," I answered.

"Twenty?"

"Yep, besides Entyce and Mignon, I got  a few more new chicks from Eatonville starting tonight. And it might be a few more I haven't counted yet."

"Damn, Mike, don't you think we got enough?" she asked.

"Not really, Kitty. You know how you guys get. It's like, some of you guys get on one guy and stay on him all night," I told her, "and to make matters worse, the guy y'all on don't even be tipping but y'all will keep right on dancing on the damn guy."

"You must be talking about the other females," Kitty replied.

"I tell you what, follow me to the living room and I'll bring your concern to everyone's attention."

We stepped back out into the living room. Half of the girls

moved about half naked, getting dressed before our departure.

"Excuse me, ladies, can I have everyone's attention really quick, please? I was just talking with Ms. Kitty about how some of you ladies tend to dance on a guy and remain on that one guy even after the song changes. Especially the guys with dreadlocks whose mouths are filled with gold teeth."

"You must be talking about Lil Kitty and Strawberry," Nicole said quickly. They the ones who be tripping on them guys with dreads and gold teeth, Michael." She paused and picked up one of the couch pillows. She placed it between her legs and allowed it to rest against her throbbing pussy.

"Nicole, you ain't even gotta go there," Lil Kitty interjected, "you be foaming at the mouth over them same niggas." She displayed her signature smile.

"All I'm saying is last night I watched a couple of you girls dance on the same guys and they weren't even tipping. And then at the end of the night when it came to paying your tip out fee, some of y'all had your mouths poked out 'cause you didn't have it. It's not fair to the other girls who pay their fees the night they're due, and those of you who don't, can't pay until the following night. When that happens, y'all end up paying double and you wind up putting yourself behind the eight ball," I said to the entire group. Each girl looked around at the other.

"That's right, ladies, 'cause if you all ain't gonna pay, I don't wanna pay either." Ms. Kitty replied.

"Anyway, now that we got that out of the way, you know who you are. Y'all go ahead and continue doing what you were doing so we can go ahead and leave for the club."

As soon as I finished up the meeting some of the other females started showing up at the apartment. They wanted to get dressed at my place with the other girls to make sure they didn't get left behind.

It was around ten o'clock. Some of the ladies were putting on make-up, while others adjusted their outfits. Me on the other hand, I was starting to get a little nervous since it was our first big show.

# The Murder Queens

I sat on the edge of my bed and all kind of mad thoughts went through my head.

Then, in walked fine ass Mignon.

"Excuse me, Mike, could you fasten this up for me?" I looked up and realized she wanted me to fasten her bra; however, I couldn't but notice she didn't have any panties on. She stood in front of me ass naked. Her ass was like a ripe cantaloupe or a honeydew melon. It was so soft, my fingers seemed to melt down in it as soon as I touched it. She turned around to face me. When I saw her nicely trimmed her vagina, my dick got rock hard. At first. I wanted to pull her fine ass right down on my rock-hard dick and start fuckin' her right there on my bed.

"Excuse me you two. ... I hope y'all wasn't about to start something without me."

"No, Kitty. Mike was just hooking up my bra for me. It wasn't anything like that, boo."

"No problem, ma. I was just saying."

Mignon quickly walked back out and into the living room. I watched her walk away.

"You were about to fuck the shit out of her wasn't you, Mike?" Kitty asked.

I made a stupid mistake when I stood up seeing that John Boy was still fully erect.

"No, Kitty, why do you say that?" I asked unknowingly.

"Michael, your dick is about to explode right out of your pants, so stop fuckin' lying." I looked down  and John Boy had his ass fully erected as If he was about to put in some serious work.

"If you had of fucked her, I would've come right in here and fucked both of y'all up! Believe that shit, Michael," Kitty said in a jealous tone. She headed to the bathroom to finish putting on her makeup

Damn, Kitty was just too much, and she had caught me right before I was about to ram all my ten and half inches of solid rock-hard meat inside of Mignon's fine red ass. After thirty minutes of Kitty and me going back and forth about nothing, it was evident that it was time for her to make her exit from the group. There was no way I could manage the girls and have her as my girlfriend too. She was just too damn controlling.

***

WE ARRIVED AT THE CLUB around eleven thirty. Judging the line wrapped around the corner, it looked like it was gonna be a good fuckin' night. I had the females take their time getting their things while I went to see how we would enter inside the club.

Before I could get to the door, Disco spotted me around the corner.

"Mike, you and the ladies come through the VIP door," he told me. Then, he instructed one of his huge security guards to come with us so no one would try to harm the females.

"Okay, girls, listen up and stay together. Follow me," he said, "we're going through the VIP entrance. So we won't have to stand in the long ass line. Besides, they want y'all dressed so y'all can walk on stage and let the guys see who'll be working the boom-boom room."

As soon as they got inside the room, I heard J.K.'s voice. "I told y'all the club would be packed!"

"Yeah, but that's for the club J.K. How many guys you think coming back here to see us?" Lil Kitty asked. She slid her small size panties down her lil' narrow cute ass.

"I can answer that for you, Lil Kitty," Sexy Redd said, as she took off the tight black skirt she was wearing. "It's going to be up to all of us to make the guys come back here and throw money. First, we gotta make sure we're looking our best. Then, when we get on stage, we need to make sure we mesmerize each and every nigga out there in the crowd."

"What about the females, Sexy Redd?" Pussy-ass eating Strawberry yelled out. "We can bring them back here, right?" "Yes, Strawberry," Sexy Redd said, as she laughed her ass off. Sexy Redd walked around and asked the girls for something to wear.

"And make sure you females who be foaming over them niggas with dreads and gold teeth make your money tonight or Mike is gonna make y'all start paying a fine for being late on your tip out fee," Ms. Kitty instructed them, as she unfastened her bra.

Her big ass tittles fell onto her chest. She put powder under them like she was caressing a new born baby's ass. The females continued to get dressed while Disco and I discussed how he wanted things to run. Although he was talking to me, he couldn't seem to stop looking at Sexy Redd.

"Mike, where in the hell did you get that one from?"

"Which one would that be, Disco?" A shy grin spread over my face.

"You know which one, nigga," he said and laughed, "the one they call Sexy Redd. Man, she is so damn fine. If I wasn't married, I'd make her my fuckin' wife," he said. He sipped his Remy and Coke.

"Yeah, I hear you. I'm thinking about making her my wife too," I replied, as I drank from a glass of Pepsi.

Minutes later one of his D.J.s walked up to Disco. "Yo'," he greeted him.

"Yeah," Disco answered.

"They want you on stage, man," the DJ told him.

"No problem, I'm on the way."

"Yo', Mike, I'll send somebody back to get you and the ladies in a few minutes."

"Cool, we ready when you are, playa," I said. On his way out, he accidentally bumped into the door as he looked back at Sexy Redd's fine ass.

"Damn, she's fine as hell, Mike," he said again. He had managed not to spill his drink when he hit the door. As he walked back inside, I stood in amazement as I looked around at the twenty-five naked women getting dressed in front of me.

By now I had a serious crew of females on my team and two more from Winter Haven, Florida had decided to join the squad. They were two cornbread-fed ass females which meant their bodies were "phat da def".

First, there was Tiger. She stood around five foot seven and weighed around one hundred thirty-five pounds. Her breasts were a size 36B. Her ass was fat and round like a Christmas Turkey, and I wanted to pluck it when I first saw her. She had a smooth, cocoa-like complexion with serious, deep, seductive eyes.

Her cousin was a fine quiet female with a pretty face. She went by the name Butter Pecan. The name was just right for the way she carried herself. She stood around five-six and probably weighed around one hundred thirty-five pounds. She had a nice chest size of 32B that accentuated her nice curvy ass. Both females made nice additions to the team.

Just as I walked outside to get away from the temptation inside of that damn room, I bumped into the last person I expected to see that night, before I made it out the door. Yeah, you guessed it, Ms. Fine ass Sharon Connolly.

"Well, well, well look who it is girls, Mr. I'm-always-too busy Valentino," she said, as she stood there looking as good as always. I was stuck. For the past few weeks I had been putting her off. What was I going to do now? I damn sho' wasn't about to let her know about the girls, and I sure as hell wasn't about to tell her I worked for the club.

"Hey, you what's up?" I smiled and asked. "I was gonna call you earlier today but somehow got side tracked." I lied.

"Yeah, I bet you were gonna call me, Michael. You know, it's funny how when you met me you told me you were not about the games. But that seems to be what you're playing, a fuckin' game, Mike! "And I don't wanna play no fuckin' games, Michael," she said. Her expression was one of confusion. I looked around to see how many people were standing around listening to how she talked to me.

"Hey, listen, boo, there's no need for you to get all bent out of shape. I meant what I said. I don't wanna play no games with nobody 'cause I don't want nobody playing games with me. So, I tell you what. After the club, I'll call you and we can go from there," I suggested.

"No, Michael," she disagreed, "why can't we just leave the club right now and go back to your place and then go from there?"

The Murder Queens

"First of all, Sharon, ain't you here with your girlfriends?" I asked, not able to hide my frustration.

"Fuck that shit, Michael! I can do without them. The way I see it, I'm standing here arguing with my supposed-to-be man right now!" she shouted. The people around began to stare at us.

Damn, I was stuck between a rock and some good ass tight pussy. To make matters worse, she looked like brand new money. She'd worn a nice tight pair of black Baby Phat Jeans that fit her ass like a fuckin' glove. To match, she'd put on a red Baby Phat shirt that complemented her nice titties. My mouth watered as I eyed her. To top off the outfit, she had on some expensive ass red Prada shoes that revealed a set of freshly pedicured toes, on each foot. Her nails matched her toes and the overlook was flawless. Sharon looked like a beautiful runway model. Her hair hung down the sides of her and made her look like a Nubian Princess. Truthfully, if I hadn't had so much going on, I would've left the club with her right then and there. I would've gladly given her some of what she wanted. Not surprisingly, I couldn't.

So, instead I said, "Sharon, listen. … I gotta stay here at The Chili and meet with some business partners to discuss the business I'm trying to start. Why don't you just go home and I'll be by there after the club closes."

Just as she opened her mouth to speak, Disco's deep baritone vibrated over the speaker system. "Let me have your attention, please! Give it up as my man, Michael Valentino, brings some of the most beautiful women in Orlando out to the stage! They go by the name of The Florida Hot Girls! Y'all give it up for 'em and show some love," Disco shouted.

As if moving in slow motion, I turned around and all of my females walked towards the stage right past Sharon and I.

"All right, Mike, we about to shut this muthafucker down tonight," Lil Kitty said. As she passed me, she bounced up and down like a fuckin' rap artist about to perform and goon the stage.

*Oh, no Lil Kitty, not now, not here, not in front of Sharon!* I thought, as I tried to hide my nervousness.

Sharon looked at me. Her face grew lines of wrinkles and her mouth twitched from side to side. "What did that bitch just say to you, Michael?"

For starters, I've never been one scared to speak when spoken to, but in that moment I couldn't say a damn thing. I was fuckin' stuck, frozen in place as all twenty-five of my girls took over the stage.

"Wait a minute, Mike, before you say anything, are those The Florida Hot Girls? And did he just say 'Michael Valentino'!" Sharon snapped.

"Yes, Sharon, they are," I confessed. "Why do you know them?"

"No, my baby daddy is supposed to be fuckin' one of them nasty ass bitches! But fuck that, why did Disco announce *you*, Michael Valentino, as the one bringing them nasty ass hoes to the stage," she asked. She *demanded* to know.

"Hold on, baby, what's the female's name your baby daddy is fuckin'?" I asked and ignored her question.

"I think it's the one they call Tiny. Why? You know them hoes or something?"

I opened my mouth to speak but only managed to get out a stutter,

"Michael, please don't tell me you fuckin' one of them nasty ass bitches!"

I couldn't say a damn thing. Sharon looked at me with fire in her eyes and waited for me to answer her.

"Say something you pretty muthafucker," she yelled.

One of the security guards walked over to us and said, "Mike, they need you on stage."

As I walked away from Sharon, headed towards the stage, I heard her question the security guard.

"Why in the hell they need his black ass on the stage with them nasty ass hoes?" Sharon questioned the guard.

He looked down at her cute ass and politely said, "Because he's the man who put this shit together. In other words, ma'am, he's the owner of the Florida Hot Girls!"

## CHAPTER SIXTEEN
### BREAK BREAD

While on stage with my females, I could see the anger in Sharon's eyes from a mile away. She couldn't believe I was on stage with the Florida Hot Girls. She already felt some type of way about them, considering Tiny, one of my dancers, was screwing around with her baby daddy.

Sharon turned to one of her girlfriend, Tamika, in disbelief. I could only imagine what they were saying to one another as they gazed toward me and the twenty- five beautiful women on the stage.

"Girl, I cannot believe the man I've been fuckin' for the past few months is the owner of them fuckin' whores on stage," Sharon said to her girlfriend, Tamika.

"So, he never told you he was the owner of the group?" Tracey, another friend of hers asked, as she sipped on a drink called sex on the beach.

"No, bitch! And to think, he left his nice ass job with the Wages Program to be a fuckin' pimp," Sharon told Tamika. She rolled her eyes at me.

"Bitch, that's not what I heard," Tracey said. She sat her drink on top of the bar.

"What?" Sharon was appalled.

"Bitch, I heard he got fired for flirting with his clients or something like that," Tamika said, as she slurped on her drink of choice, a hard Rum and Coke.

"Nah, girl," Sharon shook her head in the negative.

"Yes, chick, that's what people saying," Tamika said. The three of them backed up and rested their backs against the bar.

"I find that hard to believe because I went to his office one day without any panties on, trying to get him to turn my food stamps back on. He didn't even attempt to ask for my number," Sharon said. She held in a smile and sipped on her an Amaretto sour with crushed ice. It was a drink I'd introduced her to but the crushed ice was a lil' twist she'd added to the drink.

"Damn, trick, you just a little nasty ass bitch, ain't you?"

Tamika said and giggled. Sharon laughed as she thought about what she'd just said. She laughed so hard she covered her mouth to keep the drink from seeping out.

"Bitch, I was just trying to get my stamps back on, and to see what he was all about at the same time," Sharon said. She wiped away the saliva that had spilled out of the side of her mouth.

"Whatever, chick! You was trying to get you some dick, so stop lying to me and to yourself," Tamika said. Tracey just stood there laughing at both of their drunk asses.

"Whatever. Like I said, he didn't flirt with me that day."

"Well, whatever happened, I see you ended up hooking up with his ass later," Tamika remined her.

"Yeah, that's because he left his funny acting wife who wasn't taking care of his sexual needs or doing her job as a fuckin' wife," Sharon told her friends.

"So, I guess that's where you come in at right?' Tamika asked. She was no longer laughing and her tone was serious.

"Girl, let's just say, I try to take care of his sexual needs and whatever else pleases his fine black ass," Sharon said. They couldn't help but to admire the beauty of all the women I had on stage.

"All right, ladies and gentlemen, the Florida Hot Girls are going back inside of Disco's Boom-Boom Room! For your entertainment, cover charge is ten dollars at the door! Make sure you get ones at the bar, and like my man Mike just said, 'everybody Break Bread'."

Disco had the fellas so turned up, they couldn't wait to get back there in that damn room. By the time I got to the entrance of the room, there was a line around the club. Both females and guys were trying to get in to see what the Florida hot Girls were all about.

I stepped into the room to give the ladies their last bit of instructions when the young lady working the door stuck her head inside.

"Excuse me, Mike, there's a line out here so long the owner of the club wants to know when you're gonna get things started?" I turned around and looked at my females all lined up, ready to make their money.

"Tell him it starts right now," I told my assistant.

"Okay, ladies, it's the moment you and the whole world have been waiting for. Give them a show they'll never forget. Good luck, and most of all, enjoy yourselves tonight. It's all about you now."

When I opened the door and saw how many people were waiting to see the Florida Hot Girls, I was over whelmed with excitement and anticipation.

"Ladies and gentlemen, boys and girls, I present to you... the Florida Hot Girls!" Within minutes of opening the doors, I collected around two thousand dollars. People screamed for ones, and the girls yelled that their money bags were over flowing with more money than they anticipated.

"Just grab another bag and keep dancing, Carmen," Sexy Redd yelled over the loud music. Sexy Redd pushed her money over into a pile with her right foot as she continued shaking her ass for the guys she was dancing for.

After about thirty minutes of watching the girls do their thing, I decided to walk back outside to see how much money we had collected.

"Man, it's off the chain inside that room," I told Felicia. She was still busy collecting money from the people who were still trying to get in.

"Yeah, I bet it is, Michael, could you please give me a hand with all these people? she said, as she gave a little short ass guy back his change.

"Sure, not a problem, beautiful," I replied. That's when I caught this lil' Sexy red thang out of the corner of my eye.

"Pardon me, beautiful, can I help you?" I asked her. With a stack of twenties in my hand, I smiled at how fine the lil' red thang was.

"Yes, could you direct me to the manager of the Florida Hot Girls, please?" She was so beautiful as she stood there asking to speak with the manager of the girls.

She stood around five foot seven and weighed around one hundred twenty-five pounds. Her breasts were a very large size, somewhere around 38C. Her waist was small and sexy and she had a round plump ass. A beautiful reddish skin tone made her facial features glow.

"Now what does a pretty girl like you want with me?" I asked. I couldn't stop looking at how big her gotdamn titties were.

"So, you're the manager?" she asked. She smiled bashfully.

"Yep, that I am. I'm the manager and owner. Now what can I do for you, pretty lady?"

"Hello, sir. My name is Chyna," she said. Her smile was beautiful.

"Nice to meet you, Chyna. You're so damn beautiful, why don't I just call you Chyna Doll?" I said, as I looked her up and down.

"I saw your dancers, they all right but I know I can bring some extra flavor to your group."

"So, you telling me you wanna dance with the Hot Girls?"

"You could say something like that," Chyna answered.

"I'm flattered." I smirked.

"Why?" she asked.

"Because I was actually hoping a pretty lil' female like yourself would want to join my team of beautiful exotic women."

After speaking with her for half an hour, she was hired right there on the spot.

"So, just give me your number, and I'll call you to set up an interview, and then we'll go from there."

She looked up at me and said, "An interview? I thought you said I was hired?"

"You are but I still need to check that nice ass body of yours out.

"Okay, but listen, Mike, I don't get naked for nobody but my man."

"Yes, ma'am, I understand. But I am gonna need to see those two midgets on your chest."

She laughed and said, "Funny, Mike. Just make sure you call me and let me know when it's time for me to make my money."

"Yes, definitely. I'll see you sometime this weekend."

"Nice meeting you, Mike," she said, as she walked inside to watch the girls make money. I could hardly wait to see just how nice those big ass titties were.

After I finished talking with her, it was time for me to go back inside and check on the ladies.

Once back inside the room, the DJ played "Touch Me Tease Me" by Case and Foxy Brown, and the crowd was hyped.

I bobbed my head to the beat as I looked over the crowd. My ladies were doing their thing.

Ms. Kitty had her fine ass in the center of the room and three guys made it thunderstorm on her lil' ass. Tiny had a guy throwing away all of his pay check that I was sure he'd just cashed at the bar. Charlie B was over by the side door giving a married couple their honeymoon gift.

Your girl Chazz was over by the DJ booth smoking a fat ass blunt as usual, while Mignon and Entyce were on two big time dope boyz, Big Pat and his lil' brother Dinky from Medulla, Florida, located right outside of Lakeland, Florida.

Big Pat had told me they would be corning through but I didn't believe him until I saw the two of them over in the corner throwing nothing but big faces at my girl.

I casually yelled out to both of them and' lil Dinky held up his drink and continued throwing big faces. A fat ass blunt hung from his mouth. Walking throughout the club I spotted Sexy Redd off to the side with a pile of money all around her. She saw me and shouted out to me.

"Yeah, you see it, my nigga! Will you come pick my money up for me? You see that I'm quite busy and I don't have enough time to pick it all up!"

"Yeah ,Sexy Redd, I'll be more than happy to assist you with your money problems," I shouted back. She smiled at me knowing I had to bend down between her legs to pick up the money that had scattered the entire floor. From the looks of all the money scattered around her, I sensed she would have a nice night.

By now the crowd was huge, guys and girls were wall to wall. People who stood around and continued to ask the same question.

"Hey, excuse me, but do you have any more females available 'cause we have been standing here for at least fifteen minutes without any," one patron said.

"Can you please have two of your finest girls come over here and dance for us please?" another asked. Guys repeatedly expressed how they weren't being unattended to.

So, I replied, "Why of course, fellas! Give me a quick second." Now as I was standing there looking for some of my girls who weren't dancing, I couldn't help but notice a guy who looked familiar. I immediately turned around.

"Yo', homie, do I know you from somewhere?" I asked as curiosity got the best of me. The smooth looking brother turned to me while sipping on his cup of gin and grapefruit juice.

"Yeah, you know me," he said with a slight grin on his face.

"From where?" I asked. I wrinkled my forehead, deep in thought.

"Nigga, you don't know who this nigga is?" His homie butted in and shouted loud enough for the people down the street to hear him. Then just like that, it hit me right in the fuckin' face.

"Man, you that brother name Pretty Ricky, the Porn Star," I said, grinning like a chess cat.

"Yeah, that's me, lil' homie. Now can me and my bodyguard get some naked bitches over here, please?"

"Yes, sir, coming right up, Mr. Ricky," I said.

Pretty Ricky stood around five foot ten and weighed somewhere around one hundred eighty-five pounds. You know, a nice, young-looking light skin brother with a head full of dreads. He'd made it big in the porn industry doing local underground sex tapes. He was originally from Winter Haven, Florida but had moved out to California to further his career.

What I couldn't understand was why he needed a damn bodyguard. Hell, he looked as though he could handle his own weight seeing as though he was all cut up. But he had a body guard with him whose name was Big Jenkins. His bodyguard stood a mere six-two and looked like he weighed a cool two hundred pounds. Big Jenkins was a former Cowboy football player whose career was cut short by a few nagging knee injuries.

Anyway, I scanned the crowded room looking for a few of my

The Murder Queens

available females.

"Hey, Lil Kitty, grab Nicole and Carmen and come over here and dance for Pretty Ricky and his bodyguard, Big Jenkins."

Lil Kitty looked up and saw all the money they had in their hands and the gold teeth Ricky had in his mouth.

"Hell, yeah," she said with dollar signs in her eyes. They got all that money in their hands, gold teeth, and long ass dreads," she said. Ain't he the one who be making them fuck movies with the local chicks?" her lil' narrow ass said. She started taking off her clothes and they hadn't even thrown any money her way.

I slowly walked away as Nicole placed Big Jenkins' head in between her legs and made him smell how her vagina. I spotted Strawberry and Do-Dirty over in a corner turning two niggas the fuck out.

J.K. and her crew were busy turning in ones when Tiny walked over to me. "Mike, do we have to pay for drinks 'cause I'm thirsty as hell!"

"Nah, babygirl, go over to the bar and order yourself a drink. You guys don't have to pay for shit," I said. I looked around the club and checked out my surroundings.

"Excuse me, Mike," my assistant said, as she stuck her head inside the room.

"You got a few females at the door who wanna speak with you."

When I got out front Sharon and her two girlfriends, Tamika and Tracey were waiting to see me.

"Damn, now I hope that these females ain't about to fuckin' jump me," I mumbled under my breath.

"Yeah, Sharon, what's up?" Before she could open her mouth, a cool laid-back-ass brother tried to walk right by me and the security guard without paying.

"Yo' excuse me, cool breeze, you gotta pay to play," I told him.

He turned around and said, "Oh, my bad, home slice. I'm here with Pretty Picky and Big Jenkins. Please, let me introduce myself. The name is Clyde Johnson. I'm the producer of all the Pretty Ricky porn tapes. Excuse me for walking past you and all these fine ass ladies," he said, trying to act all fuckin' smooth and shit.

179

"Nah, excuse me for not recognizing you as soon as you hit the door. How do a nigga like me get in one of your flicks?" I asked.

"Here's my card, I'll get your number before we leave and we can go from there. In the meantime, let me get in here and get with my boys and watch these females turn the fuck up." You see, Clyde was the producer who'd got Pretty Ricky in the business. Hell, I was trying to get in the business too.

"Felicia, please show Clyde here to Pretty Ricky's table and make sure t they have plenty of drinks, and make sure their table has enough females dancing at it, please."

"Yes, Mike, whatever you say, boss," Felicia said, as she walked inside the room with Clyde. He smiled at how fine Felicia was.

He turned to me before entering the room and said, "Make sure you give me a call, playa. Keep your hoes tight and everything will be all right."

"That's a smooth ass brother," I said out loud. Sharon and her girlfriends had been listening to our whole conversation.

Then fine ass Sharon looked at me with a smile on her face and said, "I *thought* I saw Pretty Ricky's fine yellow ass walk in the club How could I not recognize his sexy ass? I have every fuck flick he's ever made."

"Yeah, including the one you stole from my house, young lady," I said with a lil sarcasm.

"Whatever, Mike. If it's going on like that inside let me and my girlfriends in for free. I wanna get an autograph from my favorite porn star," she said, as she smiled from ear to ear..

*Damn, Sharon was just arguing with me then she found out Pretty Ricky was inside the spot, and her pussy got all wet 'cause she wants to see him. What a fuckin' night! Can you believe this shit?'* As I was standing there debating on letting her and her sidekicks inside the room, I looked around for my damn assistant.

"Sharon, you and your girlfriends can go on inside while I speak with these nice gentlemen really quick." Her and her girls were inside before I could even finish my sentence.

I peeped my head inside the room and the lil' heifer was in there taking her clothes off for some damn money. I had only told her ass to go inside and make sure the guys were okay. Now, she was in there dancing too.

I was on the door collecting money when four cowboy-looking-ass niggas stepped up to me about a bachelor party they were having the upcoming weekend.

I turned around to speak to the guys about the bachelor party. The guy in charge asked, "Do you have any females available this weekend for a bachelor party for one of my homies?"

"Well, I haven't really done one yet, so I'm still new to the game. I do have some females who will be available though. How about I'll just charge you guys a hundred twenty-five dollars for four or five of them? And then your guys can just tip them for dancing." The four men looked at each other and talked it over for a few minutes before turning back to me.

"Yeah, we cool with that," the same guy doing the talking said, "here's the money along with the address. Have them there around ten o'clock Friday night, cool?"

"Cool," I said, confirming the deal. "Nice meeting you guys I'll see you Friday night."

My dumb black ass had just made one of my biggest mistakes ever when it came to being the manager of the Florida Hot Girls. But in the end, it would be the four cowboy-looking-ass niggas paying for my mistake with their lives—something I still have nightmares about to this very day.

It was now two thirty in the morning, and the club was about to close. I was busy counting the money from the door when Sexy Redd came out of the room.

"Michael, is there anything you need me to help you with?"

"Yes, have the girls go ahead and dress and collect their bar fee for me, please."

"Yes, Michael." She then kissed me on my cheek so gently and whispered in my ear, "I can't wait until it's my time to have you all to myself, Mr. Valentino."

"Girl, stop teasing me." People had started coming through the door as she walked back inside. Pretty Ricky, Big Jenkins, and Clyde Johnson walked back by me.

"There's an after party back at the downtown Hilton, room 216," Clyde Johnson yelled out to the crowd as they were walking out of the door. To all the females who may be coming, please don't wear any panties 'cause me and my homies are making a muthafuckin' movie!"

Minutes later, half of the people who had been inside the boom-boom room were following right behind them, headed to the after party.

"Mike, the girls are all dressed."

"Thanks, Sexy Redd."

Then my short ass assistant walked back out and said, "Mike, you don't have to pay me 'cause I made $560.00 dollars inside.

"Yeah, I know, but you damn sho' have to pay me for taking your ass inside and shaking it for some cash!" I told her.

"Why, Mike?" she replied with disgust in her face.

"Because you went inside and started dancing," I said.

This time, she surprised my black ass with her response. "That's because I want to be a Florida Hot Girl, you didn't know." She winked her left eye at me as she counted out her bar fee and turned back at the girls who were walking behind her.

"I guess I'll see you girls this weekend 'cause I'm one of the newest members of the Florida Hot Girls Team," she said with a smile across her face. She walked away still counting her money.

## CHAPTER SEVENTEEN
## THE AFTER PARTY

"Mike are we going to the after party Clyde J. was    talking about?' Chazz asked, as everyone  got their bags together.

"I really don't feel like being around all that noise since we just finished up with the club," I answered.

"Well, they want Nicole, me, and maybe a few more girls to go to the party." Lil fast ass Kitty yelled back loud enough for the rest of the females could hear her.

"Lil Kitty, are those niggas gonna pay y'all for going? No, they're not," I answered for her, "all they wanna do is smoke weed and then fuck the shit out of whoever decides to go to the party."

"They already throwed me and my girls enough money. Hell, we just going to the party to chill, Mike," she yelled back at me.

"Kitty, trust me when I tell you, them niggas are all juiced up and ready to fuck something. And it'll probably be your lil' hot ass 'cause you like niggas with dreads and a mouth full of gold teeth."

"What, you jealous?" she asked, laughing at the same time.

"Hell nah," Ms. Kitty said with her mouth twisted in a frown. "Why would he be jealous when he has all of this to fuck, Lil Kitty?" She turned around as if she were modeling, showing off her fine ass body.

"Yeah, I hate to say it, Lil Kitty, but Clyde did say for all the females not to wear any panties 'cause they were making a movie tonight. So, you wanna be a porn star now, huh, Lil Kitty? Nicole asked her, as she placed her heels inside of her bag.

Lil Kitty looked at everyone with a stupid look all over her face.

"Listen, ladies, we've all made a lot of money tonight. There's no need for us to still be out trying to make more. Let's just call it a night and start fresh later this week," J.K. said in her squeaky lil voice.

"Yeah, Lil Kitty. Let's just go get some breakfast and just chill the fuck out," Carmen said, while pulling her pants up over her nice round ass.

"By the way, ladies, speaking of this week, a few of you have a bachelor party this Friday, so get your rest and I'll see you on Friday," I said told the females, as we were walked out of The Chili. After speaking with them inside the room it was time to go. I paid The Chili their percentage and walked out with the females and back to our van. It was around three thirty in the morning, so we decided to head off to get some breakfast.

We did the usual and headed straight for the Waffle House for morning breakfast.

We sat and ate breakfast for at least twenty minutes. Clyde's slick ass pulled up in his limo to pick Lil Kitty, Strawberry, and Tiny up.

"All right, I see y'all are the same three who be foaming over them niggas with the gold teeth and long dreads.

Lil Kitty slung her money bag around her wrist as she stood up. "Whatever, Mike. We just going to chill, that's it."

"Well, why Strawberry don't have any panties on if y'all just going to chill?" Sexy Redd asked as Strawberry stood up to join Lil Kitty and her crew. Everybody burst into laughter as the three ran out of the Waffle House and jumped in the limo.

Clyde and Pretty Ricky stuck their head out of the sunroof and shouted, "We're about to make a movie with the fuckin' Florida Hot Girls!"

*Them slick ass muthafuckers.* All I could do was just take that one on the chin as I saw them pull away with three of my dancers. I just told their dumb asses what was up.

While sitting there chewing on my pork chop, I made a decision. I leaned over and told the females at the table, "If I see a fuck-flick with any of those females in it, I'm gonna fire each and every one of them."

"I don't blame you, Baby. You did warn them about the rules," Ms. Kitty said, while stuffing her mouth with bacon.

Later that day after I had slept in for at least nine hours, I was on my way to Metro West to meet with the realtor about the house. I had convinced Ms. Kitty to sleep in so I could meet up with Sexy Redd so we could do a walkthrough together and decide if we wanted to purchase the house.

The house was located within a nice, gated community which was fine with me. The more security the better off I would feel. The realtor left special instructions with the guard at the gate to let us in upon our arrival.

Once I drove through the gate and noticed the beautiful two-story homes within the community, I was already sold.

We pulled up to the house the address belonged to and couldn't believe how spectacular the house was. *Everything about the house is beautiful and fit for a king,* I thought as I stepped out of my car to stare at its beauty.

"Baby, I can't wait to step inside to see how it looks."

"Yeah, me too, baby, but listen, don't look so excited. She'll think we've never been in anything nice before.

"Okay, baby. I got you."

We walked inside and the house was as spectacular inside as it was on the outside, with two big spacious living rooms and a big ass kitchen to boot. The first living room had a beautiful chandelier fixed high above. That room alone looked like it could seat ten to twenty people in it. All the bottom floor bedrooms were huge bedrooms with full walk-in closets and their own bathrooms. The stairs were aligned in a circular position that went all the way to the second floor, where the master bedroom was magnificent. Just the right size for a King and his Queen.

"So, Mr. and Mrs. Valentino, how do you like it?"

Before I could even open my mouth, Sexy Redd said to the lady realtor, "We love it. Let me call my father and have him get with you so we can finalize the deal." Sexy Redd then took the realtor by the hand and walked away.

Meanwhile, I was looking at Sexy Redd like what in the hell is going on, and why did that lady just say Mr. And Mrs. Valentino? I just kept looking through the house while they were talking to one another. I walked out back, looking at the huge ass pool that had a pool house that was just as big as my apartment.

'Man, I can't believe I'm standing here in this big ass house with all this space and luxurious atmosphere. There is no way we're going to be approved for this nice ass house.

*Who in the hell am I fooling?* I was still thinking to myself when Redd came outside to me.

"There you are, honey. Good news! Welcome to our new home, sweet heart," she said all excited. And then as if someone had pushed me from behind, I fell face first into the pool from the shock.

As I sank deeper and deeper into the water, it dawned on me that my dumb ass had forgot I couldn't fuckin' swim.

"Help! Help!" I screamed, while throwing my hands up over my head.

"I really don't think he can swim," the realtor said.

Redd jumped head first into the pool like a professional swimmer to save my black ass.

The first thing she said to me as she rescued my dumb ass was, "Michael don't tell me you can't swim?" she said, as she pushed me to safety, off to the side of the pool.

"Nah, baby, I never really thought I had to learn but now that we've got a pool, I guess I should learn," I said, as I tried to catch my breath. I looked up to the heavens and said, "Thank you, Lord, for saving my life and answering my prayers."

Both of us dried off and signed the papers. Minutes later, the realtor handed us the keys to our very own house.

"Now, Michael, please understand one thing. My father purchased this house for you and me. Once I've gotten rid of Ms. Kitty, you and I and the rest of the females can move in. Not until then. Now, get me back to my car so I can transfer some money from one account to the other one, before she checks my account balance."

"Whatever you say, Redd, but why did you tell her we were married?" I asked, as I backed out of the driveway.

"Michael, I know how you feel about me. I see it in your eyes every time you look at me. Hell, Kitty knows it too. It's just a matter of time before she's replaced, trust me."

While driving back to drop her off, she looked over at me with those big ole pretty brown eyes.

"Michael, there are a lot of things that you don't know about me. One of them is, as long as you are with me, money will not be a problem. My father has a lot of it by the tons. No matter what I need, he will always make sure I'm taken care of."

"I'll explain everything else to you once we move in together."

"Let me ask you something?" I said to her. My eyes couldn't stop looking at how beautiful she looked.

"Go ahead, baby."

"How much did that house cost?"

"Believe me, you don't want to know, Michael." She smiled at me as she got out of my car and into hers. Then, she blew me a kiss. "I'll see you later tonight."

I blew her a kiss back and she pretended to catch it in midair. She smiled at me as she drove away.

By the time I got back home, Kitty and the others had struck out for the mall. She had left me a note saying they were out shopping for new outfits which was fine by me. I still had some business to tie up with Sharon. So, I decided to call her since I'd told her I would, the night before, at the club. She answered on the first ring. I lit up after hearing her lovely voice.

"Hello?"

"Hey, you, what's up?"

"Nothing. You finally decided to give me a call, I see." "Sorry, boo, I was taking care of some important business." "Yeah, with your strippers, I'm sure."

"Nah, Sharon, it was something else."

"Okay, what's up?" she said with a little attitude towards me.

"I was wondering when it would be a good time to hook up with you so we can talk."

"I don't know, Mister. Since you've become the owner of the world-famous Florida Hot Girls, it seems like you're the one with the busy schedule."

"Come on, Sharon, I didn't call you to argue about my dancers."

"Okay, Michael, let's go out to dinner tomorrow night."

"Sounds good. Where do you want to go?"

"You know I'm a black female and we love some Red Lobster."

"Okay you, Red Lobster it is. I'll pick you up around nine

tomorrow night. Until then, be safe, and I'll see you soon."

After hanging up with Sharon, I lay across my bed thinking about the new house Redd had just purchased. I couldn't believe I had finally made it. A nice home, a perfect business, money in the bank, and, to top it all off, a beautiful woman by my side who had money to burn. What else could a single man like me want out of life?

***

FRIDAY NIGHT ARRIVED FASTER than I anticipated. It was already around eight-fifteen. I had spoken with them cowboy-looking-ass niggas, and they were cool with me dropping the girls off earlier so I could get to my date on time.

"All right, ladies, listen, I'm dropping you guys off here. The guys throwing the party said everything is a go and that you should make a lot of money here tonight. After the show, you all need to get some rest, cause we're travelling to Jacksonville tomorrow so we can find a club to dance at."

"All right, baby, we'll call you as soon as the show is over," Ms. Kitty said, as her and the rest of my girls climbed out of the car.

As soon as my door closed, I was on my way to pick Sharon up for our dinner date. I got to her house around nine-fifteen. She came to the door dressed in a nice, black silk-like dress and a nice sweater covered her shoulders. Her hair was done up real nice like she had just left the hairdresser. She looked like a cute black Barbie doll. On her feet, she had on a pair of brand new Prada shoes. I looked down at the shoes and then looked her in her beautiful light hazel-brown eyes.

"You really like them Prada shoes, don't you?" I asked jokingly.

"Michael, what do you know about Prada shoes?"

"Enough to know that they're some expensive ass shoes

"Yeah, that they are, but I can afford them."

"I see. Seems like that's all you wear is Prada shoes."

"Baby, you must don't know me yet. Everything I wear is name brand. Believe that," she said sarcastically.

"Sharon, let me ask you something? You have a nice house and nice car, and you seem to always have money. So why are you on the Wages program?"

"First of all, let me explain something to you, Mister-wants-to-know-everything. My dad used to play for the Steelers and he makes sure that his little princess is always taken care of. I'm on the Wages program 'cause my sorry ass baby-daddy is on child support with the state and you know how them crackers get down."

"Damn, I didn't know your dad played professional ball."

"Yeah, he played for about thirteen years before retiring." Oh, by the way, Mike, you can have that fuckin' Pretty Ricky porn flick back. I threw all the ones I had in the fuckin' trash."

"What? Not you who wanted to get his autograph the other night. You were acting like your lil' twat-twat was wet the other night when you saw his red ass."

"Let me tell you about that fake ass nigga. The other night after the club, right . . . how about both of my girls went to the afterparty they had."

"Yeah. The one with Big Jenkins, Clyde, and Pretty Ricky the Porn Star."

"Yes, Mike. How about she was about to let Pretty Ricky fuck her. She said when he pulled his dick out, it was nowhere near the size it is in them movies they be making."

"What?"

"When she asked him why his dick looked different than it did in his movies, he told her when it comes to the fuckin' parts, Clyde, the producer, steps in and fucks the girls. They use his face and body for the eating pussy and sucking ass parts."

"That's fuckin' crazy! So, they just use his face and body for the pussy and ass eating scenes?"

"Yep, and Clyde does all the fuckin'. And all this time, I thought Pretty Ricky was the one fuckin' them bitches with that big ass dick and pretty ass face," she said. She looked just as pissed off as she sounded.

"I threw all his fuckin' fake ass movies in the trash. My girl Tamika said Clyde, who sometimes goes by Captain Dingaling, came in the room and fucked the shit out of her ass while Pretty Ricky just stood there and watched. Talking about how he wanted to eat her pussy and suck out her ass when Captain Dingaling finished. I can't believe as fine as he is, he just wanted to eat her out and then suck out her ass."

"Damn, Pretty Ricky." I laughed my ass off as I drove down Highway 50 to Red Lobster. "Fake ass brother."

"She said he claimed he had been smoking on some good ass perp and his dick wouldn't get hard because of that." Sharon rolled her eyes and shook her head in disbelief. Shit, my girl Tracey said the guy named Big Jenkins had all three of your dancers in his room having a damn foursome."

"Damn, a foursome? How in the hell he did that?"

"Beats me, baby. I'm just glad I wasn't there. I would've slapped the shit out of Pretty Ricky for showing up with that little ass dick of his."

"Damn, you act like if he would've pulled out a monster sized dick you would have fucked him."

"Hell nah, you're the only nigga getting any of this good ass pussy."

"All right, don't let me catch you cheating on me."

"Whatever, Mike. I would never do that."

"Okay, I'm glad you weren't there too, baby. Hell, if you're lucky tonight, you can have some of this dick right here," I replied and nodded my head down toward John Boy. I was still laughing and driving.

Meanwhile, Kitty and the crew were getting pissed off with them cowboy-looking-ass niggas. I was just pulling into the parking lot of Red Lobster when she texted me claiming they weren't tipping. She also said the party was boring as hell. I had Sharon go in and get our table so I could call Ms. Kitty.

"Hello?"

"Kitty, what's going on?"

"Fuck what's going on, Michael! You should have stayed here with us instead of leaving us here with these clowns. Where are you anyway?" she pried, "sounds like a lot of people in the background."

"Kitty, I'm out recruiting more girls for the group."

"Whatever, Mike. We don't need any more fuckin' girls in this damn group. We have enough bitches already. Damn, you sent too many here with me tonight! Just come get us right now!" she said in an angry tone.

"I'm clear across town right now, Kitty, just call a cab and pay for it out of the money y'all made over there. I'll give it back to you when I get home."

"That's the problem, Mike. We haven't made any money."

"What?"

"Yeah, this nigga claims he already paid you our money. He said we're supposed to just dance and do whatever and then leave."

"Hell nah, that fuckin' nigga is fuckin' lying! He only gave me a hundred and twenty-five dollars for all of y'all."

By now, Sharon was walking around the restaurant looking for me.

"Listen, get home and I'll go from there." I hung up, pissed off that those niggas had played me like that. And to make matters worse, they had my girls over there and hadn't paid them at all.

"Hey, Mike, listen. I know you have a business to run, baby, so you don't have to lie to me when you need to make a phone call. I made up my mind last night, I'm not gonna trip on you for working with those girls. Just know that I'm here for you when you need me to be. I'd rather have half of you, then none of you at all."

*Damn, did she just say what I thought she said?* Hell, she was gonna be down for me! That's all I needed to hear. She would be my ride-or-die chick no matter what happened.

Ms. Kitty was about to be history. Not only was Sharon down with me but so was Sexy Redd. There was no need for me to have Ms. Kitty around fuckin' up my circle of love.

I got me a quickie in before I dropped Sharon off. By the time I got back home it was around twelve midnight. As soon as I got in, I noticed Kitty, Mignon, Entyce, and Sexy Redd were all gone.

"Strawberry where did the other girls go?" I asked her. She was watching television.

"I don't know, Mike. They got here, took off their outfits, and then got dressed in all black and took off again."

"Put on some black clothes? What the hell? So, what's this shit Kitty said about them niggas not tipping?"

"They wasn't. And then they had me and Nicole do girl-on-girl and didn't pay us a damn thing."

"Well, that will never happen again. From now on, I'll be at every bachelor party y'all do."

After talking with Strawberry, it was after one thirty in the morning, and I was tired as hell from everything I'd gone through that day. I lay across my bed and must have fallen asleep ' cause I didn't wake backup till around ten thirty the following morning. Kitty was lying next to me sound asleep, so I quietly inched my ass out of the bed without waking her up.

I stumbled to the kitchen to get myself something to drink. I poured myself a glass of juice and walked over to the living room area to see which of the females were at the apartment. Everyone scheduled to ride to Jacksonville that day was already there. After looking at each one of them laying there fast asleep, I walked back to my bedroom and turned on the television.

While flipping through the channels, I came across breaking news on Channel 5:

> "This is Latasha Willis with Channel 5 Breaking news. There was a home invasion in which four gentlemen were found beaten to death. The murder weapon appears to have been a pair of red stiletto high heel shoes which were found beside each one of their bodies. A pair of thongs had been stuffed in the mouths of victim, and all of the men were naked with cowboy boots on."

I dropped the remote and looked over at Ms. Kitty laying there in the bed. She rolled over and saw me looking at her.

"Yep, that's exactly what them niggas get for fuckin' with the Florida Hot Girls like they did! Punk ass bitches!"

## CHAPTER EIGHTEEN
## OVER A FEW DOLLARS

The ride to Jacksonville on Saturday was somewhat somber all the way there. The girls appeared to be in some kind of trance. When I tried to bring up what happened the previous night, no one wanted to talk about it.

Sexy Redd was the only one with something to say. "As a group, we didn't like how things went last night, Michael. Next time, we would prefer you come with us or at least give us some money upfront for going by ourselves."

"You're absolutely right, young lady. I'll make sure everything is handled next time an event like that comes around. No one should have to lose their life over a few dollars."

"And what's that supposed to mean, Michael?" Sexy Redd asked with a puzzled look on her face.

"Girl, he saw the report on the news this morning. The news reporter announced how them same fake-ass, cowboy-looking-ass niggas got fucked up last night," Kitty replied.

"What?" Sexy Redd said. She sounded surprised.

"Yes, girl, somebody killed them niggas last night," Kitty said, as she looked out the passenger window. She had a fucked attitude and a frown was spread on her round ass face.

"Aw, man, that's so fucked up! You mean after we left last night somebody took them niggas out?"

"Yes, Redd, and the news reported that the murder weapon was some stiletto shoes that were found next to the victims."

"Well, Mike, I hope you don't think we had anything to do with that," Sexy Redd replied.

"Well, if you ladies didn't have anything to do with it, you won't mind showing me your shoes, right?" I asked.

"Mike, you are so crazy. I got my stilettos on right now," Sexy Redd answered.

"So do I, Mike," the rest of the girls said, one after the other. Each girl eyed the other suspiciously.

I continued driving toward Jacksonville wondering what had

really happened to them cowboy-looking ass niggas. *If my girls hadn't done it, who did and why? Had my girls almost witnessed a murder? If they had stayed there longer, would they have been killed too?*

Now I was worried that someone could be watching me and my girls trying to do the same thing to us.

Hell, I didn't know if they got robbed or if anything was even missing. The only thing the news reporter said was they were found beaten to death. Damn, what a way to go. It really put me in a bad place to know I had just talked to them brothers and now they were gone.

They were still on my mind when Sexy Redd spoke up.

"If it'll make you feel any better, I'll send some flowers to their families for the funerals, Mike." Her tone was calm and shit.

"Yes, Redd that would be nice. Thank you for the thought, I replied.

"Yeah, Redd. Make sure you send their families a thank you card too. For having some fucked up ass sons," Ms. Kitty said, looking all mad and shit.

The next thing I knew, everybody in the car got in to a heated argument. "Damn, Kitty, did you really have to go there?" Sexy Redd asked.

Ms. Kitty turned around and pulled the covers from over her head and looked at her. "Let me tell you something, Sexy Redd. Whatever happened to them sick ass muthafuckers, they fuckin' deserved it. I'm so fuckin' tired of these fuckin' men out here who treat women like us, like fuckin' dirt!"

"Kitty, what really happened at the show to make you feel like that?" I asked.

"Mike, you really don't want to know. Those guys had something else on their minds last night," Nicole replied.

I pulled over to the side of the road. "Okay, somebody tell me what the fuck really happened last night. Hell, when I got home, Strawberry told me you guys took off your outfits and put black clothes on before you left the house."

"Yes, we did, Michael. When we got there we all got out, went to the door to politely ask for our fuckin' money. But before we could even knock, we heard a bunch of noise going on inside. We peeked inside and saw a bunch of strippers already there so we jumped back in the car and hauled ass," Sexy Redd replied.

"So, what you're saying is some other chicks beat you all there and took them out instead?" I asked. I was confused but I desperately needed to know had transpired.

"Hell, how are we supposed to know, Michael?" Ms. Kitty yelled at me.

"Wait a fuckin' minute, Kitty, you don't have to be yelling at me. Damn!" I replied angrily.

"Well, yo' dumb ass asking all these fuckin' questions like you the fuckin' police and shit," Ms. Kitty replied.

"I just wanna make sure whoever took them niggas out ain't out there thinking about taking us out too," I said angrily.

"What the fuck ever, Mike. Them fuck ass niggas deserved whatever their fuck asses got. Now get our black asses to fuckin' Jacksonville. I'm tired of riding in this goddamn car."

"Kitty, you don't have to talk to him like that," Sexy Redd replied.

"Whatever," Ms. Kitty replied back with fire in her beady lil' eyes.

"You know, Kitty, you are a nasty mouth bitch," Sexy Redd said.

"Well, Redd, if you wanna do something about it you know how to get it," Ms. Kitty replied.

"Come on y'all', were a family. We don't have to do it like this," Nicole said, as I merged back onto I-95, heading towards Jacksonville.

"Nah, fuck that, Nicole. I've been waiting to dig off in that bitch ass from the first moment her pretty wanna-be-ass got in this fuckin ass group," Ms. Kitty replied angrily.

I was back on the road driving and in traffic when Sexy Redd went off. "Kitty, if I didn't care about how Mike felt about us fighting, I would drag your little rat looking ass through the fuckin' mud, bitch! You ain't nothing but a little project hoe anyway."

"Wait a fuckin' minute!" I yelled and silence fell throughout the car. "Both of you shut the hell up! How we supposed to be a team and shit and y'all two wanna fuckin' kill each other? Just last night y'all wanted to kill them cowboy-looking-ass niggas," I replied.

"Like I said, Redd, you know how to get it if you want it. Fuck this group. If he fires me for fuckin' you up, then so be it. I'm bad enough to be on my fuckin' own anyway. I don't need you or this group to make my damn money," Ms. Kitty replied.

Now I was pissed off. If she felt like that why was she still hanging around? Nasty mouth bitch.

"Kitty, when we get to Jacksonville, me and you need to sit down and talk 'cause you really tripping now," I said. I rolled my eyes at her short ass, and she just sat there, waiting to pop off.

Everybody had calmed down after the heated exchange of words and feelings had been expressed. But I was still somewhat disturbed by Ms. Kitty's display of such a nasty ass attitude. If something really went down last night, she wasn't telling me, and I didn't know who to talk to in order to find out. Hell, the niggas were dead so I couldn't talk to them. So, who would it be?

Still driving, I looked in my rearview mirror and  saw Sexy Redd staring at Ms. Kitty. She looked as though she wanted to jump over the seat and stomp the shit out of her lil' short ass.

I think Ms. Kitty had reached the point of thinking she was bigger than the rest of the group. If she felt like that maybe she was right. Maybe she was bigger than the group. Now I had to show her how big the group really was and how much bigger it would be without her foul ass mouth.

"Are you okay, Michael," Nicole asked me.

"Yeah, I'm fine, lil' one. We should be in Jacksonville within the next ten minutes," I answered. *Damn, she fine*, I thought to myself, as I looked at her seated next to Sexy Redd.

She curled up next to Sexy Redd and tried to get some needed rest before we reached our destination. I continued driving, but at the same time, I couldn't stop cutting my eyes over at Ms. Kitty.

We finally arrived around four that evening. When we got there, we checked into the same room so we could save money and try to keep the peace between everybody in the group.

After we were all settled in, we struck out for the Golf Fair Flea Market.

Once we got there, we split up and asked different people which strip club would be nice to dance at. After about two hours of walking around, we finally decided which club we would dance at. After that, we decided to head to Red Lobster for something to eat.

Like Sharon always said, 'black women love them some Red Lobster.

Once inside Red Lobster, I had a meal that consisted of crab legs, lobster tail, and shrimp scampi. Ms. Kitty had the crab legs with a side order of shrimp. Sexy Redd had a salad with a shrimp pasta, and Strawberry ate the free biscuits. For some reason, her money was short. Come to think of it, her money was always short.

Lil Kitty felt sorry for her and ordered her some shrimp scampi along and crab legs.

"All right, Strawberry, I'm gonna need mines when you make some more money," Lil Kitty said, as she chewed on her shrimp.

"I got you, girl. You know I'll pay you back," Strawberry said. First, she inhaled the food instead of eating it to show how fuckin' hungry she was.

"All right, Strawberry, you know what happened to Lil Mama when Lil Kitty bought her some shrimp the last time we ate at Red Lobster," I said to Strawberry while smiling.

She lifted her head and stopped eating from her salad. "Nah, I wasn't there. What happened?" Strawberry asked.

"Now, see, what happened is the bitch didn't have enough money for her dinner. I paid for it and she promised me she would pay me back as soon as we got to Orlando. Well, when we finally got back she acted like she forgot about my money and I dug off in her lil' yellow ass," Lil Kitty said. All the ladies at the table burst out laughing at the way Lil Kitty told the story.

"So, Mike, why didn't you fire them for fighting?" Nicole asked while sipping on a tall glass of Strawberry lemonade.

"Because Lil Mama owed her some money. Hell, I wasn't

going to pay it for her."

Everybody burst into laughter again, including Ms. Kitty's badass-attitude-having ass.

By the time, we finished eating, the tension from earlier seemed to have calmed down. Ms. Kitty was chatting among the girls, and so was Sexy Redd

Minutes later, Ms. Kitty said, "Excuse me, ladies. I wanna apologize for the way I acted earlier in the car. I was just pissed off about what happened last night."

"Kitty, you don't have to apologize. We understand what you're going through, girl," Nicole replied.

Sexy Redd and Mignon continued sipping on their drinks, watching everything unfold. Ms. Kitty looked over at Redd while sipping on her Strawberry Daiquiri.

"And I really wanna say to my girl, Sexy Redd, how sorry I am for acting like that with you earlier," Ms. Kitty added, trying to sound sincere, "I hope and pray you can forgive a sister for acting like that."

"Ms. Kitty, I don't feel no anger towards you, babygirl. We all go through something when dealing with all types of creepy ass niggas out here. But we family, baby, we should always have each other's back out here in these streets," Sexy Redd replied back to her.

"Man, now that's some deep ass shit you just said, Sexy Redd, and you muthafuckin' right! In order for us to be a perfect fuckin' group, we gotta stick together and be there for one another," Nicole replied.

"Man, don't no fuckin' group stay together forever. Hell, look at The Jackson 5, they broke up. And what about the Backstreet Boys, they broke up too," Strawberry's dumb ass said, as she tried to eat up everything on her plate.

The other girls looked at her and let out a fit of laughter.

"Girl, what in the fuck are you talking about?" Lil Kitty asked her, still laughing at her.

"Strawberry, baby, listen, we're not a group like those people were. We're something totally different, baby," Sexy Redd said.

"Oh, my bad," Strawberry replied.

"Okay, ladies, I'm glad we've apologized to one another. Now, let's pay for our food and get out of here," I replied.

"Excuse me, waitress, can we have the ticket, please?" Sexy Redd asked the waitress as she walked by.

The waitress looked at me and asked, "Will that be one ticket, sir, or do I need to separate them?"

"You can put it on one ticket. I'll take care of it," I replied.

"Hell, Mike, if we had known you were gonna pay for it, we would've ordered the most expensive shit on the menu," Lil Kitty screamed while laughing.

"I know. That's why I didn't tell y'all slick assess. Hell, I ain't nobody's fool," I replied.

When the waitress returned with the bill the ladies stood then went to the restroom. Sexy Redd stayed back with me while I paid for the food.

"Here you go, sir," the waitress said. She reached her hand out to give me the bill then asked, "Would you like any to-go bags?" she asked politely.

"Yes, could we have some please?"

Before I could take the bill, Sexy Redd snatched it out of her hand. "I got this, baby. Like I told you earlier, when it comes to money, my family has a lot of it."

"Damn, could you at least tell me how much the bill was?" I asked.

"Why? I told you I got it." She flashed me a sexy smile.

When the girls returned to the table, Sexy Redd stood up and decided she needed to go to the bathroom too.

When she passed by me, she discreetly dropped a credit card onto my lap. "That's your personal Black Card. Don't fuck it up," She winked at me just as she'd done earlier when we'd left the new house.

She walked away and I glanced down at the card and picked it up. Out of nowhere, Ms. Kitty reached over and snatched it out of my hand.

"Damn, baby, I didn't know you had a fuckin' card. Damn,

nigga, what type of business do you really have?"

"Girl, give me that damn card," I said simultaneously rolling my eyes at her.

After she gave it back, I looked at inscription—the card had my name, Michael Valentino, engraved in gold, and underneath my name were the words: The Florida Hot Girls. That damn Sexy Redd had opened a Black Card account with my business and name on it. I wondered what else had she done without me knowing.

Hell, she had already paid for my watch which looked so damn good on my arm, and, on top of that, she had paid for the new house we'd be moving into. Now, she was giving me a damn Black Card I could use at my own discretion. When I least expected it, she was always there for me.

"Okay, is everyone ready to go?" I asked, once everyone was back at the table.

"Yes, seems like everyone has everything," Nicole replied, still sipping on her drink.

"Oh, and by the way, Kitty, I wanna apologize for the things I said to you earlier also," Sexy Redd said, as we made our way the exit, "there's no need for us to act like that."

"Now that's what I'm talking about. We should all do one big group hug," I interjected.

"Whatever, Mike. Redd, it's cool, boo. I accept your apology," Kitty replied.

*\*\**

WE GOT BACK TO OUR HOTEL about nine thirty that night, just in time for the girls to get dressed up for the club. Once inside our hotel suite, I went to my bedroom area, jumped on the bed, and turned on some ESPN. My girls were all in the living room area looking at each other's outfits, and I could sense they had overcome what they'd gone through earlier.

It was a good feeling to know my girls could go through something devastating one day and overcome it the next. They were turning into more than just a group of beautiful females, they were becoming a group of beautiful women. They had a mindset to turn a tragic situation into a mere thought; in other words, they had put it all behind them. They were ready to move forward with one goal in mind, and that goal was making money.

While lying in the bed it one girl after another entered my room to ask me how her outfit looked, or one would ask if her hair looked nice enough for the night. I always answered every question they asked, making sure I gave each one of them my undivided attention.

"Okay ladies, it's eleven-fifteen and the club wants us there by midnight. How much longer y'all need before everybody's ready?" I asked, as I looked around at a living room full of butt-naked sexy ass females.

"Mike give us like twenty more minutes. We're still trying to do something with Strawberry's hair," Lil Kitty said. She stood above Strawberry's head with nothing on but a bra and a pair of narrow ass thongs that appeared to be crooked and up inside the crack of her small but cute buttocks.

"Okay, I guess that means I'm going to have to fine every one of you girls for being late!" I told them all.

"Fuck that, Mike we're ready," Mignon said, as she slid a nice tight-fitting pair of jeans up over her beautiful, naked vagina.

"Fuck this," Lil Kitty said to the rest of the girls, "we'll do her fuckin' hair when we get to the fuckin' club." So, without further delay, we made it to the club right before midnight.

The manager was just as happy to see us as we were to see his ass. The girls were escorted to a nice dressing room in the back of the club. Once inside the room, they were back out, and ready to dance, within thirty minutes.

The reception the girls received in the club was no different from all the rest. As usual, the girls in the group who loved the golds and dread heads went straight for them. Ms. Kitty and the rest of the girls hit up the guys at the tables. Sexy Redd went over by the bar and got mad attention from some Puerto Rican brothers. Lil Kitty and Nicole posted up on the pool tables and didn't hesitate to spread their pussy lips wide open. Strawberry was by the stage area trying to find her rhythm when the D. J called her up on the stage.

"Strawberry can't fuckin' dance," I mumbled and shook my head. *What in the hell is really going on?* I thought to myself. I quickly ran over to the DJ's booth.

"Hey, wait a minute," I told him, "call up Sexy Redd or Mignon. Ms. Strawberry can't dance."

"My bad, Mike, I didn't know," he replied, while holding back a smile. *That was a close one.*

Strawberry looked over at me and yelled from across the club, "Thanks, my nigga 'cause you know a sister can't dance!"

I smiled at her and nodded my head.

"Hey Mike, how long do we get to dance on stage?" Nicole asked.

"I think about three songs, but you might wanna ask the DJ to be sure," I added.

"Okay, because I'm looking up at the stage and your girl Sexy Redd is making a killing up there. Hell, I need some of that bread she making," she said, as she looked up at me and smiled with her pretty white teeth.

"All right, just go let the DJ know you wanna dance on stage."

"Okay." She walked away and her nice, fat, red ass mesmerized me and caused my manhood to rise. At that moment I wished I could've had her back in my bed again fuckin' the shit out of her. Ms. Kitty didn't realize what she'd started by allowing me to fuck her and Nicole at the same time.

It was the first time in my life I had experienced a threesome, and I must admit, it was the best thing since apple pie and ice cream. The thrill of being with two women at the same time had me look at what I was doing in a different light. Now, I wanted to be with two females every chance I could, something I knew Sexy Redd wouldn't approve of.

While watching her walk off the stage that night I started wondering what her intentions with me were, why she was there for me the way she had been, and why she always gave me money? I knew she said the money was coming from her father, but I had never met the man. Hell, come to think about it, I hadn't met any of her relatives. I didn't even know where in the hell she came from.

# The Murder Queens

As she walked towards the dressing room to change her outfit and count the money she'd made on stage, I turned back toward the bar and saw my reflection in the mirror. I sat there looking at myself in the mirror with all kind of mad thoughts going through my confused mind. *What was I becoming and why was it happening to me? Was this the life I wanted, or was it something meant for me to do?* Whatever the answer was, I didn't know it, and I sure as hell wasn't going to find it inside of no damn strip club. My head lay on top of my arms and my mind was off in wonderland.

"Hey, you, the bar isn't made for people to sleep on," Ms. Kitty said, just as she walked up behind me, "so wake yo' black ass up," she joked, and snapped me from my daze.

"Nah, I was just thinking about something, that's all."

"Well, I hope you were thinking about how you gonna fuck me tonight, 'cause I'm horny as a muthafucker." She placed her hand between my legs and grabbed my dick. "Yeah, that's right," I said it. "You fuckin' me tonight, mister!"

*Damn, if she only knew how bad I want her, Nicole, sexy ass Mignon, and of course, Sexy Redd.* "Yeah, whatever you say, lil' mama. We still need to talk about that lil' attitude you had earlier, before we do anything," I replied. I looked away and tried to ignore her.

"Damn, Mike, I thought all of us had apologized and moved on from that?" She pretended to be sad as she gazed at me with puppy dog eyes.

"Yes, you ladies did, but not me. I'm still concerned about your comments."

"Babe, look at me. I'm sorry and I won't do it again. I promise," she said, like I was supposed to believe her this time.

I looked up noticed Sexy Redd staring at us with daggers in her eyes. As soon as we made eye contact she put her hands up under her throat and moved it in a horizontal slicing motion, which I read as signal to say she would cut Ms. Kitty's head off. However, then she pointed at Ms. Kitty and moved both of her lips and said she was cut from the team. Ms. Kitty turned around to see what I was looking at seconds before Sexy Redd put her head down and continued walking into the dressing room.

Minutes later, Lil Kitty propped her narrow ass up on one of the bar stools next to me.

"I really like this lil' club, Mike. I can see us making a lot of money here once we promote it just right."

"Oh, you can see into the future, huh?" I forced a smiled.

"Nah, silly ass boy. I'm just saying look how many people we got to come out here tonight just to see us."

"Okay, y'all got a few guys up in here," I said.

"Whatever, Mike, wait until the whole team comes up here next weekend. It should be around fifteen girls here next Friday and Saturday," Lil Kitty said. A lingering smile stayed displayed over her small ass face.

"Yep, you're right, and y'all will be promoting on both days so that means everybody should make a nice bit of money," I replied. While we were all sitting there talking, Mignon and Entyce came over.

"Hey, y'all."

"What's up, ladies?" I replied.

"Excuse me, Ms. Kitty and Mike, and of course your lil' short ass Lil Kitty. How much is our tip out fee tonight, Mike?"

"Um, let me see. . . . how much did y'all make?"

"Don't worry about that homebody, just know that we made that paper tonight," Entyce said, holding up her money bag so I could see how full it was.

"Okay cool. Well you ladies shouldn't have a problem paying fifty dollars per girl," I said.

Mignon replied, "Hell, that's it?"

"Damn, you got it like that, Mignon?"

"I didn't say all that, Michael, but since you paid for our dinner earlier, I'm paying you sixty dollars."

"Okay, now that's what the fuck I'm talking about. Thanks, boo," I replied in an excited tone.

By now, Sexy Redd and the rest of the girls were all standing around me talking amongst each other.

"So, what's going on over here?" Nicole asked. She looked

down at herself to make sure her outfit still looked good around her thick, red ass.

"Nothing, girl. Entyce and Mignon just asked Mike how much our tip out fee was for tonight, right?" Ms. Kitty asked the girls for confirmation. "Mike said fifty dollars, and Mignon told him since he paid for our dinner, our fee should be sixty dollars."

"Well, Mike I haven't made the type of money Mignon made so can I just pay the fifty dollars instead?" Lil Kitty asked, looking at Strawberry who still owed her money from earlier.

"That's fine, Lil Kitty, just pay the fifty. Mignon if you wanna pay sixty that's okay too." I directed my answer to her as well as the rest of the small crew of females I had with me that weekend.

They all laughed and hugged one another. All of the girls said they really liked the club and couldn't wait until the following weekend when the rest of the team would be there.

The night turned out to be a good night after all. We had run into a bump in the road earlier that day, and I was sure it wouldn't be the last bump we'd run into. Nevertheless, I'd be ready for the ones we would run into in the future.

The entire weekend had been a learning experience for me and the girls, but, hell, it was just another day in the life of the Florida Hot Girls. ...

Michael Gallon

## CHAPTER NINETEEN
### HER DEMISE WAS IMMINENT

The weekend in Jacksonville was more like a vacation for me, but for the girls, it was just another day at the office. The club they decided to dance at was a nice small club located off of First Street in downtown Jacksonville.

It had been several years since I had been there, and I had to admit, now that I had dancers, the city looked a whole lot different than before. By now, week to week, each city I traveled to with the girls seemed to look different compared to the last time I'd been there—especially since life as I knew it was changing from day to day.

It was Monday morning and things were about to really change for one of the females in the group and I couldn't wait. I just hadn't figured out exactly how I was going to rid the group and myself of this particular female. So, as I sat there on the edge of my bed that morning, I contemplated my next move.

I turned on the television and saw the news reporters still broadcasting the home invasion of the four cowboy-looking-ass niggas. My main concern now was that someone might've been stalking my girls thinking they saw something that night. And if so, would they come looking for them to keep them from going to the police.

As I stood up from the edge of my bed, I happened to look over at a half naked body. At first, the idea of making love to her crossed my mind, but as soon as I saw the face the beautiful body belonged to, I quickly changed my mind. Instead, I stepped over to the balcony of my apartment to look out at the people who were busy getting their day started. When I heard my phone vibrating inside my pant pocket, I pulled it out before it could wake Ms. Kitty. I looked at the screen and it was someone calling from a 305 area code.

*Now who in the fuck calling me from Miami?* I thought to myself before answering it. "Hello."

"Yo', is this Mike?" asked the caller.

"Yeah, and who is this?"

"Yo', it's C-Jay, from Miami," the voice on the other line said excitedly.

"Jay from Miami?" I echoed the name as I searched my memory bank for where I knew this fool from.

"You don't know me but one of my Rap Artists, Mike D, said he was at one of your shows the other day."

"Okay." *I'll wait*, I thought, wanting him to get to the point.

"He said you had some very nice ladies who would be great for the photo shoot we're doing tomorrow."

"Oh really," I said in a nonchalant manner.

"Yes, what will it take to get you and a few of your girls down here?" C-Jay from Miami inquired.

"I don't really know about that. My girls just got played the other day by some lame ass niggas so they really don't wanna go anywhere without me."

"Well, Mike if we could get your girls down here, we would love for you to come with them," he said, sounding more serious.

"Man, not to be rude or anything, but I don't like Miami like that. Ever since my old college days down there running track at Florida Memorial, I seem acquire a very bad taste in my mouth where Miami is concerned."

"Hey, man, I can understand that. But let me reassure you that your girls will be safe with me while they're down here."

"Okay, how many females do you need and how much are you paying for each girl?" I asked.

After talking to C-Jay for thirty minutes or so, it was established that I would send him a few females, and he would pay for their travel expenses, along with their room and board.

We hung up and I immediately sent him over the information so he could wire the necessary funds to take care of everything. Now all I had to do was convince the girls to travel down to Miami without me. Something that shouldn't be so hard to do since they were getting a thousand dollars apiece up front.

They were in the living room talking about everyday gossip when I entered the room with the news.

"Excuse me, ladies can I have your attention really quick." I explained how I had just got off the phone with the CEO of Chris Styles Entertainment, and how they wanted a few of the Florida Hot Girls for a one day photo shoot. I informed them they'd be paid a thousand dollars up front for going at the last minute.

Thirty minutes later, they were packing their individual bags as though they had forgotten all about what happened just three days prior. It appeared as if they had put the whole ordeal out of their minds and simply moved on. It was understandable since they claimed they didn't have anything to do with what had happened to the four brothers. I was just afraid they wouldn't want to travel without me, especially since they had been lied to before about money. But since I was giving them the money upfront, everything seemed like it would be okay.

I walked back into the bedroom where Ms. Kitty had already started packing. She looked up at me and said, "Michael, I really don't wanna go anywhere unless you're going with me." Crocodile tears streamed down her face. I knew it would probably be the best way to get her out of my life, especially since she had showed her ass over the weekend. Her demise was now imminent.

A lot of things had transpired, not just with what had happened over the weekend, but with something a bit more serious than that. It cut me deep, very deep. ... so deep, it put a very bad taste in my mouth every time I thought about it.

I walked behind Ms. Kitty to hug her from the back since I couldn't stand to look her in her eyes. She tried to convince me not to make her go.

"Kitty, listen, boo, everything is going to be fine. I'll be at the airport to pick you guys up when you return. It's only for a day. Y'all got one photo shoot to do and you'll be right back home tomorrow," I said.

As I walked away from her, she pulled my arm and turned my body so I'd be facing her. She wanted me to see the tears in her eyes as we just stood there looking at one another.

"Michael, I love you so much. Why don't you just send someone else in my place? Please," she pleaded, "then me and you can stay here and enjoy some alone time together."

Standing there listening to her plead her case, the mere thought of her sleeping with another man kept running through my head. At one point in time, I really did love Ms. Kitty, but finding out she fucked another brother in my fuckin' bed took all the love I had for her and threw it out the fuckin' window.

The only thing I was in love with now was the Florida Hot Girls, and nothing or no one was going to keep me from taking them to the next level. Whenever I felt threatened, I had to take drastic measures to make sure nothing stood in the way of the pure perfection of the monster I'd created.

Without answering her, I walked out of the room and headed straight to Western Union to pick up the money for the girls, so they could be on their way without any hitches.

Then, Sexy Redd called me.

"Hello," I answered.

"Hey, Mike, I got your message, what's up?"

"I'm on the way to pick up the upfront money. You guys have a flight to Miami at six o'clock this evening."

"Miami, for what Michael?"

"Chris Styles Entertainment needs five of you girls for a one day photo shoot."

"Okay, who's all going?"

"Well, if I called you Redd, that means you're one of the girls going."

"Is Ms. Kitty going too?" she asked me.

"Yes, Redd, she's going too. But she won't be returning," I concluded.

"Why, what happened?"

"I really don't wanna talk about it right now. It puts a bad taste in my mouth every time I think about it."

"I tried to tell your ass how trifling her rat-looking ass was, but nah, you didn't wanna listen to Ms. Sexy Redd," she said being a smart ass.

"I hear you, Redd," I said.

"Whatever, Michael. What time do I need to be at your place?"

"Well, it's three right now and your flight leaves at six, so I say, at least, before five. The limo will be at my place at four forty-five."

"Okay, Michael, let me throw a few things together and I'll be there in a few."

"Are you gonna be okay?" Sexy Redd asked.

"I'm fine, baby, but I'ma need you to stay in my corner 'cause things are about to get a little complicated."

"You know I will, Michael. Anything for you," she said sincerely.

"Cool, thanks, Redd."

"No problem, baby. So I guess this means we'll all be moving into the house when we get back?" she asked curiously.

"I guess so."

"All right then since we only gonna be down there for one day I'll just pick up something down there. I'm on the way to your place right now."

By now, I was only a few minutes away from my crib when I made a phone call to Sharon. When she answered I told her I would be calling her later so the two of us could get together for the evening. By the time I finished talking with Sharon I was at the door of my apartment. I opened it up and was met by Strawberry. She was standing at the door with a big ass sandwich and a glass of orange juice in her hands.

"Hey, Mike, when is my girl Sexy Redd gonna get here?"

"She said she would be here shortly, Strawberry. Are you all packed and ready to go?" I asked her.

"Yes, all of us are but Ms. Kitty isn't," she replied.

I walked into my bedroom and Ms. Kitty was laying across my bed crying. Mignon and Entyce were trying to console her.

"Hey, you guys can let me handle Ms. Thang. Y'all go back out front and make sure y'all got everything ready. The limo will be here in about an hour to take you guys to the airport," I said.

Kitty turned around and looked at me. "Damn Mike, you're not taking us to the airport either? Don't you at least wanna see us off and make sure we're okay?" she asked.

"Trust me, Kitty, everything will be okay. You guys are about to head to Miami with money in your pockets and you'll make even more once y'all touch down."

Kitty and I went back and forth talking in the bedroom,. Sexy Redd showed up with a few small bags in her hand. I could hear the girls in the living room talking amongst one another about Miami.

"Girl, I ain't never been to Miami. I've always wanted to go but never had the time or money to make the trip," Strawberry said to the girls. She was seated on my damn expensive ass couch, eating that big ass ham and cheese sandwich. She had spilled juice on my living room table.

"There's nothing but palm trees and blue waters there, and if you have any questions, I can answer them for you," Sexy Redd said to a wide eyed Strawberry. Strawberry gulped down the glass of cold ass orange juice and let out a thunderous burp, while hitting herself in her chest.

"Okay, Redd, do you know where all the nice shopping malls are located?" Nicole asked, as she zipped up her Louis Vuitton bag and checked her look in the mirror. She always made sure she looked the part whenever she walked outside. Even her bra and panties matched whatever she was wearing.

"Yeah, but Michael said we were only gonna be down there for a day so we won't have much time to do much shopping," Sexy Redd replied.

I walked out front and handed the girls their upfront money.

"What's this for Mike?" a dumb ass Strawberry asked me.

"It's your upfront money, silly," Sexy Redd said as she laughed at her.

After handing the girls their money, I walked back to my bedroom. Kitty looked at me. Her eyes were bloodshot from all the crying she'd done.

"So, you're sending your Puerto Rican bitch to keep an eye on me, huh?"

'I don't give a flying fuck what your lil' short ass does down there. As far as I'm concerned we're fuckin' done', I wanted to say, but as usual, I lied.

"Kitty, please, now you know if I wasn't sending her with y'all you would have a fuckin'fit."

"Yeah, you're probably right, Michael, but you think your ass slick."

"Kitty, I trust you, boo. Whatever you decide to do, that's on you. Just call me when you guys get to Miami. And remember, I love you," I said.

"I love you too but I really don't want to go." As she stood explaining how she really didn't want to go, I started thinking of all the good times we'd had verses the bad times.

It was all the bad times that outweighed all the good times. I thought back to the time she caught me about to have sex with one of the new chicks in the group . . .

*I thought she had left with some of the girls to go to the store but I was wrong. She burst through the door and caught me standing with my manhood in my hand about to insert him inside of this cute fine red thang.*

*Kitty came through that door screaming, "I'm gonna kick your ass, bitch, and then I'm gonna fuck your ass up, Michael, for trying me with this lil' hood rat bitch!"*

*The young chick pulled her panties up so quick, she threw a quick spin move on Kitty before she could catch her. I just stood there with my hard dick in my hand.*

*The lil' red thang ran out that door so fast, it was like she was a fuckin' track star. Hell, she ran all the way home. Once she got there we never saw her lil' cute ass again. It was as if she just fuckin' vanished.*

*Poor thang, she was fine as hell and I really wanted to fuck her lil' fine red ass that day, thanks Ms. Kitty.*

*By the time, Kitty got to me, I gave her some lame ass excuse and ran out the door myself. She ran behind me with a big ass butcher knife. But what made my feelings grow cold toward her was the lil' fight we got in after that day.*

*I had to slap the shit out of her for trying to lunge at me with the butcher knife. Her face was swollen so bad, I decided to leave her home that weekend. She paid me back by fuckin' the loud mouth nigga from across the hallway— the same one she shined on the day we met Nicole. She fucked him while I was out of town doing a show. I had to hear about it in the streets one day when I was at the local car wash.*

*Two niggas had come up to me. "Hey, ain't you the dude with all them badass hoes who be dancing at the club and shit?" the skinny, tall one who went by, Skinny Pimp asked. He started squeezing his dick as though he had to piss really bad.*

*"Yeah, that's me. Why what's up? You fellas need a private show?" I asked.*

*"Nah, man, where's the lil' shorty they call Ms. Kitty?" a guy they called Q asked. He smiled at me.*

*"She's home, lil' playa," I answered him.*

*"I want to see that lil' hood chick. My dawg said he fucked her about two weeks ago while her man was out of town. He was talking about how he had left his shitty ass boxers inside the nigga's dirty clothes hamper," Q said.*

*Man, I drove home so fuckin' fast. I was pissed the fuck off. I went straight to that damn dirty clothes hamper to see if the shit Q had just told me was true. I guess Ms. Kitty found them first and disposed of the evidence he'd left behind.*

I must admit, luck was on her side that day because if I would've found them, her ass would've been disposed of that very same day. By now, everything had built up in me so much, I needed to dismiss her from my presence immediately.

Even though she became the first official Florida Hot Girl, she had changed, and not for the good of the team, but for the worse. It had got to the point where she didn't want certain females in the group so she would fire them for no apparent reason.

Eventually, she would've destroyed the team if I had allowed her to remain a part of the group. She had become so hateful towards some of the females, some of the females said they didn't wanna be on the team as long as she was the manager.

Some said they felt more comfortable with Sexy Redd being the leader of the group. So, it was evident. I had to make a change for the group of girls who called themselves the Florida Hot Girls.

## CHAPTER TWENTY
## QUESTION MARK

As the long, white stretched limo made a left onto Pine Hills Road heading to the airport, I could only hope for the best for Ms. Kitty. Simply because she deserved the best. Hell, she was one of the best at what she did and how she did it.

I couldn't fault her for loving a man like me. In the short time she'd known me, she had fallen so deeply in love, she couldn't see past me. In other words, she always felt like every girl who joined the group wanted me or I wanted them. After a few times of the same scenario, she'd left me with no other choice but to get rid of her ass.

I watched as the white limo made the turn, and she looked back at me through the passenger side window. With my hands in my pockets, I walked back up the stairs with my head held down.

One of my neighbors stuck her pill- headed ass out of her door way to being nosy and shit. "Boy, you look like you just lost your best friend, Michael." I held my head up but all I could see was my neighbors face since the rest of her fat ass was hidden behind the door.

"Nah, I'm just taking out the trash, that's all," I said. A shy ass grin, like the one Prince had in the movie Under the Cherry Moon, spread across my face—Prince played the role of Christopher Tracey, a world renown playa.

Upon entering inside my apartment, my phone started to ring. At first, I thought it was Ms. Kitty calling to tell me she didn't wanna leave. So, I casually pulled my phone from my pocket and looked at the number, a number I didn't recognize.

"Now who in the hell could this be?" I said to myself, as I hesitated to answer the phone. "Hello."

"Hello, may I speak to a Michael Valentino, please?" the baritone voiced gentleman said over the phone.

"Speaking," I revealed.

"This is Detective Tyrone Protho with the Bridgeville Police Department," he said with authority laced in his deep, bass-toned voice.

"Yes, sir, how can I help you?" I asked him. I sat up in my chair and proceeded to give him my undivided attention. At first, I thought he was calling to tell me my fuck-ass probation officer had violated my probation.

"Yes, it appears your name and number came across my desk. I need to speak with you about a little situation we have here," he explained.

"Okay, can you please tell me what this is all about, sir?"

"No problem, sir; however, I would like to speak with you face to face if that's possible? Let's say first thing in the morning?" he suggested.

"Fine, Detective," I agreed, "I'll see you then." *Damn, I knew the shit that happened the other night was gonna turn around and bite me in my fuckin' ass. But hell, my females said they didn't have nothing to do with what happened to them cowboy-looking-ass niggas. So fuck 'em. Whatever he has to say to me can't be that fuckin' serious, I thought. Hell, I wasn't there so I'm good anyway. But, still, I wonder what made them call my black ass.*

I sat there on my couch, worried about what lie ahead for me and my females. There was only one thing to do in order to relieve the unwanted stress and tension. And we all know what and who that was, yes, sir, Ms. Fine ass Sharon Connolly.

So, I hurriedly called her lil' red ass so she could come over and help me release the stress and tension I was going through. She must've already been on her way because she arrived at my apartment thirty minutes later.

She knocked on the door and I jumped up off the couch to answer it.

"Hey, Michael," she said. She stood in the doorway dressed in a pair of tight ass boyshorts that made her camel toe stare straight at me.

"Hey, you," I greeted her. Please, come in before someone sees that lil' fat-fat of yours." I smiled.

"Boy, you so crazy. It doesn't matter who sees this phat ass pussy of mine 'cause it only belongs to your black, handsome ass,"·

216

she said.

We kissed each other as if it was our first day of school and we were two school kids newly in love. She walked over to the couch and sat down on the gold mine of an ass she had.

"I must say, I was surprised when I received your call earlier today," she said.

"Why?" I questioned her, "you said you would be there for me whenever I needed you."

Yes, but I didn't know it would be this fast."

"Girl, whatever. You know you stay on my mind constantly."

"Whatever, Michael. You probably tell all the females that."

"Nah, Sharon. It's only you, boo. You the only woman I talk to. No one else has a place in my heart as you do." Even though I had Sexy Redd on my team, I was being truly sincere with Sharon that evening.

"Whatever, Michael. I know you don't think I believe that big ass lie."

"There you go," I said and chuckled. "Why don't you just bring that lil' fine ass of yours in my bedroom so I can show you just how much you mean to me."

"I was hoping you'd say that, Michael."

"What?"

"Nothing, let's not talk right now. I wanna feel you up inside of me so damn bad I can taste it," she said. She took off the tight ass shorts that looked as though they were holding her pussy hostage due to the way they hugged her ass.

As she stood there undressing, I was busy throwing on some nice, ass slow music. The song by Keith Washington "Make time for Love" played through my sound system.

She turned her naked body around and screamed, "Awww, Michael, that's my muthafuckin 'jam!" Then, she pushed me back on my bed and tore off the hundred-dollar fuckin' pair of black slacks I had on. She took my manhood by the base and gently placed it inside her warm ass mouth.

She thrusted my shaft back and forth and spit on the top of the forehead. Within minutes, she had me at a full erection. She tried hard to deep-throat all ten and half inches of it.

As I lay back on my bed with my eyes looking at the top of my ceiling, I couldn't believe how this fine ass female was sucking all the life out of my black ass. I leaned forward and picked her butt-naked ass up. I positioned her on top of me so we could be in the 69 position.

She looked back at me and uttered the words, "I love you so much, Michael fuckin' Valentino." I laid back and started sucking the juices out of her vagina and ass at the same time. *Yeah, so does everyone else*, I thought.

Twenty minutes later, she was begging me to let her ride me. So, me being the gentleman that I was, I quickly obliged as she turned her fine ass body around and climbed on top of me. She eased her soaking wet vagina down the shaft of my erected manhood.

Her back faced me while her ass was right there in front of my face. She slowly went up and down on my manhood which was engulfed inside of her tight vagina walls. For ten minutes she enjoyed herself on top of me. With my eyes focused on her cute, tight asshole, I finally said, "Girl your lil' asshole looks so inviting, why don't you let me try some of that question mark out?"

She turned back around and looked at me. "What in the hell is the question mark?" I laughed at her as I pushed her up so I could explain it to her.

"It's nothing really. My Uncle, Wesley Valentino, told me years ago, when my father had just got home from the Army, he had this chick he was chilling with for the day.

Well, when it was time for him to have sex with her, she informed him she couldn't because her period was on. So, my dad looked at her and said to her, ""Damn, baby girl, you mean to tell me I took you shopping and out to eat, and now you tell me I can't make love to you because your period is on—

"Okay Michael, so what happened after that," Sharon asked, as she lay butt ass naked with my brand-new silk sheets wrapped around her.

"Well, that's when my dad said, "Well, since your period is on, why don't you just bend over and let me have some of that question mark," Sharon damn there busted a gut laughing after I finished telling her the story.

She looked at me and said, "So, now you telling me you wanna hit my question mark?"

"Yes, beautiful."

"Michael, I have never had anyone fuck me in my ass. It's gonna hurt." She looked at me with those cute hazel-brown eyes.

"Nah, I gotcha," I said, "let me put some lubricant on you real quick." She rolled over on her back and I went to get the lubricant. She lay there in my bed staring at herself in the mirrors on top of my water bed.

I walked back out of the bathroom with the lubricant, and my manhood standing straight up. "What are you thinking about, beautiful?"

"Nothing. Just asking myself why I'm so crazy in love with your black ass, Michael."

"Oh, that's it? Well, let me show you why then." I turned her over and gently rubbed some of the lubricant on her lil' tight asshole. Then, I made sure my manhood had just the right amount on it before I slipped it in her tight, sweet asshole.

She turned around and looked back at me. "I can't believe I'm letting you fuck me in my ass with that big ass, long-hard dick of yours. I must be fuckin' crazy," she said, as she buried her head in my pillows and screamed as I pushed deeper inside of her swollen rectum.

"Nah, you're just in love sweetheart," I said, as I continued to make love to her tight, sweet asshole.

"It's not that, Michael. It's just that I'm doing all this shit with you, and how do I know you won't leave me for some other chick down the road?"

"I won't, baby," I told her. "I'm always gonna be right here for your sexy fine ass. Now be quiet and let me tear a hole out of your ass."

"Whatever, Michael. Don't get mad if I tell you to pull out 'cause this shit really hurts," she said. Her face had turned red.

"Girl, just lay there and enjoy all this meat I'm packing in your tight lil; asshole. I told you I'm not going to hurt you or leave you."

"I hope not, Michael, 'cause I have never loved a man as much as I love you."

I wasn't paying any attention to what she was saying because I was so caught up in trying to get my nut off.

Minutes later, I was pulled my manhood out of her ass. I made sure it didn't have any feces on it, then proceeded to wipe it off before placing it back up inside of her wet ass pussy.

"There you go, baby. Hit this pussy," she said, as she began to scratch the shit out of my back.

"Sharon, please calm down, baby. You're scratching the hell out of my back," I told her as I nibbled on her ear.

She whispered in my ear. "That's so if you do try to fuck another bitch, she'll see where I left my nail prints in your fuckin' back, you long, big-black dick muthafucker."

I laughed as I bust a nut.

"What's so fuckin' funny, Michael?" she asked, as I rolled over in the bed laughing my ass off.

I stood up to change the song on my CD player. "Did you just call me a long, big black dick muthafucker?"

"Yes, I did," she answered me. "You got my ass all swollen and look how you done beat up my lil' twat-twat."

"My bad, ma. I told you your sex is good as hell."

As she lay there in bed trying to fan her swollen ass and vagina, I sang along with Prince's "With You" as it blasted through the speakers of the CD player. . . .

♪ "I've held your hand so many times/ But I still get the feeling I felt the very first time/ I've kissed your lips and laid with you/ And I cherish every moment we spend in each other's arms/ I guess my eyes can only see as far as you/ I only want to be with you…

We've come so far in so little time/ Sometimes I wonder if this is meant to be/ Sometimes you are so very kind/ That the nights you're not with me I'm scared that you're gonna leave/ I guess you could say that I'm just being a fool/ But I only want to be with you/ I guess you could say that I'm just being a fool/ But I always, always want to be with you…" ♪

Prince Rogers Nelson, one of the world's best singers and songwriters that ever lived on God's green earth.

When I finished singing to her she lay there in my bed crying like a newborn baby.

"Sharon, what's wrong, honey?" she looked at me with those cute hazel-brown eyes of hers.

"Michael, you were singing that song as if it was meant for me at this very moment."

"I know, baby, it was."

"And it's amazing how you sound just like Prince."

"I know right, trips me out too. I've been singing all of his songs since my old high school days. Now, let me make you a nice, hot bubble bath so you can soak your aching body," I said, as I walked into the bathroom. Sharon followed behind me.

"So how did you enjoy it, Michael?" she asked.

"I enjoyed every minute of it, Ms. Lady."

"I'm glad I was able to satisfy you, sir."

"I hope I satisfied you also, Ms. Lady."

"You did more than that 'cause you also got my asshole hurting."

I started laughing again and she throwed a towel at me.

"That shit ain't funny, Michael. I hope I'm able to use the bathroom without being in any pain."

"Girl, you gonna be okay. Your little, tight asshole went back into place as soon as I pulled this long, big-black dick out of it."

While standing by the bathroom sink, she looked at me and said, "Oh, so you a doctor now?"

"No, but hell, it isn't going to stay open just 'cause I fucked you in the ass."

"Whatever, boy. Move your silly ass out of the way," she said and laughed. "I'm about to soak for a few hours. You can join me if you want."

"Go ahead. I'll be in there in a few minutes."

As she walked past me to get to the bathtub, I couldn't help but notice how fine she really was. How could I not want to stay with such a beautiful ass female for the rest of my life? That was a question I would ponder for many years to come. I guess the business had me so far gone, I couldn't see what Sharon really meant to me.

I walked back into the bedroom and found my phone vibrating on the dresser. I picked it up and noticed I had a few missed messages.

"Michael, where are the clean bath cloths and towels?"

"Hold on," I said, "they're inside the dryer," I told her, as I checked to see who had left the messages.

"Are you coming in here with me 'cause I'm gonna need you to wash my back for me?" I handed her a towel and a bath cloth.

"Yes, punkin, give me a minute. I need to check my messages really quick."

"Okay, don't take all day 'cause I'm still craving for some more of ole John Boy."

"Girl, you done turned into a lil' freak since you met John Boy."

"Shut up, Mike."

As I walked back into the living room, the first message I heard was from Sexy Redd…

> ☽ Hey, bae, we finally touched down in beautiful Miami. The flight was quick and somewhat comfortable. I'll try to call you again once we get to our hotel. I don't know why you didn't answer your phone. You better have a good reason when I speak with you later. Bye, big head. ☽

The next message was from a few chicks who wanted to join the team of beautiful females I had already put together. I made myself a mental note to call them after I finished giving Sharon some more of what she'd been missing for a few weeks.

I quickly put my phone down and jumped in the tub with the beautiful Ms. Sharon, and picked up where we'd left off.

Meanwhile, down at the bottom of the map, the beautiful group of women known as the Florida Hot Girls had landed in Miami.

"Excuse me ladies, you girls must be the Florida Hot Girls," the tall dark skinned gentleman said, in his deep foreign accent..

"Yes, we are," Nicole replied.

"Perfect. My name is Polo, I'll be your personal driver while you ladies are here. The CEO of Chris Styles Entertainment sent me to pick you ladies up to take you to your hotel suite.

"That's fine with us. Wow, I feel like we're some type of celebrities with this type of treatment," Entyce said, as the ladies climbed inside of the nice, plush, black limo.

"Girl, you haven't seen nothing yet. Wait until you get to the hotel suite," Sexy Redd said, looking from one girl to another. They looked around in amazement of their surroundings.

"Damn, I wish we could stay here longer than one day so we could do some shopping and sightseeing," Mignon told Sexy Redd. She stared out the passenger side window in awe.

Moments later, they pulled away from the airport and headed to their suite. Ms. Kitty sat quietly. The dark shades she'd worn covered her eyes so no one would see her reddened, tear-stained eyes. She'd cried half the way to Miami because she didn't want to go.

"Kitty, what's wrong? You haven't said one word since we left Orlando," Mignon asked her. She was concerned as to what Kitty may have been going through.

"I really don't feel like talking right now. I just wanna get this damn photo shoot over with and get back home to Michael," she said, as she placed her Chanel jacket over her and balled up in the seat of the plush, luxurious limo.

"Well, excuse me for asking, Ms. Kitty. I was just concerned," Mignon snapped back at her.

"No need to worry about me. I'll be just fine. I'm just a little homesick, that's all," Ms. Kitty said, as she tried to get comfortable in her seat.

Sexy Redd rolled her eye sat Ms. Kitty. "Sometimes you just need to worry about yourself instead of others, Mignon," Sexy Redd said.

*I don't know why she so worried about going back to Orlando. Mike already said her days as a Florida Hot Girl are over,* Sexy Redd thought as she gazed over at Ms. Kitty.

The limo driver rolled the partition down. "If you ladies want anything, there are drinks and snacks located inside the compartment on your left-hand side. I will have you ladies at your hotel suite in about thirty minutes. For now, please enjoy the condiments and the ride. And once again, welcome to beautiful Miami."

"Entyce, pass me a water and some of those peanuts in there."

"There you go, Nicole," Entyce said, "always wanting nuts in your mouth." The rest of the girls burst into laughter. Entyce looked in the compartment for the nuts and passed them to Nicole.

"You must have me mixed up with your sidekick, Strawberry. Bitch, you know damn well I don't suck no dick or fuckin' nuts," Nicole said.

"Whatever, Nicole. I don't suck nuts either, I just lick them. And for your information, chick, there called balls, not nuts," Strawberry said, as she looked around at the girls who were laughing, including Ms. Kitty.

"Damn, Strawberry, somebody said you really know how to eat the dick off the bone," Sexy Redd said, while pouring her something to drink.

"Yes, I do. I'll show you dick-sucking-hoes when we get back if y'all want me to."

"Nah, I'm good, Strawberry," Sexy Redd said back to her. She sipped on her the cold refreshing Pepsi.

"Girl, Mike has to bring us back down here so we can dance at some of these clubs," Entyce told the girls. She looked at all the greenery and beautiful landscapes they passed.

"Hell, Entyce, if y'all want to, we can go check out some of them tonight," Sexy Redd replied.

"You think we can dance in one of them tonight?" Nicole asked, as she looked out the window. She took in the sights and crunched on a mouthful of assorted mixed cashews.

"I don't see why not. We just as bad as the next female down here trying to make a living," Sexy Redd replied.

"I tell you guys what ,as soon as we get to the hotel, I'll call around to a few clubs and try to get us in one of them," Mignon said staring at the way Nicole smacked on the nuts.

"Damn, Nicole you must really like them fuckin' nuts," Strawberry said. Her face was twisted in disgusted frown as she listened to Nicole smack her mouth.

"Why you say that, chick?"

"Because your ass is over there smacking so damn loud, I can hear you all the way over here."

"Nah, it's just that I'm hungry as a muthafucker. I haven't eaten anything but that fuck-ass snack we had on the plane," Nicole said, as she continued to smack on the mixed nuts.

A few hours had gone by, and the girls had been going since their plane landed. By now, they were hot and jetlagged.

"Okay, ladies, were going to shoot the swim suit photos, break for lunch, and then you guys are finished for the day," the photographer in Miami instructed the ladies. They were tired from all the pictures they'd taken.

"Can we just go ahead and skip through lunch so we can finish up the photo shoot a little earlier?" Mignon asked the photographer.

"Yeah, we already ate a big breakfast so we good," Sexy Redd added.

"Okay, ladies, that's fine with me."

*** 

SHARON AND I WERE BACK at my place having dinner. "Thanks once again, Michael for having me over and ordering takeout from my favorite restaurant, Red Lobster."

"Hey, that's the least I could do since you had no problem coming over at the last minute."

"Anything for you, Michael," Sharon said. She cracked one of the crab legs and dipped it the hot butter sauce.

"Hey, Michael, not trying to be in your business and all, but why was there so much female stuff in your bathroom?" Sharon cleared her throat and asked.

"Oh, that's some of the ladies' things they left over here. You know they get dressed here sometime before we leave to go to a show."

"All right, Michael. I sure hope you're not fuckin' one of them," she replied. She took a bite of one of the fried shrimp and placed it in her mouth.

"Sharon, I already told your lil' ass the answer to that."

"Whatever, Michael, 'cause your little dancer who's fuckin' my baby daddy is a hot mess."

"You know I asked her about that and she said that she ain't fuckin' him. She claimed he tried to get at her but she don't do lame ass niggas."

"Well, my girl Tracey said he's fuckin' one of the Florida Hot Girls."

"Well, I don't know which one it is, and to tell you the truth, I'm really not concerned about who he's putting his dick in. I'm just concerned about you and I."

As we continued eating and watching television, a breaking news flash came over the TV screen.

The Bridgeville Police Department has new evidence in regard to the home invasion that took place last Friday night at 1125 Pine Crest Street. This is the police footage of some females who were running away from the scene of the crime.

If you know any of these females, please contact the Bridgeville Police Department, or your local crime stoppers, with any information to help catch these armed and dangerous females who might have something to do with the murder of the four innocent victims.

I was shocked when I saw the faces of the females running away from that house that night. Sharon dropped the lobster tail she was eating onto her plate.

"Michael, those girls look just like some of your girls! Matter of fact, they all look like some of them damn Florida Hot Girls!"

"Damn!" I shouted.

Shit was about to hit the fan.

Michael Gallon

## CHAPTER TWENTY-ONE
### THE MORNING AFTER

As I lay there in that bed that early Tuesday Morning staring at myself in the mirrors of my brass water bed, all I could do was wonder what the fuckin' police wanted with my black ass regarding those cowboy-looking-ass-niggas getting what they had coming to them.

The mental picture of my girls running away from the crime scene was etched in my mind. Detective Protho had put a sense of fear in my black ass by wanting to talk with me.

*I wonder what gave his ass the idea I might know something about their timely demise. Why was I even contacted, and how in the hell did he even get my phone number in the first place? Someone had to give the police my information for them to even want to speak with me.*

As I got out of bed and walked into my living room, I left the beautiful Sharon Connolly in bed looking like she still yearned for more passionate love making. The thought crossed my mind but due to my situation, the other part of my mind wouldn't wake John Boy up.

My head was just too cloudy now to even think about making love to her. I was just too far gone with the mere thought of seeing the police that day. And to make matters worse, by now I was sure my lame ass Probation Officer had issued a warrant for my arrest, so I was really tripping.

While I sat there in the dark, pondering all the mad thoughts, I could only hope and pray that my females didn't have anything to do with the murder of them clown ass brothers.

I walked back to my bedroom hoping to fall back asleep, but instead, I woke Sharon up by knocking over the stack of magazines I had on my nightstand.

"Michael, what's wrong baby, are you okay?' she asked, as she rolled over and yawned. She stretched her arms. She got up to use the bathroom, still totally naked. I looked at the beauty of her face and body.

"Yes, sweetheart. I'm sorry. I didn't mean to wake you."

"Is there anything I can help you with, honey?" she asked from behind the bathroom door. I could hear the tinkling of her using the bathroom.

"Nah, I'm good. Let's just try and get back to sleep," I said when she walked out of the bathroom. She picked up my wifebeater T-shirt that was lying on the floor. She put it on over her full size breasts before crawling back in bed and snuggling me closely.

"You seem as though you have a lot on your mind, Michael."

"Yes, I do."

"It's the girls, isn't it?"

"Yeah, seeing them on the news like that really has me tripping.

"Baby, if you said they didn't have anything to do with it, why worry yourself to death about it?"

"Yeah, you're right, Sharon. Just put your arms around me while I try to get back to sleep," I told her. Since I was used to sleeping with slow music playing in the background, the sound system was still playing slow music from earlier that night.

The song "Whose is It" by Melvin Riley, former leader of the group Ready for the World, played in the background as Sharon gazed at me with a smile over her face.

"That's exactly how I feel right now about my lil' cute kitty kat."

"And what's that?"

"It's all yours, silly boy. Goodnight, Michael," she said, as she continued to smile. She looked just like Nia Long, the lil' cute shorty from the movie Friday.

"Goodnight, baby." We fell asleep around four thirty that morning, but it wouldn't be for long.

Around eight thirty-five early that morning, Detective Protho and his tall, slender ass partner were knocking at my apartment door. Once inside they asked me all types of questions about the home invasion. They explained that my car had been seen at the victim's house earlier that night and that's how they were able to place me at the scene of the crime.

"The females that we saw running from the house had been

dropped off earlier by you."

"Yes, sir," I admitted. "I was there, but you said you saw me drop them off and leave," I said to the Detective as they both looked over my apartment for any type of clues.

"Yes, sir, Mr. Valentino. The footage also shows the females leave in a cab two hours later, but then, they returned in black clothing forty-five minutes later. It seems like it was some type of set-up on your behalf. Where were you around ten forty-five that night?"

"I was with my girlfriend having dinner at Red Lobster."

"We were both there around that time, Detective," Sharon said. She had come out of my bedroom with nothing except a thong and the robe she'd wrapped around her voluptuous body. I could see both detectives undressing her with their eyes as she sat down beside me.

"Wow, you show a striking resemblance to the chick who played in the movie Friday. . . what's her name again?" Detective Marty Pass asked her.

"Nia Long, sir," Sharon replied. She smiled at both of them and kissed me on my lips before she got comfortable beside me.

"Excuse me, ma'am, and you are?" Detective Pass asked, as he continued to undress Sharon with his small, beady eyes. His eyes looked as if they were about to pop out of his small ass head.

"Sharon Connolly, his girlfriend. We were both out to dinner around that time. If you like, I'm sure you can call Red Lobster and have them verify us both having been there around that time."

"Well, Mr. Valentino that covers you, but what about your female friends? Are they here also? We'd like to question them as well."

"Yeah, where are those hot ass females everyone says you have locked away here inside of your apartment?" Detective Pass asked, while grabbing his crotch area and chewing on a piece of old ass spearmint gum.

"They're not here, officers."

"Do you know when they'll be returning, sir?" Protho asked. Although he was talking to me, his focus remained on Sharon as he stared at how beautiful and fine she was.

"Not off hand, sir. But when they do return, I'll call you and your lanky ass partner!'

"Hey, lil' nigga, you got one more time to call me tall and lanky and then it's gonna be me and you, toe to toe," Detective Pass said to me, while looking as though he was mad at what I had just said to him.

"And by the way, tell the one they call Sexy Redd to call me personally. My oldest son is getting married soon, so I'm going to need her for a bachelor party. With the way, everyone is talking about how fine she is, I might want to see for myself." He grinned and grabbed his crotch at the same time.

"Yes, do that. The quicker we speak to those girls, the quicker we can solve this case," Detective Protho said, while chewing on the dirty ass toothpick hanging from his pink and black crusty lips.

"Do you have any more evidence in the case?" I asked Detective Protho, as I walked them to the door.

"Yes, it appears the owner of the house has a car that seemed to have turned up missing, as well some other small items of concern."

"Well, Detective Protho, if you need help with anything else, you have my number. And as soon as the females return from their photo shoot, I'll be in touch with you."

"Thank you, Mr., Valentino. You and your beautiful girlfriend have a nice day, and sorry for troubling you so early in the morning."

"No problem, sir. You have a nice day as well."

"Must be nice to see naked women all day," Detective Protho said, as he walked back down the stairs.

"Yeah, it's okay, I guess. It's better than seeing dead bodies all day, you fuckin' pervert," I mumbled under my breath.

When they were no longer in sight, Sharon put her arms around me and gave me a gentle squeeze of assurance. "Bae, don't worry, I'm sure everything will be all right. I gotcha no matter what happens."

"Hell, I didn't kill them niggas so I'm good."

"Alright, Michael, just make sure you call me later. I gotta get ready and go so I can go get my baby and head back to my house. Will I see you later tonight?" she asked.

"Well, when the ladies get in later today, we've got a show later tonight in Tampa. I'll hit you before we head out."

"Okay, be good and I'll see you soon," Sharon said. I kissed her on her soft ass lips and watched her drive away.

Then, I heard that familiar voice again.

"Boy, you are a hot mess, you got more holes than a golf course," the familiar voice, as I climbed back up the stairs to my apartment.

"Now why you gotta say something like that, young lady?"

"Because just yesterday, I saw you watch a limo full of girls leave, and I just saw you watch another beautiful girl leave your apartment."

"Yeah, that's how we playas do it," I said. I smiled at her fat, lil' short ass and closed my door before she could say anything else.

As soon as I was back inside my apartment, I got busy and called the females who would be going with me to Tampa later that evening. I had to call a few of the new ones to be sure I'd have enough for the night. By now, instead of a basketball team of beautiful women, it was more so a damn football team of them. I had so many females, I couldn't keep track of them all.

The night would be an exciting one since it would be the first night for Stephanie a.k.a. Suga Bear, the sister of Chazz.

Along with Suga Bear, was her sidekick Peekachu, their friend Shorty, and a thick ass chick who went by the moniker, Lovely. The roster was getting bigger and bigger every day.

Now, all I had to do was secure additional transportation for tonight's show. And I knew exactly who to call. My good friend Preston had a limo service that the Valentino family had invested quite a bit of money into it. It had been a sound investment, especially since I'd gotten the strippers. Instead of me having to do all the driving, I would utilize his company for the benefit of the Florida Hot Girls.

It was two thirty-five in the afternoon and I hadn't heard from the females since they'd touched down in Miami.

So, I decided to give Redd a call. As usual, she answered on the first ring. "Hey you."

"Hello to you also, what's up?" I asked.

"I should be asking your black ass that Mr. Don't-answer-your-phone."

"Now why you say that, beautiful?" I asked.

"Don't play with me, Mike, I called your phone as soon as we touched down in Miami yesterday. You're just calling me back now?" she sassed me.

"My bad, shorty, it's been mad crazy around here since you guys left."

"Yeah, I bet. Your black ass probably fuckin' everything that moves," she said with anger in her voice.

"Nah. Why would you think that, beautiful?"

"Whatever, Michael. Don't let me find out, nigga."

"What time is the photo shoot over with?" I asked not bothering to answer her question.

"We finished up about two hours ago, baby. Why?"

"Okay, cool. I need y'all to take the first flight out of Miami immediately."

"Why, baby, what's up?" She sounded worried. What's wrong? You did say everything was *mad crazy.*"

"They got y'all on the news here, and to make matters even worse, a detective and his partner stopped by this morning asking questions about y'all's whereabouts that night," I said, as I explained what had transpired.

"What?" Redd replied as if she was totally taken aback. She got quiet and I could hear her beathing heavily. I pictured her holding the phone with her mouth dropped and opened.

"Yes, so get on the next flight home so we can handle this shit ASAP," I ordered her.

"Okay, I'm getting the girls together as we speak. But, Michael," she said.

"Yes, Redd."

"Ms. Kitty is nowhere to be found."

"No problem, Redd, just get to the airport and I'll worry about the rest later."

"Okay, baby, we're on the way there right now. So, what should we do about Kitty's clothes and shit?"

"Shit, just leave her shit there. Right now, my main concern is getting you ladies back here so we can get your names cleared as soon as possible."

"All right. I'll call you back to let you know what time we'll be landing in Orlando."

"Peace. But is everyone else okay," I asked.

"Yes, baby, we all good. We danced at the Rolex last night and made a nice lil' bit of change so we all Gucci.

Ms. Kitty's grown ass left about an hour ago, with a bitch who was throwing her rat looking ass big faces all night."

"I see. Well, that's fine with me. I'll see the rest of you girls when y'all touch down back in O-Town. Until then, be safe."

After we hung up I thought to myself. ... *Redd is gonna be very helpful to me now that Ms. Kitty is gone. If I would've kept her around, there's no telling what would've become of my precious, Florida Hot Girls.*

Michael Gallon

## CHAPTER TWENTY-TWO
### HANGING OUT OF THE LIMO

"Okay, ladies, listen up, and listen up closely," Sexy Redd said to the females down in Miami. She had gathered them around to relate the information she'd received from Michael.

"I just got off the phone with Michael. He said we need to get on the first flight back to Orlando, as soon as possible. Somehow, our faces are all over the news regarding the home invasion that happened the other day."

"Oh shit! Are you fuckin' serious?" Nicole asked. Her face displayed an expression of guilt.

"Yes, girl, so we gotta get to the airport ASAP, so we can catch the first flight back to Orlando!"

"What about Ms. Kitty, Redd?" Mignon asked. She rushed around the suite grabbing her things one by one.

"Mike said to leave her shit right here and just get to the airport so we can leave. Now if you wanna stay here with her things, that's up to you," Redd told Mignon. As she spoke, she stuffed pieces of clothing inside her bag. She had already called a cab, and she'd just hung up the phone with them after giving them the address of the hotel.

"Hell nah, I'm not staying," Mignon snapped back, "as far as I'm concerned, the nasty-attitude-having bitch can stay the fuck down here by her damn self!" Mignon glanced at the mirror to check her makeup.

"For real, seeing the way that bitch acted over the weekend, I don't care what she does. If it doesn't concern me, I'm good," Nicole replied.

"Fuck Kitty, the po-po is the fuckin' problem now," Sexy Redd said.

"Entyce, hurry up out of that bathroom, girl! We ain't got that much time! The cab will be here at any minute to pick us up," Strawberry called out to Entyce from outside of the bathroom door.

"Okay, I'm coming! Whatever I ate last night decided to come back out of my ass at the wrong fuckin' time," Entyce replied from behind the slightly-closed bathroom door.

"Oh, my God! Spray some perfume or something in there, girl! You smell like something crawled up in you and fuckin' died," Mignon yelled back to her. She pinched her nose to keep from inhaling the awful stench escaping under the bathroom door.

"I just told y'all crazy ass bitches whatever I ate last night is tearing my stomach up!" Entyce shouted back. She flushed the toilet a fifth time.

"I know one thing, Entyce, if your ass is still in there when the cab pulls up, you gonna be shit -out-of-luck. We gotta get the fuck out of here," Redd yelled to Entyce.

The toilet flushed again.

"Alright, you guys got everything?" Nicole asked.

"Yes, I'm good over here," Mignon responded."

"Entyce, I'll put your things with mine," Strawberry told Entyce, who was still flushing the toilet.

"Okay. I should be done in a few minutes, girls, so please don't leave me," Entyce screamed. At last, she was finally done destroying the restroom of the nice hotel suite.

"Girl, ain't nobody gonna leave yo' stanking ass. Go ahead and jump your stank booty ass in the shower, 'cause Lord knows yo' stank ass ain't gonna sit by me on the plane smelling like curry goat and rotten cabbage," Nicole said, laughing at the same time.

Meanwhile, back in Orlando, my phone hadn't stopped ringing since the girls had been seen on television. It seemed everybody knew one of the faces on the TV screen. All I could do was tell everyone the females they'd seen on the new hadn't been one of my girls, instead, it had been some girls who looked like them. But my explanation was to no avail because they would just call right back still talking about it.

"Nah, Mike, that sure as hell looked like Ms. Kitty, and the other girl looked just like Mignon, your girl from Tampa."

It got so bad, I had to turn my damn phone off to get some peace and quiet for, at least, an hour or so. But as soon as I turned it off, there was a knock at my door.

I walked over to the door mad as hell. "Who in the fuck is it?" I said to whoever it was knocking at my door. Then I looked out of the small ass peep hole and saw that it was just J.K. and her crew of girls.

"Hey, come on in. I'm sorry for answering the door like that." She and her crew came in.

J.K. was wearing some tight ass jeans that hugged all her phat, stupid, black ass. At the moment, I wanted to squeeze her ass but I knew how she felt about me grabbing her ass. So, I just fell back and held my composure.

"No problem, Mike, we saw the girls on TV and shit," she said, before greeting me with a simple hello. "What's really going on?" she asked in her squeaky voice. She fell down onto my couch, and I told them the whole story.

"Man, them silly ass girls done got themselves into some kind of trouble. You see what happened is we had met these cowboy-looking-ass niggas at the Caribbean Beach Night Club last week. They wanted the girls to dance at their bachelor party last Friday night so I told them I would charge them around one hundred twenty dollars for four or five girls."

"Damn, Mike, that's cheap ass fuck for four or five girls."

"I know right, and that's what I found out later that same night. Well, I dropped the girls off and assumed the guys were going to tip the girls a nice lil bit of change. Then I get a text message from Ms. Kitty telling me the niggas wasn't tipping and shit, and that they were ready to be picked up. Well, I was clear across town and knew I couldn't get there in the time frame they wanted me to. So, I told her to just catch a cab home. Well, they caught a cab back here and changed into some black clothing before deciding to head back over to where those guys were."

"What?" J.K. and Kizzy said in unison. They laughed at what I said.

"Yes, wait there is more," I said. "Then, them crazy ass girls went back over to the nigga's house to ask for their money. But, when they got there, they saw some other females inside the house putting in work on them niggas. Kitty and the crew of females she had with her, got scared and hauled ass back here."

"Wow, Mike. You mean to tell me all that shit happened Friday, and you didn't know nothing about it?"

"Shorty, I didn't know nothing until the very next morning. I was watching television and the news came on, and the reporter announced the home invasion and said the guys were all dead. Now, at the time, Kitty, who was laying next me, rolled over and said, 'that's what them niggas get for fuckin' with the Florida Hot Girls.' Like they were the ones who murked them niggas and shit. But the real people who did it still out there somewhere chillin'."

"Mike, that's crazy," Kizzy said, as she went to my kitchen to look for something to eat.

"Yep, tell me about it."

"So, where they at now?" Seneavu asked. She stood her black ass up and looked like she had just stole something.

"Man, they down in Miami finishing up a photo shoot."

"What? A photo Shoot," Kizzy called out from the kitchen, sounding excited. "Mike, why we ain't at no damn photo shoot?" J.K. asked. She looked mad and shit.

"Because y'all asses wasn't nowhere to be found when they called me at the last minute about some females," I calmly replied. "Just be thankful y'all here for the show tonight, I said. I stood up and walked away, headed to my bedroom. I sat down and waited for the rest of the girls to get in.

Shortly after J.K. and her crew had arrived, half of the remaining females had gotten dropped off at my apartment. The rest were on their way. Just as another group of girls came in, I remembered I had turned my phone off earlier.

I quickly turned it back on and realized Sexy Redd had called me to let me know she had already arranged a ride to the crib, and they would be here shortly. The next message I had was from my dear cousin Richard Valentino asking for a job. Once again, I made a mental note to get back to him when I had some free time.

While running back and forth throughout the house trying to put things in the right perspective, Sexy Redd and her crew of females walked in. Sexy Redd spoke to everyone before kissing me on my lips. Then she walked straight to my bedroom. All the girls looked at me.

"Damn, Mike, you a bad man. You get rid of one Hot Girl and get another one just like that, huh?" J.K. said. I looked at the room full of ladies with a sly ass grin over my face.

"Well, J.K., if you would've given me some of that good ass kit-kat you got, it would have been you next in line."

"Whatever, Mike," she said, smiling at me.

As I walked to the bedroom behind Sexy Redd, Nicole yelled out, "We missed you, Michael!"

I stopped and turned around. "How y'all miss me and you were only gone for one day?" I replied.

"Okay, ladies, while Redd and Mike are getting ready, I'm gonna need you all to go ahead and get ready. We'll be leaving around nine o'clock, so that means we got at least two hours to get dressed," Mignon announced to the ladies. They listened as she took control of the group.

While they were in the living room getting ready, I nervously walked back into my room because I didn't know what to expect from Sexy Redd. Here it was she was finally in my bedroom after all the times I'd wanted to really put it in on her fine sexy ass.

But how would I approach her? I knew she had some strong feelings toward me, but was the time right for me to make my move?

I looked down at John Boy who looked back up at me as if to say, *'hey man, what the fuck are you waiting on? You got that fine ass Puerto Rican chick in here, just waiting on us to do our thang. Let's go 'head and get some of that'.* "But I don't know if I'm ready, I thought. For the first time I'm fuckin' nervous and scared." That's when he looked right back at me and said, *'just follow my lead, homie, I gotcha. Have I ever let you down before?'* "No, I don't ever recall a time when you have let me down John Boy."

Suddenly, she walked out of the bathroom after taking a shower. "Michael, who were you in here talking to?"

I pointed down at the hard erection in my pants and answered, "John Boy and I were having a man-to-man conversation."

241

She laughed as she stood naked in front of the mirror, drying her beautiful, long, black hair. Her phat juicy ass stared back at me. She stood around five foot eight and weighed a hundred forty-five pounds with a stupid soft ass. Along with having 36B breasts, her skin complexion was a high-yellow caramel-like color. Her beautiful vagina looked like it was calling my name as she stood there drying off. In other words, she was a fuckin' goddess. I just stood there staring at her.

"So, what are you going to do? Just stand there and look at me, or make passionate love to me, silly boy?" she looked at me and said.

"Man, I'm about to suck the hell out of your pretty ass pussy first, then I'm gonna turn you over, and kiss all over your phat stupid ass. Then I'm gonna make passionate love to you for at least an hour or so."

"Just as long as we not late for the club, Michael. Now get your black ass over here and give me what I been wanting since the first moment we met."

"Redd, where did we first meet in the first place?" I asked, as I crawled in between her luscious thighs.

"Winn Dixie, Michael. That night you were going home to cook steak and lobster, remember?" she said, as she rubbed the back of my head. I wrapped my mouth around her clit and gently held it in between my two front teeth.

"Oh, now I remember. You was the lil' Puerto Rican cutie who told me I better call you."

Minutes later, I was sucking on her lil' man-in-the-boat as though it was a piece of candy. Then I made love to her like I had never made love to any female before her.

She called out my name over and over in my ear, and it made me go crazy. We made love for about an hour and thirty minutes before the girls knocked on my bedroom door.

"Okay, we're getting ready! Give us like twenty more minutes, please," Redd yelled to the girls. They were hammering at my bedroom door due to all the noise making they were hearing coming from inside.

"Whatever, Redd!" Mignon yelled back.

AT NINE FORTY-FIVE, THE LIMO picked up the last female and we were all on our way to Tampa, fifteen girls deep inside of a nice, white stretch limo. As soon as we got on Interstate 4, the girls started asking questions about the incident that took place on Friday. They wanted to know if everything all right and if anyone got hurt. Then they wanted to know how much money the girls had made.

Of course, Ms. Nosy Ass Lil Kitty had to ask the wrong question. "Hey, where is Ms. Kitty?" Sexy Redd looked at her like she wanted to pick her up by her braids and toss her little small ass out of the limo.

But instead, she chilled and answered her. "Ms. Kitty is still in Miami. She decided she wanted to stay down there for a lil' while longer and whenever she's ready to return is entirely up to her. As far as Michael and me are concerned, when it comes to Ms. Kitty, she's terminated from the group known as the Florida Hot Girls," Sexy Redd said to Lil Kitty, with a show of sarcasm.

The ride the rest of the way was quiet and peaceful until Lil Kitty's smart mouth ass uttered under her breath, "Well I guess there's only one Kitty in the group now."

"Shut up, Kitty," Mignon told her, as the rest of the girls giggled at her.

After dancing at Apollo that night, we went straight to LouDoc's for the after-hour jump off. Since Smitty claimed he owned the club, we thought we wouldn't have any problems with the police or nothing. Yeah right, truth be told, Smitty didn't own shit, and he wasn't even supposed to be operating a fuckin' club.

Now, he had all these people inside the club, including me and my girls, trapped inside when the local police decided they wanted to raid the club. The doors were shut tight and no one was allowed to leave. The cops had locked every exit door and I was stuck right dab in the fuckin' middle of a bunch of people, one looking just as stupid as the other.

My phone started to ring. "Hello."

# The Murder Queens

"Mike?"

"Yeah," I answered.

"What do you want me to do?" The limo driver asked. I looked around the club for some type of an escape route.

"Okay, listen. ... Pull up to the front of the club, over in that field across the street. Open the rear passenger door on the driver's side and pull the limo the long way," I told him.

"Okay, what else boss?" the driver asked.

"Keep the motor running. In about five minutes, we gonna run out and jump inside the car. Be ready for a quick getaway, my boy, 'cause we gonna be coming in hot, meaning we coming in fast and in a fuckin' hurry."

"Okay, I'll be there waiting on you and the girls."

"Yep. And stay inside the car with your foot on the fuckin' gas pedal. Peace!"

As soon as I hung up with him, I was in Sexy Redd's ear.

"Go get all the females and bring them back here next to me. We're about to make a smooth getaway. I just have to figure out what our distraction is going to be."

"Okay, baby. I'll be right back." She quickly ran back upstairs to get the rest of the females just like I'd told her. By the time all of them came down the stairs, I had the rest of the females standing right beside me.

"All right, are you guys ready?"

"Yes, Mike," Lil Kitty and the rest of the girls answered. All the girls looked like a bunch of school kids who had gotten in trouble.

"When you guys see that door over there pop open, run as fast as you can towards the limo, which is parked right out front of those doors."

Just as the words left my mouth, one of the cops slammed his nightstick on the ground and shouted, "Okay, this is how this shit is going down! I need everyone to pull out their ID, and if you don't have one your black ass is going downtown to be finger printed."

"Oh shit, I don't have my ID, and on top of that, I might have a warrant due to my probation, so I know I'm not staying around here for that shit," I said to the girls who were standing around me, looking like they had warrants for their scary asses too.

Suddenly, this fat ass female started screaming at the top of her lungs, and somebody bum-rushed the door the skinny white cop was standing at.

Every one of us ran straight for that door and ran the skinny white cop the fuck over.

The limo was parked exactly where I had told the driver to be. The door was wide open just as I had instructed the limo driver have it. Of course, I was the first one to jump in and Sexy Redd was right behind me. The rest of the girls were running behind her. One of the cops was standing outside the club. I guess he was expecting some shit like that to happen because she started walking over to the limo like a nigga wasn't going to run his white ass over.

"Man, pull the fuck off ," I shouted to the limo driver. And then out of nowhere, yep, you guessed it, your girl, Strawberry came running towards the limo at top speed, trying to catch up to the car. First, one of her heels flew off her feet, then she stumbled as her other heel on the her shoe broke.

You could hear Lil Kitty scream at her. "Hey, those were my good muthafuckin' heels, bitch!" I laughed my black ass off as she ran behind the limo trying to get away from the club. She stumbled again while trying to run with one heel on.

The damn driver turned around and said in his deepest voice, almost in slow motion, "Close. The. Damn. Door!"

Strawberry must have heard him because suddenly, the heifer picked up some more speed from somewhere and ran down the limo. By now, I was laughing my muthafuckin' ass off.

Lil Kitty was screaming, "Hurry up, bitch, your dick-sucking-ass is about to get left down here in Tampa!"

"No, you're not Strawberry, go ahead and jump! I gotcha, "Sexy Redd yelled out to her.

"All right, go ahead and try to be super-save-a-bitch if you want to. When her weight pulls your ass right out of the car with her, don't get mad at me when both of y'all end up with a bunch of scratches all over y'all bodies.

"Run, girl, run!" Nicole screamed out of the sunroof. The limo was about to get onto the main road as Strawberry leaped at the car for dear life. Half of her body hung out of the car as the car drove down the road.

After we'd made it a few blocks or so down the road, the limo pulled over so Strawberry could look over her body for any scratches or cuts she may have acquired from her miraculous escape from justice. The entire car load burst out into laughter after we realized what had just happened.

After that night, Lou Doc's was shut down for a few weeks until Shitty Smitty got his shit together. But after that night, we also decided Lou Doc's wasn't worth going to jail for.

***

THE NEXT MORNING, SEXY REDD and I were up early with the movers, ready to move most of my furniture into our new home. The other females who were living with me, were busy packing their belongings.

Then, Detective Protho called me. "Hello."

"Good Morning, Mr. Valentino."

"Morning, Detective Protho. What can I do for you?"

"We looked back over the footage from the home invasion and we saw where the females in question did, in fact, leave the scene before any crime was committed."

"Okay, so what are you saying?"

"Basically, they're not the main suspects anymore, but we would still like to speak with them, at some point and time, to see if they may have seen the actual suspects."

"No problem, sir. I'm in the middle of something right now but I'll get back to you when they're available."

"Thank you, Mr., Valentino."

"You're welcome, sir."

"Hey, pimp, tell one of them hoes I wanna suck her toes!" Detective Pass yelled to me from the background.

"You have to forgive him, Mr. Valentino, he gets like that from time to time, ever since his wife of twenty years left his ass."

"No problem, sir. Have a nice day."

I informed the females they were no longer considered the main suspects anymore, but that the police still wanted to speak with them in regard to the investigation. In the meantime, it was business as usual. Everyone was so excited about moving into our new home, time just flew by. But to me, it was just another day while being the owner of the world's famous Florida Hot Girls.

## CHAPTER TWENTY-THREE
## BABY LACK
## FLORIDA

Things were flowing just right for the Florida Hot Girls and me. Ms. Kitty was gone, and I was happier than a faggot with a bag of dicks. Our popularity had flowed everywhere, and it got even bigger when we met the world-famous Baby Lack and DJ Lick'em muthafuckin' Low.

The Florida Hot Girls had landed a spot on one of the hottest underground radio stations in Central Florida. Owned and operated solely by Dawg Man Entertainment, it was an up and coming radio station located in the heart of Orlando. Baby Lack and DJ Lick'em low loved the Hot Girls so much, they invited them to make guest appearances on their individual shows. The ladies were in full swing. Not only was Baby Lack interviewing them and allowing them to help assist him at all his local events, but he was also our full-time DJ whenever we had an out-of-town show to attend.

One weekend in particular, things went south for Baby Lack and one of my premier dancers in the group. I had set up a show in a small ass town known as Jasper, Florida; the town was so small, there were probably three traffic lights throughout the whole town.

The town was nice and quiet. Well, that was, until the Florida Hot Girls invaded it that dreadful weekend. The name of the club my girls were dancing in was called E and J's, a nice two-room house trailer that had been modified into a nice ghetto club outside of town. It was located in an old, run down cow pasture that the owner used for a make shift parking Jot.

It seemed as if the only excitement the town of Jasper, Florida ever had was when the Florida Hot Girls came through that weekend. Not only were the guys getting the Florida Hot Girls, but the ladies in the small ass town were about to get the first sight of the Florida Hot Boyz.

With Baby Lack hosting both shows at the same damn time, like I said, Jasper, Florida was about to get something that had never been done before—The Florida Hot Girls and The Florida Hot

Boyz, dancing at the same time, in the same fuckin' club.

While on the long ass drive to Jasper, Baby Lack and Keyonna couldn't seem to get enough of each other. Keyonna was from Lakeland, Florida. She stood a mere five foot five with a nice pecan-tan complexion. Weighing one hundred twenty-eight pounds, she was equipped with a nice fat ass, and a breasts size of 34C. She had a cute baby face to go along with everything else she had to offer.

Poor Baby Lack just couldn't keep his hands off of her, and she just couldn't seem to control herself when it came to him either. It was as if he was the first man to ever have her head so far gone, she could only see as far as him.

We arrived in Jasper around three that afternoon. I didn't feel a need to go out and promote, so we checked into our hotel rooms. The ladies paired up and purchased their rooms, while Sexy Redd and I purchased our own.

Now Baby Lack and Ms. Keyonna purchased a room also, but it was more like the two of them were on their honeymoon. Whatever went on in that room that weekend remains a mystery. Let's just say, their futures would be linked together forever from the events that took place between them.

The show that night went as planned until one of my females crossed the line by trying to fuck someone's man.

While I was collecting the money and making change for the guys and women, Ms. Fast Ass Tarshay decided she wanted to take a customer in the female's bathroom. The show was at full capacity until a fat ass woman weighing around two hundred seventy-five pounds walked in the club and shouted out her husband's name. She must have had one of her girlfriends in the club watching out for her, 'cause she went straight to the bathroom where Tarshay and her husband had gone.

A few minute later, Tarshay's little, short ass flew past me like she had just been shot out of a fuckin' cannon. Before I could ask her, what happened, out comes this guy with his pants hanging down, with his fat ass wife running behind him, beating him with a thick ass leather weight trainer's belt.

Every time she swung her large overweight arm, she would catch him right across the small of his back. He tried to get away from her, but to his dismay, she was keeping up with every step he took. By the time his ass got outside the club, his wife beater T-shirt was just that, as it was hung from his bleeding back.

Tarshay didn't even run outside to say goodbye to the badly beaten lover. Afterall, she was somewhat at fault since she'd tried to have a romantic escapade with him in the female's bathroom. Besides, her little, short black ass knew fuckin' customers was a no-no. The girls weren't permitted to partake in any kind of sexual activities with customers, period. Now Ms. Grown Ass Tarshay feared for her safety, so she decided to hang out with security for the rest of the night. She tried to explain what happened, but if you knew Tarshay like I did, you'd be a fool to believe half the shit that came out of her mouth.

Needless to say, the show went on without a hitch. The females made their money and the guys made theirs as well. However, following the show, we got the shock of our lives when we opened the door to get inside of the limo. To our surprise, when the driver opened the door, there were five local females inside the car.

I poked my head inside. "Well, hello, young ladies, to what do I owe the pleasure of meeting you beautiful women?"

"Umm, we wanna dance with the Florida Hot Girls, sir," the leader of the group answered. The rest of them sat there looking as if they were sure I was gonna say yes to their asses.

Now, don't get me wrong. There were five girls and I already had twelve in total for the show. Five more would've been entirely too many people in the limo.

"Okay, ladies, all of you look nice and all, but I only have room for two girls at the moment. If three of give my assistant your info, I'll come back for you at a later time and date." The ladies agreed but decided all five of them would wait. With that said, me and my girls drove off into the night. Truth be told, there were only two who could've gone with us night anyway. The other three wouldn't have cut it in the world of the Florida Hot Girls.

On the trip back home, the ladies let me know they preferred traveling for shows versus doing local shows. So, it was established we'd stay on the road more in the future. Aside from everything else that took place, one thig was for sure, Baby Lack and Keyonna were now a couple. All she talked about for the next few weeks was Baby Lack's damn short ass.

In Baby Lack's mind, all he was doing was testing out the merchandise before he purchased it. I wish somebody would have told Keyonna that because she never got the memo. And the one rule I preached to the girls to this very day was: 'there is no love in the stripping game'. From that weekend to now, I had witnessed so many females on the team meet some guy and fall in love, only to get their hearts broken the very next day. Some would even go as far as leaving the group, only to return weeks or months later asking for their jobs back.

After Keyonna found out Baby Lack wasn't feeling her as much as she was him, she dropped a bombshell on him. She told him she was pregnant and that she was keeping the baby. She ended up quitting the group and moving back to Lakeland, Florida. She ended up having a beautiful baby girl who, some said, looked just like the father, Baby Lack.

Keyonna eventually went back to dancing years later. I would run into her from time to time in different strip clubs. She made enough money to put herself through college in Miami, and afterwards, she opened a few daycare centers on the East Coast. Now, she was living life to the fullest.

Baby Lack went on to broadcasting and hosting shows for Dawg Man Entertainment. The last time I'd spoken with him, he had become the DJ at a popular strip club in Orlando by the name of Cleo's. He was still best known for the signature catch phrase that got him started in the radio business, "Baby Lack, Florida, put that dick up in your Daughter".

And that's how it went. Every weekend there was a story to tell about what happened the previous weekend, while we were out of town making money. If you were one of the unfortunate ones who had missed a weekend, you were fined for missing work. You were also one of the first females to call one of the girls who were there so you could find out what happened.

\*\*\*

WE RETURNED HOME FROM JASPER, FLORIDA that week and before we knew it, it was time to travel back to Jacksonville. We hadn't been in Jacksonville in the last month or so, since we, or should I say me, had got played doing one of the shows.

You see, it all started the weekend of Homecoming for FAMU's Football team in Tallahassee, Florida. It appeared Uncle Luke was doing his Freak Fest Volume Five at the same damn time as Homecoming. Frank, the guy who owned the club in Jacksonville where the girls would dance at from time to time, couldn't make it that weekend with his girls. He asked me if I would mind taking my girls in their place since Luke needed some girls for his Freak Fest. I was flattered.

Not only would we be on video, but it would give us the much needed publicity we needed—or at least, that's what I thought. But little did I know, I was getting set up in the worse way a nigga like myself could be set up.

The plan was for me to take my girls to Tallahassee first. Once there, they would meet up with Uncle Luke to help promote the night's event. After that, we would meet at club V-12, in Quincy, Florida, another small ass country town in Florida.

We got to Tallahassee early that afternoon. As soon as we got there, Luke wanted us to ride on his rented tour bus with him so the girls could get the word out about the show. Then, he wanted us to go with him to the local radio station to talk with the listeners to hype up the event.

Yours truly, Chyna, had all the attention centered on her. First, while on the radio, she proceeded to do all the talking. Then, as we rode around on the bus, she hung onto Luke's arm promoting the show as if it was all about her. The rest of us hung around as if we were only tourists or something.

It was supposed to be one of our finest moments to shine, especially since the squad I had with me was definitely on point. To name a few, there was Sexy Redd, Lil Red, J.K., Chazz,

Diamond, Strawberry, Lil Kitty, White Chocolate, Charlie B., Stephanie a.k.a. Suga Bear, Peekachu, Shantel, Chyna, Lovely, Ashley, Kizzy, Monique, Tarshay, Keyonna, Tiger, Do-Dirty, and fine ass fuckin' Jasmine. Man, I had so many females with me you couldn't tell me a damn thing that weekend.

I thought, or felt like, I was the muthafuckin' man. Little did I know, I *was* the man. The man who was about to get played by the man Luke and the manager of Club V-12.

Anyway, we finally stepped off the bus and into the club. My girls were rushed off to the VIP room. Once inside the room, the girls were told to get dressed in their dancing outfits. In the meantime, Luke explained how he wanted the show to go that night.

Now, when we had met Luke earlier that day, we had all eager to meet his squad of girls. We just knew he had some badass sisters since he had come from Miami. Nonetheless, he told us he hadn't brought any females with him. He let me know it would only be my girls, along with some females from Georgia who went by the name Georgia Peaches.

It was at that very moment that I quickly found out that *this* was the game, and I was about to be the part of the game they played. You see Luke hadn't brought any females with him, because if he would've, he would've found out like I did years later, you *cannot* transport anyone to make money and not have the Government receive any taxes from it. It's called depriving the Government, and we all know the Government don't play when you owe their ass. Now, on the flipside, they can owe you forever, but if you owe them one penny, you'll find your black ass somewhere like I did fifteen years later.

The DJ called the ladies up on stage in front of the packed house. I was in a daze as I looked at my beautiful ladies on the stage that night. *What are they supposed to do on stage now?* I thought to myself. On stage with my girls were these huge women from Georgia. Every single Florida Hot Girl just stood there. They didn't even move. Not a single one. Instead, they looked at one another as if they were scared to death to be up on stage, like it was their first time. When they turned and looked at me, all I could do was laugh. They weren't prepared and neither were the Georgia Peaches. But then, taking everyone by surprise, one of the Georgia Peaches pulled this lil' short ass nigga out of the crowd and up on stage. She flipped him upside down and sucked his ass crack completely dry, before sucking his two-inch manhood, right there on stage. Everyone laughed.

Luke commented, "Another fuckin' Luke Freak Fest!"

Afterwards, the ladies got a chance to dance inside the VIP room and make money there. I just watched and waited on my big payday. At least, that's what I thought it was going to be for the Florida Hot Girls and me.

Michael Gallon

## CHAPTERTWENTY-FOUR
### NO MONEY AT ALL

Now the club that night was charging twenty dollars a head to get in, when we arrived it was already packed to capacity. I figured I would get a stack or two for bringing my females, so I kicked back and tried to enjoy the rest of the show. Boy was I wrong. After the doors were shut and the club secured, everyone was counting money except my black ass. I casually walked to the manager's office where I found Luke and the manager, Coach, busy counting nothing but big faces. I quietly knocked on the door and both looked up at me standing there looking like I had just caught somebody fuckin'. They looked at each other, and I could of sworn I heard Luke ask Coach, 'what this lame ass nigga want?'

I cleared my somewhat-dry-ass throat and said in my coolest voice, "Ah, yes, excuse me. I ain't got paid for bringing my females to your event at the last minute. sir."

The manager looked at me with his cigar hanging from his mouth and Luke just continued counting his money.

"Oh, didn't Frank tell you?" he asked, with a stack of hundred dollar bills in his hand.

"Tell me what, sir?"

"That you would make your money from the tips that your dancers made." I stood there with my mouth in my hands looking dumbfounded.

"But since you drove up here on short notice, here's a few dollars for gas and a bite to eat," he said. Then the big-headed ass muthafucker handed me a hundred dollars.

I looked back at him like, *what am I supposed to do with this? Buy some coffee and fuckin' donuts?*

Luke looked at me and cracked an evil ass grin and said, "Hey, man, your girls did their thang on that stage tonight. You think you could bring them to the show I got coming up in a few weeks, down in Orlando, at the Hard Rock Cafe?"

"Sure, Luke, anything for you, man," I said with a straight face. "Just hit me and we'll go from there."

"Oh, by the way, it's Mike, right?" he asked with a stupid smirk on his face.

"Yeah, Luke, my name is Mike," I said dryly.

He took out his silver two-way pager and beamed me over the name Caligula and his number. Now if you don't know who Caligula is, he's supposed to be the Roman Emperor who had the first fuckin' orgy known to man. Leave it up to muthafuckin' Uncle Luke to know that shit.

The only way I found out was, one day as a lil' kid, my family and I were over in Orlando from Lakeland visiting my uncle and other family members. As we sat around listening to the grown folks converse, my uncle's two oldest step-daughters decided they wanted to take the kids to the movies with them and their friends.

I was supposed to be off in another part of the theater watching some fuckin' kid's movie, when my lil' grown ass went into the movie the older people were watching. I had to be at least eight or nine years old when I took my ass into that damn movie. It blew my lil' ass mind when I saw all that fuckin' on the movie screen.

My life was changed forever after I saw that movie. I walked my young, black ass back into the kid's movie with a hard on out of this fuckin' world. Needless to say, that very, day I was introduced to the wonderful world of sex.

"Make sure you bring the same females with you," Luke said, never losing count of the money.

"Yeah right, Luke. I'll bring the same ones, I sure will," I said, insolently.

As I walked away, I heard Suga Bear say to Peekachu, "Girl, Mike gonna cry in the car."

"Why you say that, Step?" Peekachu asked her, as I headed for the nearest exit.

"'Cause them niggas just "Debo'ed" his black ass out of his fuckin' money, Peekachu!" Peekachu and Step laughed as they walked to the van and counted their money.

I was so fuckin' mad, right then and there I vowed to never take the Florida Hot Girls anywhere unless I received some type of deposit up front first.

# The Murder Queens

\*\*\*

AFTER THE CLUB THAT NIGHT, the girls talked me into driving to Tallahassee. While there, they crashed someone's homecoming party and continued to make more money.

Sunday morning didn't come quick enough for me. I called Frank to let him know how I got played.

"Hello," he answered in a groggy voice.

"Frank."

"Yeah, it's me Mike, what's up?"

"Man, why didn't you tell me I wasn't getting paid for taking my girls to Luke's Freak Fest?"

"What? He didn't pay you anything?" he asked, trying to sound all attentive and shit.

"Man, them clowns paid me a hundred dollars and then told me to have a nice fuckin' day!"

"Wow, dawg. I'm sorry about that but what do you want me to do about it?"

"Nothing, Frank, it's just a bitter pill to swallow, I guess I just got played since I'm new to the game. All right, Frank, thanks. I'll talk at cha later. I'm still on the road headed home"

"Mike, before we hang up, can we expect you and your girls to be at the club this weekend?"

*No this flat faced ass nigga didn't just ask me if was bringing my girls to his fuckin' club for the weekend.* "Yeah Frank, anything for you, dawg."

Man, me and my girls didn't go back to Frank's club for a minute after he sent me on that wild fuckin' goose chase.

It had been the weekend after Jasper and we were on the road to Jacksonville. I had located another spot for the ladies to dance at. It was located near the entrance of Jacksonville. It was a nice, small club but with plenty of potential. It was located in the nice, classy vicinity of Jacksonville. I just didn't know about the type of environment I was introducing the ladies to. So, when I was told about the high drug area on that side of town, I was at a complete loss.

You see, I really didn't like the ladies to partake in any types of drugs. I mean, no type at all. Not even the sticky-icky.

But I would find out sooner than later that I had some real characters on my beautiful squad of ladies. Lil Kitty along with your girl, Chazz, were some real high rollers when it came to the smoking off the herbal essence known as weed. At one time, I thought they were having a battle between them to see who could smoke the most weed in a day.

Now you could always tell when Lil Kitty was high, due to the way she looked. She always looked like she was taking a shit, which made her look like she was constipated. She would still have that smile on her small ass face as if something was funny.

Now Chazz on the other hand, you couldn't tell if she was high or not because she always looked the same fuckin' spaced-out way. The only way you would know if she was high or not was because she would actually tell you. And that's if you were lucky enough to get her to open her mouth. You see, the moment she got high, she would just shut down and stare off into space as if she was talking to aliens or something.

I really wasn't aware of any other drugs in the group until that night in Jacksonville. The ladies were dancing at our new spot, making mad money.

Stephanie a.k.a. Suga Bear walked up to me with a serious ass look on her wide fuckin' ass face.

"Excuse me, Mike."

I was standing over by the bar area watching the ladies. I turned to her and replied, "Yes, Suga Bear."

"It's Peekachu."

"Okay, what's wrong with her lil' red ass now?" I asked.

"Follow me," she said. Walking in front of me, her thick red ass switched from side to side.

I followed her to the dressing room where Peekachu was lying on the floor, sweating and shaking with her mouth twitching from side to side, as if she was trying to say something, but couldn't the words out of her little ass mouth.

I looked over at Suga Bear, shocked out of my mind. "What in

# The Murder Queens

the hell is wrong with her Bobby Brown looking ass?" I asked.

"She took an X pill."

"And what in the hell is a fuckin' X pill, Suga Bear?" I looked at her and waited for an answer.

"It's the new drug everybody taking."

"It can't be, Suga Bear," I said, as sweat began to run down my face like I'd taken one too.

"Why is that, Mike?"

"Because I sure as hell ain't took one and don't plan on taking one," I said, "especially if it's gonna make me look the way her retarded ass is looking. She look like she done lost her-rabbit-ass mind. And why in the hell is she shaking like that? Is she fuckin' cold or something?" I looked at Peekachu wondering what the hell was going on.

"I think she's tweakin' right now," Suga Bear informed me.

"And what the hell is tweakin', Suga Bear?"

"I guess her body is having some type of chemical reaction. What you want me to do with her?" she asked.

"Oh, now you ask me? After she's half-dead?" I shook my head from side to side.

"See, Mike, you making jokes and shit. What do we do with her?" Suga Bear asked again. I could see the fear and nervousness in her eyes. It was almost as if she thought Peekachu wasn't gonna to make it.

"I don't know what you gonna do with her crazy looking ass, but what I do know is I'ma about to go back out here and watch my money!"

"C'mon, Mike," Suga Bear pleaded, "what do you want me to do?"

"Oh, so if you can ask for my opinion now, why couldn't you ask for it before she decided to take that damn X pill?"

"Mike, for real," she said louder, "she needs your help right now!"

"Man, put her lil' doped up, Bobby Brown looking ass in the back of the truck. Throw a blanket over her crazy looking ass so no one sees her out there. Don't want her scaring the shit out of people

261

with them big fuckin' ass eyes of hers. And by the way, Suga Bear, who gave her the fuckin' pill in the first place?" I asked. I wanted to know.

"I don't know, Mike."

"It doesn't matter anyway," I said, "whenever she comes down from her high, make sure you tell her shitty ass, she owes me a fuckin' fifty-dollar fine for not being able to perform."

"Don't worry, Mike, I'll pay it for her," Suga Bear said.

"Yeah, you should, since you're the one who gave her the damn pill, smart ass," I rolled my eyes at her right before she got one of the club bouncers to help her take Peekachu to the truck.

That weekend was a learning experience for the females, and myself, one that made me realize there were a few females I needed to pay very close attention to—if not, they could turn what I was trying to build into a fuckin' drug hangout for a bunch of doped up females.

After that weekend, things went back to normal for me the Hot Girls, or so I thought. I found out two of the cutest females in my group were beefing with one another. A beef between Lil Kitty and Chyna that had me a bit on edge. It had gotten to the point they weren't even talking to one another. I didn't like that kind of animosity between the females in the group. I wanted them to have a family-type relationship between them since we were always together.

The beef stemmed from Chyna calling my assistant manager, Dre, who was also Lil Kitty's boyfriend. Chyna would always call him to ask what we had planned for the week as if she didn't already know. Lil Kitty felt as though Chyna was being somewhat discourteous by her calling him all the time. I thought I had everything under control until the night of one of our shows. That particular night, it all came to an awful head between them.

We were all on the way to a show in Winter Haven, Florida. We stopped by the 7-eleven off John Young Parkway to get gas and snacks before getting onto Interstate 4. I was inside the store browsing the cold drinks. I happened to look to my right and saw small ass Lil Kitty standing with her hands on her small ass sexy hips. A very disturbed look was plastered on her cute ass face.

"Mike?"

"What, Lil Kitty?"

"I'm telling you right now, I'm so sick and tired of Chyna calling my man," she said in an angry tone.

"Kitty, she only called to ask him for the weekly schedule," I tried to tell her.

"Nah, Mike, she's calling my man with all kinds of non-sense, and I've had enough of it!"

"Kitty, you gotta let that shit go, boo," I said, trying to calm her suspicions, "it's nothing like that. Anyway, ain't you and Dre good?"

"Yes, we are, but I still don't like her red ass calling my muthafuckin' man."

"Kitty, he's my assistant manager so you can't trip out when one of the females call him for questions about our schedule."

"Well, she needs to be calling you instead of my man!"

"Listen, Kitty, let's just go make this money and we'll handle this once we get back in town."

"I don't know if that's gonna happen, Mike," she said, with fire in her beady eyes. She walked out of the store shaking them small ass hips of hers like she was a damn bear or something.

Not two minutes later, some guy came running inside the store screaming, "Hey, man, the Florida Hot Girls outside fighting in the parking lot. Man, them hoes going blow for blow outside!"

I ran outside and just like he'd said, Lil Kitty and Chyna were going at it like two professional boxers.

Now your girl Chyna outweighed Lil Kitty by at least twenty-five pounds, but she had her hands full with Lil Ms. Firecracker Kitty.

Chyna was throwing straight body punches while Lil Kitty threw straight jabs that connected to Chyna's beautiful face. After about ten minutes of those two fighting each other, I had to step in and break things up before two of my most beautiful females messed each other's face up.

Now if Kitty would have gotten ahold of Chyna's shirt and

pulled it off, man there would've been titty juice everywhere—something I would've loved to have witnessed, but I had bigger things on my mind at the time. There was money to be made and that little catfight was holding me up. Nobody actually won the fight because both females were skilled with her hands.

"Okay, break it up Chyna! Let her go, Lil Kitty! Y'all stop swinging before one of y'all hit me in my face," I shouted. All the other females in the group just stood around watching without even trying to break it up. "Stop Kitty! Let her go, Chyna! Move out of the way! Damn, why y'all fighting anyway," I yelled at them.

"She started it, Mike," Chyna said, "she just came out of the store and bum-rushed me from out of nowhere!" Chyna tried to fix her hair. Then she straightened her shirt that threatened to reveal the eighth wonders of the world, her big ass fuckin' titties.

"Nah, Mike! She tried me again after I came out of the store. She had her lil' red ass posted up all by my man. I told her ass not to try me like that and that's what she did! So I gave her red ass some of what she was looking for," Kitty yelled liked a mad woman. She swept her hand down the length of her hair and tugged at her ripped clothes.

"Okay, Dre, listen. Take Kitty home. The rest of you girls get in the truck. We got a show to get to."

"But, Mike, why do I have to go home? What about Chyna?" Lil Kitty asked, with tears about to well up in the bottom of her pretty lil eyes.

"Kitty, listen, boo, your hair is all fucked up and you're not gonna be able to dance looking like that."

"Okay, am I fired?" Kitty asked, trying to hold back her tears of anger.

"Nah, Lil Kitty. You're not fired. Just take the night off and be ready for the next show. Chyna, you and Kitty both just earned y'all selves a fine for fighting," I said. "And I should fine the rest of you ladies for letting them fight."

"Nah, Mike, we tried to break it up but them two was bent on fighting so we let them go at it," Sexy Redd said. I directed the ladies to get into the different vehicles that had been waiting on us.

# The Murder Queens

Whatever the case was that night, a few weeks later those two eventually worked out their differences and the group continued to blossom.

***

BY NOW, TIMES WERE GOOD. We were living damn good and we were definitely eating good. Money was coming in faster than we could count it. And females were coming from every direction trying to land them a spot on the team. I had to actually turn some ladies away due to having so many ready, and willing, to work.

The females who lived with Sexy Redd and me were enjoying life to the utmost. They were living in the lap of luxury. By now, Sexy Redd had even hired a nice cleaning service to work at the house since it was so damn big, and hard to keep clean.

But even with things going as good as they were, there was still something beyond the horizon waiting for the girls and me. We just weren't prepared for what was about to take place in our lives. But low and behold, you always have that guardian Angel on your side, and that's exactly what the Florida Hot Girls and I had, we just didn't know it at the time.

Michael Gallon

## CHAPTER TWENTY-FOUR
### PHYLLIS

It was Friday morning, another start to a beautiful weekend out of town, and I couldn't wait. Neither could the females who were already running around the house preparing to leave. There were about six females at the house, packed and ready to go, and a few more were enroute.

Chyna's big titty ass was in the kitchen telling the other girls how she wanted a manager position. Before she could even finish her sentence, Sexy Redd emerged from around the kitchen corner sipping on a tall cold glass of orange juice.

"Excuse me, ladies, since Chyna Doll here, seems to have everybody's best interest at hand, let me interject on her request. First, I thought the problem of any females in the group wanting to be one of the managers was solved with the exodus of yours truly, Ms. Kitty. Now, it seems like someone else wants to take a vacation right along with her short rat-looking ass," Sexy Redd said. The females gathered around listening to Chyna grouch about her status in the group.

"No," Entyce said. Her eyes looked as though they would pop out of her pear-shaped head. She sounded like the guy in the movie Friday when Debo asked him if he wanted to be knocked out like he had knocked his son out over his bike.

"Who in the hell is Ms. Kitty? Is there more than one Kitty in this group?' Chyna asked unknowingly. The rest of the females just stood there waiting on the display of fireworks between the two of them. Everyone knew the tension had built up in the air between the two high-natured females.

"Ms. Kitty was the first manager we had before Sexy Redd took over. But something happened to her when we went down to Miami for the photo shoot," Mignon said, as she walked over and stood next to Sexy Redd.

"My fault," Chyna said. She looked around at all the girls in the kitchen who had shifted over to Sexy Redd's side of the room.

"The only manager in this group, other than Mike and Dre, is me, and there's no need for another one at the present time."

"All I'm saying, Redd, is that I can bring a lot of females to this group, and I can set up a lot of shows for us," Chyna told her, "way more shows than any other female in this group," she said. She felt isolated from the entire group of girls who had stood beside her before Redd entered the room.

"That's all good, Chyna Doll, but all we need you to do is play your part. In other words, fall back, and if I need you to step up to the plate, I'll let Michael know, and he'll take it from there."

"So, let me understand this again," Chyna said, as if she were totally confused. "Sexy Redd are you saying you're the boss of the Florida Hot Girls?" she asked. Her tone revealed her attitude.

Sexy Redd took a firm stand. She prepared herself as if she was waiting for Chyna to jump at her.

"Now let me tell you and whoever else needs to know. I'm the bitch fucking the boss, and until another bitch comes in here and moves me out of that big ass fuckin' bed upstairs in that master bedroom, I run this shit! Now does any one of you females have a problem with that?" By now she had slammed her glass down on the marble countertop which caused glass to disintegrate everywhere.

"Maria, could you please come in here and clean this mess I've made in here. And if you ladies don't mind, would you all please put your bags inside of the truck. It's almost time for us to be leaving."

I was around the comer listening to Redd's little speech and thought to myself … *She don't play the radio. Shit, she just the type of female I need to help me run this group.*

After Sexy Redd had that brief meeting with the females that morning, the ride to Jacksonville was quiet and peaceful. We reached Jacksonville before I knew it. We got into town around two-thirty that Friday afternoon and went straight to the Golf Fair Flea Market. We shopped for a few hours before heading to our hotel. While at the Flea Market, the girls busied themselves shopping and letting the guys know the club they would be dancing at that weekend.

Me on the other hand, I was busy looking for more recruits to join my elite team of beautiful females.

"Hey, Redd."

"Yes, Michael."

"How much money do you have on you?"

"Why, Michael? What you need me to do?"

"Listen, I know you're about to pick you out a nice outfit for tonight."

"Yes, you already know."

"Well, pick me up something to wear also and I'll pay you back when we get to the hotel."

"Michael, you know you don't have to pay me back. What's mine is yours."

"Thanks, Redd. And what's mine is yours also."

"I already know, Michael. Now you go ahead and recruit some females while we go shopping." Just standing there observing her walk away made my manhood rise to the occasion. The way them tight ass jeans hugged her tight ass turned a nigga on. If Redd wasn't the finest female in my group, she had to be one of them. It seemed the more I fucked her, the finer she got.

Loyalty and honesty were Sexy Redd's strong points. If she wasn't with me, she wasn't with anyone else, and that's exactly what I liked about her. I never had to concern myself with the idea of her sleeping with any other guys. She wouldn't even let another guy see her vagina while she was dancing. She always said that was for my eyes, and my eyes only. And that's what made her the difference between the other nonessential females in my somewhat confused life.

So, standing there observing her walk away, I was once again tom between two beautiful females in my life—her and the fine, beautiful, Sharon Connolly. That is, until *she* walked in the side entrance of the mall.

I was standing by the hotdog stand ordering a slaw dog when the cutest lil' female in Jacksonville walked inside. She stood around five foot two and weighed around one hundred twenty-five pounds. Along with a set of 34C sized breasts, a nice, round, fat ass poked perfectly from her backside. Her skin complexion was like pure butter. A pair of small-framed glasses sat atop tiny nose and decorated her face just right. She looked educated, like she could've been someone's first grade school teacher. She was pure attractiveness in motion. I stared at her for about five minutes before I got up enough nerve to ensue her.

"Excuse me, beautiful."

"Hey," she said back to me. A great big smile graced her face. She must have noticed my charm immediately because she came right over to me without me asking her to.

"And what's your name, beautiful?" I asked, with my best Denzel Washington smile on my handsome face.

"Phyllis," she answered.

"Well, hello. The name is Michael. Nice to meet you," I said, as she smiled back at me.

"Nice to meet you, Michael," she said. I couldn't help but notice how elegant she looked.

*Now why in the hell would anybody want to name their child Phyllis, especially as fine as this lil' thick chick is,* I thought to myself. *Her name should have been Ms. Phat Da Def 'cause that's exactly what she is. Phyllis sounds like someone's grandma's name. Oh well,* I thought.

"So, Phyllis, do you have a job at the present moment?"

"No, I don't, sir, and I sure as hell need one right about now," she said, as she leaned on the counter of the hotdog stand.

"Well, let me ask you something, if you don't mind?"

"No, I don't, go ahead," she said. She gazed at me as if I was a brand-new one-hundred-dollar bill.

"Have you ever thought about dancing?"

"Somewhat," she answered, "it has crossed my mind," she added. "Why do you ask?"

I knew I had her then when she asked me *why*, so I quickly responded. "Well, I have a group of females known as the Florida Hot Girls. We travel all around, dancing at different clubs and doing bachelor parties."

"Y'all be some of everywhere," she said. Optimism filled her voice. "I heard about your group a few months ago," she told me.

"Oh, so you've heard of them? Cool, 'cause that's why in in town now. My girls actually have a show tonight at one of the local clubs in town. The ladies are in here now looking for some things to wear."

"Well, in that case, yeah, I would love to dance. How much will I get paid for dancing?" she asked, straight and to the point.

"Babygirl, that's totally up to you. It basically depends on how you dance and how you go about doing it," I answered truthfully.

"Okay, so how do I join the group?" She smiled and her eyes sparkled. I could feel John Boy trying to get my attention, but I willed him to be respectful. His introduction would come at a later date.

"I thought you would never ask, Phyllis. All I have to do is take you back to the hotel, check out that fine body of yours, and then, we can go from there," I explained.

"That's it? Well, I'm ready right now," she said. She clasped her hands together as the corners of her mouth turned upwards. A slight twinkle flashed around her pupils as she smiled in glee. She was delighted and so was I.

"My truck is parked right out front," I said. I extended my hand in front of me and welcomed her to follow my lead. "Let's ride, Miss Phyllis."

On the way back to the hotel we talked briefly about the possibility of her traveling with us. She was so stimulated about becoming a dancer, it seemed like that's all she'd ever wanted to be in life.

Twenty-five minutes later, we were walking into my hotel room.

"Wow, you guys are staying here?" she asked.

"Yeah, we always stay here when we're in town."

"I heard the rooms here were like $200.00 dollars a night."

"Yep, sounds about right," I agreed. "This one cost me a little bit more since it's the presidential suite. You like it?"

"Man, I fuckin' love it! I could stay here for the rest of my life," she said, as she looked around the room in sheer astonishment.

"Damn, Phyllis, you like it that much?" I laughed jokingly.

"Yes, gosh, look at your bed! It's big enough to make a person wanna roll up in it and stay all day and night."

While looking at her standing there, I thought to myself, *and that's exactly what I had in mind.*

"So, Michael, what do I need to do first?" she asked. I sat down on the huge bed. We were about to venture off into some serious love making.

"Well, all I have to do is check out your body to see how fine you really are."

"That's it? Well, all I have on is this dress 'cause I really don't like to wear any panties." Then she pulled off her dress, and just like she'd said, she didn't have on panties. Her titties stood out, on her chest, like ripe honey dew melons. She had her vagina shaved with just a small hairline going down the front and center of it. She looked as though she'd been born to be a dancer.

"Well, do you like what you see, Michael?" Before I could respond to her question, she placed her lips gently against mine.

"Don't say anything, Michael. I can tell by the erection in your pants, you like what you see." And just like that, she slowly unzipped my pants. I was so embarrassed when my manhood shot out of my pants like a loaded pistol, cocked and ready to fire. All I could do was just think to myself, *damn, it's good to be the manager of the Florida Hot Girls.*

## CHAPTER TWENTY-FIVE
### PURE INNOCENCE

As I stood there holding my manhood by the base, she looked at it, as its size grew fully erect manhood as if to say, 'damn, where you gonna put all of that at?'

"Damn, Michael if your dick gets any harder, it might knock down the walls of the hotel room," she said. She stared at the size of my erect penis, knowing it would soon be engulfed inside her lil' sexy ass.

"Nah, if I get up in that cute lil' vagina of yours, I'm gonna knock down *your* walls," I joked.

By now, I had to take charge of the situation because I didn't want to disappoint her by cumming too fast. So, I quickly hit her with a simple question to throw a curve in the game. "As cute and enticing as you are, do you mind if I savor a bit of that nice looking vagina of yours?"

"I'm gonna say yes because I like the way you put those beautiful words together. I love the style and finesse you seem to have about yourself. So, go ahead, it's all yours, Michael," she said, as she lay back on the big king size bed.

I smiled at the way she looked while sitting there stark naked. Then, I navigated her in to the position I wanted her in.

"Why don't you lay down on your back. Now relax and just open your legs wide enough so I can nibble on that beautiful vagina of yours." I sucked and slurped on her sweet tasting vagina as she softly rubbed my head. She lay back and relished the attention her tight lil' vagina was acquiring.

"Michael, could you turn your body so we can get in the 69 position?" she asked, in her cute, provocative voice.

"Now Phyllis, what do you know about the 69 position?" I asked, as I positioned my body so both of us could partake in the festivities.

"Michael, I may look young, but I know more than you think I know," she said, as she grabbed John Boy and placed him inside her warm mouth. She began to suck on him as though she was a newborn baby with a huge bottle in her mouth. That is, until John Boy began to swell up inside her mouth like a big ass Ball Park Frank. I could hear the sounds of her slobbering and sucking as she tried to prohibit it from going down her small throat.

I looked back at her. "You alright back there?" I asked. She tried to answer but my swollen manhood was inside of her small ass jaws.

She pulled my manhood out of her mouth by the base. "Damn this is a fuckin' mouth full."

"Yep, that's what they usually say," I told her. "Just wait until I get it up in your lil' ass stomach."

Then, I got out of the bed and laid her head toward the head of the bed. I opened her legs just wide enough to lay on top of her comfortably. As soon as I entered her, she tensed up and tried to catch her breath. Before she knew it, I had pushed every inch of my manhood up inside her tight vagina. She grabbed a hold of my back as if I was going too deep inside of her.

She placed her succulent mouth on my right ear lobe and whispered, "Michael, do you do all the girls like this? If so, I know you must have a lot of girl's head over heels about you and this big ass dick you're placing inside of my small ass stomach."

After fifteen minutes of me inserting her tight vagina, she was having her first of many orgasms. Ten minutes later, she was scratching the shit out of my back. By now, I had her legs up on my shoulders. I guess you could say, I was balls deep up inside of her.

"I've never had this much dick up inside of me like this, she said. "I can feel you all the way up in my fuckin' chest, Michael."

"Girl, stop," I said. While she continued screaming, I continued lunging inside of her lil'sweet ass. You can say, I was bent on teaching her a lesson for not wearing any panties around me.

After about forty-five minutes of nonstop fuckin', she thought it was over. I pulled my dripping-wet manhood out of her swollen vagina. As I stood there butt naked, and soaking wet from perspiration, I looked at the way her vagina lips were all swollen up, due to the beating I'd just put on her young, tender ass.

"Go ahead and turn around," I said, "so I can make love to you from the back."

# The Murder Queens

She looked at me with eyes as big as grandma's country flap jacks and said, "Are you fuckin' serious? You mean to tell me you ain't came yet? Because I have. At least five times already," she said.

"Okay, I'll cum in a few minutes. Just turn over and put your head right here inside this pillow so the other hotel guests don't hear you screaming."

When I finally got back up inside of her, I could feel her vagina muscles grabbing my manhood. By now, I was in full stride, stroking her back and forth, and then going around and 'round, up inside of her tight ass vagina. She turned her head around and looked at me with those cute brown eyes.

"If you keep fuckin' me like this, I might not be able to dance at the club tonight!"

"Just a few more minutes and I promise I'll be done."

Thirty minutes later, I was erupting inside of her.

"Now see, Michael, you done nutted all up inside of me and I'm not on any birth control," she said. She fell out of the bed and stumbled to the bathroom. She sat on the toilet and tried to push all of my semen out of her so she wouldn't become fertilized with my child.

"Don't worry, beautiful, you're good. I'm not trying to have any kids any time soon. And besides, you are only fertile for twenty-four hours after your last period," I said. I walked in the bathroom and saw her fine ass sitting on the toilet, trying to urinate so my semen would come out of her.

She looked up and said to me, "Michael I think something is wrong with me because I can't feel my legs!"

"Don't worry, you will in a few minutes," I told her. "That seems to happen to a lot of females after they finish making love to me."

She smiled at me and said, "Okay, Michael, did I pass the test?"

I bent down and kissed her, oh so lightly, on her lips. "Why of course you did. You were elegant as you laid there and had hot, passionate, sexual intercourse with me. You passed the test as soon as you took off that dress and I saw that fine ass body of yours."

She stood up from the toilet after wiping herself clean and kissed me as if we were two passionate lovers in love.

"You really fucked the shit out of my lil' ass. Can we take a quick nap before we go back to the Flea Market?" she asked, as she stood back and looked at our reflections in the bathroom mirror.

"We really don't have much time. We still have to meet up with the girls by six so we can have dinner. And by the way, what size do you wear? I'll have one of the females pick you up an outfit for tonight's show."

She stood there for a minute, still looking in the mirror. "You know, Michael, we would make a nice couple if we were ever to pursue such a thing. And I wear a size seven," she said, as she bent over to turn the water on in the shower.

I stood there for a minute while I took in the sight of her bent over the bathtub. I wanted to infiltrate her once again but I had already pounded the poor girl for at least an hour. I knew most females couldn't take that much affliction. So, I ushered her into the shower with me and washed off my scent off of her. I also washed her scent off of me so Sexy Redd wouldn't smell it when I met up with her at the restaurant.

After we took a nice hot shower, I placed a call to Sexy Redd. I told her to have the girls catch a cab so they could meet Phyllis and me at Red Lobster once they were done shopping.

"So how was she, Michael?" Sexy Redd asked, before I could hang up the phone.

"What are you talking about, Redd?"

"Mike, listen, I've been with you since day one, so please don't try to insult my intelligence. I know damn well when your black ass is up to something!"

"Okay, Redd, she was all right. I think she can make some serious money with the right teacher.''

"Okay, I hear that but my inquest to you is did you fuck her?"

"Redd, I'll talk to you when I see you at the restaurant."

"Alright, Michael. It's like ten of us here, so that means we're gonna have to take two cabs."

"Just tell the cab company you got at least ten people in your crew so you'll need a van."

"Don't worry, Mike, I'll get us there. I know what to do."

"By the way Redd, pick her up something nice to dance in tonight, please."

"What's her size?"

"She said a size seven."

"Okay, Michael. I'll see you soon," Redd said. "I love you."

"Love you too, Redd!" I hung up with Sexy Redd. As Phyllis stood behind me and dried off, she looked like she could stand another round of love making.

"Well, I guess, there won't be any relationship between us," she said, as she put her dress back on, and over that beautiful vagina of hers.

"Now why do you say that, beautiful?" I asked.

"Whatever, Michael. I just heard you tell that female you loved her. I don't want to be nobody's side chick."

"I can understand that. You deserve way more than that," I said, as I walked over to put my clothes back on.

As we got dressed, neither of us said another word. Truth be told, Phyllis was a beautiful girl and I possessed feelings the minute she placed my manhood inside her mouth.

On the way to Red Lobster, she was even more excited about being a member of the group. She was about to eat at Red Lobster and meet the world-Famous Florida Hot Girls at the same time.

We pulled into the parking lot and I could see the girls at the table. They looked out of the window, trying to see how the new girl looked.

We entered the restaurant and I heard Chyna's mouth as soon as we got inside. "She alright but she ain't all that," she said as we walked in.

"Damn, Chyna do you have to be so fuckin' contradictory all the damn time?" Mignon asked. She told Phyllis to sit next to her.

"That's right, Chyna. Damn, she's new. Can you be a little more courteous please," Sexy Redd said, as Phyllis sat down next to Mignon.

"Yeah, y'all right. I'm sorry. Hi, I'm Chyna, and this—

As Chyna introduced Phyllis to the rest of the girls, Sexy Redd quickly grabbed me by my arm.

"So, I'm gonna ask your ball-face ass one more fuckin' time, Mr. want-to-fuck-everything-that-moves, Did you have sexual intercourse with her?"

"Yes, Redd! Damn, why is it so important that you know if I fucked her or not?"

She grabbed me under my short ass neck and looked me directly in my eyes. "So, I don't have this lil' hood chick all in my face and shit smiling, trying to get to know me and she done fucked my fuckin' man, that's why!" She let go of my collar which she had just wrinkled up. She walked to the restroom and left me standing there. I felt like I had just shot and killed someone.

Now I understood why she wanted to know. It was a girl-code thing. Who would want to be in someone's face and they had slept with your significant other? Now one thing about Sexy Redd was she had class and style, and most of all, she had pride. The secret of it all was that she knew how to hide it. You would never know if she was mad at you unless she told you.

She came back out and walked by me. "Well, I hope you enjoyed it because it's going to be a while before you get back up in this pussy here, playa," she said with irony.

"Damn, that's how you feel? C'mon, Redd, don't even act like that. You know I had to check out her body."

"Yeah, Mike, you did, but you didn't have to fuck her, did you?"

"But it wasn't even like that. You see one thing led to another and then it just happened."

"Mike, your black ass wanted it to happen as soon as your black ass walked out of the mall with her lil' tender ass. It ain't like you walked outside and fell off in her pussy just 'cause it was there, nigga."

She was absolutely right. Who in the hell was I fooling? I was dead wrong, but shit, I couldn't help it. She was fine as a muthafucker. Once she pulled off that lil' skirt and I saw that pretty

278

ass vagina along with her beautiful face, I was turned on. I had to have her just to see how good her vagina was.

While I stood there looking for something else to say, Phyllis slid her fine ass over into our argument. "Excuse me, you're Sexy Redd, right?"

"Yes, honey, I'm Sexy Redd. What can I do for you?"

"Strawberry told me to ask—

"I know honey," Redd said, cutting her short, "you don't have any money, right?"

"No, ma'am!"

"You don't have to call me ma'am, sweet heart. Don't worry about it. Go ahead and order whatever it is you want to eat. Michael here is going to pay for it since he fucked you earlier. And always remember, baby," Redd said, "always get your money up front when you let a man get between your beloved lil' legs, mama."

"Thank you. And by the way, you are so gorgeous," Phyllis told her.

"Thank you, boo," Redd said. Phyllis walked back to the table with the rest of the girls. Sexy Redd looked at me and shook her head.

"Oh, by the way, your outfit came to like two hundred dollars, Michael. And hers," Redd pointed at Phyllis, "came to two hundred fifty dollars. I want my fuckin' money, Michael. And you better hope her little country ass don't eat that much!" We smiled at her cockiness as we joined the rest of the group to order our food.

"Can I have your attention, please, I would like to give a toast to our newest member to the Hot Girl family." Redd stood her proper acting ass up and said, "And by the way, we definitely have to change your country ass name." Everyone fell out laughing, including Phyllis.

As we ate and laughed with each other we'd almost forgotten we had a show in just a few hours.

\*\*\*

THAT NIGHT, WE DANCED AT FRANKS CLUB. The crowd was nice, and the niggas had mad money to spend. I had just what they wanted: them badass women from Orlando, Florida. By now, everyone was talking about them. Frank noticed some of the new females I'd added to the group since the last time we'd been at his place.

He really liked Phyllis. He watched her flow while on stage as she danced on the pole. He turned to me as I sat drinking on my cold glass of Pepsi. "Mike, who is that new lil' cute thing you got up there on my stage?" Frank asked.

"I don't know her stage name yet. I met her earlier at the Flea Market and she's been with us ever since. Sexy Redd came over to the table as Frank and I were conversing about a stage name for Phyllis.

"Hello, Frank," Redd said.

"Well, hello, to you too, Sexy Redd."

"Her name is Innocence," Redd said.

"Whose name?" Frank asked Redd.

"The new broad on stage you just asked Michael here about," Redd answered.

"Damn, how did you know I asked him her name?" Frank asked Redd curiously.

"I read your lips from across the way, Frank."

"Damn, Mike, she's good." Frank laughed and shook his head in amazement.

"Yes, she is. Hell, I didn't even know she was observing us talk."

"Yeah, Frank, Mike said she's pretty good," Redd said in a sarcastic tone. "She's one of your local girls here in town. Yeah, Mr. Mike her gave her an interview earlier by fuckin' the poor girl's brains out back at our hotel. Didn't you, Mike? Why don't you tell Frank how good her lil twat-twat was."

Frank couldn't help but laugh as Redd continued to pull me through the mud. I just sat there and let her vent as I continued to sit there looking like I was the innocent victim.

"Oh, by the way, Mr. Want-to-Rescue-Everybody," you know ole girl doesn't have any clothes with her. And please don't think that I'm going to buy her any."

"No, I don't expect for you to buy her any clothes. You know the deal. They make their own money for their own clothes."

Frank threw a few dollars at Ms. Innocence as she danced on stage doing her thing. After a few songs, it looked as though Ms. Innocence knew exactly what she was doing. Frank continued to fill the stage up with ones. He threw them all at her which was a surprise to me, because Frank rarely threw money at any of the girls. He was always about making money instead of throwing it away. But I guess ole girl must have struck a nerve in Frank by the sheer beauty of her appearance.

Innocence walked off stage and came over to me. "Excuse me, Mike," she said as she smiled at Frank.

"Yes, beautiful, what can I help you with?" I asked.

"Here you go. This is the money for my outfit," she said as she continued smiling at the both of us.

"Nah, ma, you keep that. As good as that pussy was, and the way you took all that pressure, that outfit is on me," I told her.

"You better not let your girl hear you say that," she responded, with her genuine smile.

"Hear what, young lady?" Sexy Redd walked up on us just as the words had left Innocence's mouth.

"Nothing, I was just telling Michael about the money for the outfit that you bought me earlier today."

"Girl, you good. Always make a nigga pay for your clothes, especially if you giving up the pussy. Nothing is free, including your precious lil twat-twat ma." She smiled at Sexy Redd when she pointed down to what was between her legs.

"Thank you, Sexy Redd," she said.

*I'm glad as hell Sexy Redd didn't put her hands on me for fuckin' her man*, Innocence thought.

Redd gave her a hug and then told her to go and make her money. She told her if she needed anything else to let her know. Now, I could see why the girls in the group looked up to Sexy Redd as their leader. She was always the one to admit when she was wrong or rude in any kind of way. She had a real take-charge attitude that made the girls feel comfortable around her.

That night, the girls became closer to one another. By now,

there were at least sixty girls in the group and new ones were trying to get in every day. But the group of girls I had with me that night had developed a bond between them that just couldn't be broken.

After the club that morning, it was breakfast as usual at the nearest Denny's. The ladies were hyped about the money they'd made and couldn't wait to go shopping the next day.

Sexy Redd and I sat alone in a booth near the back of the restaurant. "Michael, I may have overreacted a little earlier today when I saw you with the new broad."

"Oh, you realize that now." I smiled.

"Shut up, Mike, I'm not finished," she said, "but as I was saying, I had to try and perceive why I was getting upset about you being with her. Then it hit me as to how much I really care for your black ass. I guess what I'm really trying to say is if you continue to really put it on these young ladies, their feelings are gonna get involved and then they're not gonna wanna pay you at the end of the night."

She was definitely right. After having sexual intercourse with them, they would feel as though they didn't owe me anything since they had already given me free sex.

*Oh no, we can't have that,* I thought, as chewed on a piece of hickory smoked bacon.

"So, from now on, Redd, I'm not gonna let my manhood come between you and my job anymore."

"Mike, you mean that now, but as soon as another pretty face walks through that door, you're gonna want her just like all the rest. So, save the bullshit for the birds," she said and rolled her eyes. "Just always remember this: don't lose sight of what you have in front of you for something you might think is better down the road." She got up and walked away and her hips twisted from side to side.

I sat back and gazed at her walk from table to table, acquiring my bar fee from the females. My mind went a drift thinking about how nice it was to be the manager of all those beautiful females. There was just something else bothering me. I just couldn't put my finger on it at the time.

## CHAPTER TWENTY-SIX
## YOU CLOWNS TRYING TO ROB ME

We spent the rest of the weekend in Jacksonville, shopping and just hanging out. The girls danced at Frank's club that Saturday night. They expected a nice crowd since they had been promoting all day at the Arlington Mall. The promoting really paid off for all the females that weekend because they all made well over three-thousand dollars apiece. We returned to Orlando around six that Sunday evening, and as usual, I dropped the females off at their individual homes. When I got to Chyna's place of residence, Innocence got out with her.

"Okay, Innocence where do you think you're going?" I asked, as she helped Chyna secure her bags.

"She's staying with me, Mike," Chyna responded with an attitude.

"Chyna, I wanted her to stay with the girls and I," I replied.

"There's already enough of the girls staying at your place, Mike, and besides, Sexy Redd already said it would be okay for her to stay with me."

"Okay, Chyna," I agreed, "she's your responsibility, so if anything happens to her it's on your head," I said, as I pulled off mad and frustrated. I didn't like the fact that Innocence had decided to stay with Chyna without consulting me.

I really didn't like the females to hang with each other after a long weekend. I didn't want anything to happen between them that resulted to a fallout. It only caused trouble by putting me in the middle when they no longer want to work with one another. In other words, they would want me to leave whoever they fell out with home. It was just a bad idea for the girls to be around each other, unless we were at work.

While driving away from Chyna's house, I couldn't wait to get home. At this point, I was just getting used to our new neighborhood. However, something just didn't feel right, especially since I had the new chick, Jasmine, with us.

It was just something about her that always left me with a very bad vibe. She was a friend of one of the girls in the group by the name of Do-Dirty. Do-Dirty had got fired for trying to steal Nicole's money bag one night after leaving the club. Jasmine was staying with us until she could make enough money to find her own apartment. And that was where things had gone south for everyone who stayed at the house.

We had just pulled up to the guard gate when I rolled down my window to put my security code in. I noticed there wasn't a guard at the guard gate.

"That's strange, Redd," I said.

"What's that, bae?" She turned away from what she was looking at through her passenger window.

"There's always a guard at the gate but I don't see one tonight."

"Oh yeah, you're right, she said, after she noticed the gate had been left unsecured.

I pulled into my driveway and pushed the button on the garage door opener before proceeding to drive inside the garage.

Within minutes, the ladies and I were inside the house. We put our bags down and proceeded to settle in.

Out of nowhere, I got hit across the side of my face. I fell to the ground, holding my jaw in sheer pain. Sexy Redd had gone through the den area and somehow managed to get upstairs without being noticed.

"Get down and stay down!" the heavy-voiced man said as he stood up over me with a chrome plated .380 pointed at my dome. "You bitches put your hands behind your fuckin' back and don't fuckin' move! Tie their asses up," he yelled to one of his henchmen."

I rolled over to four masked gunmen standing inside my house. I looked over and realized Mignon, Strawberry, Nicole, Entyce, and Jasmine had all been tied up.

Still somewhat dazed, I thought to myself, *where in the hell is Sexy Redd?*

The leader of the masked group sat me up in one of the dining room chairs. "Okay, Mike, this can be over in a few minutes, or we can take all fuckin' night kicking your ass and fuckin' these pretty ass bitches since you don't never let nobody fuck 'em. Your black ass know what time it is, nigga, so let's not waste each other's time or get nobody killed over a few measly dollars."

"Hey, man, hold up," one of the henchmen yelled to the leader of the group. "It's supposed to be six bitches in here with this fuck ass nigga. Where that bitch they call Sexy Redd?"

The first guy turned around to poor Strawberry and asked her. "Where is Sexy Redd, bitch?"

"I don't know who you're talking about," she said with her head looking downward. *WHAP!* He slapped poor Strawberry so fuckin' hard across her red face, she fell to the floor. Blood squirted from the right side of her lip and face, as tears of anger filled her eyes.

"C'mon, man, you didn't have to slap the shit out of her like that!" I yelled.

"Shut the fuck up, nigga! I'ma slap yo' punk ass just like that, if that bitch of yours don't show the fuck up in five fuckin' minutes," he barked in my face.

"Man, she ain't here! You don't see her, do you?" I snapped.

*SWAT!* The next thing I know, the big, black ass muthafucker slapped me across my face with his pistol and my jaw began to swell instantaneously.

"Man, listen, if it's the money you want, man, y'all can have it!" I said. "Just untie me and I'll get you the money," I told him, trying to bargain with him. He instructed a slim nigga to go upstairs to check for any other females who might've been in the house.

Doing as he'd been told, the slim guy quickly ran up the stairs carrying a rusty, old ass gun that looked like his grandfather might've given it to him. Once he was up there, I could hear his footsteps as he walked from room to room, looking for anyone else who might've been hiding inside the house.

"Now, Mike, back to you, pimp," the lead man said, "we understand there's a safe in here somewhere." He paused and looked around as if it would magically fall out of the air. "We want everything in it, plus all the cash these pretty ass hoes made over the weekend. I heard they made quite a bit," he said, "somewhere in the neighborhood of three-thousand dollars apiece, right?"

As I listened to him talk facts, my mind raced. *Damn, this nigga even know how much money everybody made over the weekend. One of my girls must have set us up.*

By now, the ladies were crying their eyes out—everyone except Jasmine.

"Hey, we don't wanna die over no fuckin' money. Y'all niggas can have this shit," Nicole said angrily. Her face was wet with tears and her pretty face was smeared with snot and makeup.

"Mike, please do something," Strawberry said. The blood from her lip oozed down her chin, and the mascara she'd been wearing made her look like she had racoon eyes. Her lip grew bigger by the minute and she reminded me of Eddie Murphy in the movie "The Nutty Professor".

"Y'all bitches stop crying and shut the fuck up," the gunman said. He looked from one girl to another, which caused his eyes to move around rapidly. "Y'all don't be acting like this when y'all be taking our fuckin' money in the strip club and shit," he said. He pointed his gun at Strawberry's head. One of the guys sounded so fucking familiar, and he was the same one who looked at the girls and unzipped his pants.

"Man, let me put this dick in one of these bitch's mouth, since Mike don't let these hoes do no fuckin' after the club." He laughed. "Let me see how this bitch with the fat, red ass can suck on this big ass dick," he said, as he stepped closer to Nicole. "Open your fuckin' mouth, trick!"

"Muthafucker, I'll take a bullet to the head before I suck your little ass, dick-in-the-booty-having-nigga, bitch," Nicole said with anger in her voice. She coughed up some yellowish-colored phlegm and spat at his black ass.

"Hold on, nigga, we came here to get this bread, not fuck these hoes," the leader of the group said to his partner. His partner still had his limp manhood out. He tried to get it up so he could make Nicole take him up on his offer.

"Man, after we get this money, I'ma fuck that little red, loud mouth bitch in her fat lil' ass!" the familiar voice said, as he zipped up his Wrangler jeans. He wiped the phlegm off that had landed right on top of his shoe.

Realizing how long the slim dude was taking upstairs, the leader of the group yelled out to him. "Yo', nigga, you found anything yet?"

"No, not yet!" Right after he answered, a loud, thunderous *thud* sounded from upstairs. The floor above shook and a picture fell from the wall. The skinny nigga came tumbling down the stairs hollering in agonizing pain as he hit the bottom of the stairwell.

"What the fuck!" the leader of the group shouted. His eyes bulged from his head, as he gazed at his partner lying on the floor. When he bent down to assist his homie, Sexy Redd came running the stairs, taking them three at a time, with a chrome .380 automatic aimed and loaded. She came down so fast, it was as if she'd had wings.

"Drop your muthafuckin' guns or I'ma split your Goddamn heads in two like a fuckin' watermelon," she shouted, as she simultaneously jumped over the guy.

Perplexed, they dropped their weapons.

The guy on the floor yelled out to his homies. "Man, this pretty ass bitch broke my fuckin' jaw and pushed me down the fuckin' stairs. I think my fuckin' leg is broken too," he said, as his leg lay twisted up by his head. "The rest of my body is facing another fuckin' direction," he said in disbelief, and began to cry.

"All you broke ass niggas move your black asses over there out of the muthafuckin' way," Sexy Redd yelled out to them. "Baby, are you alright?" she asked. She handed me the chrome .380 automatic, and I pointed it at the nigga who had hit me in my fuckin' head.

"Yeah, boo. Untie the girls." As I was getting up, Redd untied Strawberry. Strawberry walked over to the guy who had slapped her and slapped the shit out of his black ass before she spit in his face.

"Damn, Strawberry, wait until the nigga takes his mask off before you spit in his face!"

"Oh, my bad. I ain't never been robbed before, Mike," she said, as she bent over and picked up the rusty, old ass gun that had fallen from the nigga's hand.

"Alright, you busta-ass niggas. Take off your masks and keep your hands where I can see them," I demanded.

To my surprise, it was the niggas from the carwash. Lil Q, Badass Mikey, and the pussy-eating-ass nigga who went by the name Goldmouth. I don't know why they even called him that, 'cause that nigga didn't have a gold tooth nowhere in his fuckin' nasty ass mouth.

The guy who was lying on the floor crying about his leg was called Skinny Pimp. First of all, his breath smelled like he had eaten two shit sandwiches for breakfast, and he had no teeth in his fuckin' stank ass mouth. I looked at him crying on the floor.

"Man, why they call you Skinny Pimp?" he turned over slightly, as he moaned in pain.

"Cause I used to pimp your mother, nigga!" he said back to me, as he held his broken jaw.

"Now you didn't have to go there," I said calmly. "Do you even know who my mother is?" Before he could respond to my question, Sexy Redd kicked him so fuckin' hard, he farted and passed out.

Strawberry threw his rusty piece of a gun at him while he lay there on the floor in a dead sleep.

"Why did you do that Strawberry?" Sexy Redd asked, with a surprised look on her face.

"Man, that wasn't a fuckin gun! That was some old ass piece of scrap iron made to look like a fuckin' gun!" Strawberry said, as she kicked Skinny Pimp in his back.

"So, you young cats were just gonna come up in here and rob a brother and his employees, huh?" I asked.

"Mike, you have to believe me when I tell you, it was some of your own dancers who set this fucked idea in motion! They told us you always up in here flossing about how much money you be making, and how all the females be up in here walking around butt ass naked!"

"So, that gives you the right to come in my crib and slap one of my dancers in the face so hard she probably won't be able to dance for a whole fuckin' month? And then cause her to bleed all over my ten-thousand-dollar Persian rug? Not to mention, you tried to rob them of what they made over the weekend."

Sexy Redd was standing to the side of me with her chrome .45 pointed at them. "Not to mention, Mike, they were going to kill all of us after they robbed us!"

"Mike, that was them niggas and them silly ass hoes of yours," Badass Mikey said. "I told their dumb asses yesterday this was a bad idea. But, nah, they had to listen to them stupid ass bitches. Mike, man just let me go, and I promise I won't say anything to nobody. I swear on my mama," he said.

I just looked at him and thought, *man, you must think I'm stupid or something?*

"Nah, Mike, this one wanted to fuck me in the ass," Nicole said, and kicked him right smack dab in his nuts, with her heels on.

"Baby, just let me do these clown ass niggas now and get it over with," Redd said. She pointed her gun at the leader of the group.

"Hold on, Redd, we can't just kill all four of them right now," I told her. "Hell, you don't want Detective Protho and his tall lanky ass partner to come hanging around here, do you?" I asked.

"Yeah, you right. So, what do we do with them then?"

"I tell you niggas what we're going to do. Bring me the females who helped you set this bullshit up. When you do that, we'll dead this and just forget it ever happened," I said.

"Hell, nah, Mike!" Mignon screamed, "if we let these fuck ass niggas leave, how sure are we they won't come back to finish us off?" The whole time she was standing there talking, the guy they called Lil Q had this shitty ass grin on his small ass face.

"Yo', lil' homie, why you all over there smiling and shit?" I yelled to him. Sexy Redd kept her pistol on all of them.

"Nah, it's like your lil' shorty right there is sexy as fuck. I just wanna fuck the shit out of her right here in front of everybody," he said, while standing there holding his dick in his hand, as if she had agreed to fuck him.

"Nigga, I don't do punk ass bitches who go around robbing people for a living!" Then, Mignon spat in his face too. He just wiped it off with his hand. Then, he licked it as he continued to smile at her.

"That's exactly what I like for a bitch to do. Spit on my dick while she choking on all this meat," he said and laughed out loud.

Mignon grabbed one of the guns that was off to the side of the countertop and pointed it straight at Lil Q's fuckin' head.

"Say something else, lil' ass nigga and I'll take your head clean off!" He laughed and tried to say something else.

Then, Skinny Pimp woke up. "Man, just shut the hell up before we all get killed. 'Cause if they shoot one of us, they gonna have to kill all of us!" Sexy Redd kicked that nigga right back to sleep. This time she kicked him so hard he shit all over himself.

"Damn, Redd, you do know someone is going to have to clean that nasty ass shit up, right?"

"Yeah, one of his fuck ass homies are gonna clean that shit up with they fuckin' shirt."

"Okay, this is how we're gonna do this, Goldmouth. Here is the number to call when you find me those bitches who crossed my girls and me. You have exactly one week to come up with those females. If not, Redd here will be paying each one of your mothers a fuckin' visit to leave them a black rose to remember you by.

"Nah, instead of paying them a visit, baby, I'ma buy their mothers a black fuckin' dress so she can wear it to their funeral!"

Goldmouth held up his head. "Now why there gotta be a funeral, beautiful?" I slapped him right across his face for slapping me and caused one of his teeth to fly out of his mouth and onto my kitchen floor.

"That's for you dumbass niggas fuckin' with the Florida Hot Girls, bitch!" I told him. "Now pick up your fuckin' tooth and get the fuck out of here before I start popping rounds off in y'all dirty muthafuckin' asses. Bitch niggas!"

To Be Continued…
The Murder Queens 2
Coming Soon

**Lock Down Publications and Ca$h Presents** assisted publishing packages.

**BASIC PACKAGE** $499
Editing
Cover Design
Formatting

**UPGRADED PACKAGE** $800
Typing
Editing
Cover Design
Formatting

**ADVANCE PACKAGE** $1,200
Typing
Editing
Cover Design
Formatting
Copyright registration
Proofreading
Upload book to Amazon

**LDP SUPREME PACKAGE** $1,500
Typing
Editing
Cover Design
Formatting
Copyright registration
Proofreading
Set up Amazon account
Upload book to Amazon
Advertise on LDP Amazon and Facebook page

***Other services available upon request. Additional charges may apply

**Lock Down Publications**
**P.O. Box 944**
**Stockbridge, GA 30281-9998**
**Phone # 470 303-9761**

## Submission Guideline

Submit the first three chapters of your completed manuscript to ldpsubmissions@gmail.com, subject line: Your book's title. The manuscript must be in a .doc file and sent as an attachment. Document should be in Times New Roman, double spaced and in size 12 font. Also, provide your synopsis and full contact information. If sending multiple submissions, they must each be in a separate email.

Have a story but no way to send it electronically? You can still submit to LDP/Ca$h Presents. Send in the first three chapters, written or typed, of your completed manuscript to:

**LDP: Submissions Dept**
**Po Box 944**
**Stockbridge, Ga 30281**

*DO NOT send original manuscript. Must be a duplicate.*

Provide your synopsis and a cover letter containing your full contact information.

Thanks for considering LDP and Ca$h Presents.

Michael Gallon

## <u>NEW RELEASES</u>

THE COCAINE PRINCESS 3 by KING RIO
THE BILLIONAIRE BENTLEYS 3 by VON DIESEL
COKE GIRLZ by ROMELL TUKES
VICIOIUS LOYALTY 2 by KINGPEN
THE STREETS WILL NEVER CLOSE 3 by K'AJJI
THE MURDER QUEENS by MICHAEL GALLON

# The Murder Queens

# Michael Gallon

KINGPIN KILLAZ IV

STREET KINGS III

PAID IN BLOOD III

CARTEL KILLAZ IV

DOPE GODS III

**Hood Rich**

SINS OF A HUSTLA II

**ASAD**

RICH $AVAGE II

**By Martell Troublesome Bolden**

YAYO V

Bred In The Game 2

**S. Allen**

CREAM III

THE STREETS WILL TALK II

**By Yolanda Moore**

SON OF A DOPE FIEND III

HEAVEN GOT A GHETTO II

**By Renta**

LOYALTY AIN'T PROMISED III

**By Keith Williams**

I'M NOTHING WITHOUT HIS LOVE II

SINS OF A THUG II

TO THE THUG I LOVED BEFORE II

IN A HUSTLER I TRUST II

**By Monet Dragun**

QUIET MONEY IV

EXTENDED CLIP III

THUG LIFE IV

By **Trai'Quan**

# The Murder Queens

THE STREETS MADE ME IV

By **Larry D. Wright**

IF YOU CROSS ME ONCE II

By **Anthony Fields**

THE STREETS WILL NEVER CLOSE IV

By **K'ajji**

HARD AND RUTHLESS III

KILLA KOUNTY III

By **Khufu**

MONEY GAME III

By **Smoove Dolla**

JACK BOYS VS DOPE BOYS II

A GANGSTA'S QUR'AN V

COKE GIRLZ II

By **Romell Tukes**

MURDA WAS THE CASE II

**Elijah R. Freeman**

THE STREETS NEVER LET GO II

By **Robert Baptiste**

AN UNFORESEEN LOVE III

By **Meesha**

KING OF THE TRENCHES III

by **GHOST & TRANAY ADAMS**

MONEY MAFIA II

LOYAL TO THE SOIL III

By **Jibril Williams**

QUEEN OF THE ZOO II

By **Black Migo**

THE BRICK MAN IV

THE COCAINE PRINCESS IV

# Michael Gallon

**By King Rio**

VICIOUS LOYALTY III

**By Kingpen**

A GANGSTA'S PAIN II

**By J-Blunt**

CONFESSIONS OF A JACKBOY III

**By Nicholas Lock**

GRIMEY WAYS II

**By Ray Vinci**

KING KILLA II

**By Vincent "Vitto" Holloway**

BETRAYAL OF A THUG II

**By Fre$h**

THE MURDER QUEENS II

**By Michael Gallon**

## Available Now

RESTRAINING ORDER **I & II**

By **CA$H & Coffee**

LOVE KNOWS NO BOUNDARIES **I II & III**

By **Coffee**

RAISED AS A GOON I, II,  III & IV

BRED BY THE SLUMS I, II, III

# The Murder Queens

BLAST FOR ME I & II

ROTTEN TO THE CORE I II III

A BRONX TALE I, II, III

DUFFLE BAG CARTEL I II III IV V VI

HEARTLESS GOON I II III IV V

A SAVAGE DOPEBOY I II

DRUG LORDS I II III

CUTTHROAT MAFIA I II

KING OF THE TRENCHES

By **Ghost**

LAY IT DOWN **I & II**

LAST OF A DYING BREED I II

BLOOD STAINS OF A SHOTTA I & II III

By **Jamaica**

LOYAL TO THE GAME I II III

LIFE OF SIN I, II III

By **TJ & Jelissa**

BLOODY COMMAS I & II

SKI MASK CARTEL I  II & III

KING OF NEW YORK I II,III IV V

RISE TO POWER I II III

COKE KINGS I II III IV V

BORN HEARTLESS I II III IV

KING OF THE TRAP I II

By **T.J. Edwards**

IF LOVING HIM IS WRONG...I & II

LOVE ME EVEN WHEN IT HURTS I II III

By **Jelissa**

WHEN THE STREETS CLAP BACK I & II III

THE HEART OF A SAVAGE I II III

299

# Michael Gallon

MONEY MAFIA

LOYAL TO THE SOIL I II

By **Jibril Williams**

A DISTINGUISHED THUG STOLE MY HEART I II & III

LOVE SHOULDN'T HURT I II III IV

RENEGADE BOYS I II III IV

PAID IN KARMA I II III

SAVAGE STORMS I II III

AN UNFORESEEN LOVE I II

By **Meesha**

A GANGSTER'S CODE I &, II III

A GANGSTER'S SYN I II III

THE SAVAGE LIFE I II III

CHAINED TO THE STREETS I II III

BLOOD ON THE MONEY I II III

A GANGSTA'S PAIN

By **J-Blunt**

PUSH IT TO THE LIMIT

By **Bre' Hayes**

BLOOD OF A BOSS **I, II, III, IV, V**

SHADOWS OF THE GAME

TRAP BASTARD

By **Askari**

THE STREETS BLEED MURDER **I, II & III**

THE HEART OF A GANGSTA I II& III

By **Jerry Jackson**

CUM FOR ME I II III IV V VI VII VIII

An **LDP Erotica Collaboration**

BRIDE OF A HUSTLA **I  II & II**

THE FETTI GIRLS **I, II& III**

# The Murder Queens

CORRUPTED BY A GANGSTA I, II III, IV
BLINDED BY HIS LOVE
THE PRICE YOU PAY FOR LOVE I, II ,III
DOPE GIRL MAGIC I II III
By **Destiny Skai**
WHEN A GOOD GIRL GOES BAD
By **Adrienne**
THE COST OF LOYALTY I II III
**By Kweli**
A GANGSTER'S REVENGE **I II III & IV**
THE BOSS MAN'S DAUGHTERS I II III IV V
A SAVAGE LOVE **I & II**
BAE BELONGS TO ME I II
A HUSTLER'S DECEIT I, II, III
WHAT BAD BITCHES DO I, II, III
SOUL OF A MONSTER I II III
KILL ZONE
A DOPE BOY'S QUEEN I II III
By **Aryanna**
A KINGPIN'S AMBITON
A KINGPIN'S AMBITION **II**
I MURDER FOR THE DOUGH
By **Ambitious**
TRUE SAVAGE I II III IV V VI VII
DOPE BOY MAGIC I, II, III
MIDNIGHT CARTEL I II III
CITY OF KINGZ I II
NIGHTMARE ON SILENT AVE
THE PLUG OF LIL MEXICO II

# Michael Gallon

By **Chris Green**
A DOPEBOY'S PRAYER
By **Eddie "Wolf" Lee**
THE KING CARTEL **I, II & III**
By **Frank Gresham**
THESE NIGGAS AIN'T LOYAL **I, II & III**
By **Nikki Tee**
GANGSTA SHYT **I II &III**
By **CATO**
THE ULTIMATE BETRAYAL
By **Phoenix**
BOSS'N UP **I , II & III**
By **Royal Nicole**
I LOVE YOU TO DEATH
By **Destiny J**
I RIDE FOR MY HITTA
I STILL RIDE FOR MY HITTA
By **Misty Holt**
LOVE & CHASIN' PAPER
By **Qay Crockett**
TO DIE IN VAIN
SINS OF A HUSTLA
By **ASAD**
BROOKLYN HUSTLAZ
By **Boogsy Morina**
BROOKLYN ON LOCK I & II
By **Sonovia**
GANGSTA CITY
By **Teddy Duke**
A DRUG KING AND HIS DIAMOND I & II III

302

# The Murder Queens

A DOPEMAN'S RICHES

HER MAN, MINE'S TOO I, II

CASH MONEY HO'S

THE WIFEY I USED TO BE I II

**By Nicole Goosby**

TRAPHOUSE KING **I II & III**

KINGPIN KILLAZ I II III

STREET KINGS I II

PAID IN BLOOD **I II**

CARTEL KILLAZ I II III

DOPE GODS I II

By **Hood Rich**

LIPSTICK KILLAH **I, II, III**

CRIME OF PASSION I II & III

FRIEND OR FOE I II III

By **Mimi**

STEADY MOBBN' **I, II, III**

THE STREETS STAINED MY SOUL I II III

By **Marcellus Allen**

WHO SHOT YA **I, II, III**

SON OF A DOPE FIEND I II

HEAVEN GOT A GHETTO

**Renta**

GORILLAZ IN THE BAY **I II III IV**

TEARS OF A GANGSTA I II

3X KRAZY I II

STRAIGHT BEAST MODE

**DE'KARI**

TRIGGADALE I II III

MURDAROBER WAS THE CASE

# Michael Gallon

**Elijah R. Freeman**
GOD BLESS THE TRAPPERS I, II, III
THESE SCANDALOUS STREETS I, II, III
FEAR MY GANGSTA I, II, III IV, V
THESE STREETS DON'T LOVE NOBODY I, II
BURY ME A G I, II, III, IV, V
A GANGSTA'S EMPIRE I, II, III, IV
THE DOPEMAN'S BODYGAURD I II
THE REALEST KILLAZ I II III
THE LAST OF THE OGS I II III
**Tranay Adams**
THE STREETS ARE CALLING
**Duquie Wilson**
MARRIED TO A BOSS I II III
**By Destiny Skai & Chris Green**
KINGZ OF THE GAME I II III IV V VI
**Playa Ray**
SLAUGHTER GANG I II III
RUTHLESS HEART I II III
**By Willie Slaughter**
FUK SHYT
**By Blakk Diamond**
DON'T F#CK WITH MY HEART I II
**By Linnea**
ADDICTED TO THE DRAMA I II III
IN THE ARM OF HIS BOSS II
**By Jamila**
YAYO I II III IV
A SHOOTER'S AMBITION I II
BRED IN THE GAME

# The Murder Queens

**By S. Allen**

TRAP GOD I II III

RICH $AVAGE

MONEY IN THE GRAVE I II III

**By Martell Troublesome Bolden**

FOREVER GANGSTA

GLOCKS ON SATIN SHEETS I II

**By Adrian Dulan**

TOE TAGZ I II III IV

LEVELS TO THIS SHYT I II

**By Ah'Million**

KINGPIN DREAMS I II III

**By Paper Boi Rari**

CONFESSIONS OF A GANGSTA I II III IV

CONFESSIONS OF A JACKBOY I II

**By Nicholas Lock**

I'M NOTHING WITHOUT HIS LOVE

SINS OF A THUG

TO THE THUG I LOVED BEFORE

A GANGSTA SAVED XMAS

IN A HUSTLER I TRUST

**By Monet Dragun**

CAUGHT UP IN THE LIFE I II III

THE STREETS NEVER LET GO

**By Robert Baptiste**

NEW TO THE GAME I II III

MONEY, MURDER & MEMORIES I II III

By **Malik D. Rice**

LIFE OF A SAVAGE I II III

A GANGSTA'S QUR'AN I II III IV

# Michael Gallon

MURDA SEASON I II III

GANGLAND CARTEL I II III

CHI'RAQ GANGSTAS I II III

KILLERS ON ELM STREET I II III

JACK BOYZ N DA BRONX I II III

A DOPEBOY'S DREAM I II III

JACK BOYS VS DOPE BOYS

COKE GIRLZ

**By Romell Tukes**

LOYALTY AIN'T PROMISED I II

**By Keith Williams**

QUIET MONEY I II III

THUG LIFE I II III

EXTENDED CLIP I II

By **Trai'Quan**

THE STREETS MADE ME I II III

By **Larry D. Wright**

THE ULTIMATE SACRIFICE I, II, III, IV, V, VI

KHADIFI

IF YOU CROSS ME ONCE

ANGEL I II

IN THE BLINK OF AN EYE

By **Anthony Fields**

THE LIFE OF A HOOD STAR

**By Ca$h & Rashia Wilson**

THE STREETS WILL NEVER CLOSE I II III

**By K'ajji**

CREAM I II

THE STREETS WILL TALK

**By Yolanda Moore**

# The Murder Queens

NIGHTMARES OF A HUSTLA I II III

**By King Dream**

CONCRETE KILLA I II

VICIOUS LOYALTY I II

**By Kingpen**

HARD AND RUTHLESS I II

MOB TOWN 251

THE BILLIONAIRE BENTLEYS I II III

**By Von Diesel**

GHOST MOB

**Stilloan Robinson**

MOB TIES I II III IV V

**By SayNoMore**

BODYMORE MURDERLAND I II III

**By Delmont Player**

FOR THE LOVE OF A BOSS

**By C. D. Blue**

MOBBED UP I II III IV

THE BRICK MAN I II III

THE COCAINE PRINCESS I II

**By King Rio**

KILLA KOUNTY I II III

**By Khufu**

MONEY GAME I II

**By Smoove Dolla**

A GANGSTA'S KARMA I II

**By FLAME**

KING OF THE TRENCHES I II

by **GHOST & TRANAY ADAMS**

QUEEN OF THE ZOO

# Michael Gallon

By **Black Migo**

GRIMEY WAYS

**By Ray Vinci**

XMAS WITH AN ATL SHOOTER

**By Ca$h & Destiny Skai**

KING KILLA

**By Vincent "Vitto" Holloway**

BETRAYAL OF A THUG

**By Fre$h**

THE MURDER QUEENS

**By Michael Gallon**

The Murder Queens

**<u>BOOKS BY LDP'S CEO, CA$H</u>**

TRUST IN NO MAN

TRUST IN NO MAN 2

TRUST IN NO MAN 3

BONDED BY BLOOD

SHORTY GOT A THUG

THUGS CRY

THUGS CRY 2

THUGS CRY 3

TRUST NO BITCH

TRUST NO BITCH 2

TRUST NO BITCH 3

TIL MY CASKET DROPS

RESTRAINING ORDER

RESTRAINING ORDER 2

IN LOVE WITH A CONVICT

LIFE OF A HOOD STAR

XMAS WITH AN ATL SHOOTER

Michael Gallon